REMO COBB SERIES

BOOKS 1 - 4

MIKE MCCRARY

REMO WENT ROGUE

REMO COBB # 1

PART I

SUCH AN ASSHOLE

1

L eslie likes to fuck men. Sometimes she ends up bedding
some dudes that she doesn't really like. It happens.
So what?

When you're a thirty-three-year old woman living in New York
and you like to fuck men, you may find yourself bedding a few pricks.
Yes, the literal nature of that statement is understood, but you get it.
An attractive woman in a demanding job, working ridiculous hours,
surrounded by men of loose moral fiber may have to drop her standards in order to get some.

Sex or the high road. The low road has an impressive win/loss
record. Again, it happens. All of this swirls around Leslie's pretty little
head as she nudges back and forth on her back. On a desk. In the
dark. Having sex with one of those previously-mentioned pricks.

It's not so much that Remo is a prick, really. Actually, she doesn't
even know him all that well. Probably best. What she does know is
that he talks while doing the deed.

Like, a lot. He's been rambling practically the whole time. With
hump-altered speech, Remo tells a story. "There's this pack of vicious
assholes who decide to hit a bank on a random Tuesday..."

Remo describes a seemingly normal weekday morning in the big city. Every day New Yorkers file into a Midtown bank as it opens. Good folk enter before work, grab some cash, make a deposit, bitch about a fee. All walks of life. Men, women, kids. The wealthy, the middle-class, the just-getting-by. A cultural and financial melting pot. None of them have a clue what's coming.

A van sits parked across the street. Six men wait inside the van, dressed for bad things. Armed and ready.

Three of them are the Mashburn brothers. They sit along one side. Dutch, the oldest brother, is both experienced and damned evil. The middle Mashburn is Ferris, a sharp-minded, ice shard of a man. The youngest, a wiry wacko called Chicken Wing.

On the opposite side of the creepy rape van sit two more members of this crew. Garden-variety crime boys. A slick criminal called Bobby Balls, and a young punk of a bastard called Country.

Their real names escape Remo at the moment. The final crew member is the driver, Lester, an aging career criminal who's never moved up in the ranks. Lester looks uneasy.

Uncertain. Uncomfortable. Dutch, the obvious leader, gives the nod. Dutch has his craft down, and has developed some simple rules for working jobs.

Rule # 1: He sees no reason to get creative with dead president masks or all that movie horseshit. Be nondescript; don't give the law something exotic to look into. Hmmm, where do you find this unique, hard-to-find mask? Run a check on all retailers that might carry masks like it, pull the security camera video and sync it with the register on the date those masks were sold. Any shit-stain who caught five minutes of any of the ten *Law & Order* episodes last night could piece that together. Just use something to cover your fucking face.

The crew pulls down classic black ski masks.

Rule #2: Don't use semi-automatics when doing banks. Don't use a weapon that spits out evidence like a PEZ dispenser. All those shell casings bouncing off the floor looks fuckin' cool in the movies. Glocks going crazy, lead flying in slow-mo...but in the real world—Dutch's world—it only creates evidence for cops to bag and help them tell a story.

.357s don't leave casings.

You say, "But what if you need more bullets? You have to reload, Old West style." If you need more than five guys with seven rounds a piece to do a bank you don't deserve the take. Go suck a dick. Now if the cops join the party, that's different. The AKs on their backs are for that.

Rule #3: In case of emergency, use AK. The crew readies the guns. All nickel plated, rubber-gripped .357 magnums. AKs strapped on their backs.

And, oh yeah, Rule #4: Witnesses are like shell casings. They should not be able to help tell a story.

The van doors bust open and the masked crew pours out, armed to the teeth. One throws an innocent bystander to the concrete en route to the bank door.

The five men rage into the bank like cowboys from hell.

A relentless rat-tat popping of gunfire echoes from inside the bank. Screams wail behind the closed doors. People on the street scatter in every direction.

Lester watches from behind the wheel. His eyes drop, each pop of gunfire seeming like it physically hurts him. He rubs a small cross hanging around his neck. He hates all of this, and he doesn't even know why. He's struggling with this. It's not like he's never been around killing or killed anybody before. God knows that's not the case. But today for some reason the pounding blasts from inside the bank, the obvious outcome from those blasts, are almost too much for Lester to bear.

A final bone-rattling shot sounds from inside the bank.

Remo powers on with his mid-sex tale: "Sixteen dead. Three point two million gone. Over in two minutes and eleven seconds."

At some farmland just north of Where-the-Hell-Are-We U.S.A, the bank crew digs a massive hole to stash the cash. Large money bags drop in. Dirt falls. Another thought from Dutch, possibly Rule #5: *Don't get caught with the money.* This isn't an international crime crew of sex symbols off the lot at Warner Brothers. They don't evade laser sensors and they don't have the capacity to launder that kind of green within a day of stealing it. They need to keep it safe until the heat subsides a bit. The first forty-eight hours are dicey, but after a few days you can get your money and get on with your life. If you get pinched holding bags of money, well, your options are somewhat limited.

The crew holes up in a tiny dump of a cabin in the New Mexico mountains, living like the fucking Amish on a bad day. They make it a day, two tops before a swarm of lawmen arrive with zero warning. The cabin is surrounded by police, and they are not in the mood for any shit.

Dutch peels back a rag posing as a curtain. Like a switch is flipped, a balls-out gunfight ignites. Shotguns and handguns punch at the shoddy construction.

Bullets fly in every direction. Back and forth like a ballistic shit-fit. Fire begins, spreads to a blaze throughout the cabin. The police hold steady. Dutch and the driver, Lester, fly out the door, fire and smoke pouring out behind them.

The cabin goes up like it was newspaper soaked in gasoline.

The police jump on Lester and Dutch. Dutch looks back at the burning cabin with a knowing sneer...

Remo, in mid-stroke. "Most of the crew dies in the fire, including two Mashburn brothers."

Leslie flips a light on, one of those banker's lamps with a green shade.

It illuminates her face as she moves back and forth rhythmically. Around the office is a smattering of quickly removed clothes and empty booze bottles. The 30-something intellectual beauty looks up at Remo, completely shell-shocked. He stares down at her. What?

Remo is older than Leslie by almost ten years, but a damn handsome man with a bar-boy charm that has served him well over the years. It's been stated before that Leslie does this with pricks, and Remo more than qualifies. None of that bothers her right now. It doesn't.

It's not that he's been talking the whole time. Sure, she'd rather the talk be dirty or not at all, but it's not that.

It's not even that she is the Assistant District Attorney assigned to prosecute the very bank crew that Remo has been rambling on about.

What bothers Leslie about all this, what's really throwing a wrench into this potential pleasure fest, is that Remo is one of the top defense attorneys in New York City. Sorry, *the* top defense attorney in New York City, and this bank crew, Mashburn brothers, Lester and the others are. . .

Remo's fucking clients.

2

"Stop," snaps Leslie.

Remo explains. "The math on this is simple."

"Can you stop?"

"It's a huge case. I have a bulging box of evidence. You can put them away forever."

"What?"

"What, what?"

"To be clear, you're admitting while we're having sex that your clients are guilty."

"Too weird for you?"

Leslie scrambles off the desk and pulls on some of the balled up clothing on the floor. Her confusion is surpassed only by her hostility.

"You unbelievable shithead."

Drunken state showing, Remo stumbles while trying to find his pants, yanking open the curtains as he falls and hits the hardwood. It's the middle of the day and sun lights up the room. Through the window is a magnificent view of Manhattan.

Leslie wants out of there, fast. She tries to get her head around this situation.

This Remo Situation.

"I am the fucking prosecuting attorney, and you're telling me how to put your clients in jail forever?"

Remo slides over to the cabinet, pouring himself a foot-sized tumbler of Johnnie Walker Blue. He gives her that damn smile.

With her last bit of dignity, she fires, "Fuck you, Remo. My team is going to win this case . . . cleanly."

"Highly doubtful." She'd defend herself, but he's right. Damn it. He takes a large gulp of booze, then pulls a box from under his desk. The box is packed. You can't even close the thing, files and photos almost spilling out. A bursting, spewing, geyser of evidence. Leslie's eyes nearly pop.

"I can't take that."

"It's not that heavy."

"Remo, I cannot accept the box."

"Leslie, your team is fairly shitty."

Complete disbelief that he said it, but she knows he's right.

"You will lose," Remo clarifies. "Look at it this way: you get to help the world be a better place, with orgasms to boot. That's as Kennedy as it gets."

"Orgasms?"

"Seemed like your eyebrow twitched."

"Why are you doing this?"

Remo pops a pill. Ritalin. It's a delicate balancing act with the booze, but Remo has mastered the chemistry. He washes it down with a gulp of Johnnie Blue. Pours a fresh one. He'd rather not give his reasons.

Leslie has heard the rumors. Remo has had a few problems, to put it mildly. Something about a wife who left, and a kid. Somebody said something about that during a lunch, but Leslie can't remember the details. One of those things you hear and give a forced-compassion response like, "Oh, that's horrible," or "Man, that's tough. Is he ok?"

That kinda shit.

Leslie gives a similar response now, thinking she knows what's up. "You're going through a rough patch."

Remo barely appreciates her efforts, gives her his rebuttal. "I'm living a dream."

"Come on, even an emotional dumpster fire like you has to acknowledge it. Everybody knows. The drinking, the pills, the whatever...and now you're throwing cases. Your behavior is suspect, at best."

Remo is a blank slate.

She tries to pry the humanity from him. "Your wife went bye-bye. Have you ever even met your son?"

"That . . . that has nothing to do with this thing . . . here." Now it's all over him, because it has everything to do with this thing here. He redirects. It's what he does for a living, for Christ's sake.

"You have sex with the defense, I win your case for you, and you call me a shithead. Flat-out fucking rude."

She continues getting dressed.

Remo continues drinking.

She says, "Healthy people have a cathartic moment of clarity and give up the pills and sauce."

Remo mulls that idea for a second. "That sounds awful." He pushes the box toward her. "This is a onetime thing."

She thinks, then asks, "The money?"

"Wow. Hookers are less direct than you."

"No, fucker, the money from the bank. The three point two million they stole."

"Oh, I dug that up."

"What?"

Remo shrugs.

"Well fucking hand it over."

"Don't fucking have it."

"Where the fuck did it go?"

"You know that foundation for the families of the bank robbery victims?"

Leslie nods.

"Gave it to them."

"What?"

"The city offers health insurance. Your hearing is horrible."

"Bullshit. Which locker at what train station is it stuffed in?"

"I. Don't. Have. It. Gave it to a good cause. That so hard to believe?"

Leslie's eyes bore through him. Yes, it's extremely hard to believe that a guy like this even knows how to do that. You could hand him a donation bag of used clothes and shoes, drive him to the front door of the local Goodwill, he still couldn't pull it off.

Remo replies, "Take the box. Win the case and you'll get hired to a better gig. Or you can run the risk of being that prosecutor who tried to trade sex for a guilty verdict."

Leslie stares daggers as she struggles with her whirling thoughts. Is he right? Yes. Does she have a choice? Yes, but the right choice, not taking the box, does her no good whatsofuckingever. Eventually, as per usual, the low road wins. She grabs the box as she heads for the door. "You are a stunning asshole. Thanks for the guilty-in-a-box and the god-awful sex."

Remo stops her, his face now reflecting a surprising, almost alarming amount of sincerity. All the bullshit is gone, the slickness washed away. "Promise me these monsters will never be able to do this again."

Leslie takes in his complete shift in tone, his new body language, and can't help but be moved. This is the man who got her into bed...well, on a desk. This is a man with a heart and perhaps, God forbid, a soul. She understands there is a real reason for what he is doing. She hopes it's a good one, and not that he stole the damn money to flush it away on hookers and blow.

Realistically, she knows that cocaine and boob jobs are exactly where that boatload of blood money is headed, but for the moment, this moment, she'd like to believe Remo is better than that.

The idealistic, hopeful little girl in her can't help but respond, "I promise."

3

The plan?
  Simple.
  Murder multiple motherfuckers, save one asshole.
  This is the strategy of one Lester Ellis, a former criminal, former wheelman, current man of the Lord. Lester's résumé, if he ever felt the need to pen one, would read:
  "July 1968 to February 2012: Murdering Thief -- Team player. Individual contributor. Fluent. Six Sigma.
  "February 2012 to Present: Servant of God -- Six months experience. (But a good six months, you judgmental ass.)"
  Lester: weathered, seasoned, bleary-eyed, and beaten down by years of dirty deeds. He stands along an empty road some thirty-odd miles north of New York, surrounded by not a whole helluva lot. Behind him lies the unmistakable outline of a sprawling fifty-five acres on the east bank of the Hudson River known by most as Sing Sing maximum security prison.
  His body is a wandering contradiction of personal philosophies. Tats tell the tale of a confused, or at the very least conflicted, man. A Swastika rests on one side of his neck, with a sad clown on the other. A large cross with Jesus nailed to it is scrawled from blade to blade on

his back. "FuckU" on one of his shoulders. The cherry on top? On the fatty part of his right paw, etched in crude prison-blue fashion: "Right Hand of God."

He carries few earthly possessions in his thick hands save for his prized cigar, which is barely holding together, a plastic bag that contains a roll of duct tape, and a Bible. The guard working the release counter thought it was kinda strange when Lester asked for the duct tape. Lester proceeded to point to the holes in his boots. What the hell does the guard care? Lester readjusts the crude silver tape job that holds his footwear together.

His fingers rub along his Bible, caressing it. This is not some cheap-ass Motel 6 bible. This thing has some weight, with a hard binding built to stand up to time, and gold accents with touches of tough leather designed to protect the word of the Lord.

Thoughts bounce. Thoughts of the life he's led. Thoughts of the life he's going to lead. Thoughts of how he's going to find salvation for the wicked he has done, if that's even possible. Can you forgive the killing? The stealing? The severing of limbs? The blood Lester has spilled during his lifetime could fill an Olympic-size pool. The money he's made off of it could fill a needle...and it did. Can all the wrongs be washed away by recently letting the Lord in? By performing a righteous act or two? Can that kinda shit be forgiven?

Good Book says it can. Sing Sing preacher man says it can. Gotta give it a shot, what the hell else is he gonna do? Go back to that life? Back to the shit that put him in a hole for the better part of his life, shoved him farther and farther away from the Lord? Not fuckin' likely. To Lester, this is a new day with a new path. One that will deliver him from evil...even if that means inflicting a touch of evil in the process.

Lester closes his eyes tight while he mutters a few holy words under his breath.

Pops his lids open. He's ready now. A horn blares, jolting Lester from his perfect moment of introspection. His eyes squint, verifying the vehicle kicking up dirt is headed his way.

Yup, that's his ride.

A slightly used black Escalade—a fine mode of criminal transport a few years ago—dented here and there with four unmistakable bullet holes peppered around the hood. The Escalade makes a sudden stop, a drop of the power window revealing the driver—Bobby Balls from Remo's story.

But unlike in Remo's story, he's very much alive.

Bobby Balls smiles wide while greeting Lester. "You ready, sweetheart?"

Lester checks the back, spotting two other criminals. The young one, a punk of a bastard begging to show you how hard he is, answers to Country.

On the other side sits an ice shard of a man with a piercing gaze that makes pit bulls piss. A man who'd gladly cause the suffering of fools way before he'd even consider suffering one himself. One who's spent his years without knowing remorse. Goes by the name of Ferris Mashburn.

Yup, all three of them are very much alive. Sizing up the occupants of the car, Lester makes his way to a passenger-side door. He tosses the cigar, grips the plastic bag in one hand, bible in the other. As he takes in a deep breath of fresh air, he looks to the heavens and mutters a few more silent words before plopping down in the Escalade's passenger side.

Ferris starts in. "We cool?"

Lester gives a nod as he rubs a finger across the bible.

"Fuck yeah we are," from Country. "That fucker is dead as Dillinger."

Nothing but a searing gaze from Ferris, then, "Nobody touches the lawyer until Dutch gets loose." Eyes Country in the back. "Get me?"

"Fuckin' why?" fires Country.

"Because that's how Dutch wants it—"

"Fuckin' retarded."

"—which means that's how we want it. More importantly, that's how a subhuman half-wit like you wants it. Clear enough?"

Lester slowly removes the duct tape from the bag. No one notices.

Country starts in again. "I know big man Dutch wants to be the one to end the motherfucker, but he's locked up, and we're out, and I'm really fuckin' tired of being in hiding. It sucks. We got Chicken Wing on the lawyer right now, watchin,' just waitin' for the green light. We go in, blow that legal eagle to shit, get our money and ride off into the sunset as soon as Dutch joins the party. Pretty fuckin' simple if you ask me—"

Ferris stops him midsentence. The heart-freezing glare, along with Ferris's fingers tightening around his voice box, puts an end to Country's debate. They roll on in silence, the energy in the car having been sucked up and held hostage by Ferris.

"We've been in hiding, that's correct. What's also correct, the point you're missing, is that we've been waiting for the right time, and that time has presented itself. Now."

Country gives a guttural sound, works as a *yes*.

Ferris eyes Lester. "You're a quiet prick."

Lester caresses the Bible. Country continues to gasp and squirm.

"Heard Lester found Jesus or some shit," adds Bobby Balls.

"I did," Lester replies.

Lester watches the countryside, but not for the view. He's looking for something in particular. Setting his bible down next to him, he rests the plastic bag on top, starts to peel a small bit of the duct tape off the roll. Makes a starting pull at the tape as discreetly as can be. No one notices, except Ferris, who's starting to eye the back of Lester's head.

Country is a second or two from passing out. Ferris releases him from his near-death grip. Country slips into a ball in the corner of the backseat. Where he belongs.

Bobby Balls continues, "Tell me, why do you people always find God in the joint? Is it to cling to something, or is it more about hope? Hoping that some magic man in the sky will help you while you're taking five black cocks in the shower?"

Country cackles with laughter, starting to feel his blood flowing again.

"Something like that, I suppose," says Lester, still scanning the outside world.

Without looking down, he has taken the plastic bag in one hand and attached the free bit of duct tape from the roll. Has a finger gripped around the roll as if ready to pull, plastic bag at the ready in the other.

"I mean, seriously. When they say find Jesus...the fuck does that even mean?"

Ferris keeps watching Lester. Lester keeps watching the road. Country keeps laughing.

"What is Jesus going to help you do? I mean, now that you found his ass." Bobby Balls giggles childlike, amused with his own questions.

Lester's eyes stop. He's found what he wants through the front window.

"Come on, man, I'm just fucking with you. But really, what are you and Jesus going to do?"

Lester cracks the slightest of grins as he gives his answer. "Murder multiple motherfuckers, save one asshole."

Everyone except Lester has been slapped with a healthy dose of "what the fuck?" A perfect, silent slice in time. The plastic bag flies over Bobby Balls' head. In a single move, Lester rolls the duct tape around Bobby's neck two, three times, sealing the bag. The words "Right Hand of God" flex on his hand as Lester works the tape. Leaves the roll attached, bouncing as Bobby Balls fights for air, plastic sucking in and out with a panic-stricken rhythm. It's sick, lacks compassion, but it does give a nice beat you can tap a toe to.

"The fuck?" Country screams, making a dive from the backseat toward the front, 9mm pulled. As he does, Lester grabs the wheel, cutting hard toward a line of trees just off the road.

The Escalade slams head-on into a tree, a jarring collision of bark and steel. Country launches from the backseat—a low IQ javelin— face-first into the windshield. Nose-first, actually, with a crunch of bone and snap of spine, leaving a pulp-faced corpse.

Air bags deploy a fraction of a second after Country's lifeless body bounces from the glass. Ferris's seatbelt snaps him back, as does Lester's. The whole string of events takes only a few seconds. One dead. One working on dying. Two left to kill each other.

The Escalade ricochets off the tree, skidding to a stop. Fluids spit from the hood. Windshield's a spider web, with clumps of Country's face and hair stuck in it. Bobby Balls gives a couple of dying jerks and spasms.

He's hanging in there. God bless him for trying.

Ferris pulls his .357, squeezing off two blasts at Lester. An air bag takes the blast as Lester pops the seat belt free, spinning out the door.

The eerie quiet that comes after a car crash fills the air. All that violent, sudden energy expended in a sliver of time, leaving you with a pile of life-altering devastation. Granted, most car crashes are not the byproduct of a recently released Jesus-freak suffocating the driver with a plastic bag, but it's the same result as a soccer mom blowing through a stop sign while on her cell babbling about shoes—shit you don't want.

Ferris stumbles out, his .357 tracking as he makes his way around the back. Legs wobbly as he tries to get his post-car-wreck bearings, he clears the back bumper and is met by the solid binding of Lester's Bible, which makes a low, muted thwack, connecting with Ferris's face. Leaves his vision spotted with white blobs of light. It only lasts a moment, but that's just enough for Lester to get to his feet and land a crack-punch. Drops Ferris to the dirt. They go at it like wild dogs fighting over the last scrap of meat. Not elegant. Not choreographed. Criminals are beating one another's ass, life and death on the line.

A 4Runner filled with high school kids pulls up. The bearded, hipster driver pokes his head out the window.

"You guys ok?"

Lester pops up, having wrestled away the .357. Ferris bolts, putting a foot on the 4Runner's hood as he springs over. Opening fire, Lester's shots pop holes across the kid's hood, barely missing Ferris as he escapes into the woods.

Kids in the 4Runner give bloodcurdling, scared-shitless wails as they haul ass outta there. Lester lowers the gun, less than satisfied at

Ferris giving him the slip. Bobby Balls falls from the car, still hanging in there. God bless him. He's managed to pull the bag off and is crawling away. Lester casually puts two bullets in him.

His mind drifts back to the second bullet point of his plan.

Oh yes, something about saving one asshole.

4

"Asshole?" Mr. Crow barks. "Have you listened to one damn thing I've said?"

Crow, a dapper, well put-together criminal of means, sits across from Remo Cobb, his high-priced defense attorney. Not a hair out of place, suit immaculate. Watch costs more than your car.

Remo gives the tiniest flash of eye contact. "All ears on this side of the table."

Not really; he's preoccupied. He's attempting to bounce a pill into a half full scotch glass that has been carefully positioned between him and Crow. A fun little game of pharmaceutical quarters.

Crow grows more and more annoyed with each bouncing Ritalin. "If the bitch would have just done things right we wouldn't be in this spot."

"Meaning you would have stopped just shy of crushing her windpipe?"

"It got out of hand. She got out of line. I was having . . . a what? A 'day,' let's say. She just ... stopped breathing."

The two men are surrounded by wall-to-wall leather- bound legal books, polished oak and brass. A private meeting area at the most prestigious New York legal firm that ill-gotten gains can buy. Same office Remo was in with that prosecutor, Leslie. People are still getting fucked, but a much different meeting is in progress.

"I did it. Can't lie. But she pushed me. She pulled a blade for Christ's sake."

"Shit." Remo's response has nothing to do with Crow's story. He missed the damn glass again.

Crow grows more annoyed as a pill flies by his face. "My sight went white. Next I know she's not breathing."

Remo misses. "Cocksucker."

"Am I bothering you?" asks Crow.

Remo glances up. Now he's growing annoyed at his client for interrupting his efforts.

"No?" asks Crow.

Remo is not nearly as well put together as his client. Suit's a mess. Eyes like red pinholes. He was a good-looking man at one time. Now he looks like he's been on a multiyear bender. Crow, previously completely focused on his dead-hooker dilemma, suddenly realizes this asshole attorney, the one he's paying a mint for, is not even vaguely paying attention to his plight. And in Crow's mind, there's a massive bit of plight, goddamnit. "You think you can pay attention, you son of a bitch prick cocksucker?"

Remo bounces a pill, landing one with a plop in his glass of Johnnie Walker. Shoots his arms up in the air as if draining a buzzer-beater at the Sweet 16, then raises a single finger, stopping the now red-faced Crow before he can lay into him with a blitz of heartfelt profanity. He throws back the booze, along with the swimming pill.

It's hard to decipher if Remo has more disdain for his job, life, or Crow. Silence permeates the room. They sit eyeing each other like fighters circling, determining how to dismantle each other. Crow hates that he needs Remo almost as much as Remo hates that he needs Crow. Crow stops himself from blowing up, slips into a smile, deciding to break his lawyer down with a different method. The truth.

"Remo fucking Cobb."

"Present."

"Straight outta Cut and Shoot, Texas."

"Great town. You'd do well there."

"Daddy died in a backroom card game. Mommy? Nobody knows. You're a walking, talking hillbilly lullaby."

"That's the rumor," Remo says after a gulp of scotch.

"Made a name working small cases around Texas. Then you caught the eye of a big swinging dick firm in New York City. Got some motorcycle gang off or some shit, right? Must have been hard shedding that dumbass Texas accent while chewing up d-bag, Ivy League Jews." Crow takes a calculated dramatic pause for fun, then, "Also managed to lose a family along the way."

The family statement sticks at something in Remo, deep. He shakes it off, pushes it down. Swishes a mouthful of Johnnie Blue while eyeballing Crow, absorbing the unrelenting, unnecessarily hurtful truth Crow is telling.

"This path of most resistance made you into the man you are today, and that man? This Remo? Is a USDA certified, Grade-A, grain-fed asshole."

Remo's had enough. "The body gone?"

"The body?"

"The girl. Her body. The shell that carried her soul. Remember? You killed her with your bare hands? Sorry, the one who stopped breathing. I mean, let's table your unfortunate murder habit, and forget the people who might care about these women."

"This isn't my first rodeo," sneers Crow.

Remo pours another drink.

Crow, slightly offended: "You gonna offer me a drink?"

"You shouldn't drink."

"Should you?"

"Absolutely."

"Can you take care of this thing or no?"

"Yeah."

"Yeah?"

Remo shakes his head. It truly yanks at his guts to say but he says it anyways, "I can ease your troubled mind and heal your heavy heart."

"Fuck you, Remo."

"Much appreciated." Remo gulps, then slams the empty glass down.

Every word out of Crow's mouth was accurate. Why the hell does the truth have to come from a wretched human being like that guy? That fucking guy? Remo doesn't go to a therapist. He should, heaven knows he should, but he doesn't. Doesn't see the point, doesn't believe in it, and, damn it, he's not going to. However, his inner thoughts and feelings—some may call them demons—seem to come to the surface while talking to these dregs of society.

Should he just lie on the couch while taking these client meetings?

Remo knows the truth of his life. He's lived the history. Which is precisely why he drinks and pops those pills.

Fucking *duh*. Not a supernatural mystery of the universe. He's no Bigfoot. Unfortunately, substance abuse doesn't make memories or present truths or lifelong demons disappear. It might later on in life, but even if Remo makes it to old age and can't remember the past, who gives a shit? It's today that's rough for him. The here and now is a fucking mess. Besides, if his current behavior can shave those later shitty years off his life, so be it.

Remo knows his life. Doesn't necessarily hate it. Doesn't exactly love it either. It is what it is. That's what people say when they can't, or don't want to, explain a fact of life, right?

All this fuels the synaptic fireworks that are Remo's mental state as he stumbles through the city, in and out of crowds, hours blurring until he finds himself at Gramercy Park. He watches kids playing at a crazy pace, an army of youth without a care in the world. Dogs being chased and giving chase in return. Moms and nannies keep a watchful eye. A safe distance away, a distance where he can't be seen, Remo sits, still dressed in his pricey, mussed up suit which hangs on him like a hanger made of old bones.

He pulls a small pair of binoculars from his coat pocket. He keeps them there, just in case. He begins spying on the children. Actually, he's spying on one child and mother in particular. The three-year-old boy is Sean, his beautiful mother, Anna.

Remo's not a perv. He is a lot of unsavory things, but pervert isn't on the list. Well, not the kind who goes to the park to look at little boys. Jesus, how fucked up is the world when you have to explain that in order to clear the air?

It is what it is. Remo knows Anna and Sean. Cares about Anna and Sean. Anna picks Sean up, spinning him around. Happiness doesn't begin to cover it. Remo watches on for a moment. It's hard to make out his purpose. He sets down the binoculars. Shades of sadness and rising ripples of regret hit him. He wishes he were with them. No time for that shit—that thinking, feeling shit you hear so much about. Remo sparks a one-hitter, looking for some clarity, letting the smoke roll into his lungs and back out.

Flushing out his system. A mother with her newborn bundle of joy pushes an all-terrain jogging stroller near Remo. He's now all but spread-eagle in the grass. She stops, giving him more than a hint of disapproval. *What is wrong with this city?* She moves closer to get his attention, thinking her mere look of disdain will somehow shame this disgusting man into submission.

Remo rolls over, notices her and her look. "Go fuck yourself, lady."

Remo falls into his apartment, flipping on the lights, exposing a magnificent two bedroom in a Murray Hill high-rise. Most would kill half, or all, their family to live here—the best of everything, with a jaw-dropping view of the city. The space is big, filled with many expensive things, yet feels empty, deeply hollow.

The silence is deafening.

He checks the fridge. Nothing but three variations of mustard, some fancy imported beer and a pizza box.

Turns on the TV. Flips around. All dog shit. Checks the fridge again. Hasn't changed. He slips on some headphones, plays some old Violent Femmes. He loves music, even more when he's completely ripshit-hammered.

Uncorks a bottle of wine. Pours a glass. Pops a pill. Drinks.

Tries to sing. Tries to dance. Sucks at both. Catches a glance of his rhythmic ineptitude in the mirror. "Jesus." Grabs his keys, exiting as quickly as he can. Remo's destination is a hipster bar if ever there was one.

Wall Street masters of the universe, young law firm royalty and generic d-bags of all shapes and sizes mingle in the elite watering hole. Men and women trolling for a hook-up. Remo cuts through with drunken grace, with purpose. His target is clear.

At a far end of the room is the quintessential hot bartender. Her name escapes Remo at the moment. Late twenties, Old World gorgeous with New World tits. She works magic, slinging sauce in every direction—a blur of booze and mind-bending sex appeal. Men kneel and worship at her feet.

She knows it. It's what keeps her in business, and business is good. Her focus is unbreakable until she spots her man. Her present love, her way out of an hourly wage.

Her meal ticket.

She stops everything and lights up of the sight of Remo. "Hey, baby."

There's some sexual history here. Everyone sees it. Pisses off the army of hard dicks hoping to be the one she'll pick. She never does—most hot bartenders don't—but it doesn't stop the boys from playing the lottery. Got to be in it to win it, and somebody has to win... right?

She leans over the bar, putting her hands on Remo's face while laying on a sloppy kiss that would strike down mortal men. Breasts saying hello. A twenty-two-year-old bond trader may have passed out. Remo knows they're all watching him. He loves that they're watching. He loves her. Well, not *her*. Loves her chest. Of course he does. It helps to fill the pit a bit. It won't last. Like eating Chinese food or sniffing glue. All good for a while, but it doesn't stay with you long.

They retreat to a converted warehouse loft in Midtown. Nice place, but trying hard not to be too nice. Cool, but trying hard not to be too hip. Expensive, period. On the bed, the hot bartender rides

Remo with abandon. Bites her lower lip, squealing like an over-caffeinated porn star.

Remo is bored out of his mind, his dead eyes staring at her and her show.

Glances at the clock, then back to her. Formulates a plan. Remo forces out some bad acting. "That's it. There it is."

"Oh yeah? Do it, Remo. Come for your girl."

He gives it final thrust, adds a twitch to make it look good, along with a somewhat convincing grunt. He lies still, hoping she bought it. She stops bouncing, a little confused and not sure how to handle this.

"Did you come, Sugar Bear?"

"Yup, mind-bending."

"Really? It just didn't seem like you did."

"I have a condom on, so it's not really the bareback kinda fireworks."

"I know, but—" She slides off him. Something is bothering her as she pulls her clothes from the floor. Sure, she likes not having to pay for things. Nice things. She likes having the little things that make life special for her. But dammit, there needs to be a little respect, too. Just a little bit. She deserves that much. Sex with someone you don't like isn't as easy as it looks. She starts to say it, stops, then says it anyway.

"You don't respect anything about me."

Remo sinks. "Ah, fuck."

"No, really. What do you respect about me?"

"There's so many."

"Come on, Remo. One thing. Name one thing."

"I—look, you're a great girl."

"Thank you. And?"

He thinks. It hurts. It hurts to think at all, given the booze, pills and fake orgasms, but it's even harder to come up with a single thing to tell this woman. Whatever her fucking name is. She becomes more and more pissed as the pause drags out. She looks at him as sincerely as a naked, surgically-enhanced woman can.

"Well?"

With no other options, Remo attempts the truth.

"You're a twenty-eight-year-old bartender with a BMW, condo, and tits, who I happily picked up the tab for—what's not to respect?"

Without even a "fuck you," she throws her shirt on in a huff, heading for the door.

Not a great time for the truth. Remo does respect the tits, just not what they're attached to. He tries to make a quick, last-ditch effort to bring them back.

"My place in the Hamptons this weekend?" The door slams behind her. "Sugar Bear?"

That could have gone better. It started out nice. Fuck it.

Remo's hungry.

5

Remo takes refuge at an all-night Chinese joint. He's nestled himself into a throne of a booth in the 24/7 dive. Red table-cloths, cheap paper lanterns. A drunk's after-hours haven. His mind drifts as he stares out the large picture window. He lets his head unwind as he watches New York breeze by effortlessly, people moving through the city, through their lives. He looks on glassy-eyed. Lost. Wanting. Like a puppy left in the rain.

He gets caught up in the pace of his wandering mind. There's a lot going on in that head. Still can't shake his conversation with Mr. Crow. The sting of his words hasn't faded. People have said many horrific things to him before— nothing new—but that conversation is doing a number on Remo. His memory slams back to his father. It always does. Daddy Cobb was a hard, hard man. Loved the sauce, hated keeping a job, not much use for Remo. The day Remo's mom went AWOL, Remo remembers asking his dad, "Will she be back?"

"No."

"Where is she?"

"Does it matter?"

"Is she ok?"

No response. Later, when Remo was around ten, he found out she left them; remarried and even had a new baby. Can't blame her. Remo never looked for her. Even with the vast resources currently at his disposal, he's never tried. His firm could find anybody, anywhere, but she wanted out, so she's out.

It is what it is.

Not many people these days have their dad die in a gunfight while cheating a card game. Remo did. In a way, he takes pride in it. Others might say, "My dad died from Alzheimer's at this nice home we found for him," or "He fought the good fight, but cancer ultimately won." Not Remo. "My dad shot two men down after he caught a hanger off the bottom of a stacked deck and, shortly after that, caught two slugs from a .45—one in the chest, one between the eyes."

How would you rather go? Again, it happens. A fifty-something Asian waitress drops off a plate of shrimp fried rice as big as his face, along with a cup of black coffee. At fifty-something, she looks twenty. *These people don't age,* Remo thinks. He addresses the shrimp-laced pile with a fork in hand. Pauses, pushes the plate away. Pulls a silver flask, twists off the top and pours some booze into his coffee, stirs it with his finger.

Remo is forced to hit "pause" on memory lane as some guy tries to get his attention.

The guy does more than that. The guy slides into the booth across from Remo.

Weathered, seasoned, beaten by years of dirty deeds. Body art a wandering contradiction of personal philosophies.

A confused, or at the very least conflicted, man. Lester speaks.

6

"Remo Cobb." Remo barely glances up from his plate—hurts to focus—and the expression he manages to pull together is one of indifference and intoxication.

Lester sits and rubs his bible while staring at Remo. Watching, taking in everything about him, studying him, working through his feelings about this man and suppressing the ill will. Remo takes note of Lester's appearance, tries to place the face. He can't seem to remember this guy, but feels like he should.

Some burn-out from high school?

That crazy ass-clown from down the dorm hall in college?

Booze typically makes positive recognition challenging, but this one is particularly difficult. Remo attempts, nonetheless, to identify the man sitting across from him, asking, "I know you?"

Lester sits stone-faced for a moment that stretches forever—beyond and back again—then utters, "You do."

Remo's brain gives off a vague spark, ignites a flicker of recognition. "Client?"

"I was."

"All right. What the hell you want?" Remo drifts back to his meal, with its coffee and sauce chaser.

"My name is Lester, and I'm on a mission of mercy."

Remo spots the God tat on his hand, then the Bible. *Jesus freak. Fuck me.*

Lester continues, "I was imprisoned. During that time I learned the grace and glory of a righteous path. A road to redemption, the way the Lord wants me to be. Wants me to save you." Lester is well aware the ears across the booth from him are deaf to his words, but feels he has to at least say these things. Sort of like a disclosure statement for a car ad ("professional on a closed course, do not attempt"), or a cigarette box ("smoke these and die slowly and horribly"). Everybody knows, nobody cares, still, it has to be there.

Remo halts his rice and spiked java intake. "Fan-fucking-tastic."

"Please don't interrupt me, sir."

"Please go away, cocksucker."

Lester feels the rushing wave of anger rip down his spine. He remembers a time when that ripping sensation meant someone was going to be hurting, really bad, really soon. That was a different time, a different Lester. He holds those bad thoughts back now. The thought of jamming that fork into Remo's eye? Currently on the back burner. The idea of dragging Remo from this booth and stomping a boot through his teeth? Held back. That simple notion of wrapping his fist around this lawyer's neck until there's a single snap? Please hold. In lieu of these proven problem-solving techniques, Lester grits his teeth and goes with the coping mechanisms he learned inside. Breathes through his nose. Finds his calming voice, his happy place. Exhales the hate and says, "I'm asking you politely to listen to what I have to say. I've come a long way for you."

Remo, who considers holding back and exhaling hate techniques for pussies and homos, opts for another method. He covers his face with his hands. From behind his fingers, he replies, "When I move my hands, I'd like you to be gone." He gives it a beat and then removes his hands.

Lester's still there.

Frustrated, annoyed and flat-out fucking done with God Boy, Remo barks out, "Pretty please, fucking dissipate."

Lester slams his Bible to the table. Hard. The kind of slam that makes one think, *I shouldn't have said that.* Shrimp and coffee jump as Lester's cold, hard eyes burn with an unmistakable intensity. The room drops to a low murmur. Other tables look on while trying hard not to seem like they are. The uncomfortable seconds crawl. The air feels tight; at least it does to Remo.

Lester lets the entire restaurant off the hook by finally speaking. "You have wronged people in your life, correct?"

Nothing from Remo. He's pretty sure Lester knows the answer without him saying it.

Lester asks harder this time. "Correct?"

Remo gives in. "One or two."

"Yes. Yes, you have." Lester grabs a giant scoop of shrimp fried rice with his bare hand, inhaling it. Remo is trying hard not to be disgusted by this poor man's Tebow shoving his paw into his food.

He asks, "You mentioned saving me?"

Lester gives a nod.

"From..."

"Men are coming to kill you." Lester wipes the excess rice from his mouth.

Remo watches a carrot cube land on the table, then asks, "One more time?"

"You recall a devil named Dutch? Evil brothers named Mashburn? Ferris? Chicken Wing?"

Remo's life hits pause. Face drops. Heart freezes. Every molecule of his being slams on the brakes, flips and catches fire. Oh hell yeah, he recalls. Throwing the case. Digging up the money. Fuck. Fuck. Fuck. Total recall sets in, Remo now remembering how he knows this man. "You drove getaway."

"Yes." Lester flicks the carrots cube away.

"How the hell are you out?"

"An organization named Prisoners for Faith got me a new attorney and found some holes in the case against me."

Remo's blood pressure spikes. How could Leslie fuck that up?

Lester takes Remo's shaking hand. "I'm a man of the Lord. I've been given a second chance and I cannot, will not, allow them to hurt you. I'm here to save you."

Remo pulls away. This is entirely too much for him to process in the moment. Hard to process in a lifetime. Too much for anybody to process, but for Remo, in his condition, this is just too damn much.

Lester prompts, "You threw our case."

Remo knows the truth will not set him free in any way, shape or form. He attempts to cover the obvious truth, but Lester cuts him off. Saving Remo from throwing one more lie on the fire. "You lost on purpose. You lost the case against Dutch and me. It's all right, Remo. No hate from me. I'm a better man for it."

"I didn't throw your case. I got beat. Big difference."

"You stole their money."

"What? What money? I did nothing of the sort."

Lester's dagger-stare puts an end to Remo's bullshit.

Remo recoils, leaks out, "Okay. Fine. Got me. I threw the case, but I don't have the money. I gave it to a good cause."

"Of course you did."

"I did, damn it."

Lester smiles as he snatches another handful of rice, thinking how damn good it is. He thinks about ordering some more. Perhaps an egg roll. Pork, not that vegetarian shit. He's for God and all, but the man enjoys meat. Maybe some of that fried pork with the red shit on top.

Remo's mind couldn't be any farther away. He's thinking of red shit all right, he's thinking about his blood seeping out from multiple bullet wounds. Hell, that's if he's lucky. These Mashburn boys like to get creative when disposing of people they dislike. With Remo sitting at #1 atop on the Mashburns' most wanted list—yeah, they'll work up something really super special for their best buddy Remo. His defense mechanisms kick in, and he thinks *this can't be happening.* Thinks *it is simply not possible.*

Thinking out loud, Remo utters, "Dutch is in jail. His brothers and the rest of their crew are corn-holing Hitler in hell."

"They didn't die in that fire," says Lester, trying to flag down a waitress. "Some are dead now of course, by my hand. But the Mashburn brothers? Oh, they've been waiting for the right time to present itself, and they are very alive and very upset with you."

Remo swallows a bit of vomit. Terror-shakes set in, rattling their way down to his toes. He says, "You're out of your skull. Nobody's coming."

Lester looks to Remo with surprisingly kind eyes. "People will come, dear Remo. Nasty, filthy, scary people. People with bad childhoods and questionable morals will descend upon you with guns, bloodlust, and visions of murderous mayhem dancing in their heads. Make no mistake. They are coming."

Remo sits back, letting this life-altering news wash over him, through him. This kind of news is on par with "you've got cancer" or "your liver will explode in 3 to 6 months" or "your balls are going to fall off." He rubs his face, then takes a hard swig from his flask. Skips the coffee. Lester gets frustrated with the waitress, who is clearly ignoring him, and motions to Remo about his plate of unattended fried rice. May I?

Remo pushes it towards him. *Oh please, help yourself.* An ever so delicate sound stops Remo.

Tink, tink, tink.

It's coming from outside the restaurant.

Tink, tink.

Remo looks to the window. A man in a hoodie, dark glasses, and what looks like a very fake beard is tapping on the window with car keys, trying to get Remo's attention. Remo gives the man a *what the fuck now?* look. Lester notices nothing, oblivious, with his face buried in the blissful freedom of Chinese food.

The Hoodie Man points down toward the ground. Remo doesn't get it. The man pulls a nickel plated .357 with a rubber grip. Remo gets it.

Drops down, sliding under the table lightning fast. Hoodie Man opens fire on Lester without a hint of mercy. A relentless pounding of lead blows out the window, glass exploding in a scattershot of bouncing shards which blanket the table and surrounding area.

Bullets rip the air, tagging Lester in multiple points of entry, spinning and whirling him out of the booth. Pulpy pops sprout from his body like springtime flowers.

Restaurant patrons scatter like roaches when the lights turn on, screaming and running for the exits. Tables fly, chairs skid across the cheap floor, plates break—this is what happens when bullets come for dinner.

Remo hits the floor under the table, the falling rain of glass dancing around him, contorting into a fetal position in a feeble attempt to gain some form of comfort.

Comfort is now a distant, distant memory for Remo.

One final, bone-rattling blast sends Lester to the floor. The mysterious, gun-toting hostile Hoodie Man bolts into the night, escaping into the cover of darkness.

Lester's body falls, flopping face-to-face with Remo on the floor. Remo tries to find his breath while looking into a dying man's eyes. Blood begins to slowly roll into pools of deep crimson, engulfing the cheap black and white checkered tile. Fear has rendered his legs numb. Breathing is past the point of controlling. Remo fights to stay calm, or as calm as a man can be when his heart is seconds from jumping out through his throat.

As calm as a man can be staring eye-to-eye at his future.

This is the day his life will surely change.

PART II

WHAT THE HELL IS WRONG WITH ME?

7

An hour later and Remo's face is still plastered in the controlled mental meltdown expression he had on the floor face-to-face with Lester. His mind is a spiraling whirlpool of *what the fuck?* Realizes he could still be having sex with a gorgeous bartender rather than this.

This!

What the hell is wrong with me? What's going to happen to me? Fuck me. The place is now swarming with police, surveying the area, picking through debris for evidence, working the scene. Not much around to pick or work though. Only things there are a blown out window, a shot to hell Chinese joint and a tatted up ex-con clinging to the rim of life. Lester is carted off by EMS. Words and phrases like, "Not gonna make it," "Not looking good," and "Fucked" are thrown around casually.

Remo sits at a table sipping coffee. Across from him is Detective Harris. There's a certain amount of uneasiness between them, people with an unfriendly past. A ton of hate bubbles within Harris, just beneath the surface. He keeps it there in order to maintain a certain level of professionalism, but it's very hard to do. He's held back from beating rapists, murders, and others into unrecognizable puddles, but—like a lot of people—Harris can taste the burning fantasy of beating the piss out of Remo.

Harris is exactly what you'd expect. Big. Fat. Bald.

Asshole.

Harris says, "In your line of work, your sense of right and wrong must be like a pretzel. Meet a lot of hefty bags of shit, don't ya?"

"Clients," replies Remo. Speaking is difficult for many reasons at this moment. The fact he really doesn't want to talk to Harris doesn't help.

"This guy Lester, he one of your shit bags?" asks Harris.

No comment from Remo.

"He say anything of note?"

"Yeah, 'of note'."

"Ya know, off the record... I don't like you. At all."

"Painfully aware."

"Last April you toasted me pretty good on the stand."

Three uniformed cops, along with a few detectives, now stand around. They all stare at Remo like he fucked their sisters then didn't call. Not lost on Remo, he recalls April clearly. Really he just wants Harris to shut the hell up. Perhaps that guy in the hoodie can come back and shoot Harris—or Remo. At this point it doesn't matter to him. Harris keeps riding his train of thought.

"And that disease of a human you set free? The one who killed four more people less than a day later? You recall that little moment, fuckface?"

Remo redirects. "Can we talk about tonight?"

"Sorry, excuse me. On the record again."

"He said people are coming to kill me." A long, silent beat to go with the long, blank stares from Harris and his fellow officers. "You catch that, Detective?"

"Oh, yeah, I got it."

"Thoughts?"

Harris delivers his explanation like he was reading the daily lunch specials. "It's New York. People say shit all the time. I had a homeless guy tell me today that lesbian mutants were planning a global rebellion."

Cute, Remo thinks, but he can't help but consider this may be more of a real threat than the good Detective's dismissive evaluation.

"You said this man at the window instructed you to get down?"

Remo nods.

"Like he was telling you to get out of the way? As if he was only after Lester?"

Remo knows where this is going. "Maybe, but—"

"Doesn't sound like you were the target of any violence here. More like Lester was the one in trouble."

Nothing from Remo. Why argue with a man who doesn't care, hates you, and worst of all... is making sense?

Harris, an annoying gleam in his eye, offers to help. "If, of course, you feel uncomfortable or threatened in any way, I can have some of my best men keep a watchful eye over you."

Remo looks to the gallery of armed lawmen who despise everything about him.

Harris leans in. "Off the record, they hate you too."

No shit.

Outside the eatery, the sun is starting to rise. Through the blown-out window, people are watching real-life crime TV. They can't help but watch as Remo has his little love chat with Detective Harris. Across the street, a small crowd has gathered to gawk and rubberneck at the crime scene. Early morning fun for those coming off the grave-yard shift, and even better for those still drunk from last call.

Nestled among the crowd of onlookers is the man in the hoodie. The man with the .357 who shot Lester all to hell. He's lost the glasses, the hoodie, and the beard, now looks like his true self: a frail, coked-up, weasel of a man who wears a crooked smile and has crazy eyes.

Eyes that are locked on Remo like he was dinner.

This would be Chicken Wing.

8

Chicken Wing. A.K.A. the youngest Mashburn brother. At the tender age of 23, Chicken Wing is clearly the most dangerous of a dangerous bunch. He carries a seemingly endless surplus of nervous energy, fueled with a mix of angst and narcotic-enriched psychosis. By any normal standard, an unemployable disaster of a human who operates without remorse, reason or the vaguest sense of right and wrong. Of course the Mashburn family business has a much different set of standards.

The 'Chicken Wing' handle was lovingly given to him by his brothers. When he was a kid, his scrawny frame produced arms that resembled—you got it—chicken wings. He can't remember which one saddled him with the name, but it stuck. Nicknames, a lot like herpes, don't leave you. Ever. He's older now, but still a skinny guy, and his muscle mass hasn't grown enough for his brothers to change the name. Only Chicken Wing's anger and violent tendencies have grown.

His cell rings. He knows who it is without looking. Chicken Wing steps away into a nearby alley. "Yo." A familiar voice crackles on the other side of the call.

A family voice. "You on him?" asks Ferris.

Just as Lester had said, Ferris is alive and well and standing in the middle of a suburban home that looks like it was ripped out of a Pottery Barn catalog. Every knickknack has a story. He plays with a wooden rooster as he talks to his fucked-up brother on a prepaid cell. He smiles, thinking how Chicken Wing would giggle hysterically about Ferris playing with a cock.

"On him? Surely am. Haven't seen any money—"

"He's not going to walk around with three million and change. Probably has it in several safe spots around town." Ferris walks into a warmly decorated living room. He's lived through problems with Chicken Wing, problems that arose from his little brother failing to follow the simplest of orders. Not because the kid is stupid, but because he's an impulsive little nut bag. Ferris knows he has to be very clear with his little brother. "Hear this now. You stay on him. Lester lost his shit today. He took out half the crew."

Chicken Wing grows a big, knowing grin. "Just saw Lester. Put a bucket of bullets in him."

"When?" Ferris closes his eyes, freezing off this new info – *What the fuck did he do? What the FUCK did he do?*

"Just now. He was talking to Remo and—"

"Remo? What did he say to him?" Ferris is about to jump out of his skin, mind flipping through worst-case scenarios. Chicken Wing scenarios.

"How the fuck should I know?" Chicken replies, beginning to simmer toward a boil because of his big brother's big-brother tone.

"Chicken Wing, we talked about control. Remember our talk? Do not—"

"Yeah, I know, Ferris. I saw Lester having dinner with Remo. Didn't look like a good thing, so I took care of it."

Ferris recognizes the defensive spike in his brother's tone, registers it, and pulls it back a level or two, trying to soothe the conversational tone. "And you were right . . . this time. But we can't go reckless with something like this."

His efforts are not working. At all. Chicken Wing's agitation multiplies with every word. "I heard you, for fuck's sake. You always fucking... you worry about your own goddamn chores." Chicken Wing considers throwing the burner phone against the brick wall, but hangs up instead.

Congratulates himself for his maturity.

Ferris pockets his phone, walks into the living room, and takes a seat on the couch. Clearly, he's not happy with his little brother. He can't help but blame himself a bit for putting Chicken Wing in a position of potential failure. Then again, the kid has to grow up sometime. Can't keep mothering the motherfucker. Mutters to himself something about that dumbass little shit fucking up everything.

His self-contained conversation is interrupted by a muffled yelp from the corner of the room. Ferris turns, puts a finger to his lips and waves a cold no-no finger toward a woman balled up on the floor.

A bound, gagged and terrified woman.

When she hand-picked all these knickknacks for her dream house, she never thought life would end up like this. While she carefully scoured countless thrift stores, pored over catalogs and searched online, she never thought she was decorating her own tomb.

Her lips quiver, fighting to obey her home invader's—she didn't catch his name—request for quiet.

Ferris turns on the TV, putting his feet up as he opens a bag of Baked Lays. Baked Lays? Just buy the fucking real ones. Unbelievable. He turns up the volume, ignoring the cries from the woman in the corner.

A picture of a glowing couple rests on a corner table, the woman on the floor during a much happier time. In the picture, she's wrapped in her husband's arms. Her eyes lock on the picture. She thinks that if only her broad-shouldered, strong, courageous husband were here none of this would be happening. Frank would kill this fucking asshole. This fucking asshole who's eating their Baked Lays and putting his feet up on their brand new Hyde turned-leg coffee table... oh, this fucking asshole.

What she doesn't know, couldn't possibly know, is that her husband is actually painfully aware of what's going on. He's not happy about it, but he knows nonetheless.

He knows because her husband, her Frank, is the same Frank as—

9

The broad-shouldered, strong, courageous prison guard stands monitoring the island yard.

Rikers Island to be exact.

Unlike in the happy picture with his wife, Frank's face is wrapped in worry. Smile gone. Beyond tense. The thought of Ferris Mashburn spending some quality time in his home, with his wife . . .

He scans the yard filled with convicts of all makes and models. It's a criminal soup of races, tats and mental twist-ties. Frank zeroes in on one inmate in particular, walking a hard line toward Dutch Mashburn.

Dutch stands alone, watching an inmate basketball game. Whites against blacks. Sure, it's all about race, and does nothing to soothe ethnic tensions, but it does make keeping track of who's on whose team very easy.

Dutch, older than Ferris and considerably older than Chicken Wing, is the undisputed ruler of the Mashburns, the crew and, now, Frank and his wife.

In short, Dutch = Scary Dude.

He was born with the glow of filthy, nasty intelligence, and has the look of a man who would gut your family and then post it as an anatomy lecture on YouTube.

Frank moves closer to Dutch, trying to have an inconspicuous conversation while they watch the nearby game. Struggles to find a tough, strong tone as he speaks. "The bus is set. They're moving some of the more violent inmates to another facility."

A tough and strong tone means little to nothing when talking to Dutch. All he gives in return is his standard, ghastly disposition.

Frank continues, "I got myself scheduled to work the bus. That means you need to find a way on it." He pulls out a crude, prison-made knife, or shiv to those in the suburbs, slipping it discreetly to Dutch.

"Only inmates get hurt. No guards, right?" asks Frank.

Dutch still offers nothing. Frank hates having to act like customer service to this bastard. He knows the situation, sure, but he has his limits, and he's just about pushed to the edge. He looks at Dutch, raises his voice to a harder tone. "Listen, you piece of shit. If that monster of yours hurts my wife in any way..."

Dutch's face doesn't even attempt to alter expression.

His heartbeat rests comfortably, as if he were lying on a raft drifting in a pool in Vegas. Dutch was threatened, beaten, shot and stabbed—all before he could he could drive a car. Not too long after that, Dutch was the one delivering the threats and beat downs. He's shot more people than the LA and Detroit PDs combined. Butchered more poor bastards than Jason Voorhees. Not a whole helluva lot shakes Dutch's tree. Certainly not some prison yard bull who Dutch has by the balls. Which is why Dutch doesn't even give the courtesy of eye contact as he simply replies, "What?"

Frank's blood boils, working him into a lather as he attempts to retort.

Dutch cuts him off. "Was that your big plan? Raising your voice?"

Frank stands down.

"We have a deal, sweet-ass. You do what you want to do and we won't." They lock eyes. Frank has no choice but to trust him. The whole time, Dutch never loses concentration on the basketball court.

"Now, please. I need to go get violent for a moment," says Dutch, whistling as he strolls toward the court. He cuts through the game without pause, forcing the players to alter their movements. He strolls to the center of the court, the mean, high-intensity game in full swing.

Dutch couldn't care less.

He parts the players like the Red Sea, bringing the game to screeching halt. The players surround him. Black and white alike, they've found a common enemy. A mountain of muscle steps up, itching to throw down a ton of unpleasantness. Any reason to unleash pain on someone is an excellent reason. He towers over Dutch.

Mountain snarls, "The fuck, Dutch?" The players crowding around are dying to tear this old guy apart.

Other guards start to take notice.

Dutch, calm as a Hindu cow, gives a disarming crack of a smile before ripping the shiv across the Mountain's neck. So fast, so clean it doesn't even bleed at first. It starts to spit slowly, then gushes like water from a burst dam. The Mountain grabs his neck, blood rushing through his thick fingers.

Shock and disbelief are stuck in his eyes as his life spills out onto the court.

Dutch spins, a devil's holiday, jamming the crude weapon into anyone unfortunate enough to be around him. Inmates fall back, bleed, drop.

Cutting. Plunging. Ripping. Multiple stab wounds for each.

Sounds of thick flaps puncturing skin followed by the stomach-turning tearing from the blade's exit. Dutch moves like a man possessed, lightning fast, an impressive, beautiful blur of violence.

He releases an inhuman, hollow wail. His face expressionless. An atypical outburst for a man like Dutch. He usually conserves his vocal cords, only using them as necessary, but in this situation, he feels it's just the right finishing touch.

The right amount of violent crazy to get him on that bus.

Frank gives it a standing eight count before rushing over to join the other guards as they swarm the scene. They push their way through the crowd, stepping over, and sometimes on, wounded and dying inmates. The group pins Dutch to the court with hands and knees, fat sausage fingers.

Dutch's eyes flare, the pleasure he's drinking in, the excitement, permeates his very bones. Veins pop on his forehead, an insane smile spreads. The ecstasy of the moment, this is what Dutch lives for.

Violence. Death with a purpose. His purpose.

Dutch doing what Dutch does best.

10

The morning sun illuminates the stainless steel fixtures, polished hardwood floors, and high-end upgrades in Remo's apartment. Showroom-quality living, fit for a king.

Remo staggers through the front door looking like he's been hit by a truck then dragged for miles. The events of the previous day have taken their toll. His keys get tossed in one direction, and his shoes fly in another as he storms through the living room en route to the bar.

He pulls his tie free, dumping it into a silk lump on the hardwood. Gulps some Johnnie—sweet, sweet nectar make the bad man go away —while trying to pull himself. Thinks, *Who lives like this? I gotta get my life in order. This is no way for a man to live. Need to start exercising, eating better, be kinder to animals . . . perhaps people.*

Fuck people. Grabs a banana, pours a fresh scotch. It's a start. An envelope slips under the door.

Remo stops cold. His cheeks balloon, filled with Johnnie like a drunk chipmunk.

Remo eyes it, his heart revving, pushing the needle deep into the red. Sets down his scotch and gingerly moves toward the door. Pokes his head out into the hallway, then allows the rest of his body to follow.

Empty. Nothing. Nobody.

Remo slips back inside, locks the door. He slowly picks up the envelope, treating it like it was a special delivery of anthrax. Takes a long moment, as if not opening it will end whatever the fuck is going on. As if denial will call off the dogs.

The Mashburn family. If only. He slides his finger along the flap, creating a slow tear, opening it ever so carefully. In the back of his head, he thinks of the Road Runner's creativity while trying to elude Wile E. Coyote. With one eye shut, he rips the rest of the envelope open. No anthrax or bomb, but he does find a crudely written note. It reads like an inbred five-year-old— or a profane Santa— crafted it.

We no when U R sleeping. We no when U R awake. Sleep tight, cunt.

Remo's balls might have climbed into his sinuses. His hand shakes as he guzzles more Johnnie. It should burn as it slips down his gullet. Remo's senses are so dull he doesn't even notice. He races to the bedroom. Clothes scatter in every direction as Remo digs through his dresser.

"Come on. Fuck, fuck, fuck. Ah, there you are," he says, finding the Glock 9mm he has tucked away, just in case.

Hello, lover.

He inspects the Glock like he knows what he's doing. Pulls at it, picks at it. "Shit." The clip falls out, dropping to the floor. The Glock was a gift from a client to show appreciation for a job well done. When Remo opened it years ago, his first thought was, *how many times has this been used?* What a nice, tidy way to get rid of a murder weapon—give it to your attorney.

Unbelievable dickhead clients.

Now, however, Remo thinks it's the most thoughtful fucking gift he's ever received. He just wishes he'd gone to the range or taken some damn lessons or something. He jams the clip back in and yanks back the slide like they do on TV.

Blam!

The blast blows out his bedroom window, a deafening sound

reverberating through the apartment. Remo makes a mental note to come up with a good lie before calling maintenance with this one. He slips the gun back into the dresser drawer, covering it with underwear. Perhaps going to the gun was a bit premature. He's pretty sure the neighbors are out of town. He'll lie later if he has to.

Remo heads back into the living room, yanks the sprawling picture window's curtains shut.

Throws the remaining three locks on the door. Slides the chain on. Checks the peephole. Jams a chair under the knob.

He doesn't know what else to do. He's defended people who have caused situations like this one. He's even torn apart on the stand the people who were their victims. But he's never been the target. He's not a fan.

Remo digs through the hall closet, finds a baseball bat and backpedals out. *Okay,* he thinks, *you're okay.* On second thought... he switches off the lights.

"Shit," he yelps as he bumps into something, falling to the floor of the now pitch-black apartment.

Fumbling in the darkness, he manages to get a candle lit and sits at the dining room table. Smells like jasmine. Would be a romantic setting, if things weren't so damn shitty.

He takes out his cell and scrolls through the contacts. He stops on one, looking long and hard at the name. Anna. His thumb inches toward "select."

Stops himself. Not the time. Not sure if there *is* a good time. He scrolls on and goes with another number. New York City ADAs are somewhat used to receiving phone calls at all hours, but the rude awakening still pisses Leslie off.

She manages a groggy, "Hello?"

"You fucking suck," Remo announces before hanging up.

Downs the Johnnie and pours a fresh one by dancing candlelight. A self-satisfied smirk spreads across his lips. He can't help but think, *Even in the face of death, I've still got it.*

11

They say when you drink to the point of passing out you don't ever truly achieve a deep sleep. Something to do with the fact that your body is fighting off the alcohol and is unable to relax enough for your mind to completely let itself go. That or maybe your body has some sort of mechanism just underneath the surface that's acutely aware your drunken ass could puke at any moment. Believe it or not, your body doesn't really want you to die choking on your own vomit while passed out. Self-preservation doesn't take nights or weekends off.

Of course, you can override this mechanism by sucking down so much sauce it short circuits nature's little self-preservation helper—see former AC/DC frontman Bon Scott for details. Death by misadventure does not look pretty.

Your brain will allow you to dream while in this alcohol-induced limbo. Perhaps not as peaceful as normal sleep would be, not as fluid. More of a herky-jerky kind of sleep that starts and stops, hits pause, rewinds, then records over the good parts. Over and over and over again, until you wake up feeling like you crawled out of a goat's anus.

Remo prefers this to lucid dreaming.

It's not the sole reason he drinks the way he does, but it's a side effect he welcomes. Real dreams can unlock the head or unconsciously unwind things that are better left in a twisted hairball in the corner.

His dreams tend to be more superficial mental exercises. Comfort food dreams. Something for his brain to chew on while Remo falls under the spell of Ritalin and Johnnie Walker Blue. R&B, he calls it. He saw something somewhere, maybe *60 Minutes,* where college dickheads were taking Ritalin to increase brainpower, allowing them to study/cheat in school. The drug was designed for hyperactive children, but apparently when adults take it the results are slightly different. Instead of mellowing out hyper Jenny or Jack, it allows adults to focus—like really fucking focus—and absorb information at a much greater rate. Of course, there's also talk about it elevating blood pressure, causing strokes and the like, but hell, McDonald's can do that too. Not to mention, Mickey D's does nothing for your grade point average and can make you fat as fuck, so what's a boy to do?

Remo likes the Johnnie Blue, but he's a high-priced, high-profile attorney who needs to be able to focus, be sharp, and retain large amounts of information. The sauce can cause more than a few hiccups with those needs, so it makes perfect sense to welcome the pills to the party.

Mr. Blue does what he does, little boy Ritalin does what he does, and Remo comes out smelling like a rose.

Of course, it hasn't been perfect. Working out a system takes time, and there were moments, especially in the beginning, when he struggled to get the timing, dosage and mix just right. Painful, socially uncomfortable moments. But after a relatively short amount of time Remo got it down and, depending on your personal moral code, he's been pretty successful.

Alcoholics sometimes refer to their time being drunk as "being on the island." Remo thinks those AA cocksuckers probably invented it.

Quitters.

Not that "being on the island" is a bad description. It just sounds so, so...

Fuck it. Remo just doesn't like it, that's all.

Now, during Remo's time on the island, his thoughts tend to bounce and skip from memory to memory, with the occasional blip of fantasy.

Tits and pussy, booze and pills, big-ticket luxuries. More tits. More pussy. Remo surrounded by tits and pussy while in a massive hotel suite, getting a blowjob in a limo, sex with a woman while skydiving, her form flipping between different nationalities and ethnic origins like that chick from the X-Men. Fairly certain there's a blue girl in there somewhere.

Then, surprisingly, his mind goes black.

The kaleidoscope of pornographic images is wiped from his mind, replaced by total, swallowing darkness.

In his dream a door opens. It leads into a dimly lit room. A room lit by the soft glow a child's nightlight. In the room, a young boy is sound asleep, wrapped up in bed with the covers pulled up to his chin. Remo slumps in a leather office chair nestled in the corner of the room. He wears his best suit and holds a bottle of Johnnie Blue in his hand. He watches the boy but is unable to see his face. The boy's back is turned to him as he lies facing the opposite wall.

A baby cries in the background, somewhere Remo can't see. The sound is piercing. Through the door storms a pack of men armed with shotguns and assault rifles. Their faces are blank, like a pillow-case of skin has been stretched over their skulls.

They stop to look to Remo, then turn their attention to the boy in the bed.

The baby screams louder. Remo looks on emotionless, takes a swig. The men pump their shotguns, lock and load their assault rifles. The baby's screams stop, leaving an eerie silence in the air. The young boy pops straight up in bed as if it was on fire.

His face is pillowcase blank as well, but Remo can still make out his mouth beneath the strained skin. The boy reaches out for Remo and screams in terror.

Remo tries to jump from his chair but falls hard to his knees, fingers fumbling mere inches from the faceless boy.

Shotguns explode. Assault rifles rattle endlessly.

This is not REM sleep.

This is REMO sleep.

12

Remo jolts awake. Not completely awake. It hurts to get there. He cracks his lids open, finding himself still at his dining room table. The candle has burned down to a purple cow turd. He sits upright in the stiff dining chair. All seems well, save for the fact his Johnnie bottle is completely empty.

His head feels like it's on fire, and he realizes he still holds the bat, clutched tightly to his chest. Remo jolts back in the chair when his cell starts ringing, tipping over and landing less than gracefully on the floor. He springs up, bat in hand, fighting to gain some semblance of control. Answers the call.

"You thinking about making it in today, snowflake?" asks the gravel-grinding voice of his boss, Victor.

Remo squeezes his eyes shut, "Rough evening. Cover for me?"

"Fuck you, cover for you. We're buried here."

"Things . . . things are bad," grunts Remo.

"Fascinating. Get in here or I'm sending people to come get you."

Victor's words spark an idea. Remo hangs up, bolting for the door.

Remo looks a mess as he pushes his way through the crowded streets. He constantly checks over his shoulder, working sideways glances to scan faces as they pass by him. His heart pounds at the thought that someone could gun him down at any moment. Can't help but think again, this is no way to live. Thinks about Harrison Ford in *The Fugitive*. That makes his situation seem sexy-cool for about five seconds, then it's back to the sickening tumbling in his gut, a feeling that's starting to become his normal state of being. It's odd, but this feeling is starting to become almost comforting.

Everyone else seems to glide along without a care in the world. Just fluttering about their normal day like all is fine and dandy. Have they no idea about the pain and struggle of others? Actually, Remo realizes he's never given a second thought to any of these things either. Decides to let it go.

Someone bumps into Remo and he jumps back, raising a fist.

"What the fuck?" barks a kind-looking little old lady.

Nice. Even the elderly are giving him shit. Remo tries to get a hold of himself as she passes, muttering something about him being a fucking cocksucker. Lovely woman. Remo cuts through the crowd and enters a building, heading for the floor of his law office. Office of the Gods. He barely makes eye contact with his co-workers. A few try to engage in a "good morning" or two. He stops just short of telling them to fuck off, actually. Remo hates morning chit-chat on a good day, and he sure as hell isn't interested today. Singular focus as he moves to a corner office.

He reaches his corner fortress of solitude, shutting the door behind him. Fires up his laptop while pulling multiple files from a cabinet. In the files he fumbles through photos of now familiar guys. Candid photos, multiple mug shots, and other random photos of Dutch, Lester, the Mashburns and other assorted assholes doing unsavory activities. There's a shot of masked gunmen taking down a bank, followed by a great team photo of the crew—you could put it on a Christmas card. Next ones he pulls are stills of a shot-to-hell bank lobby taken from the surveillance cams.

Pools of blood.

Tape outlines of bodies.

Some, very small bodies.

He turns to his laptop, scanning seemingly endless legal PDFs and .doc files, before finding a video file. Remo leans back. He knows this is the one he was looking for. The one that frightens him. Remo hesitates before clicking it open, knowing what's on it. Wishing he'd never seen it. But he has to see it again. He clicks.

A surveillance video of the bank lobby opens on the screen.

Calm at first, filled with people doing their business. Remo's eyes zero in on a young mother holding a newborn child. He'd warn her if he could. *Run! Get the hell out of there, lady.* It's too late, of course. Hell busts loose as five men in ski masks storm in, armed to the teeth.

The Mashburn crew, crashing the party.

Remo's eyes never leave the mother and child. He knows what's coming. Hates what's coming. Hates what he's seen. Not just here, but what he's seen and defended over the years. He feels sick again, and this time not because of the people coming to kill him. This time he feels sick because he defends these people. He's been paid well for defending these people.

Who does that? He does that. His thoughts are ripped back to the screen by the mix of screams and thundering gunfire. He closes his eyes and covers his ears, trying to force away the horrible sights and sounds of senseless violence. There are a lot of bad things on that video. Bad things that can't be unseen.

Remo pops a pill. Slams the laptop closed. Pulls his iPhone, flips to a picture of a three-year-old boy. Sean from the park. Remo storms into Victor's office, one which leaves no question this is where the boss does his thing. Pleasant work environment doesn't even begin to cover it. Victor, a silver fox of a defense titan, sits, working someone over hard on the phone.

He massages the words like a tiger playing with a ball of yarn. "Maybe he burned down the building, maybe he didn't. Arson is a strong word to use so casually . . ."

Remo grabs the phone and hangs up.

You'd think Victor'd be pissed, but he's not. An effective leader, Victor knows you have to treat individuals differently. If you produce for Victor, you get the spoils. If you don't, you get a sideways foot up your ass. Remo gets the spoils, and the benefit of doubt that goes along with it.

"Well, fucking hell. You look like you crawled out of a goat's ass."

Remo shuts the door, starts closing the blinds.

"What the hell are you doing?"

Remo paces. "I need help."

"No shit."

"People are trying to kill me."

"Who?"

"Bank crew, about a year ago."

Victor scratches his head. "Need more."

"Mashburn brothers."

Zero recognition from Victor.

Remo explains. "Oldest one, Dutch, touch of a violent streak. Middle fucker, Ferris, cool as a cucumber but mean as a snake. Then there's the little whackadoo they call Chicken Wing."

"Oh, yeah. Right, right."

"Their getaway driver, dude named Lester, came to me last night."

"You lost that case." Victor likes Remo, but you have to remind even your best employees every once in awhile about their failures. He remembers reading that in some book once during a long flight.

"Big loss. You should have won, if memory serves." Victor gets up.

Remo follows him out the door and they continue their chat while moving through the busy floor. Remo can't help but be annoyed by the conversation—I mean, shit. *People are coming to kill me, you insensitive prick.*

Instead, Remo goes with, "Victor, I know, but—"

Victor cuts him off. "Got a lot of ink. Not favorable ink."

"They think I threw the case."

"Did you, asshole?"

"No, of course not. They also think I stole their money from the bank job."

Victor cracks a grin, speaks in a low, between me and you tone, "Did you, asshole?"

"No. My income clears seven figures by March. Why would I . . ."

"Don't get sensitive, just asking."

"What would I need the money for?"

Victor hits the down button for the elevator, thinking as he says, "Oh I don't know... booze, drugs? Snatch?"

"Victor, I think they're really going to try and kill me."

Victor stops, attempting to fake some concern. "Talk to the cops?"

Remo looks at him, incredulous.

"Sorry," Victor laughs, "They may shoot you themselves."

"I need protection."

"Call Hollis."

"You're full of fucking giggles this morning."

"He's the baddest man I know."

"We're not currently pals," recalls Remo.

The elevator arrives and they enter a car packed with workers from other floors. Remo and Victor slide to the back. Most people wouldn't think a public elevator is the best place to discuss matters such as this, but Victor and Remo aren't most people.

Victor continues. "That will happen when you fuck a hitman's wife . . . sorry, wives."

"Only fucked one wife," Remo responds.

The other elevator passengers alternate looking at the ceiling and their shoes. Wanting to get the point of this conversation, Remo asks, "Look, Victor, didn't Schmidt use a bodyguard service a couple of months ago?"

"Yeah, that gang shit-show went sideways and he needed a little looking after. Got him set up with this protection outfit, supposed to be the best in the city. Schmidt's still breathing, so . . ."

"Yeah, them. Set me up with them."

Earns an eyebrow raise from Victor.

"What?" Remo demands. "You want a please, cocksucker?"

More uncomfortable looks from their fellow elevator passengers.

Victor rubs his fingers together. "They ain't cheap, Big Fun."

"You're fucking kidding me, right? What was my number last year? Last month? Hell, last week—"

"Fine. Damn, you bitch a lot." Victor pulls his Blackberry, scrolls through a few things. "But Hollis is your best bet." He sends a text to Remo's phone, which buzzes. Remo reluctantly checks, finding a text that says HOLLIS, along with a phone number. Remo looks at it like Victor sent him a nude picture of his mother.

"He used to like you," Victor points out. "Make him like you again."

The elevator reaches Victor's destination floor as he pushes his way out. "Can we talk frankly for a second?"

Remo shrinks. "If we must."

"You've got demons. I know it and am fine with it because you always deliver. But when a Five Diamond criminal like Crow with a habit of killing hookers comes to me, concerned about you . . . Sweet fancy Moses, man, that should give you a moment of pause. Maybe dry out for a spell?"

Complete disbelief from Remo. "That's sweet, boss, but could you call the bodyguard before these animals eat my heart and make my corpse their girlfriend? Could I trouble you to make that fucking phone call?"

The elevator doors shut in his face in answer.

13

Remo sits in an Irish pub across from a stern-looking wall of a man. His new bodyguard. Goes by Seck. They sit in uncomfortable silence as the place moves on around them. Remo tries to break the ice with some banter. "So, you from New York?"

"Yes." Seck likes the ice where it is.

"I'm from Texas originally."

Remo receives a blank.

"Little town you've probably never heard of."

Nothing.

Remo's working way too hard at this. "Tiny, tiny town."

Seck finally responds. "Mr. Cobb—"

"Thank God. You do know how to speak."

"Your firm is paying me to protect you. Keep you out of harm's way"

"That's the idea. "

"Keep you alive?"

"At the minimum," replies Remo.

"Right. That's what bodyguards do. We guard bodies. We are not escorts. This is not a date. If you're lonely, call somebody else. We understand each other?"

Remo smiles. "We're gold."

"Stupendous."

Seck and Remo move their conversation out onto lower Broadway. The client and his new bodyguard pass around and through the masses on the streets of NYC.

"Now, what's the issue with regard to your personal safety?" Seck asks as he scans for predators, checking reflections in the passing store windows, always on the job.

Remo tries to explain. "Nutshell, there's a few people running around who would like to kill me."

"Happens."

"Yeah, well, not to me. I mean, sure, there are a ton of folks walking the earth who don't really care for me, but they don't want to kill me. Not in a realistic sort of way, right? I'm sure plenty have entertained the idea of me dead, though none have actually gone this far. But I have it from a reliable source there is a particularly high threat level. I'm pretty certain someone will try to take me out in the very near future."

"Who's the source?"

"This dead Jesus-freak dude," Remo responds, in as matter-of-fact a way as he can. "Most guys find out they're dying from a doctor who starts off the conversation with, 'You've got a horrific disease.' Me? I get the 'Agitated psychos are coming to kill you' heads up. All from an ex-con neo-disciple of Christ who gets shot to shit while shoveling down fried rice—my fried rice."

"You don't need to worry, Mr. Cobb."

"Well, come on. Need to worry a little. Who doesn't worry when people are coming to kill them?"

Seck stops in the middle of the street and gives Remo a strong, reassuring look. "Mr. Cobb, I am the best at what I do."

Remo relaxes a bit, feeding off Seck's calm and confidence. He enjoys the feeling of security, thinks about how he's always taken that feeling—the feeling most people have pretty much all their lives, that they are safe going about their day-to-day business—for granted. Until now. He lets that feeling sink in, allows it to take hold.

With a nerve-shattering crack, part of Seck's head explodes.

Remo's new bodyguard wilts to the concrete, a decapitated flower. People scream while parting like the Red Sea. The street becomes a rippling wave of chaos. Remo ducks, fear tearing through every cell in his body.

No sign of the shooter anywhere, only people running for their lives. Remo rises to his feet, about the join the stampede, when he spots a man standing across the street. Stops dead.

Have I seen this guy before? Maybe. Fuck, have I? Remo can't place him, but of course the last time Remo saw him it was dark and the guy was wearing a bad beard, dark glasses, and a hoodie. This time he's able to get a good look at the youngest Mashburn.

Chicken Wing stands still among the bystanders scurrying for safety, staring directly at Remo. His mouth cracks into a bone-freezing grin, followed by a finger curl wave.

The blood drains from Remo's face as Chicken Wing gives a bounce-step and starts toward him. Chicken Wing walks a straight line through the masses running in every direction—a shark fin cutting through the water.

Remo takes off, pursued by Chicken Wing. He loves it when they run.

In and out of the crowds, they slice between gridlocked cabs, limos, and delivery vans. Remo darts in front of one of the few vehicles moving, a cab which stops just shy of taking off Remo's leg. He jumps, rolling across the hood, back bouncing hard off the windshield before tumbling back to his feet on the street.

Horns blare. Profanity flies. Chicken Wing's still on him. Remo cuts through Macy's, trying to find cover among the patrons long enough to catch his breath. Turning, looking, he doesn't see the man chasing him. Taking a beat, Remo works to gather his senses.

Chicken Wings springs through the store doors and scans the floor, wild eyes looking for his unwilling playmate. Remo runs for all he's worth up the nearest escalator, Chicken Wing back in pursuit.

Second floor. Remo pushes and shoves his way through a Women's Sports Wear Sale, doesn't slow down or look back. His heart feels like it's pumping battery acid as he races to an exit door. He finds an employee-only stairway and takes the concrete stairs two, three at a time. Lungs on fire now, but he can't stop, flying to the emergency exit covered in alarm warnings. Remo pushes through, alarm screaming, and hits the street like he's shot from a cannon. Runs wild without knowing where he's going, only that he can't stop. The feeling of safety he soaked in just minutes ago gone as quickly as it came.

He spots a cab pulling out up ahead and chases it down, beating on the roof, slapping a palm to the window. The cab finally stops.

Remo dives into the back, a bona fide mess. Barely gets out, "Anywhere," to the cabbie before the cab door opens. Remo almost jumps out of his skin as Chicken Wing slides in.

"You mind if we split this? Got a flight to catch," Chicken Wing says with a shit-eating grin.

Remo can't speak. The cab takes off.

14

The cab cuts through the packed New York streets where it can, weaving in and around traffic and civilians who are completely unaware of the situation playing out in the cab's backseat.

This is possibly the single most unnerving moment of Remo's existence. He's been in proximity to a lot of unpleasant individuals, no questions, but not like this. He's not completely sure it's number one, but sharing a cab with a psycho who murdered two people and intends to kill him is at least in the top three.

A silent ride, save for Remo trying to catch his breath, which isn't going too well. He keeps his eyes actively looking for an exit. Chicken Wing pulls a New York Times from the floor. They don't make eye contact. Remo labors to the get a hold of himself.

Chicken Wing breaks the silence. "Where ya headed?"

Remo can't believe the question, but he answers. "Away."

"Must be nice to have that kinda freedom." Chicken Wing puts the paper down and leans in close. Uncomfortably close.

"More freedom than you gave my brother."

Remo jerks back. "Stay the fuck away from me."

"I'm just saying." Chicken Wing goes back to the paper.

"Who are you?"

"You know me, man."

"Sorry, I don't."

"Friends and family call me Chicken Wing. To you, it's Mr. fuckin' Mashburn." Remo's blood stops. He's seen pictures, heard stories, but has never had the displeasure of meeting Mr. Chicken Wing Mashburn face-to-face.

The cab driver looks in his rearview, not liking where this conversation is going. "Everything okay back there?"

Chicken Wing says, "We're cool man. We're actors. I'm running through a . . . what's it fucking called? An improv. Isn't my buddy here good? Looks scared, doesn't he?"

The cab driver surveys them, says, "Yeah. You're pretty good, bro."

Remo's growing tired of Chicken Wing's bullshit, his little improv. "I don't know what you want, but—"

"Nothing really. Just the fucking money you stole from us. That's all. If you don't get us that, then we'll take your head. Your balls."

Remo beats on the separation between him and the driver. "Stop the cab."

The cab slows. Chicken Wing isn't interested in ending their talk. He beats harder on the glass. "No, good sir. Keep going, please." He turns to Remo. "You can't run away from this. You can try, but we'll find you." He flashes his .357.

"I didn't do whatever you think I did."

"No? Think about it good. Pretty sure you did."

"I don't have any of your money and I can't control the legal system. The judge ruled—"

"The attitude is unnecessary, dude."

Remo scrambles for something to say. "Okay, look. It wasn't supposed to happen like this. I've made mistakes."

Chicken Wing squeezes Remo's cheek, hard. "We're the sum of our mistakes, right? Dutch always says that shit. Lester shouldn't have come to you, and that bodyguard was unwelcome." He lets go of Remo's cheek with a slap, leaving an outline of his fingers, a pinkish hue behind. Lester?

Remo suddenly realizes Chicken Wing was the guy in the hoodie. Pictures Chicken Wing's face with the bad beard and dark glasses, remembers the reckless violence. His memory is now crystal clear as he relives Lester spinning like a blood-soaked top on the floor of the Chinese joint.

Every part of Remo shakes.

The cabbie glances in the mirror again. "You really are pretty good."

Remo's eyes dart uncontrollably, scanning the streets. *What do I do?* The cab stops abruptly, inches from the bumper of a delivery truck, cabbie slapping the wheel in frustration. Now or never. Remo pushes the door open, exploding out into the street with arms and legs pumping like pistons firing. He pinballs through people crowding the streets but keeps moving, blocks passing in a blur. He reaches his apartment building in a balls-out sprint, flies through the lobby, and attacks the stairs two at a time all the way to his front door.

Pulling a leather duffel bag down from a shelf, he stuffs it like he was on the clock cleaning out a bank vault, cramming in items without any real thought or plan: socks, underwear, toothbrush, Q-tips...whatever he can find. He rifles through the closet, yanking ten-grand-a-pop suits off hangers and tossing them aside like they were last summer's Old Navy bargain graphic tees. He pulls down the last one, revealing a large safe in the wall.

Remo punches the code into the safe's digital keypad, and the door opens with a click.

Inside is a stack of cash. A nice stack of cash, sure, but nothing vaguely close to the 3.2 million the Mashburns are all hot and bothered about. Looks like a few grand, tops.

Remo pauses briefly. He takes a hard, thoughtful look at the blown out window from his recent gun experience. Yeah, that didn't go well. But this is one of the situations where it's better to be a well-armed idiot than an unarmed dead man. He yanks open his dresser drawer, grabs the Glock and stuffs it in the bag.

Remo rushes through the apartment building's subterranean parking garage, duffle over his shoulder. Clothes peek out from the bulging, unzipped bag. He tosses the bag into the passenger seat as he falls in behind the wheel of his Mercedes CL600. Remo pushes the ignition button, jams the shifter into D and speeds the hell outta there, the CL600 scraping the curb as it tears out of the garage.

Remo takes alleys at high speed, running rip-shit in and out of traffic—offensive driving at its finest. He makes New York cabbies seem tame and neutered in comparison. The Mercedes races across the Brooklyn Bridge, breezing past the other cars at a frantic pace, as if they were standing still. Escape and self-preservation are Remo's only concern as he taps nervously on the steering wheel, constantly checking the side mirrors. It's fight-or-flight in action, and flight has won by an overwhelming margin. Remo's been reduced to moving on instinct, and instinct is screaming to get the fuck out.

Peeling off an exit ramp, Remo's CL600 reaches a red light and comes to a stop. Remo's breathing is slowly but surely returning to normal. He's still on edge, but coming down a bit. He's bought himself some time to think about what the hell he's going to do. He tries to, anyway, but his thoughts are complete shit.

Who would know how to help me?

His mind drifts.

He grabs his iPhone and flips through it, eventually finding what he's looking for: a video he'd taken of Sean playing in the park.

He stares at the screen, almost through it. He wants to jump into the video and join that place—a place he gave up.

Remo stops just short of running his finger over the boy on the screen's hair. The boy is bursting at the seams with life, so happy, no sign of hate or anger. *What's that like?* wonders Remo. Can't remember ever feeling like that. Maybe he never did. He's transported to another world, a better world, where things make sense. This one makes no sense. Not now, not ever. Not Remo's world.

The light turns green and Remo's foot slides over, reaching for the accelerator . . .

Smash!

The driver's window explodes from the impact of a crowbar. It's a jarring moment of mind-bending confusion, punctuated by a fist crunching into Remo's jaw. He takes another blow to the jaw, then another that dots his eye. Spit and blood scatter. The hand now tugs at Remo's suit jacket, trying to pull him from the car. The seatbelt prevents Remo for being dragged from the car, keeps pulling him back into the driver's seat.

Remo thanks God for that.

A tactical knife comes in, sawing away at the seatbelt, through it. in seconds. The door's pulled open, spilling Remo out into the street where he rolls on the concrete. Fights to get his focus back, then he wishes he hadn't.

Above him stands Chicken Wing, .357 in hand. It's not aimed at Remo though, even though Chicken Wing would like nothing more than to execute this fucker right here and now. No, not yet. He holds the gun by the barrel.

Like a blunt weapon.

Remo knows what's coming as he mutters, "Sean . . ."

Chicken Wing whips the butt of his .357 into Remo's head.

PART III

LIVING A DREAM

15

This is not REM sleep. This isn't even REMO sleep. This is what happens after a guy called Chicken Wing beats you to a pulp. There are no dreams. No tits, no pussy, and no aerial sex with a blue chick. There's only a thick, swollen mass of nothing.

A cerebral shit sandwich.

If there's a state of being wedged somewhere between awake, asleep and dead, this is it.

Remo drifts in and out of consciousness a handful of times. There's a flash of being dumped into a trunk and landing on a spare tire. He vaguely remembers not liking it. Later there was a red glow, of brake lights he guesses, flashing off and on while Remo rolled back and forth like a grocery sack.

Other than that bit of fun, all Remo knows is that it feels as if his skull was thrown down a hole, with demons and ghouls spitting on it all the way down. He also retains a smeared vision of Chicken Wing wailing on him, and noticing that Mr. Wing was really, really enjoying it. Remo can't wait for Johnnie Blue to take that memory out of his head. That is if he ever sees his good buddy Blue, or his favorite mix of R&B, again.

During one if his brief blips of consciousness, Remo thought he was going to die. For a fraction of a second, before he drifted off again, he thought that Chicken Wing was going to cut him up and spread his remains all over the city.

His eyes go heavy.

Roll back.

Back to black.

Remo comes back online again, remembers reading in the files that the Mashburns have done this bit before. They caught up with a witness, a cab driver who said something he shouldn't have...the truth. They hacked the guy into pieces with an axe and then fed those morsels, bones, guts and all, to some pigs down south.

He thinks it was in Georgia, maybe Arkansas.

Fortunately, Remo's been unable to maintain a consistent state of consciousness. Thank God for that. Not that Remo is a religious person at all, but where else is he supposed to go with this? He'd rather not watch the axe come down. Rather not be a treat for a pen of pigs. He'd rather just wake up later, in heaven.

That's right. Remo thinks he belongs in heaven. Fuck you for thinking otherwise. He feels the car slowing down. Remo's mind scrambles, screaming inside his head, *Please let me pass out again.*

The brakes squeak and the trunk lights up red as the car comes to a complete stop.

Remo's heart races, skipping beats, slamming harder and harder into his chest. His lungs can't find air. His mouth robbed of all moisture.

He can't tell if he's in his head or screaming out loud, but the message is clear: *Please. Help me. Please let me pass out now.*

A swollen, raw hamburger of an eye struggles to open. When it finally does, red spider webs decorate the white of his eye.

Remo is in a familiar spot: a stiff chair in his dining room. His face resembles road kill. His limp body hangs off the chair like a bachelor's laundry. Looking around, he's not sure how he got here. Sitting up, he scans his home, wincing the whole way. Even his hair hurts. Nothing is out of place, not a single thing moved, everything right as he left it. The front door is closed.

The leather bag he packed for his escape rests next to him. Even his baseball bat is against his chest, wrapped in his arms. He sees his customary bottle of scotch, a full glass on the table in front of him.

For a moment, he thinks maybe this isn't really happening. Like in the movies. It was a dream or he is dead—well, not that—or something along those lines. How sweet would that be? If all this shit was some big hoax his mind was playing. Or, maybe, he took a few too many whacks to the head from Chicken Wing and his brain crammed too far to one side or the other. Perhaps he had a few too many sips of the sauce and blacked out. Not like it's never happened. Perhaps he miscalculated his R&B and took a little snooze. That hasn't happened for a long time, but still, it's completely plausible. These thoughts bring him comfort until he moves the bat from his chest and finds a note pinned to his shirt.

Comfort shot to shit, he gives the note a rip. As he reads it his stomach sinks to the floor. His hands vibrate and his good eye twitches. Penned in the same writing, and skill level, as the previous note, it reads: *Told U not 2 fucking run cunt.*

Remo springs from his chair as a panic-fueled freak-out bubbles up and spills out. The chair flies backward, crashes hard against the wall, causing an overpriced painting to fall to the hardwood, breaking the glass.

He grabs the bat and searches the apartment. Races to the bedroom, yanks open the closet door. Empty. Heads to the bathroom, rips back the shower curtain.

Nobody. Back to the living room. Remo stumbles through. His eyes sink back into his skull. The weight of it all crashes down on him as Remo leans his back against the wall he slides down in a heap. Complete breakdown at his fingertips. He battles hard to keep it at bay. His options are complete shit, his life pretty much the same.

He looks to his iPhone on the floor. It lies there, mocking him, begging him to make the call. Almost slapping him with the obvious choice he needs to make.

Remo pulls up the text that Victor sent him earlier, the one with Hollis' contact info. This is the last call he ever wanted to make, but does it anyway. Like calling your parents for rent money when you've blown everything on booze, like asking your wife for one more chance, like asking someone you've wronged greatly to help save your life.

He dials. Each ring is like a vice grip to his testicles. Finally, there's an answer to his call of desperation.

A strong voice answers.

It's only one word, but it has a tone, a coolness that gives you nothing but tells you everything. The voice of Hollis answers, "Hello."

Remo has no idea how to start this conversation. Even the mere sound of Hollis' voice make him want to piss himself and hide under the table.

"Hello . . ." Hollis presses.

No choice. Remo swallows big and replies "Hollis, it's Remo."

Deafening silence from the other end of the call.

"Hollis, it's Remo. I don't know what to say here, but I need you to give me a minute . . ."

Click. Hollis is gone.

What little color Remo had in his face washes white as his thoughts do jumping jacks. He rocks back and forth, face wrapped in his hands. Pulls them away and stumble-crawls to the bathroom with as much speed as he can muster.

He flies to the bowl, flings up the lid, and vomits violently. It's the rare type of sickness that can only come from the knowledge that you will certainly die in a horrible, horrific fashion. From knowing it's all your fault and that things could have gone much, much differently if only...if only...

Fuck it. Remo falls back from the toilet, pulling down a towel from the rack.

Wipes his face and gives an oddly-timed laugh.

Deadman puking, he thinks with a giggle, a twinge of pain spiking up in every part of his body.

The cold reality of the situation hardens his expression. *I'm a dead man.*

16

The last thing Lester remembers is really enjoying a handful of that delicious fried rice. Then there was the familiar crack of gunfire, some shattering glass, screams and then darkness. Now that he thinks about it, he recalls a flash here and there of an ambulance ride. There's also a fuzzy recollection of being rushed down a corridor by many people. Words and phrases like, "Not gonna make it," and, "Fucked," being thrown around.

As he opens his eyes and looks around, he realizes he's in a hospital room.

God bless them. He did make it. Lester scans the room with his eyes. He doesn't want to make any sudden moves that might draw attention or frighten the young woman checking his vitals. She's standing next to a tray that contains an array of medical things. He can't quite make out what they are. She's pretty, he thinks, real pretty. For a moment, in his weakened state, his mind reverts back to his old self. His old self would love a piece of this young, pretty nurse. His old self would do things, even if she didn't want to do them with Lester. He was inside for a long time—a long time without the touch of a woman.

He's only a man, he thinks, and man was born a sinner. What's the harm?

He allows his fingers to graze the young nurse's hand. She jumps back, more startled than anything, as she exclaims, "Oh my God!" The words, and the sweet sound of her voice, snap Lester back to a correct frame of thinking. Like a windshield wiper on his damaged psyche, his impure thoughts are wiped away.

His head gets right. The Lord. His new calling in life. Remo.

Lester jumps from the bed, tearing the tubes from his arms. He wraps his thick, tattooed hand around the nurse's mouth. Her eyes bulge as her voice is reduced to a muffled murmur under Lester's vice grip. He shushes her with a soft, caring tone. Reassuring her that he will not harm her, he just needs a few things and some information.

He speaks to her in a warm, friendly voice, barely above a whisper. "Blink once for yes, twice for no. Is there someone guarding outside?"

She blinks her green eyes once.

"Is he armed?"

One blink.

He moves her to the window so he can get a look outside.

The windows are sealed shut—he can work around that—it's more about the height. His room appears to be a few stories up. Nothing crazy, but still a long way down. Lester takes note of the ledge along the side of the building and a dumpster farther down the way, delivery trucks passing by. At least there are a couple of options. He won't know what will work best until he gets out there, but thank the Maker there are options.

Neatly folded in the closet are a pair of sweats and a nondescript white t-shirt. They must be there for when he wakes up and needs to go down to physical therapy. He takes a moment for personal inventory. Doesn't feel great, but he's felt worse.

He scans the tray the nurse brought in. It contains gauze, tape, and some syringes.

Again he addresses her in a kindly tone as he instructs, "Please take everything off that tray, and whatever you have on your person, and place it all in the trash bag from the bathroom. I have no intention of hurting you, but I will not hesitate to snap your pretty little neck if you prevent me from completing the Lord's work."

The nurse's heart pounds, reaching a level of fear she's only seen on TV.

Lester continues, "I also need you to assist me in changing into those clothes and dress my wounds for travel."

She's frozen. Terrified. Can't even muster a nod. Lester recognizes the symptoms. He's caused this response in men and women many times before. That was in the old days, of course. Perhaps he should have left out the "snapping her pretty little neck" bit. He's still learning to maneuver within his newfound faith. But, damn, it was easier in the old days. In those days he would simply resolve the situation with some violence. It would be quick and painless, for Lester at least.

No. While following his current path, the righteous path, he must stop and seek to understand what the other person is feeling. Seeking to understand is slow and somewhat painful at times, but it does keep a man in step with the Lord. This, for better or worse, is the path Lester has chosen.

Damn, it's hard work.

Lester takes a breath, forces himself back into his calming mode, and addresses her again. "Everything is going to be fine as long as we work together on this. Can you help me? Please blink once for yes, twice for no."

She starts to calm down. There's something in his eyes. She believes him.

Lester gives her the slightest of nods as if he's willing her, leading her to the correct answer.

She blinks once.

Lester hides his shock. That worked? Perhaps this isn't as hard as he thought. One last thing before they get started. He asks, "I had a bible with me. Do you know where it is?"

She blinks once. Good girl.

As if in slow motion, Remo drags his troubled bones through the streets.

The rest of New York City moves at its normal, infamous energetic pace, paying no attention to this guy who can't get out of first gear. They pass him by, moving around him like water rolling around a rock in its path.

It's all lost on Remo.

He walks down block after block, trying to piece together some plan of action. Aimlessly stares into shop windows. With glassy eyes, he watches as street performers and homeless do their thing. He doesn't even bother scanning for Chicken Wing.

Knows he's out there somewhere. *If he wants to kill me, I'm here.* While roaming, he passes a homeless guy holding a sign that reads, THE END IS UPON US. Remo stops in front of him, engrossed by the sign. His glazed stare is stuck on the words, as if not even reading them. More like he's studying the inside of his own head, and his eyes just have to look at something while he's doing it. His stare bores through the crude sign, all en route to a spot in his mind, a hopeless little corner of the universe that only Remo can see.

Homeless guy asks, "You okay?"

"No."

"World's on a freight train to hell, brother. You ready?"

The question—*You ready?*—sparks an idea in Remo. The answer is an overwhelming *No!,* But at the same time, Remo wonders why, if he can't stop his death, can't he at least be ready to die? Is that the way to look at this? Is that the angle to play? Like those movies where the character is told he has cancer or some shit and they go through a journey of self-discovery, blah, blah, blah... yeah, those. Now, of course, Remo and self-discovery are like a porn star and virginity. You can't put the genie back in the bottle, but Remo chooses to look at it differently.

I'm going to die, and that sucks, but now what? What's the play? What's my move with this?

Remo's wandering has brought him to a coffee shop, where he's now sprawled out in a corner booth meant to seat six. A pot of hot coffee sits on the steel-topped table, his flask of Johnnie at the ready. Balled up wads of napkins are scattered among the salt and pepper shakers and the jelly tower. He works feverishly at writing something on a fresh napkin. He writes fast, pouring his mind out on the page, then stops. Crosses everything out and wads it up, tossing it to the side to keep company with the other scraps of ideas.

A young, hipster-punk waitress walks up, topping off his coffee. Tattoo sleeves wrap her arms and cover her neck. Mermaids or some shit. She could be very attractive, but damn that's a lot of ink. Nose and ears look like a pincushion.

She takes note of Remo's struggles with his writing, then asks, "Whatcha working on?"

Remo offers her nothing in the way of a response.

Undaunted, she tries again. "Looks like it's giving you some stress."

He pours from his flask into the coffee and spins it with a spoon, working to get the mixture just right. Takes a sip, adds some sugar. He'd rather not engage in conversation with this person. Drinking is a better way to spend his dwindling time on this earth.

"Oh come on, boss, I've been on since 3:00 a.m. You're the closest thing to interesting I've got." The waitress is almost begging him to engage. Remo can't take it. As if he doesn't have enough troubles, now he has to entertain this person with the remaining sand in his hourglass. He reluctantly replies, "List of shit I want to do before I die."

"Oh my God, are you dying?"

Remo covers. "No, no, heavens no. I'm good. I saw that damn movie the other night, you know the one? With the before-you-die list? I was flipping around, it got me thinking . . . not getting younger and whatever the fuck."

"Oh." She gives it a think, wondering what she would want to do before she bit the big one.

"Sunrise in Thailand?"

"No."

"Paris?"

"Could give a fuck."

"Three way with some black guys?"

"Look, I appreciate your input here. I do. But I don't have the kind of time for big-event type things."

The waitress pulls back, confused. "Don't have time? You said—"

"I mean, if or when you find out you're dying you don't have a lot of time to spend. In theory."

She gets it. "What would you do if you only had, what? A couple of days, maybe only a day left?"

"Bingo."

"I'd call my Mom."

Remo thinks, *dig deeper kid.* The waitress picks up a couple of the wadded up napkins.

"Well, what do you have so far?"

Remo tries to stop her. "Those are just notes."

"They all say, 'Meet Sean.'"

"Rough draft," says Remo, hiding the new napkin he's working on. He looks down the table so she can't see the tears forming in the corners of his eyes.

"I don't know you, but it seems to me if that's the one thing you have on a bucket list, then maybe you should go meet this guy. Who's Sean?"

Two words have never hurt more. "My son."

This is the first time Remo has said this to anyone. Sure, a lot of people knew, but Remo never discussed with anyone openly. Not with friends or co-workers or anybody. For some reason, at this moment in life Remo feels the need to share this with a complete stranger. All of this washes over Remo in an instant.

His first instinct is that he's losing it. Going soft in a moment of weakness. Then he realizes something, something so clear... something so clear that even this dumb-fuck with shit stuck in her face and retarded pictures drawn all over her body can see it.

The waitress gives an understanding nod, decides to share. "My dad left us when I was a kid, but I got this P.I. guy I was dating, well not really dating, more like a fuck-buddy situation... Anyway, he found my dad a year or so ago and I just haven't had the cojones to actually go see him."

As the waitress rambles on, her voice fades into the background noise. For the first time in days Remo's thoughts become focused— for the first time in a few years. The answer to at least part of his current dilemma has just become easily identifiable. Ideas fall in line behind his distant eyes.

He tosses a few bucks on the table, quickly leaving the booth, the waitress still yammering on as he pushes out the door.

17

Remo arrives at a downtown office tower. He plows through a floor filled with bustling cubicles in full swing, hunting for someone in particular. He looks like hell as he sticks his head in cubicle after cubicle with no success, rudely interrupting corporate drones from their tasks, coffee, and three-hour Internet breaks. A few get pissed, and a few more get really pissed. A dull murmur about the visitor buzzes around the floor.

One employee asks, "Can I help you, buddy?" Remo ignores him. Heads pop up like prairie dogs to get a look at the nuisance of the floor.

He checks the Men's Room.

Then the Women's Room, where he's met by a shriek and the inevitable, "Asshole!"

Across the floor. Anna sips coffee as she returns to her desk.

Anna is a naturally beautiful woman, with that rare light of happiness that seems to surround some people. It's a light that she can, and does, share. Some people have it. Not Remo, but some people. Not to say her life has been peaches and cream, not even close, but Anna is able to put things in perspective. Everybody has their baggage, their cross to bear and all that. But she's able to look at the world with big-picture mentality and understand that her struggles are nothing in the grand scheme of things. Through the years she's been able to gain a healthy view of life. She thinks having a child has helped her put things in their proper place. Sean is really what fuels her light.

Unfortunately, that light gets extinguished as she turns and notices Remo.

Her eyes widen, then harden at the sight of Remo disrupting the work day. She gets a sinking feeling, one she hasn't experienced in awhile. Anna never knew she had a bad side until she married Remo. He was a project, of course. Most women have one—at least one—they are convinced they can change, positive that the right woman can turn the guy around. They're completely certain there is a good, good man in there and that other people just don't see it like they do. Sometimes these women are right.

They never married Remo.

As Anna's eyes find Remo, her defense mechanism takes over. She drops down into her cubicle looking for cover, shrinking lower and lower as she hears the sounds of Remo on the hunt. She'd dig a hole under the cheap, carefully chosen corporate carpet if she could.

Shit.

This is her worst fear; this guy showing up at work. This motherfucker, here? Anna rarely resorts to f-bombs. Not that she judges those that do, it's just not her thing. Something about Remo turns her vocabulary into that of a hostile longshoreman.

She stands, closes her eyes, and finds the strength to utter a quiet, "Remo."

He doesn't hear her and keeps searching the floor like a man possessed. The entire company hates him by now. She swallows big, then tries in a louder voice. "Remo."

He stops a few rows over. The floor goes silent. Anna locks her eyes firmly on Remo.

Remo knows she's not happy to see him, but something in him melts all the same. It always did when he saw her. Even when he fucked things up, it never went away.

Remo says, "Anna. You look—"

"What..." she begins in a burst of anger. Noticing the entire company is watching, she pulls her rage back, begins again. "What do you want?"

"Can I have a word?"

"No."

"Just a few words. You can count them, then I'll leave." Anna would rather talk to a drooling mental patient armed with a chainsaw. With zero desirable options, she points toward a private conference room.

Remo stumbles, shoved into the conference room by Anna. The company's version of posh is decked out in bad art and a long, polished table surrounded by ten empty Herman Miller chairs. There's a projection screen at the far end of the room, with a ceiling projector just waiting to beam out PowerPoint genius. Anna slams the door shut.

Remo decides he should try to smooth things first by saying, "Now. I realize—"

Anna doesn't want to smooth anything. A woman scorned and ready to unleash. "What the fuck are you doing here?"

"It's good to see you Anna—"

"Oh, cut the shit, you complete fucking asshole. We agreed. The courts agreed. This . . . does not happen. No more drunk phone calls at three in the morning. No more just happening to bump into me on the street. No more motherfucking Remo."

Remo resets. "I understand I'm not your favorite person—"

"Did that just come out of your mouth? Are you fucking kidding me? Get out."

"I have to talk to you."

"No, you don't."

"No, really, I do."

"Really, you don't. Leave before I call security." She moves to a phone on the conference table and picks up the receiver. Remo scrambles for the best way to say what he needs to say.

"I'm dying."

Anna takes those words in, asks, "What?"

"I'm dying."

She puts down the phone. Sure she hates this guy, but doesn't want him dead—well, not literally. "How?"

"It's not important how, but I don't have a lot of time."

She collects herself, her thoughts, and finds her natural feeling toward her ex— animosity— resurfacing. "What the hell I'm I supposed to do with that information? You walk in here after years of shit and tell me, what, you're dying?"

"You're feeling mixed emotions, I get that."

"Fuck you," she paces. "Fuck you. Fuck you, Remo Cobb. Look at you. I can't tell if you're lying, dying or just looking for a pity blowjob."

"I'm not looking for a pity anything. I'm going to die. It's true. I just want . . ." He pauses, then says it. "I'd like to see Sean before I go."

Anna takes that like a steel-toe boot to the gut. In a way, she knew this day was coming. That some day he was going to want to meet their son. She hoped it wouldn't, but in the back of her mind she feared it. Carrying that fear just underneath the surface was her baggage, and her baggage was now standing in front of her.

"I'd like to at least meet the kid before I check out. Ya know?"

She fights the conflicting emotions pulsing through her. "You agreed to not be a part of his life, remember?"

Remo knows.

"You asked to not be a part of his life."

"I know what I said."

"We don't need you. We don't want you."

Remo recoils. "You hate me."

"You don't think I've earned the right?"

"Don't you think he would want to meet his dad?"

"I'm not even sure I believe you're dying."

"It's going to happen. Soon."

Anna's bitterness takes over. "He's already infected with your shit DNA. Nothing I can do about that. Do you really think I'm going to introduce you before you go away? Do you think I would do that to my son?"

Remo takes the hit. It hurts, and Remo's natural instincts kick in —to cut down whoever is in front of him. "Technically, *our* son."

Absolutely the wrong thing to say her.

"Please go away," Anna says, ice in her voice.

"Anna."

She looks to him, eyes begging. "Please, leave us alone."

"I only want to say hello to him."

She gives her final answer in the only way this guy will understand. "Remo, go away and die."

Her words cut, hurting even worse because he knows they were completely justified by the years of hurt he's caused, driven by all the things he's done to her.

To Sean.

It's a crushing moment of realization about the life he's carved out for himself.

He gathers the battered remains of the hope he had at the coffee shop, thinking he should have known better. It was a fool's errand while the clock is ticking on his final days, a waste of what little time he has left.

He gives an understanding, accepting nod to Anna as he exits.

Anna hates herself.

18

A prison transport bus rolls across a barren stretch of rural highway, which stretches like black arteries snaking through the land.

Steel mesh is bolted tightly to the security windows. It's just good old-fashioned, federally-funded transportation for psychos and sociopaths. Inmates are cuffed and secured to their seats. Not a word is spoken as they sway and bounce with the roads' imperfections.

Dutch Mashburn watches the world pass by, seemingly oblivious to what is about to happen.

Frank sits facing the inmates, his mind engulfed in an all-out war. He fights like hell not to show what's going to happen.

What he's going to.

What he has to do.

The battle's raging in his head—right vs. wrong, and all the wrong that will happen to his wife if he doesn't make things right with Dutch. He grips a shotgun, wipes the sweat from his brow. Wrong has an impressive win/loss record.

Dutch turns to Frank and flashes a look.

It's time, shitbird. Frank knows it's time. Every part of him hates it, but these animals have his wife. Memories of how they met, hot dates, all of their special times together, spiral into and mix with his overactive imagination's ideas of what they might do to her.

Pushing aside his internal struggle, he takes to his feet and moves down the aisle, passing inmate after inmate. Frank takes them in as he passes with unsteady steps. The choices they've made, they all deserve to die. *Fuck 'em,* he thinks. His wife doesn't deserve this. He doesn't deserve this.

The portly bus driver checks his rearview, taking in the monster cargo behind him.

Frank reaches Dutch.

They share a silent moment. It's all over Frank's face; he's losing his will to do this. Dutch's granite-gaze coupled with a mocking slash to the neck reminds Frank that his wife will die if he's not helpful, as in right fucking now.

"Everything all right back there?" asks the bus driver.

Dutch's hate-drenched eyes slip to him then back to Frank. "You going to answer him, asshole?

"Yeah, it's fine," replies Frank. He pulls a set of keys, turning his back to the driver.

Frank speaks, low and shaky. "Look in my eyes and tell me she's okay."

Dutch smiles. "What do you think I am?"

Dutch knows something Frank doesn't. He knows that not far from here Ferris is exiting Frank's home, getting into a stolen roofers' van and driving off. Ferris will check his watch. Count to five. Then Frank's house, along with his little lady, will burst into a fireball. Dutch is more than comfortable knowing all this—actually hasn't given it a lot of thought up until now. Of course Frank knows none of this as he locks eyes with Dutch, otherwise Frank would blast that shotgun into Dutch's smiling, knowing face.

Frank thinks he has no other play here, so he unlocks Dutch's cuffs and chains. Stepping back, he gives Dutch a silent finger count.

One ... Two ... Three.

Frank calls out for the benefit of the other guard and the driver. "Sit down, Dutch!"

Dutch springs up, locking his arm around Frank's throat, twists his shotgun away. The other guard gets up, trying to level his sidearm. *Blam!*

Dutch drops him, blood spray hitting the roof and front row of prisoners.

"No!" screams Frank. The site of his fellow guard being blown away, because of him, is almost too much. Because he was trying to save his wife, this guard will not be going to his home. Frank pushes that reality to the background, rationalizes something about how we all know the risks, and that's the job.

Inmates scream and cheer like it was NFL Sunday.

"Pull over," Dutch instructs the driver, calm as can be. The driver's eyes bounce between his rearview mirror and the road. Dutch fires a shot into the roof.

The driver yanks the wheel, pulling over to the side of the road. $30k a year ain't worth it. Sure, dental's nice, but fuck it. He's been thinking of going back to school anyway.

The bus is now complete chaos, escalating by the second. Rocking, bouncing and swaying, shocks and struts put to the test by the inmate's pent-up bloodlust. Still fastened to their seats, they tug like rabid animals whipped into a full-blown frenzy. They beg Dutch to set them free, calling out to him as if he's their Lord and Savior. He ignores their pleas, pushing Frank to the front of the bus.

"Open the cage," orders Dutch. The driver looks to Frank, then Dutch. "Open that door or I kill him and release the freaks on you." Again, the math is simple—not worth the trouble. The driver opens the cage door and Dutch pushes Frank through. Without a second thought, Dutch delivers a shotgun blast into the driver's face.

A roar from the fans in the cheap seats.

Dutch shoves Frank out the bus's doors, where he rolls into the dirt, reduced to a puddle of emotion. Through rage-induced tears Frank calls out, "We had a deal."

Something catches Dutch's eye; a roofers' van speeding their way.

"We did."

"You won't hurt her?"

"I won't."

The van pulls up, driver's window lowering to reveal Ferris at the wheel.

"Or me?" asks Frank.

"I won't," sneers Dutch, as Ferris fires two .357 slugs into Frank's forehead.

Frank's body hasn't even hit the ground when Dutch enters the van.

The reunited Mashburns speed off, leaving in their wake three dead prison guards and a busload of Satan's minions, still strapped to their assigned seats. The bus jolts in every conceivable direction, like it was a sack full of wild monkeys trying to fuck a football.

Dutch sits back, letting the wind blow through his rat's nest of hair. Ferris steals a quick look at his brother, allows a small smile, but says nothing.

Hands Dutch the .357.

emo's pace is that of a dead man walking. Void of any form of expression, his facial muscles hang from his skull. Throngs of busy people rush along with a vibrant pulse that matches their city, while Remo moves at a crawl.

You couldn't find his pulse with a map. He's a man who has given up, accepted his fate. Accepted what the Mashburns are going to do to him and that he can't do a damn thing about it. He remembers the pictures and reports from the numerous assaults and murders the three brothers have committed over the years: blunt force trauma, strangulation, decapitations and—when they're feeling their Christian side—gunshots. All these thoughts and more string together at random, coming together in a collage of introspection.

Do I deserve to be alive? What do I have to offer this place? Not a whole helluva lot.

Church bells ring in the distance. There's a Catholic cathedral a few blocks over. Remo's not exactly a man of tremendous religious discipline. However, he does acknowledge his Southern Baptist upbringing—which is to say that his grandmother dragged him to the Lord's house while his daddy slept one off. They had snacks. He remembers a wad of bread and shot of grape juice. And not to be a

dick, but isn't church where people go when they're dying? Where
normal people go in an attempt to make peace with the man upstairs
before they check out? That kinda thing?

Remo crosses the street, heads in that direction.

A hundred or so men and woman, all dressed in black, stand
waiting as a casket is shepherded out of an elegant hearse. He can't
keep from watching the polished oak casket moving along. The care
the pallbearers give to it. The care they all share for whoever's inside
that box. It's pretty damn moving when you think about it—that
thing looks fucking heavy.

Remo enters the magnificent house of worship. Stained glass fires
off striking beams of colored light. An organ produces a rich soundtrack, letting you know it's okay for sadness; it's okay for tears. This is
where you grieve. So, please, grieve.

He takes note of the sorrow on the faces of the people paying
their final respects to their fallen friend or family member. His body
tightens, eyes watering. Not for the poor soul in the handcrafted
wooden box; he doesn't know that man or woman. Nor are his tears
for the loved ones left behind to pick up the pieces from this person's
passing.

Remo's sadness is for himself. He sees the truth of his life, and it
hurts. There will be nothing like this when bites it. Not even close.

An elderly man passes and Remo grabs his arm to stop him.
"Yes?" asks the man.

"How did you know the deceased?"

The man delivers his answer with great warmth, from a special
place in his heart. The wrinkles in his face loosen above his glowing,
honest smile. Just talking about the departed seems to melt years off
the man. "He was a great friend to me and my family for years. I've
known him a long time—"

Remo cuts him off. "You're going to miss him?"

The question confuses the man. "Terribly."

Remo moves on, stopping other funeral guests as he goes.

Finds a young woman and asks her, "And you, you'll miss him
as well?"

"Of course, he was—"

Not needing the full answer, Remo drifts on, moving to another, and then another. He's beginning to cause a scene at the funeral he's crashing. People are staring, starting to take note of the strange and disheveled man asking about the deceased.

Remo's mind is an emotional taco salad, trying to balance the idea of this amazing mass of people gathered to honor the life of someone they cared about deeply against the crushing reality of the certain, nasty death he's facing.

The church begins to swirl and twist, the world crashing. He shuffles in no clear direction, speech reduced to the muttering of a crazy person. For a moment he turns in a slow, small circle. He's made it completely around the church, back around to the first elderly man, who stops Remo and asks, "May I ask whom you are?"

Remo ignores him, asks the older man the question of Remo's lifetime. "And when you get your ticket punched, old-timer, people will probably miss you too?"

The old man's answer is simple and so clear. "I hope so."

Those three words put Remo's mental puzzle together, slamming the pieces in place for the first time. People will miss the old man, no need for him to hope so. Remo knows he needs more than hope for people to miss him. In fact, nobody will miss him when he dies— sorry, when he gets viciously killed and left as a bloody mess for wild pigs to feed on.

He's built an impressive portfolio of reasons for people to not only not miss him, but rejoice when he dies. Hell, they might throw a parade.

Fuckers.

Sure, a few criminals will miss his legal services, but fuck those guys. Really? *That's it?* he thinks, *that's the sum of me?* Uncharacteristically, Remo hugs the man for an extended period of time, hoping maybe some of the old man's good nature will rub off on him. Perhaps the proximity of good people will help. Can't hurt. But even the kind old man has his limits. "Could you please release me, son?" Remo drifts out of the church, all eyes on him. No longer kind, understanding eyes, these are the eyes of men and women who have now joined the long list of people who don't want anything to do with Remo. He wants to thank them, but we're past that now. Remo slips out the door, making the long, lonely walk to his deluxe apartment in the sky.

20

There's a song that rattles around in Remo's head from time to time.

He avoids it when he's sober. When he's hammered, he gives it a listen. By the time the last chords of the song fade away Remo's usually in a puddle. It's an obscure Pink Floyd song from one of their lesser-known albums.

The song is "The Final Cut."

It lasts four minutes and forty-nine seconds.

There's no chorus or catchy riffs to speak of, but the lyrics?

The words, man.

Those words, Roger's, they cut right through him every damn time.

Tonight Remo is drinking like a boss with "The Final Cut" worming deep into his busted brain. Roger's words are moments away from sending Remo down for the count.

A gulp of booze.

A flood reaches the eyes.

Down goes Remo.

21

Remo sits stone-faced in his apartment, the ever-present glass of scotch in hand while seated at his long, empty dining room table. It's imported from... somewhere. He remembers that someone referred him to a gay guy who hand-picked everything in the place. Nothing here has any real meaning or history, other than Remo's memory of suffering through the gay guy's presentation of his urban chic vision.

Remo's set up a small video camera on a tripod on the far side of the table, lens pointed directly at him. A one-man press conference of sorts.

He looks long and hard into the camera's lens, struggling to capture his thoughts before starting this little exercise. Maybe this was a bad idea.

No, it is a good idea. Great idea. Just fucking do it already.

He clears his throat, starts to address the camera. Stops for a snort of scotch. Coughs and clears his throat again.

Shakes his head hard side-to-side and then starts. "Boy . . . Son . . . Sean. You have no idea who I am, and that's probably a good thing." Thinks, then goes with it. "I'm your dad."

Takes a beat to let that sink in. Sounds funny for him to hear. No one ever talks to him about Sean, and God knows he never talks about Sean to anyone else. Well, aside from the goofy waitress. He can't imagine what it will sound like to Sean.

Remo continues, "I set up a college fund for you, started it when you were born. Your mom doesn't know about it. You should go to school, drink . . . drink a lot. It'll assist in the realignment of your thinking about your old man."

Sip of scotch.

"You should drink and get weird with a lot of girls. Everybody says that kind of behavior doesn't help; they're fucking idiots. It helps. Helps a lot. Sorry, off topic."

Gulp of scotch.

"My sperm donor of a daddy died in a shootout. Unfortunately, it's looking a lot like your's might bite it the same way. His was for cheating an unfriendly poker game. Mine is, well, slightly more complicated. Same error in judgment, I suppose... fucking drifting again. Sorry, man."

Another gulp. Pours more. "You're going to hate me for a long time and you won't really know why. That's okay. I should have been around to show you shit, I know I should have."

He pushes the glass away and pops open his pill bottle, scattering out a few on the table in front of him. Preparing.

"You got good DNA kid, no question. Your Mom's a MILF, and I'm not bad either. Both of us are pretty bright bulbs, so that has to put you ahead of the curve. Good-looking and smart goes far in this life. Sucks for the armies of hideous dumbasses that clog the planet, but it is a fact. People will like you, and definitely will want to show up to your funeral. That's a long way off, but it's important."

Takes a mouthful of scotch, swishes it side-to-side before a hard swallow. He picks up a pill, getting it ready between his thumb and index finger.

"You should live like you want people to miss you. There, that's a good one. I'll leave you with that bit of wisdom."

He bounces the pill, trying to land it in the scotch glass.

"Take it easy on your mom. Take care of her. She deserved a

helluva a lot more than me. . . as do you. Just know that I think of you frequently. I've set aside some things for you. Your mom will know what to do. But Sean . . ." Remo's eyes water, but he holds it together. "All of this—me talking here, the mindless babbling—this is really me trying to say, in an extremely piss-poor fashion, that I'm so very, very sor—"

His ringing cell phone cuts him off in mid-sentence. Plop. Finally got one in the glass. Remo sees the caller ID, answers with a confused, "Hello?" Nothing on the other end.

"Anna?"

Anna clutches her cell, standing in the doorway of her homey kitchen. Unlike Remo, she picked everything out by herself.

Sean sits coloring a *Toy Story 3* picture at the table. Woody and Buzz are an odd mix of magenta and periwinkle, but the kid's enjoying himself. Anna tries hard to keep her conversation with Remo away from Sean. "Remo, I shouldn't have said those things. You deserved every word and it was the truth, but I shouldn't have said them. Are you really dying?"

Remo, touched, replies, "Unfortunately."

"Let's be clear, I will never forgive you."

"Understood."

"Stop. Let me talk. I don't like this, and I'm certain this is a massive mistake, but... you should meet Sean. If I don't let him meet you, I'll hate myself later." The conversation is emotionally exhausting for her.

For first time in a long, long time, a light shines in Remo. "Thank you, Anna."

She can hear in his voice that he means it. At least, she'd like to think he's being honest. She snaps, "No talking. I'll meet you Saturday at seven. They're doing a thing for kids at the park that night."

Remo doesn't want to make a mistake with this. "Help me out. I haven't checked a calendar in a few days."

"Today is Friday."

"Okay. Yes. Absolutely. I'll be there."

"Remo... don't fuck this up."

"No. No way. I will be—"

She hangs up.

Remo looks straight into the camera, "There."

Wipes the moisture from his eyes.

Sniffs.

"Well, okay then."

He gives a grin, his heart wide open.

His expression shifts as his mind clicks, data churning. A thought comes to light, and he hates himself for not piecing this together sooner, pissed that this is something he should have realized long before. *Why haven't they killed me yet? Chicken Wing could have easily done it by now, so why hasn't he? He can't!*

It's a fucking family dynamic issue, some bizarre organizational chart Mashburn chain of command.

He can't do anything until his brothers get here. Remo shuts off the camera and hustles out. His beloved pill sits at the bottom of the glass, dissolving into granules swirling in good scotch.

22

R emo scours the aisles of a late night convenience store. He checks his new best friend, the Glock he's tucked in his belt for safe keeping. Checks it just about every five seconds, like a newly married man twists his wedding ring after the ceremony—some things you have to get used to.

He hunts down the aisles, searching for something specific, even though he doesn't even consciously know what he's looking for.

Finally, he finds the goal of his hunt in the aisle of random crap packed high with gaudy tourist bait—worthless Made-in-Taiwan NYC souvenirs—there to amaze the taste-challenged. Remo wonders, *who buys this shit?* He picks up a Statue of Liberty, checks the weight. That's not it, but close. Puts it back, lifts a marble ashtray with a cheaply painted silhouette of the Brooklyn Bridge. He thinks this could be the one; it's heavy.

Likes it.

He continues his shopping, finding a generic white electrical extension cord. Takes two.

Outside the all-night convenience store, a late-model battleship of a black Lincoln sits parked across the street, Chicken Wing behind the wheel. He studies the store. The streets are almost vacant at this wee hour of the night. He inhales a bag of peanut M&M's as he watches. He's surrounded by a landfill of empty candy bags, Big Mac boxes, wadded up Taco Bell wrappers, crushed coffee cups, and a piss jar. Chicken Wing is on a stakeout, and fucking hates it. If it were up to him, and it's not, he would have already cut that lawyer's head off and mounted it above the fireplace of whatever house in wherever the fuck country Dutch was talking about blowing away to after they get their money. Chicken Wing allows his broken mind to imagine this unknown country. A place where he can be himself, free of all the shit that holds him back (meaning laws and his brothers), and of course a place filled with hot women who have no other desire than to please Lord Chicken Wing. What a glorious place it will be.

In lieu of that special place, Chicken Wing has been stuck in a Lincoln for days with shit grub, forced to peer through binoculars, watching this fucking cocksucker Remo like some half-assed stalker. Though it has been fun to watch Remo as he comes mentally undone. Chicken Wing has seen all of it. The zombie strolls through the city. The hanging out in the coffee shop. And, of course, that little show at the funeral. That was a good one.

His burner cell goes off.

He answers. There's no "hello." No "thank you for all you've done." No appreciation for the fact he's been pissing in a jar. All that comes his way are questions, with a hearty helping of attitude.

He fucking hates it.

Bites his tongue, answering, "How the fuck should I know what he's doing? Shopping for the Last Supper."

In the stolen roofers' van, Ferris mans the wheel while Dutch talks to his little brother. Dutch and Ferris have had their differences, sure, what brothers don't? But they share a singular philosophy on how to deal with Chicken Wing. You must be clear, be precise, and if he fucks up, be harsh.

"Do not kill him," says Dutch.

Annoyed, Chicken Wing responds, "You fuckers keep telling me that. I. Fucking. Know." He gets more worked up with each syllable. "All the fucking time with you people."

"Calm down."

"Fuck you, calm down." Chicken Wing sees Remo exit the store. "Wait. He's coming out." Remo makes a beeline toward the Lincoln with his bag of goods from his shopping spree.

"He's coming this way."

"Why?"

"He's crossing the street, coming toward me." Remo pulls out the Brooklyn Bridge ashtray as he gets closer to the Lincoln.

"What's he doing now?" asks Dutch.

"Fuck!"

Remo pulls back the ashtray, giving it a major league heave at the driver's side window. The old school Lincoln's windows shatters, a buckshot of glass shards bouncing around the interior, covering the huddled Chicken Wing.

The sounds from the other end of phone earn a look of deep concern between Dutch and Ferris.

Remo works quickly. Chicken Wing scrambles and Remo smacks his Glock across Chicken Wing's jaw, which makes a satisfying pop and crunch.

Damn, that felt good, thinks Remo.

Once more he whips the gun into Chicken Wing's face. Hell, does it again. The release of violence is intoxicating.

"You lost your fucking mind?" Chicken Wing calls out with a spit of blood.

Remo gives him another smack, enjoying it a little too much. "I'm calling your bluff." He grabs the extension cords from the bag.

"I'll kill you. I swear to fucking God." Chicken Wing thrashes with rage.

"You can't or you would have done it already, right boy?"

Chicken Wing is dazed. Bleeding. Pissed.

Remo continues his work, wrapping Chicken Wing's hands tight with the extension cords, just like he learned in Cub Scouts—knew it would come in handy someday. "Big brothers won't let you. That has to suck for you." He takes the second cord, tying it around Chicken

Wing's neck. Remo sees his cell on the seat, grabs it. "That you, Dutch?"

"Hello, Remo."

Chicken Wings struggles to get loose; it's a lost cause. Remo clutches the phone. "You want me, come get me. You'll hear from me by sundown with the location. This all stops. You hearing me, you fuckin' faggot?" Remo knows from years working with the criminal element that you can say a lot to these guys and it will roll off their backs, but "faggot" usually gets their attention.

The street is silent save for Chicken Wing fighting the cords that bind.

Dutch finally answers, "Yes, Remo."

"I'm dumping your brother at my place, pretty sure you know where it is." Remo jams the cell in Chicken Wings shirt pocket. Chicken Wing groans some inaudible, profanity-laden threat.

Remo gives him another pistol-whip, just for good measure, and for fun.

A nice, tooth-removing smack from the Glock's Nylon 6.

Remo's cab pulls to a stop in front of a gorgeous home nestled in a suburban golf community. Yard's manicured to absolute perfection. A dog barks in the distance, more than likely a pure-bred. A marriage of two Lexus in the drive: one SUV, one sedan. A very cute couple.

Stepping out from the cab, Remo looks over the place. His face hardens, neck muscles tighten. Something in that pleasant, inviting home has him scared shitless. He hands the cabbie a wad of sweaty cash, and the yellow cab peels off, roaring past the rows and rows of comfortable homes.

Remo takes a moment for personal inventory. *I don't want to do this, but do I have a choice?*

Nope.

He makes the seemingly endless death march up the shrub-lined walkway, making note of the lovely rose bushes along the way. He dodges a basketball sporting a Knicks logo before reaching the two thousand dollar, handcrafted front door that was designed to look old and worn.

Remo takes a deep breath, says a small prayer, and rings the doorbell.

Inside, a sculpted soccer mom goes to answer. Jenny, as she's known around the neighborhood, works hard to maintain and improve the genetic gifts she's been given. Her looks and the appearances that come with the zip code help to hide the truth: Jenny has a past.

It is precisely that, though. Her past.

Children whining in the background, she grabs the door handle. "Just a second, I've got to get the door."

She checks the peephole, sees Remo. "Fuck me," she says just under her breath.

On the other side of the door Remo, knows what she's probably thinking, says, "I understand you have no good reason to open this door."

A man walks up behind her and puts a strong, reassuring hand on Jenny's shoulder. He's got this. She would like to open the door and kick Remo in the nuts, but she's not that girl anymore. Instead, she walks off to tend to the children.

The man is dressed like your average dad: king of the burbs, master of the cul-de-sac. Carries the looks of a successful engineer who jogs and maybe plays tennis. Definitely plays golf. But please, make no mistake . . . he's not that guy.

Hollis is a bad, bad man, and if you force him to demonstrate that, you will not like the show.

Remo continues talking, thinking Jenny's still guarding the gate. "I really, really need to talk to him."

"What do you want, Remo?"

Remo starts squirming, the sound of Hollis's voice pushing pause on Remo's heart. All of their history, good and shitty, comes rushing to him. It's the shitty that really has Remo concerned.

He utters, "Five minutes, friend."

Hollis wraps his large hand around the knob, gripping it tight. He almost feels the steel start to dent in his grip as his knuckles go white.

He's reviewing the shitty as well. Hollis throws open the door and barks, "Two words: 'fuck' and 'no.'"

Remo jumps back, says, "You know I wouldn't come here if I had any other choice." He gives the most sincere eyes he can muster. "Please, man."

Hollis locks onto Remo, cocks his head, trying to read the most impossible man on the planet to trust. "You get three minutes."

Remo tries to step through the door but Hollis stops him cold, planting his meaty palm in the center of Remo's chest. "Not a single damn toe in my house. Back yard."

The door slams in Remo's face, yet he can't help but feel hopeful. Considering Hollis didn't rip his heart out or stomp his skull on the front porch, this is a positive sign.

Remo enters the sanctuary of the backyard through a wooden gate. Hollis waters his numerous rose bushes with an 8-Pattern, pistol-grip spray nozzle. He's chosen a fan spray setting for his rose's soil; it works the best. The care he takes is obvious. Hollis refuses to make eye contact as Remo cautiously steps in his direction. Remo's smart enough to leave some space between them, a comfort cushion.

Over the years, Remo has found it's best to open a conversation with something that makes the other person comfortable. Something that will perhaps form a bond between them, or at the very least break the icy landscape that separates them, hopefully planting the seeds of a new, stronger relationship—one that Remo can manipulate for his own wants and needs, of course. In this case, Remo goes with a comment about the man's flowers. "It's really coming together—"

"The pair of balls on you is beyond comprehension," Hollis fires off.

"You're upset, perfectly understandable."

"Appreciate that."

"But I did keep you out of ten-year jail stretch."

"You also fucked my first wife, got a handjob from the second, and tried to work a three-way with the third."

"You could thank me for saving you from those first two whores. That third one in there, though, she's a real catch."

"Two minute warning." Remo's on his heels in this discussion. Scrambling, he replies, "I've got nowhere to go with this. You're it, I'm sorry. I wish I didn't have to come here today, but I'm fucked, man. People are coming for me."

"Shocking."

"Bad men are coming to kill me and they will be monumentally successful unless you help me. You're the only one who can throw me an assist here. Please. Come on... save me. It'll do your soul a solid."

"Final minute."

"I can't fight these people alone, you understand? I will be dead. I can't run from this. . . fucking tried." His voice cracks, a slight chink in his armor that doesn't go unnoticed by Hollis, who continues to water the nicely kept rose bushes.

Still zero eye contact.

Remo continues to pour his heart out. "I'd like to live, Hollis. I'm working toward being a slightly better human."

Hollis turns off the spray. "And we're done."

The hose drops.

Remo drops the shit, digs out the truth. It's hard for Remo to find, given that he's spent the majority of his life avoiding truth of any form or fashion, has made a fortune slicing the truth up, throwing it in a blender with some bullshit alteration of the facts, then shoving it down your throat with a big smile.

Remo fumbles, but finds the heart of the matter. "I have a kid, a son, I abandoned. I turned my back on him." Remo sees he has Hollis's attention and keeps going. "I've done countless shitty things. Helped a lot of shitty people get away with shitty things . . . immeasurable moments I wish I could undo, but I can't. I can, however, maybe, just maybe, salvage something from this waste of sperm and egg I've turned out to be. I'm trying man. I'm trying hard to do the correct thing."

All defenses are gone, a raw nerve of a man. "I've been bold, now I need a mighty motherfucking force to come to my aid. Please help me."

Hollis finally looks in Remo's direction, sizes up the moisture building in Remo's weary eyes. He hates everything about this man. He can't help but glance at his kids through the window. They are fucking up the house, and Jenny's screaming at them, but they are his kids, and the love he has for them is immeasurable. Hollis remembers when his first was born. Something in him shifted; there was an actual change in his thoughts and feelings.

That change didn't happen when Jenny told him she was pregnant—a call he took mere minutes after executing five mid-level targets in Bangkok. No, it didn't register until he was waiting for the nurses to bring him into the delivery room. He was alone, dressed in scrubs, waiting for his first child to be born, and all he could think about was how he needed to take care of family. Even thought about changing his line of work. Of course, that didn't happen. Look, he's in his forties and he does what he does. He can't go back to school or start a new trade, go entry-level at some crap company for 30K a year with bennies after the first 60 days. Not when he makes high six figures in bad years, seven in the good ones. No, now he just makes better decisions about the jobs he takes.

Hollis is a first-rate killer. A global, all-star, motherfucking murder man. He's killed in hot, cold, and room temperature blood, dropped bodies on every continent, and told people they were going to die in more languages than Rosetta Stone can teach. But even he can't ignore what he sees in Remo.

"Meet me at Chili's."

23

C hili's. That bundle of glory that is Middle America's home for fine dining. Hollis sits across from Remo in a booth toward the back, a location Hollis has selected so he can view all entry and exit points, as well as keep a good line of sight on the kitchen. Just in case some fucker decides to come out blazing.

A table tent separates the two of them, proudly displaying a dizzying array of colorful drinks and towering dessert options, all for reasonable prices. Rarely is there this much tension at a Chili's, but there's been nothing but stares and uncomfortable silence between them since they sat down. Remo can't take it anymore, opens up the conversation by saying, "I can't begin to describe how much this means to—"

Hollis can't take it either. "Asshole." Hollis stops while a young waitress drops off a plate of appetizers with zero zest for life. When the abruptly delivered plate stops sliding, Hollis continues. "I haven't agreed to a damn thing. Now, what are you proposing here?"

"Bluntly speaking, we gotta kill these fuckers. Going to be three of them--"

"Probably more," Hollis states matter-of-factly, based on his extensive experience with this type of situation.

"Sweet Christ, I hope not. You think so?"

"You defended these guys?"

Remo shrinks. "Kinda."

"Care to expand on that?"

"I was going through a bit of a time during their case. The wife left me—"

"Smart girl."

"Without question. I fell into a little depression, self-loathing. The descent dumped me into the abyss, and then this case comes to me. Could have won it fair and easy; cops fucked up everything. But I couldn't do it. I've seen a ton of horrible things over the years, but this one...man. They shot everybody. Most were unarmed, face down. There was this woman and her kid. Kid ... a baby, really." Remo drifts, comes back. "They shot everyone."

Hollis watches, trying not to show sympathy for this complete waste of oxygen sitting across from him. Keeps listening as Remo goes on. "I threw the case."

Hollis's eyes go wide. "Sweet, counselor."

"That's not all. They got away with just north of three million. As their attorney, I told them I needed to know where it was stashed."

There it is, thinks Hollis, *fucking knew it.* He starts to reassess being here.

"I dug up the money," Remo confesses.

"Give it back."

"Don't have it."

That does it for Hollis. "I'm leaving." He begins sliding out.

Remo scrambles to keep him there by saying, "I didn't want that money landing with the cops, going wherever the fuck it happens to go. I gave it all away. One hundred percent."

"Where?" asks Hollis.

"I gave it to the foundation they set up for the families of the bank victims."

Hollis knows better. "You lying fuck."

"Why doesn't anybody believe me? I gave it away. Seriously, I did. Roughly ninety percent of the money went to them."

Hollis flicks aside a Loaded Potato Skin, grabs a Southwestern Eggroll. His disbelief wrapped in disapproval spins round and round. He busts into a series of uncontrollable laughs.

"Not funny. Not funny at all."

"Oh, it is. The one vaguely decent thing you've done with your miserable life is the thing that's going to get you killed." Hollis is now rolling with laughter. "Classic. I'm so glad you stopped by today."

"Glad I helped you find your smile."

"Simply awesome."

Remo tries to ignore his "buddy's" enjoyment of the situation. "I've got a vacation home in East Hampton. It's secluded, nobody else will get hurt. They think I'm handing over the money. Told them I'd call by sundown."

"What are you, Wyatt Earp?"

"So what I propose," Remo continues, ignoring Hollis' sarcasm, "is you, guns, and a pile of dead fuckers. Name your price."

"I'm not going anywhere." Hollis stuffs the once-discarded potato skin in his mouth as he starts to slide out again. Remo's heart drops, his last bit of hope fading away. He has no other plays left. That's it. It's all over.

It's really fucking over.

Hollis turns back to him. "I'm going to the mall. You in or not?"

REMO FOLLOWS Hollis as he strolls among the suburban shoppers in a mall that buzzes with parents, teens and children, as well as some elderly people using the place as a walking track. A 1,434,786 square foot monument to disposable income and the American dream.

Hollis stops at a large window outside a Gap, admiring a sweater.

Remo is beyond anxious. "No offense, friend, but I didn't come here to bond with you by sharing feelings and picking out sweaters. I need you heavily armed, bloodthirsty and pissed off."

Hollis continues his window shopping, chatting along the way. "Did you think you could just stumble into my yard misty-eyed, spewing flowering sentiment about your kid and I would gladly dive face-first into a sausage grinder? For you?"

"Yeah. I did."

"Do you completely understand my profession?"

"You kill people."

They pass an ice skating rink. Hollis shakes his head in frustration and thinks to himself, *Nobody gets my job. They think they know from watching movies and playing video games. 'Ooooh, look how cool it is to be a contract killer.' The hell with it. Just suffer the fools . . . can't kill them all.*

Hollis takes a deep breath and attempts to explain. "I'm a highly-skilled professional. I research everything. Nothing is a surprise. I monitor daily patterns. Wait. Watch. Plan. I take out targets from a hundred yards away. The goal is to work without the target, or anybody else, knowing what happened. I only go messy if a client wants to send a message, but that's an additional charge. My skill set is—"

"Calculated murder. Are you forgetting who you're talking to here?"

"It's what I do. What I don't do is kick in doors, spraying bullets like some entry-level cowboy who just jerked off to *The Fast and the Furious.*"

"What are you willing to do?"

Hollis takes a moment to ponder that while checking out the display case of one of those places with the big-ass cookies. He makes a decision while surveying the buffet and says, "I will arm you. I will arm you well. I will show you basic tactical weapons scenarios, fundamental close-quarters techniques."

Not what Remo had in mind, but it's better than his other options, which all end with him cut to pieces and his remains spread like fertilizer.

Hollis continues. "I'll assist in developing some basic situational defense plans." He pauses to chat up a cute cookie cashier. "Just one. Chocolate chip, please." He turns to Remo. "You want a cookie?"

Remo feels more like throwing up again. Hollis takes the cookie from the cashier. He moves on through the mall, smiling the whole time like a three-year-old getting a big treat. Remo is forced to catch up, and attempts to get the conversation back on track. "Well. I mean, thank you, of course, but I was hoping you might pitch in."

"Go to the cops then." Hollis bites into his cookie. Soooo good.

Remo snaps, "You know damn well I can't. They hate me too. And, oh yeah, I threw a case and stole stolen money."

"You'll be alive."

"Disbarred, unemployable, in jail."

"Maybe your son is better off without you. You think of that?"

That stings. A verbal foot to the junk. The truth is a painful thing. He has thought about that and, sadly, the boy may be better off that way in the long run. Remo pulls a large envelope from his tattered suit jacket, hands it to Hollis and says, "In there is a DVD and a copy of my will. If this doesn't go my way, please give these to Anna. The DVD is for Sean."

Hollis takes the envelope with a nod, no reason to discuss it further. He's had to sit Jenny down and show her the "worst case scenario" box he has put together. Except Hollis's box contains Swiss bank account access codes, a 9mm, passports, and approximately twenty large in cash.

"I'm the only one who can stop these guys," says Remo. "They've already dodged jail and the cops once."

Hollis gets it, but wants to make sure Remo gets him. "I've got a family, too. I've made my offer. Your call."

Remo has no play here, no leverage. There never was any. It's not a place Remo is accustomed to. He nods in agreement; he'll take what he can get at this point. Hollis nods as well, a silent agreement between two people who are the best at what they do. Up until today, however, Hollis has only taken advantage of Remo's skills, and Hollis knows it.

Next stop, Home Depot.

Remo feels like he's touching all the bases of the suburban diamond; golf community, Chili's, the mall, and now Home Depot. Perhaps they'll pull through somewhere for a diet cherry limeade and catch a dance recital. Hollis searches an aisle packed with a thousand nails and shit. Remo pushes a cart behind him.

Hollis takes the opportunity to begin his lessons and clarify some finer points of their arrangement. "That fantasy you're having of me swooping in like Han Solo . . . not realistic."

Remo snorts. "You were cooler when you had balls."

Hollis tosses him a high-powered nail gun.

Mattress Giant is destination two.

Remo follows Hollis with no idea why they are here. Hollis sucks down a diet cherry limeade as he checks the quality of various mattresses. Hollis bounces on one in particular, checks the specs on the tag. Not all mattresses are created equal, and his assessment has nothing to with the spine. He's looking for a mattress with the ability to stop, or at least slow down, a shit-load of bullets.

He flags down a dork of a sales guy. Wide as he is tall, probably been to Comic-Con ten times, and not the one in San Diego. Fuck that noise. San Diego has become all about the money, all about Hollywood's full-on rape of what was once pure. No sir, the true fanboys attend the New York City version of the pop culture event.

Hollis asks Remo, "How many downstairs windows at this place?"

"I don't know, ten maybe."

Hollis tells the sales guy, "Give me twelve of these." The sales dork has never been happier in his life; he hit his monthly nut with one customer. More *LOTR* figurines await him. He almost glides off.

"I can't turn you into Special Forces in a few hours. You ever even fired a weapon?"

"Used to get drunk in high school, shoot beer bottles with a deer rifle by the creek. Oh yeah, I shot out a window not long ago."

"Motivated Mashburn brothers might be slightly more challenging."

24

D utch and Ferris enter Remo's apartment. They find Chicken Wing hogtied on the floor with the electrical cords. His face is swollen, still pulsing from being busted up by Remo.

Ferris snickers, "Such a tough guy."

"Fuck you piece of shit fuck-face cock sucker—"

Dutch cuts in, "Get him up."

Ferris goes to his little brother's aid.

Dutch leans over Chicken Wing, looking him over. "You think this behavior somewhat dampens the element of surprise?"

"In his defense, Lester fucked that up," Ferris chimes in. With Ferris's assistance, Chicken Wing begins the process of pulling free from the cords.

He fires back with a face-saving, "And I fucked Lester up."

"You're lucky Remo didn't bounce to the cops," says Ferris.

"Remo tried to run away," whines Chicken Wing, getting more and more defensive.

"And?" prompts Dutch.

"And I tuned him up."

Ferris raise his eyebrows. "Yeah, looks like you showed him good."

If looks could kill, Ferris would have ninety-seven bullets in his brother by now. Chicken Wing, finally getting loose from the cords, tackles Ferris to the floor. They go at it as homicidal brothers will do. Every third or fourth punch lands, a stray foot here and there. They're pretty rough-and-tumble dudes, capable of taking a beating as well as dishing one out.

Dutch lets it go on for a while; they need to get it all out. He looks to a clock and decides that's enough. "Stop." They pull away from each other immediately, as if Dutch was their father with a belt. "If he hasn't gone to the cops by now, he won't. He has too much to lose. We just have to adjust our plans." He turns to Ferris. "We still got safe passage?"

Ferris shrugs. "If we can afford the freight out of town."

"Then nothing changes. Get our money, make Remo wish he'd never been born, and take a long holiday." Dutch looks around the luxury apartment. "Tear the place apart. Find out where he is. He's going somewhere he feels safe. Rather not wait for his invite."

Dutch looks around, taking in the digs where Remo resides. He thinks of his last residence. The closet. The dog pen. The 10 x 6 Rikers condo he lived in during his little stay in shit-town U.S.A.

He reflects on that first night when Rudy tried to fuck him. Literally. Rudy must have had some daddy issues—or a thing for older men—considering Dutch was at least twenty years older than the boy. Dutch remembers hating himself for choking Rudy to death, after taking out one of his eyes. Not out of some remorse for taking the life of one of God's creatures. Please. Dutch hated the idea that this sick fuck probably liked being choked like that... until he died, of course.

That time in Rikers was all made possible by one man: Remo. Now Dutch stands in this gorgeous apartment where Remo eats, sleeps, shits and fucks. Probably fucks pretty women at will. Probably lounges around watching the tube in his underwear, never knowing the fear that comes from the ever-present possibility of gang rape. Remo probably ate well, not knowing anxious moments in a chow line. Those moments of checking your blindside for some bitch who wants to show the yard how hard he is by taking down Dutch Mashburn.

No, pretty sure none of that was an issue here for Remo.

If it wasn't clear before, it's crystal clear now—Dutch fucking hates Remo Cobb.

The younger Mashburn brothers, having been given their orders, are ripping through the place, scavenging like wild bears looking for good eats. Kitchen drawers get thrown, dumped. Dishes spin like Frisbees into earth tone walls and shatter, pieces falling to the floor. Chicken Wing tosses the king size mattress aside, as Ferris digs in the dresser without regard for the fine oak finish.

Dutch watches his brothers as he calmly pores over Remo's office desk for something that will help. Let those guys do the heavy lifting. He digs through files, checks some random business cards—mostly massage parlors—some random strippers' cell numbers, and a Subway punch card. He opens a drawer, finding a stack of bills. Flipping through them, he finds a few utility bills with an East Hampton address in Remo's name.

Compares them against Remo's other bills.

Dutch smiles on the inside—smiling on the outside is for women, fags and children. He turns to a laptop on Remo's desk, pulling up Google Maps. He enters the starting and destination addresses. A nice blue line shows the way. Those prison workshops are good for something.

He calls out to his brothers. "Got him."

PART IV

THEY'RE GOING TO EAT ME ALIVE

25

The pounding sound of relentless gunfire rattles and echoes in the background.

Remo and Hollis stand over a table sprawling with guns, guns, and more guns. It's a jaw-dropping buffet of firepower. Remo is excited with a mutated form of boyish glee. Hollis looks like he's buying toothpaste.

"I need an AK, right?"

"No," Hollis replies without even looking at Remo.

"I'd like an AK."

"You'll only hurt yourself. Give me two of those, Terry."

Terry, an old war-torn strap of beef jerky, is the proud proprietor of "Click and Pow," a haven for gun enthusiasts and anyone else who likes firepower. He grunts with every move he struggles to make. The years have been tough on Terry. He hands over two shiny 9mm Sig Sauers.

Hollis calls out items like ordering at a bakery. "One of those." Terry moves down the rack behind the counter. "Stock?"

Hollis thinks. "Pistol grip. And one of those."

Remo has no idea what's going on.

At the outdoor tactical course, Hollis walks alongside Remo

through the close-quarters course designed to simulate interior combat. Hollis thinks it's a poor simulation of what it's like to be boxed in with multiple murderers. That's impossible to simulate, but it's the best they've got.

Fake walls that form fake rooms and fake hallways do provide reasonably good practice for entering and clearing rooms in a way the average person might actually find themselves forced to do. The simulation uses human-shaped targets that pop out at you without warning. Some are children with lollipops, others are masked men with .45s. They keep the targets somewhat racially nondescript so as not to offend anyone who has a profiling bug up their ass.

Remo is equipped with a pistol grip Mossberg 12-gauge shotgun.

A target jumps out.

Remo fires.

The force of the blast causes the shotgun to fly from Remo's hands, skidding across the dirt floor in a dust cloud. "Fucking shit!" Remo shakes his hands violently, trying to get feeling back in them.

Hollis steps up, holding a custom-made swivel sling he got from Terry. He picks up the shotgun then pulls out a pair of strategically-padded tactical gloves with the fingers cut off.

Remo is starting to panic as he says, "There's no way. Might as well do it myself." Only half-kidding, Remo pulls the Sig from his hip, trying to jam it in his mouth. Hollis disarms Remo effortlessly, stopping him as easily as he would his two-year-old with a butter knife.

"I'm completely fucked, right? Fucked."

Hollis gives him a calming look, a look from someone who knows a little something about the art of click and pow. He attaches the strap to the shotgun and pulls the sling over Remo's head and shoulder, essentially turning the shotgun into a purse. The shotgun hangs down by Remo's side for easy access, but doesn't leave his body.

Hollis helps Remo slip the tactical gloves—gloves specially designed for gunplay—over his pampered, manicured hands. Hollis and his buddies would guzzle beer after a successful job and make fun of people who needed these things, but now he realizes they have their place, and that place is on Remo's little bitch hands.

Hollis speaks with an even, calculated tone, not wanting to either scare or bullshit Remo. "These guys have been violent since birth. They have a huge advantage in the categories of 'balls' and 'killing.'"

"Still not helping, Hollis."

"You have home-field advantage and better tools." He points to the cardboard "bad guy."

"Look what you did to the target."

The shotgun blast sprayed the target from navel to fore- head. If it were a real person—a Mashburn—he'd be smoking a turd in hell right now.

Hollis taps the shotgun that now hangs by Remo's side. "This is a Mossberg 12-gauge gas-operated semi-automatic shotgun. Perfect for close quarters. Point and fire. Can't miss."

Remo looks at the mangled target. Starts to calm down a bit.

Hollis speaks in level tones, coaching, and teaching, working to build Remo up; trying to make him a good enough killer to survive this. "Try it again with the sling. Feel the weight, get comfortable with the sound and the recoil."

Remo grabs the grip, giving an uneasy nod. Hollis gives a wave to someone who works the course, starts moving alongside Remo again.

They round a corner. Remo scans the area with his Mossberg; it's clear. They push through an open door.

A target pops out. Remo fires. Target gets blown completely to shit. The shotgun flies from Remo's grip again, but only swings down to around his belt. Another target pops out. Remo is able to grab the shotgun from his side, comes up blasting again. Not seamless, but better.

Remo glances to Hollis. *Fine? Maybe. Okay?*

A sliver of hope.

26

L ester still can't believe how easy it was to find Remo's home address. Ask a few polite questions here and there, add in a few mouse clicks on the right websites, and what to do you know?

You can find anybody.

He gives the door a knock. He rubs his Bible while he waits, caressing the leather. He looks down, checking out his clothes. His escape-from-the-hospital garb. Sure, he's a former killer, thief, and convict, but as a newly reformed man of God, he's not pleased about running around NYC in a plain t-shirt and shitty sweatpants.

No answer at the door. He gives it another knock, pressing his ear to the door, angling for a listen inside.

Nothing.

Lester checks the hall, making sure there are no pain-in-the-ass innocents watching. He turns the knob; to his surprise, it's unlocked. He steps into the apartment, not surprised that it's a ransacked disaster. It doesn't take a criminal mastermind to deduct that Dutch and his bros were here. The place is ripped to shreds, not a single square-inch untouched. He knows it's probably useless, but he scans the place for Remo anyway, just in case he's bleeding out on the floor somewhere. There's no way Dutch would leave him here even remotely alive, but you've got to check all the boxes. He figures whiles he's here he might as well see if there are any items he can use on his mission of mercy. Lester enters the long runway of a closet, finding Remo's impressive wardrobe. He and Remo are not exactly the same size, but close enough. Fishing through the tailored garments, he comes across a nice navy blue button-down with some Italian dude's name on the tag. He tries on a couple of pairs of pants, finally finding a pair that will work for him. Nice cut, fine cloth. He completes the outfit with a pair of designer shoes with rubber soles.

At the top of the closet he spies a medium sized suitcase with rollers. He stuffs it with more clothes and slips his prized Bible between some pants and socks to keep it safe. He makes a quick stop in the bathroom and checks behind the shower curtain. No Remo. Lester takes the opportunity to take a swipe at his teeth by squeezing out some toothpaste on his finger.

Rinse. Spit. He rolls the suitcase into the kitchen. There's not much, but he finds a few non-perishable items: a can of soup, some crackers. They might get him through in a pinch. Lester helps himself to the loose change sitting in a large bowl on the counter. A set of culinary knives rests on the kitchen island in a wooden block. Lester inspects them, knowing that he will more than likely need something more than his hands and faith to stop the motherfucking Mashburn brothers. He slides the largest knife of the set out, revealing a massive butcher knife.

He slips the knife into the front pocket of the suitcase and closes the zipper. He'd prefer to keep it in hand, but knows he can't walk around NYC holding a butcher knife. He dodges the debris littered everywhere as he rolls the suitcase through the living room. The suitcase stops rolling. Leaning down, Lester notices the back wheels of the suitcase are hung up on Remo's baseball bat. Lester picks up the Louisville Slugger. Again, may fill a need down the road.

Lester gives the place another once over. He's come a long way. There has to be something here to tell him where to go. The Lord brought him here. No way his journey has ended with this. Seeing nothing, his heart sinks.

Poor, lost little Remo.

He rolls his new suitcase, packed with fresh clothes and weapons, toward the door. New items added to his meager collection of earthly belongings. Turning back, he gives the place one last look.

His eyes stop.

Remo's laptop. The screen is dark, but the little glowing green light indicates it's powered up. Lester flicks the mouse.

The screen lights up.

It still has the Google map to the Hamptons pulled up. Lester studies it, then scans the desk. Next to the laptop are the bills Dutch found.

Lester hits print.

27

F erris drives. In the passenger seat, Dutch loads a crudely sawed-off shotgun. Chicken Wing's in the back, checking his .357 and sharpening a hunting knife—the one he keeps on his ankle for up-close-and-personal work. These are not the polished, tactically sound weapons of professionally-trained killers. These are the tools of men who were schooled in the violence of broken homes, poor neighborhoods, and shitty role models.

Something is obviously bothering Ferris. He's been running through possible scenarios concerning the death-match they are headed into. This is what Ferris does. Chicken Wing jumps without looking, and Ferris thinks. He wants to look at all the angles. No matter how crude the goal, he wants to be smart. There's something they haven't considered.

"We sure he's alone?"

There's silence in the van, as even Chicken Wing gives the question its due. Chicken Wing answers with a tone of impulsive wisdom. "Of course. Everybody hates the prick."

"Lester tried to help him, even after Remo put him in jail. I'm just saying, we don't know," explains Ferris. Dutch thinks. Chicken Wing doesn't bother with thought anymore. He tried it on for size; it didn't fit. He just wants blood and becomes a difficult little boy if he doesn't get it. On the other side of the spectrum, Dutch knows the answers to most of life's questions are usually somewhere in the middle. The correct answer to a situation is rarely balls-out one way or the other. Nine times out of ten it doesn't come down to "do nothing" or "murder every fucking thing moving." That's the yin and yang of Dutch's world: Ferris and Chicken Wing's dueling philosophies. Sometimes one of them alone does hold the correct course of action, but in this case Dutch feels down the middle is the call. There's too much at stake here for left wing/right wing (or Chicken Wing) partisan bickering. Dutch gives his ruling. "Make some calls. Find some local sluggers looking for fast work."

28

E ast Hampton. Gorgeous homes sprawled on the coast of New York.

Vacation homes of the fortunate. Remo's second home. His den for meditation, his little hideaway and fuck shack. It lies in an area where the homes sit just off the water.

Great places to escape life for a while.

It's a quaint, two-story Victorian home with a sprawling, covered porch that wraps around the house. The backyard runs right up to the sand and water. A line of thick trees surrounds the front yard, secluding it from even the possibility of pain-in-the-balls neighbors looking on.

Hollis's Lexus SUV is parked in the circular driveway, two kids' car seats strapped in the backseat. Even a certified badass has to transport the kids.

In the distance, a repetitive chunking sound causes a dull echo to seep from the house. Inside the vacation home, Hollis works a high-powered nail gun. Remo helps by holding long straps of roofing material in place. They use it to secure one of the recently purchased mattresses in front of a window. Defense measures are in full effect. The other windows already have mattresses secured snugly in place.

Hollis looks around, inspecting his work. It's not bad. Not perfect, and it would never hold up in a military theater, but for a brief fire-fight among friends...it'll do. Hollis tells Remo, "You're all set upstairs, too." He gives a reassuring nod as he keeps working, surveying and planning for the upcoming attack on the house. Remo follows him like a child, watching everything and soaking up every word. Hollis knocks on a living room pillar, then another as he continues his inspection of every square inch of the home. Your average home inspection doesn't include a walk-through to assess the possibility of a battle with psychopaths.

Perhaps they should.

Hollis keeps scanning, spot-checking his work while consulting with Remo. "Don't worry about running out of bullets. I've got you stocked with enough ammo to invade Connecticut." He goes back to the middle pillar, giving it a hard shove, then tells Remo, "If you get boxed in down here and need cover, use this one. It's a support beam, it can take some hits."

In spite of all Remo's faults, he's not without gratitude, he's just miserable at expressing it. In his line of work, hell his life in general, "please" and "thank you" are not words he uses often. If he uses them at all, it's to manipulate the piss out of someone. Genuine apprecia-tion is tough. Nevertheless, Remo tries by saying, "Hey man, I just—"

Hollis cuts him off. "Remember. Shoot and do not hesitate."

"Hollis—"

"You've probably got twenty, thirty minutes tops before the cops come swarming in."

"Can I say something?"

Hollis keeps checking points off his list without pausing for Remo to speak. "Oh yeah, wait until after I've left and call the Mashburns in."

"Hollis!"

Hollis stops the battle plan run-through and turns to face Remo. Hollis has perfected a way of looking at people that gives them noth-ing. He projects neither sympathy nor kind- ness, neither hate nor disdain. It is simply something undefined.

Remo hates Hollis's undefined face, but continues all the same. "You didn't have to help me." He starts to pace, playing with the shotgun sling, picking at it like a young girl would pull at an uncomfortable Sunday school dress. Completely uneasy with this sort of talk, he looks down at his shoes. "Most people in your position wouldn't piss on me if I was on fire, but you put aside all our baggage and I just want to tell you . . ."

He pauses.

How the hell do people talk like this all the time?

Feelings spewing all over the fucking place. However, he realizes he does actually feel better by saying it out loud. The weight is starting to lift; he's thanking Hollis and he means it.

It's a start.

He feels the warmth of contentment spread throughout him as he comes to grips with this revelation, this borderline sense of pride he's feeling from this little slice of self-growth. He's almost beaming as he completes this grand moment of thanks. He looks up to find...

Hollis is gone.

Remo blinks, spins around. Hollis has left the building. Remo finishes his thought out loud anyway. "Thanks."

The reality of his situation begins to creep back. The Mashburn brothers situation. The contentment and warmth are gone. Remo resumes his frantic pacing.

Outside the vacation hideaway, a van rolls up. The bad men are here. The worst case scenario has arrived.

The Mashburns exit the van. Scan the area. Check the Google map. Check their weapons. They're just down the street from the gates of Remo's property. Trees surround the gate and the nearby area. No words are spoken between the brothers, only a singular purpose between them: get their hard earned money and kill Remo . . . in no particular order.

Chicken Wing buzzes with a manic energy.

Ferris is cautious and controlled, but ready for violence at the flick of a switch.

Dutch has the confidence that comes from being a successful, lifelong madman.

They make a determined, single-minded march, descending upon Remo like the messengers of death they are.

Inside the house, Remo is wearing out the floor, pacing like an expecting father. He's almost pulling his hair from his scalp, thoughts burning him down from the inside out. Nothing can prepare you for what is coming for Remo. He looks at the checklist Hollis prepared for him, just in case Remo freaked out and forgot. Remo pooh-poohed the very thought when Hollis suggested actually putting pen to paper and writing out a list, but Hollis was right. Remo has started to freak out and has forgotten everything, including #1.

Calm the fuck down. Remo moves on to #2. He straps on his Kevlar vest and takes a deep breath, trying to find his center, to find a place in his head where he can function. He knows there's no way out of this.

Remo checks the window. The sun is starting to set. He knows it's time to call them. Fights it, but it's time. He pulls his cell, ready to dial.

It rings before he gets the chance.

Remo drops the phone, picking it up on the second bounce. Heart in his throat, he answers.

"Great place, Remo." Dutch's voice digs a hole in Remo. Shell-shocked, panic strips Remo to the bone. He flies up the stairs with all the grace of a pregnant yak.

He skids across the hardwood in the second-floor bedroom on his knees, stumble-rolling into position in front of the sniper rifle perched at the ready. His breath is heavy, partly from running upstairs, mostly from the knowledge there are armed whackos in his yard.

He presses his eye to the scope, views the perfectly manicured yard. It's empty. Still. Peaceful. It's almost as if the plush grass is waiting for war as well.

Remo grabs his cell. He takes a big swallow, saliva hard to come by. "What do we do now?"

"Well, maybe you come outside with the money."

"It's nice in here, Dutch," says the shaky Remo.

Along the tree line, Dutch has taken cover with a good view of the front of the house. This isn't the first time Dutch has stormed a house, though usually it's a crappy apartment or some half-ass meth shack in the middle of nowhere. This is a significant step up in tax brackets, but the same school of thought applies. *This is a good spot,* thinks Dutch, *for now.*

Ferris waits a few trees over, soaking up the details of the house, listening to and observing the landscape, trying to calculate the best play here.

Chicken Wing is yet a few more trees down, Glock in one hand, .357 in the other. These are the times that make the man tick.

Ferris gives a look to Dutch, almost telepathic communication firing between the two brothers. It's clear they don't like any of this. Chicken Wing just wants to hurt someone

Dutch replies, "Why don't you come outside? Haven't seen you in years."

Remo just stares through the scope, completely frozen. He heard Dutch's words, but his focus is on not pissing himself. He knows coroner's reports, what they read and how they circulate around the city

The deceased pissed his pants before he was killed. Not how a man would prefer to be remembered.

29

R emo has the rifle's sight plastered so tight it's nearly become part of his eye.

Sweat beads, verging on pouring. Heart pounds hard against his ribs. He moves the rifle from side to side, trying to keep aim on them, trying to keep up with the Mashburn brothers. They change positions, improve their positions, constantly moving behind trees, making it damn difficult on Remo.

Not the Mashburns' first rodeo.

Outside, Dutch's eyes alternate between his brothers and the house, trying to get a read on the situation. Where's Remo's head? What does he have going on inside that house? Aside from the language, Dutch uses the tone he would take with his mother as he speaks to Remo. "Just toss out the fucking money and we can go grab a beer down the road. Have a laugh about all this."

Remo knows that's not so subtle a code for he's a dead man no matter what. Replies, "Sorry, I've got a thing later."

There's a crunch of brush behind Dutch. He turns. The local slug-gers have arrived. Dutch would smile if he believed in it. Dutch is fairly confident the advantage is now firmly in his favor, no matter what that asshole has waiting in that house. Dutch tells Remo, "Tell you what. I'm going to send Chicken Wing to the front door, and if you're less than hospitable . . ."

Remo adjusts his sight. His eyes bulge as he sees Chicken Wing step from the tree line. Remo takes a little bit of pride in the fact that his handiwork has left Chicken Wing looking like he got his ass kicked by a bad man.

He exhales deeply, says back to Dutch, "If he's cool, I'm cool."

Chicken Wing takes a couple of steps forward from the tree line into the front yard, toward the front porch of the house. He looks around; the coast is clear. Gun in each hand, he begins walking, moving out onto the lush front lawn.

From his second-floor vantage point, Remo's finger tickles the trigger, fumbles a bit. He looks away from the scope, wipes the sweat away and then goes back again. Thinks, *I really should shoot this guy.*

It's harder than he thought.

Chicken Wing keeps walking at a steady pace. Not in a rush, but not a slow walk either. The steady, determined march of a killer. His mind dances with the heart-warming thought of blowing Remo's face off. It's a beautiful day. He looks back to Dutch, gives a toothy grin and a shrug. This is going to be sooo damn easy.

A loud crack of gunfire sounds out.

The single shot explodes into Chicken Wing's shoulder. The impact spins him around, but he remains on his feet. The Glock flies from his hand, landing softly in the grass. The shot echoes, followed by eerie quiet.

The whole world seems to disappear.

Complete shock rips through Chicken Wing. This doesn't happen. For a fraction of a second, he thinks, *so this is what it feels like.* Fucking sucks to get shot. This is as close to empathy as Chicken Wing has been or ever will be. His shoulder seeps, a bloody mess.

Dutch and Ferris's surprise quickly turns into hostility. Their brother is a headache and an unquestionable fuck-up, but he's their brother and they take exception to anyone shooting one of their own.

Up in his second-floor perch, Remo can't find his breath. He can't believe he did it. "Holy shit!" He's excited, taken back to that little kid at the carnival in Cut and Shoot, Texas, who knocked over milk jugs with a baseball.

Remo finally understands what all the fuss was about, why so many of his clients take pleasure in shooting the people who piss them off. So this is what it feels like to shoot an asshole. Pretty fucking sweet.

Chicken Wing holds his shoulder with his .357 hand, twirling in circles in the front yard, trying to shake loose the pain. Sucks in through his teeth with hard, short breaths. Blood slips and spills through his fingers. Seeing red, he releases an inhuman war cry from deep inside. Wounded animals sound more pleasant than this. The hollow, angst- dripping wail cuts through the air. The streaming, blistering sound that pours out from Chicken Wing is the stuff of mythological beasts.

Remo looks on from above, boyish excitement fading. It's become abundantly clear he has simply awoken a sleeping, psychopathic giant.

Fuck.

Chicken Wing's wail continues as Dutch and Ferris spill out from the trees. They don't hesitate as they open up heavy suppression fire. Sporadic waves of bullets pelt the second floor. Dutch wraps Chicken Wing up in his arms, moving him along while blasting away.

Remo's eyes snap wide open. Bullets whizz by him, popping and zipping through the walls and windows. He pulls himself back up to the rifle, shielding his eyes from the flying glass. Before he can get his eye to the scope, he sees through the blown out window three hard-hitting, tougher-than-leather thugs spill from the trees armed for war, storming toward the house. Big as linebackers, armed like a SWAT team, they fall in behind the Mashburns. Remo hasn't seen these cats before, doesn't know who they are. This new, united army thunders headlong toward the front porch, big guns and bad attitudes at the ready.

Remo's world slips into slow motion—they say that happens during car wrecks and times of personal danger. His thoughts explode, compress, then explode again.

This is how his dad died. This is how he's going to die. This is how his son will remember him, pissing himself before dying a horrible death.

What was it Hollis had told him before he left?

Oh yeah, something about shooting and not hesitating. Remo forgets the scope and just starts firing, ripping off shots as fast as he can, shrapnel, glass and bits of house bouncing around him.

Bullets churn up the front lawn by the fistful. Most of the shots miss the impending doom coming Remo's way, not even slowing them down to a jog. Then, one lucky shot lands. A leg is knocked out from under one beefy thug. Actually, it's almost blown off at the knee. Remo takes the time to aim and fires another while the thug's a stationary target. The high-velocity round plugs the thug in the chest, sending him hard to the grass.

Remo doesn't waste time on the victory. Spit flies from his mouth as he releases his own battle cry, firing with all he has until...

Click. Click.

Fumbling for a reload, he hears sounds from downstairs. Beating. Kicking. Ramming at the front door. Glass smashes, the sound muffled by a pillow-top mattress covering the window. Remo scrambles to the stairs, shotgun in its tactical sling bouncing like a badass handbag. He takes the stairs as if they weren't there. About two steps from the bottom, the front door takes a blast from a 12-gauge, the door knob flying past Remo's head. Another shotgun blast takes out the deadbolt. A thug punches through, door flinging open to reveal a wall of a man brandishing an AR-15. He looks like a badass right up until the point he's met by a shotgun blast from Remo. Just like it did at the range, the Mossberg flies from Remo's hand, but stays close thanks to the sling. He scrambles to get control of it again. The thug falls back through the door onto the porch, body flops like a side of beef. Ferris and Dutch watch the body land, blood pouring from the wounds. Dutch motions for Ferris to go around back with the remaining local muscle.

Before leaving, Ferris gives Chicken Wing an *Are you okay?* glance. Chicken Wing waves him off. Not the time to baby the man. Rage erases all the pain of his blown out shoulder. Ferris and the thug take off around the house.

Dutch and Chicken Wing take positions on either side of the front door, Dutch calling out to Remo. "You are a cocksucker. That much is certain."

Remo listens as he rushes to the Hollis-approved pillar for cover.

Remo barks, "Aren't we way past name calling, cunt?"

At the back of the house, Ferris and the thug round the corner into the small backyard overlooking the beach. The sun setting over the water would be gorgeous if not for the bloodthirsty criminals and hostile gunplay. Remo keeps his head on a swivel. He can make out movement on the porch, also the shadows moving around back. He knows they're coming at him from all angles.

"You're boxed in Remo. Give this up," calls out Dutch.

Remo's breath shortens, blood pressure elevates. The walls are closing in.

Dutch keeps up the talk. "All we want is the money."

"It's all in nickels now. That okay?" Remo smirks to himself. It's good he can still crack wise.

Dutch shakes his head with a wry grin. Funny man, that Remo. Chicken Wing is not amused. His ravaged shoulder has robbed him of his sense of humor.

Dutch replies, "We're going to come in there, and we are going to kill you. Or, we can make one last deal. Give us the money . . ."

Remo is all ears.

"And I won't chop up Sean."

Remo's blood turns to ice. He closes his eyes tight, wishing he hadn't just heard his son's name come from Dutch's mouth. A bad situation just blew past worse on its way to unimaginable.

Dutch keeps working him. "What did you think? We wouldn't find out? That's cute. I haven't seen him myself, but I hear he's a real nice-looking boy. Why don't you come on out? You decline and every-body dies in a very nasty way."

Remo can only listen. He has no angle to play.

"How about I drag you along so you can watch what I do to the boy? That's a better idea. Yeah, I like that. Whatcha think, counselor? Sound like a plan?" Dutch talks like a man who knows he's holding every card in the deck. Except the money card, which Remo stole from him.

Ferris and the thug stand at the back, guns ready to blast open the door. Ferris has to strain, but he can hear Dutch from the front porch. He holds tight, waiting for some kind of sign from Dutch.

Dutch checks his .357, wondering which bullet will be the one to blow Remo's brains out. "Your call, counselor."

Remo's lost, thoughts racing around his head at breakneck speed.

How did it get to this?

What have I done?

I've put Sean and Anna in danger.

What do I fucking do now?

"Remo? You still with us, buddy?" Dutch is giving the performance of a lifetime. "You can save your boy's life right here and now. I hate the countdown drama, but I guess there's a reason it happens. I'm giving you a three count. If you don't come out, well, ya know, the math on this is simple."

Remo closes his eyes and listens to Dutch countdown.

"One..."

Ferris and the thug listen with bated breath from the back of the house. "Two..."

Weapons up.

Fingers on triggers.

Chicken Wing is so ready, .357 itching to go off.

"Remo? There's not gonna be a two and a half."

Remo takes a deep breath. The only thought in his head is for his son, his Sean. Probably should have been his only thought for years. Not that Sean wasn't on Remo's mind, but it wasn't enough. Even Remo knows that.

What Dutch doesn't know is that before he threatened Sean, Remo may have lost focus. If this was only about Remo, he may have slipped up, fucked up. But somehow, when it's about something bigger than Remo, he finds a new level of concentration. Caring about someone more than you do about yourself does that to a man. Remo has been forced to think beyond himself, beyond his future, his career, his wealth. He has been forced to understand that what happens here is going to affect something he truly cares about. Even if he could give a fuck or less about himself, he cares about Sean. Remo may have made a mistake without Dutch's careless threat, but the only mistake made here today was by Dutch.

He dragged Remo's boy into this, that asshole, and that fucking changes everything.

Remo's eyes snap open. He exhales with a focus he's not known before today. He grips the shotgun tight. The tension is wire tight. Everything that happens from now on, happens really fucking fast.

"Three."

30

The hinges blow off the back door.

Remo whips around, leveling his shotgun. The back door is kicked loose from the frame, sending it slamming and sliding along the kitchen tile. In the same moment, a crash sounds from a front window as Chicken Wing dives through, hurling himself into the mattress, ripping free the nails holding it in place. Chicken Wing rides the mattress down to the hardwood floor. As he slides with the pillow-top mattress, he manages to come up with his .357 pounding.

Chunks fly off the pillar Remo hides behind.

Ferris and the thug flood the room and Remo opens fire, trying to hold them back. Ferris and the thug dive in two different directions as they scramble for cover.

Dutch steps through the front door. Remo is now completely surrounded.

Chicken Wing continues laying down hammering fire, and Remo spins from the pillar, letting loose a shotgun blast that misses wide.

Chicken Wing's shot doesn't miss.

His bullets cut the air, Remo catching a bullet in the center of his Kevlar vest. It spins him like a top. Better than being shot without a vest, but still hurts like a bitch. Another shot from Chicken Wing hits Remo's arm and pain explodes, burns throughout his body. His teeth grind as white-hot pain spreads from his wounded arm. His shotgun falls to his side.

Ferris comes up behind Remo, sawed-off at the ready. Remo collapses to a knee holding his arm, still trying to find some air for his lungs after taking that bullet to the vest. As he falls to his knees, Chicken Wing unleashes a reckless barrage of .357 fire while screaming like a banshee. His uncontrolled blasts miss Remo as he thrashes from side to side.

They don't miss everyone, however.

.357 slugs tag Ferris in the chest and face tearing thick, fleshly ice cream scoop style wounds.

Chicken Wing's .357 clicks empty.

Ferris tumbles dead in a heap to the hardwood. What's left of his head bounces off the floor.

Chicken Wing stops cold. Stunned. *I just killed my brother.* That reality grabs hold, twists and strangles the youngest Mashburn's simple little head. Remo sees an opening. Now or never. Summoning every fragment of strength he has left, ignoring the greatest pain he's ever felt in his painless life, he pulls his battered body up. His feet slide and scramble to find traction as he flees down a hallway. Dutch unleashes a flurry of fire, blasts churning up the floor behind Remo's scampering feet. The thug follows suit, blasting away.

A blood trail winds behind Remo as he slips into a room at the end of the hall. He slams the door behind him, bullets tearing through the walls. Remo stands in his home office, a room lined with thick books, random office supplies, and other lawyer shit. A large, solid oak desk sits at the back of the spacious room, a long window along the far wall. Remo locks the door, wedging a chair quickly under the knob.

He regards the blood pouring from his arm. No time to fuck with it. He rushes to the heavy desk. With everything he has left in his tank, Remo pushes the desk over, toppling it to the floor. He slips down, taking cover behind it.

Back in the living room, Chicken Wing is a manic mess, his eyes flooded with tears of anger.

Chicken Wing screams silently as he holds what's left of his dead brother. His mouth is wide open, but nothing comes out. His face is a dark red, veins bulging and popping from his neck and forehead.

Dutch, cold and inhuman, allows Chicken Wing a second to grieve. That's it. He storms over, slapping the taste from Chicken Wing's mouth as he barks new orders. "Not now. Pull it in." Chicken Wing pushes the tears down, controls his breathing. Dutch loads the .357, shoves it back in Chicken Wing's hand, saying, "Everything inside you right now, use it. Feed on it...and kill him."

Huddled behind the office desk, Remo reloads the Mossberg with his good arm. Pumps. Grits his teeth. The sound of something wicked plowing down the hallway shakes him to the core.

A guttural scream from Chicken Wing gains power as he stampedes down the hallway. Stripped of all human traits, the primeval Chicken Wing slams his body into the door with all that he is, zero regard for his shoulder wound. He plunges his full weight into the door repeatedly, bloody smears from his arm's hard contact with the wood covering the door. He steps back to get a running start and lands a solid foot to the door.

Another. Then another, and another.

31

A s Hollis drives his Lexus out of town, his mind is in a twist. He turns on the radio, flipping the stations. Turns it off. He hates himself. It's all over his face. He hates himself for even thinking about Remo. "Fuck him. Fuck. Him." Hollis knows he's almost out of this; the city limits are in his sight. He's done enough for that prick. More than anybody ever should, that much he knows. He tries the radio again.

Then.

Hollis spots a black Escalade with the windows blacked out and heavy tint. A gangster ride if ever there was one. It's completely out of place here. This isn't the kind of neighborhood where this type of pack would travel. Not without a reason. Not without a score, or a score to settle. He watches the Escalade pass by him. The driver's window is down and Hollis catches a glance at the passengers. A heavy-hitting crew of bad boys.

Hollis knows they can only be headed to one place. After they pass, Hollis takes a self-loathing pause. Takes that time to try and determine the weight of the situation, understand what is actually happening here. Those guys are going to Remo's. Of course they are.

If Remo is even still alive, he won't be for long. Hollis starts beating the steering wheel. "Dammit. Fuck. Shit."

The Lexus does a screaming U-turn.

32

D utch tears up the stairs to the second floor in search of his money. In the distance he can hear Chicken Wing going nuts, working that office door like a champ. Dutch pours through closets, behind furniture.

Nothing. A new feeling for Dutch—fear. Where's the money? In the office, Remo is curled in a fetal position behind the pushed-over desk. He can only watch and wait as the door is battered by Chicken Wing's relentless attack.

It's almost open. Won't be long now. Remo's mind spins, trying to find a strategy. He pokes his head up for a look. *Smash!*

The thug flies through the window, squeezing off a couple of rounds in mid-air. Remo drops behind the desk. In the same instant, Chicken Wing finally busts through the door, his bloodlust in hyper drive. The thug lays down fire, holding Remo down behind the desk. Overwhelming fire rains down. Remo is forced to stay down, pinned behind the overturned desk.

Chicken Wing runs wildly toward the desk, dropping the .357 and pulling his knife along the way. He wants the feeling of tearing, of ripping, of cutting Remo's flesh by hand. He wants to slow-bleed this fucker.

From behind the desk, Remo hears Chicken Wing's footsteps rumbling towards him. They're slightly muted by the thug's pounding fire, but the rolling thunder of Storm Chicken Wing is coming.

Chicken Wing leaps, looking to go over the desk, looking to land his knife into Remo's skull.

Remo pops up at the last second, getting a point-blank blast off with the Mossberg. The shot catches Chicken Wing in mid-air.

Almost cuts the kid in half.

As chunks of Chicken Wing's corpse land with thick, wet sounds, his knife jams deep into Remo's thigh. Remo cries out in agony. The thug keeps firing, shots hitting way too close to the thrashing Remo. Remo manages to turn his shotgun in the general direction of the thug. Knows his shot doesn't have to be perfect—just point and shoot. He rattles off two fast blasts, blowing the thug's upper body into pulpy bits.

Remo knows this is far from over. He pulls the knife from his thigh—to say it's painful is the understatement of the year—clinching his teeth, his face draining of color.

Oh shit.

He's bleeding badly, almost every part of his body something to be concerned about. Thinks he could pass out.

Gotta make a move.

Dutch whips around the corner, firing with double-fisted .357s.

Remo drops to his belly, managing to fire two blasts which push Dutch out of the room, back into the hallway. Dutch takes cover behind the door. This is taking its toll on him as well.

In the distance, the sounds of sirens wail.

Dutch knows he doesn't have much time. He calls out to Remo. "Hear that? Cops are coming."

Nothing from Remo.

Dutch makes a silent two count and spins, coming hard through the door firing.

Remo is long gone.

He did leave behind Dutch's almost-cut-in-two dead brother and the bloody remains of a hired thug for Dutch's viewing pleasure.

Dutch has learned the valuable trait of compartmentalizing his emotions. It's a skill that will get a man through a lot of bad days inside, if you can master it without completely checking out of your head. Dutch will, at some point, grieve for the loss of his brothers.

Now is not the time for that shit. He eyes the blown out window to his left.

It's starting to get dark outside. Remo is running on fumes as he drags his beaten, barely functioning body through the woods. He takes cover, propping himself behind a tree where he has a good line of sight on the house. Remo readies his shotgun. He'll wait for Dutch to come out, end this damn thing.

One way or another.

A decent plan, all things considered. Then he notices a dead, heavily tattooed body with a single, clean bullet wound between its eyes. Way too skilled for Remo.

Who the hell?

He looks around, sees another similar body. Same perfect wound.

The guys from the Escalade.

Of course, Remo doesn't know this. Crunching footsteps sound behind him. Remo turns, readies his shotgun.

Movement from a tree not far from him.

Remo reacts without thought, doesn't have time to process who it is before he pulls the trigger. His shotgun blast hits Hollis, sending him flying backward to the ground.

No! No!

Sure he's killed Hollis, Remo dives to his side. *Please no, not this.* Remo can't compartmentalize this the way Dutch can. Hollis is a friend, of sorts, and this is a cross that Remo cannot bear. Hollis's face is cut up, a few stray hits in the shoulders and belly. Peppered buckshot shows all over his Banana Republic wrinkle-free Oxford.

However, there is no blood to speak of.

Through the holes in the shirt, shades of black show, giving the sight of the Kevlar vest Hollis is wearing. Wounded, but he'll make it. Remo breathes again.

Hollis spits out, "You are such a fucking asshole."

"Shit. Sorry."

Hollis's eyes go wide. Remo doesn't have time to turn before Dutch is on them. He rams Remo at full speed, the force knocking Remo clear of Hollis. Dutch beats on Remo while screaming out, "Where's my money? Where?!"

"Gave it away," says Remo, taking a solid punch to face.

"Where is it?"

"Look at you. Big, bad man. Listen good. Your money is with the family members of the people you and your piece-of-shit brothers murdered."

Something in Dutch comes unhinged.

Remo spits out a tooth, saying, "It's gone baby, gone."

Dutch's rage has been building for a lifetime. Taking care of his brothers when nobody else would. Years inside a cell.

Time waiting for a prize that was never even there. Someone must pay the full freight for these heavy burdens. Dutch unleashes punches backed by a primal animal furry. Face, neck, ear—doesn't matter where they land to Dutch as long as they inflect pain. His veins pop. Spit flies.

Remo is pinned down, his only option to lie there and take the beating.

Dutch feels around for something, anything, to finish the job. He fingers find a large rock. He raises it above his head, ready to crush Remo's skull.

Dutch can taste it, the moment he's obsessed about. Remo's death is in sight.

Remo can only watch, motionless, as the rock rises above him, casting a shadow across his face.

Hollis pulls his 9mm, shifting to get a clear shot. It's not there.

The solid clunk of a baseball bat connects with the side of Dutch's skull.

Lester stands over Dutch, bat in hand.

Remo watches Dutch's body wilt to the dirt, blood spreading out around his head. Sitting up, Remo attempts the impossible task of comprehending the last hour of his life.

Hollis holds his gun on Lester. Lester grips the bat, not about to stand-down. Remo can't help but notice: *did he steal my fucking clothes?* He jumps up yelling, standing between Lester and Hollis.

"No, Hollis, I know him. Lester, stand-down. You did good. You saved me. God's proud."

Lester's expression remains hard, war-ready. Not a single facial muscle moves. Hollis keeps his gun on Lester; it's what he does.

The sirens are very close now.

Remo continues talking Lester down. "We've gotta go, man."

On the ground, an indecipherable grunt comes from Dutch. Hard to believe it, coming from a man like Dutch, but it's a whimper of sorts. A dying man looking for some kind of mercy in his final minutes.

Lester nods to Remo, then flashes a cold set of eyes to Hollis before turning his attention to Dutch.

His former partner in crime. Current object of anger. Up until now, Lester has done a fine job of keeping his violent tendencies in check, stuffing his old self down under the surface where it wouldn't cause harm. Like all pressure that builds, it has to be released. Lester's under pressure, and his violence needs to be released, regardless of his newly found path of the righteous.

Lester remembers the Preacher Man saying, "Personal growth is a work in progress."

He'll ask for forgiveness later.

Lester lifts the bat high over his head and rains down a frenzy of brutal swings to every inch of Dutch's body. Bones crunch as wood lands over and over. He pulls the butcher knife from behind his back. Grabbing a fistful of Dutch's hair, he attacks his neck, sawing away with the massive carving blade.

Tendons pops. Blood gurgles. The sickening mix of sight and sound is too much for Remo.

It reminds Hollis of a night he spent in Singapore many years ago.

Remo and Hollis rush through the woods, the sirens continuing to get louder as they move out of the trees toward Hollis's Lexus. Remo wants to look back at Lester, but doesn't.

He knows that some things can't be unseen.

Pale. Bleeding.

33

Pissed, but working through it.

Hollis is laid out in the passenger seat while Remo drives away from his house in the tranquil Hamptons. A stream of police and emergency vehicles blow past them, headed the opposite way. Remo watches as they pass, checking his rearview.

Hollis is a pro, always. Even with the annoying little flesh wounds, he manages to disassemble his gun in record time and with absolute precision. He tears away from his carved up vest and dumps all of it in a black, Hefty lawn & leaf bag.

Remo alternates between looking at the road and Hollis, admiring his work and curious about what's next. His wounds throb, but Remo thinks it would be in bad taste to bitch to Hollis about the pain. You know, considering that he shot the man.

They haven't said a word to each other since Hollis called him an asshole. Remo can't take it and decides to break the silence. "Dude—"

"Shut up." Hollis isn't interested.

Now Hollis truly hates himself for going back. He could be watching the Golf Channel right now, or perhaps playing with the kids while nursing a cocktail. Worst-case scenario, he'd be attempting to talk the wife into an evening blowjob. The possibilities were endless.

Now, however, his possibilities are somewhat limited. He pulls his cell and scrolls through his contacts. To Remo's surprise, Hollis speaks in perfect Mandarin to whoever is on the phone. The conversation takes less than twenty seconds, but it's damn impressive. Hollis hangs up and barks to Remo, "Give me those." He motions to Remo's equipment. Remo pulls off the sling and vest, doesn't ask questions about the Mandarin.

Hollis stuffs all of Remo's hardware in the bag as he speaks. "You drop me off a couple of blocks from Dr. Wu's house." Motions to his wounds. "I'll take care of this, and you can go fuck yourself."

Remo bites his tongue. Again, given the fact he's the one who shot Hollis, he should just take it. Of course, that's not a truly viable option for a guy like Remo. He reflects on the day's events as he says, "Not to be a dick, but you had a gun."

"I was going to shoot him, but your whackadoo buddy showed up and—"

"You took your sweet-ass time as that animal beat the piss outta me."

Hollis winces and continues packing everything in the bag. "Shut. Up."

"Pretty sure you did it on purpose, that's all." Rolling silence.

No eye contact. "Fucking hate you," mutters Hollis. Complete silence the rest of the way.

PART V

CRAZY, CRAZY HEART

34

Children and parents are playing their hearts out, soaking up family time at Gramercy Park on a gorgeous Saturday evening. Anna and Sean sit on a bench, waiting for Remo. Sean, every bit the wide-eyed boy who can't sit still, looks like any child would if they were waiting for Santa or the Easter Bunny or meeting their dad for the first time. He bounces with anxious energy while his mom tries her best not to look how she feels. She doesn't like this, but she holds it together for her boy. There's a gasp, followed by a low murmur spreading through the park. The low hum starts to grow as whatever's going on gets closer to Anna and Sean.

"Oh my God."

"Is he okay?"

The commotion finally catches Anna and Sean's attention.

Turning, they see the cause. Remo.

A bloodied mess, he's somehow pulling himself through the park. He's barely able to walk, a staggered crawl of sorts. He stumbles through the park without regard for his body or others' for that matter.

Puts a foot in the middle of picnic blankets, in plates of food. A sandwich squirts mustard as his heel plants in the middle of the rye.

He interrupts games of catch. Knocks over a girl texting. He resembles the grace and style of a zombie with epilepsy.

It hurts to watch him move, powering through despite every cell of his body yelping in agony.

Anna stares. *What to Expect When You're Expecting* doesn't cover these moments in life. "Remo?" she asks, covering her son's eyes as Remo makes it over to them.

He stands up as straight as he can. Adjusts his shirt. Sways a bit. Although he looks like he's been touring the bad side of hell, he's glad to be there at the park. It pains him, but he gets out, "Hey, guys..."

Then falls face first to the ground like a broken pile of bones.

35

An eye fights to open. It's a real struggle, but the lid finally gives way with a slight crack of healing skin. The lid flickers slowly, reluctantly, as it finds its way to a semblance of normal. It begins blinking rapidly, working overtime to find moisture and feed an eye that feels like you could strike a match across it.

Remo's lone good eye dances around, checking out the room he's found himself in. Doesn't recognize it, but coming to in a strange room has happened before.

It's a stark, clean place. Not a bar, a whorehouse, or even a lady's strange apartment with cats and shit. Most importantly, he's woken up and not found himself in a coffin.

It's a box of a room that's trying very hard to be a livable space. Not much furniture to speak of, bland dime-store paintings hanging on the walls. The sun peaks through heavy curtains, cutting shafts of light across the white tile floor. Remo is laid out in a hospital bed. Struggling to come around, he smacks his lips.

Feels like a cat shit in there. He forces his lids to remain open. He thinks about the cartoons he watched as a kid where they used toothpicks to hold their eyes open, lids crashing down, snapping them in two. Up until now that seemed silly and unrealistic to Remo. Today, however, it's possible.

Tubes and machinery are attached to various points of his body. Something to the left drips. Another thing to the right dings softly every so often while numbers bounce across a screen. He's held together with tape, gauze and a little bit of hope, but he's alive. Pain fires through every inch of him as he sits up, trying damn hard to regain his senses.

His voice cracks as he says, "That was a horrible idea." He stops short, realizing he's not alone. There is a person staring at him. A little person.

Sean.

Perched at the foot of his near-deathbed is his son. A perfect little face rests in tiny hands, propped up by scrawny elbows. Sean has found a safe distance from which to watch, but he's close enough and curious as hell. The young boy gives a slight, apprehensive wave. Remo winces through the pain, but returns the gesture.

A hopeful splinter in time for Remo.

Remo turns, noticing that along the wall is a line of other folks who were waiting for him to wake up as well.

Folks just dying to chat with Remo.

Detective Harris leans against the doorframe, along with a pack of his fellow officers, all looking like they would like nothing more than to rip Remo's face from his skull and nail it to the wall. ADA Leslie has wedged herself in a corner of the room, sharing a similar expression.

Anna sits in an uncomfortable chair. She could care less about Remo. She's a ball of nerves as she watches Sean. *What was I thinking? I knew somehow something like this would happen. Fucking Remo.*

Detective Harris breaks the ice. "Remo. Would love a word."

Remo puts up a hand, asking for a moment. He wants to say something to Sean. No idea what, but he's gone through some serious trouble to have this opportunity, and wants to have this moment.

He starts to say something, stops. Thinks better of whatever was about to come out. Anna watches with the same level of apprehension she'd have watching a dog trying to cross a highway. Sean sits with his little heart beating fast in anticipation. Remo knows there's no way to say what he needs to say, what Sean deserves to hear, so he opts for silence instead.

Sean lets him off the hook by asking, "Who are you?"

Remo smiles, the closest thing to genuine happiness you will ever see out of him.

"One asshole."

They share a big smile as an infectious giggle rolls out of Sean.

36

T he plan? Simple.

Murder multiple motherfuckers, save one asshole.

That was the strategy of one Lester Ellis, a former criminal, former wheelman, current man of the Lord.

Mission of mercy complete.

Lester walks alone on a back strip of country road about 20 miles outside of Syracuse. A light rain falls over him. *Feels nice,* he thinks. He rolls his suitcase down the road, still dressed to impress with the clothes he borrowed from Remo's closet. The wrapped grip of the Louisville Slugger pokes out the top, zipper as close to closed as it can get around it.

Now what? thinks Lester. The Mashburns are gone baby, gone, and Remo is safe from them and their wicked ways. He hopes Remo has found a better path, at least better than the one he was on.

He has to. After all the hell he endured. Can a man not change after surviving an experience like that? There's another question that truly troubles Lester. It plays with his brain like child picking at a scab.

Who was that man Remo was with?

That man with the gun.

That man seemed to carry a heavy burden as well. A different burden than Remo for sure, but the weight of the burden that man is hauling around can't be ignored. The kind you've been carrying so long you don't even know it's there—the worst kind.

It was in his eyes.

Lester has learned how to get a lot from someone in a short amount of time. Just let him see the eyes; it's all in a man's eyes. It's really all you have to go with when a man has a gun on you, and that man would have shot Lester dead. That much Lester knows. The man Remo called Hollis has killed before, that's for damn sure.

Is Remo truly safe while he's keeping company with a man like that?

Lester thinks not.

Lester turns his suitcase around, heading back in the direction he came from. Back toward NYC. He needs to make sure. As he turns, the suitcase tips off balance, toppling over to the road. He bends down, taking a moment to adjust its contents. Unzipping the bag, he moves the clothes around, trying to get the balance back in working order. He opens a bulging black trash bag nestled among the clothes.

Inside the bag, Lester grabs a fistful of hair, shifting Dutch's head.

Once satisfied, he zips the suitcase up again and continues rolling down his path.

His newly chosen plan.

REMO WENT DOWN

REMO COBB # 2

PART I

REMO'S STILL THE GOODS, BABY

1

Remo Cobb is a fucked up mess of a man.

A worn strap of beef jerky barely able to stand upright. It's a real struggle, given what Remo's been through, but still, there he stands scanning over the tattered remains of his once glorious NYC monument to success. Not long ago, his multi-million dollar condo was the picture of New York elite living.

Now?

Now it's a busted-up shitbox. Simply a pile of broken things that used to be worth some serious scratch. Not much in the way of glory here anymore. Elite living? Not even close. That super expensive, super special glass thing that gay-as-hell decorator picked up for him in SoHo? That one-of-a-kind picture of whateverthefuck? Those things and more are shattered into millions of overpriced pieces, scattered across the floor in a super special spread of useless debris.

At one time, Remo's suit was the proud uniform of a big-time, big-money attorney. Custom tailored, high-end threads worked and crafted with amazing precision by a man named Mario, working out of The Plaza. After Remo's little conflict in the Hamptons, however, this five-figure suit is now a torn and frayed disaster. Covered in sweat, blood and fear, but with just a touch of redemption. It's the suit he wore when they wheeled him into the hospital. Despite all this destruction to everything he owns, there's an odd smile plastered across Remo's face.

Crooked, to be sure, but there is a smile.

A look of relief mixed with joy on his face, his eyes locked in a thousand-yard stare. Despite the demolition of this earthly wealth and the physical pain he's endured, he got what he wanted. What he really wanted. What he set out to get done.

He met his son.

He met Sean.

Remo grows an even bigger smile. A pure smile.

The cost of the goods that have been reduced to rubble before him is staggering, but he simply does not care. He finds an unbroken highball glass up high in the cabinet. It somehow survived Hurricane Mashburn. *Brave little guy,* Remo thinks. *It must have been a rough storm to ride out.* Remo serves himself a long pour of Johnnie Blue then moves on to the living room. Swatting away a coaster, a coffee cup and the scraps of a broken dessert plate, Remo takes a seat in a leather chair. Drinking in slowly and deeply, he lets the scotch go to work.

It burns the good burn.

His brain unwinds.

Thoughts unspool the insanity of the recent events.

Thoughts of his house in the Hamptons and the war fought (and won) against the Mashburn brothers. All the blood spilled. Some of it his. More of it theirs. Guns blasting. Shells bouncing. Bullets pounding. Hollis the hitman coming to his rescue. Lester putting a period on the thing by cutting off Dutch Mashburn's head.

Remo shivers a bit off that little golden memory.

Can still see Lester doing it. The cutting. The hacking. The sounds of it.

He drinks more. Pops a pill. He's sore as shit.

His mind drifts back to Hollis and how pissed off he was at Remo. Even though he came back to help Remo out, Hollis was so damn hostile about doing it Remo's fairly sure he will never see nor hear from the man again. Hollis will bounce the hell off the planet with his wife and kids and never be seen again. They will become ghosts. Hollis knows how to become thin air. It's what he does. Hollis is a professional killer with some special skills, and those special skills are the reason Remo knows the man.

Remo defended Hollis successfully a few times, and helped him take care of some other legal problems before they became fully fucking realized shitstorms. Remo helped with things, like where to find a clean car. Where to find a safe house. Where a few stacks of *fuck you* money were located. Those bits and bobs and more. Remo and Hollis were decent enough friends. Until Remo let his dick wander a bit.

"You fucked my first wife, got a hand job from the second, and tried to work a three-way with the third," is how Hollis recalled it. Remo knows he's not wrong.

Remo takes another slug of Blue.

He considers Hollis a friend, despite the roadblocks.

Hollis is a good one.

"Oh well," says Remo, "fuck it."

Big slug of booze, followed by another long pour, filling his glass.

His brain now slips over to Lester.

Ah, Lester.

The former criminal and current man of the Lord. Not to mention a completely insane killer with a borderline personality disorder. Lester was a member of the Mashburn crew until he went to prison and found God. He was a new man when he came out. Lester left the Mashburns—actually he tried to kill the Mashburns—and then set out on a righteous path. He considered Remo to be a sheep in desperate need of Lester the Shepherd. He truly believed Remo needed his special brand of saving in more ways than one. Remo watched Lester get shot in a Chinese food joint, then watched Lester show up later, a couple of days ago in the Hamptons, to cut off Dutch Mashburn's head.

Remo shivers again.

Drinks more.

Then there's Sean. His son. His boy. The child from his failed marriage. Remo takes some pride in the fact it's his only marriage. He still cares for Anna, but knows she's better off without him. Most people are. She's a good person. Smart. Strong. Good mom. Remo has no illusions of reconciling with her, despite his recent moral turn. Anna has warmed a bit to him recently, but nowhere near thawed enough to even vaguely consider taking him back on a fulltime basis. He knows he fucked all that up years ago, but he's truly grateful to her for letting him meet Sean.

She didn't have to.

He knows it.

Remo had given her plenty of reasons not to.

The look on his son's face when they met in that hospital room for the first time was worth everything he went through with the Mashburns. Remo would do it all again, if he had to. He'd rather not, it was a bitch, to be clear, but he would do it for his boy.

Another drink.

He thinks on the conversations he had after Sean and Anna left the hospital room.

Conversations with cops and lawyers.

Angry cops and lawyers.

Conversations that contained words like *disbarred*, *criminal charges*, *seizure of assets* and *you're fucked, you are completely fucked* and *fuck you, Remo.*

Big drink.

Now his brain slides to the future.

Remo's future.

Doesn't look all that rosy.

"Shit."

Gulp.

2

"You're saying I'm not going to practice law?"

"Remo, we talked about this. You're not practicing shit anymore. The pain pills dicking up your hearing?" Victor asks.

Victor is Remo's boss. The biggest, baddest partner at the firm. He's known as a titan in the criminal-defense-attorney circles around the city. He has a soft spot for Remo, but in this case there's only so much he can do for the guy. Remo is toxic with a capital T. Victor has his phone gripped so tight in his fist it's about to snap.

Remo called him from his condo looking for a little help and hope from his boss. Neither help nor hope is going well.

"There has to be something," Remo says.

"Your place in the Hamptons is filled with blood, bullets and bodies. The bodies, the Mashburns, were your former clients. The firm's former clients. One of them sans his head, I might add. There are also rumors floating around that you threw the case against them, which would more than explain why they would come to your house with murder on their minds."

"Dammit, Leslie," Remo mutters.

"What?"

"Nothing."

Leslie was a casual sexual acquaintance, mutually casual, and also a New York Assistant District Attorney. Remo gave her all the evidence he had against the Mashburns and their crew, then he dug up the money they stole and gave it to a good cause. Most of it, at least. Leslie must have blabbed about all that. She was the only one who could connect the dots. Can't blame her. She has to watch out for her own ass too. Still, it pisses Remo off.

Remo pauses. Thinks of speaking, knows he's got nothing. Stops.

Everything Victor is saying is true.

"You've got a meeting. A damn important meeting tomorrow afternoon with your buddy, Detective Harris."

Remo chokes as he gulps some Blue. "Harris? He hates me. He'll eat my heart and toss me in the street."

"Yes. Yes he will. Look, I can't help you. I want to, but I've got to create some distance. You're a toxic prick at the moment." Victor takes a breath, looks at a picture of him and Remo skiing in Vail. "You know the drill. Keep your mouth shut with Harris. Let the cops talk and work the best deal you can." Victor dumps the picture in the trash.

"What about money?" Remo asks.

"What money?"

"My money."

"Your assets are frozen until the Feds can sort all this out."

"No severance package from sweet, sweet Victor?"

"I can't. Wouldn't look great. Maybe when this is all over. If you need some cash to get you through, I'll be glad to—"

Remo hangs up.

He begins to work the floor at a feverish pace. Moving back and forth, back and forth, letting his mind run ripshit. Racing to his closet, he sees most of his suits are gone—no idea where they went—but there are still a few pairs of overpriced jeans and some shirts he can live with for a while. Moving to the bedroom, he dumps the things from the closet onto the bed and then fishes out a few pairs of underwear, some socks and a couple of T-shirts.

His phone rings.

It's Alex Trip. A law school friend Remo hasn't spoken to in a few years. Not since that little incident in Vegas. Long story. Odd and ugly. Shit happens. Remo tries hard to remember if he owes Alex anything or what pile of shit he might be stepping into if he answers the call. Remo quickly decides the risk is worth the potential reward and that he can use all the friends he can get right now.

"Alex?"

"Remo, long time. Look, I hate to dump this on you. Heard about your troubles. Not sure if you're in a cash crunch or not but I got something with my brother, Jasper. Might help you out. Nothing crazy, just a little money for a lead of sorts."

"I'm in."

"You want to hear what he wants?"

Remo sighs. "Fine."

"He wants to be put in touch with some bank robbers."

"That's stupid, but I'll can see what I can do."

"I know, I know. I tried to talk him out of it, but just talk to him. If you can."

"Ten grand, cash."

"A bit steep."

Remo says nothing. Testing how serious and/or desperate they are.

"Fine," says Alex. "I'll tell him."

"Good. Tomorrow, eleven a.m."

"Done."

Remo hangs up. Checks his wallet. He's got one credit card that belongs to his law firm, which has more than certainly been cancelled, and a personal MasterCard that may or may not have been frozen by the Feds. Might be maxed out too.

Remo doesn't like bills.

The wallet also holds two twenties and sixty-eight dollars in ones.

Remo does like strippers.

He looks around his bedroom then to his disaster of a living room. He quickly realizes he needs to find another place to lay his head for a few days. The thought also occurs to him that others might come looking for him as well. Other clients who might catch wind of the Mashburns and how Remo *handled* their case. Remo's clients don't like complications, and they also don't like lawyers who might have fucked them over.

Remo's mind clicks.

He created an *In Case of Emergency Break Glass* option a few years ago. An out. A fail-safe package. When you live the life Remo has, you need some clearly marked exits. Only problem is he created it when he was drunk out of his mind, so the location is a little fuzzy.

He spins around in a circle searching, not sure what for. His face heats quickly from a surging blood pressure spike. Fishing around the wreck that is his desk, he thinks of something. He starts looking for something very specific. Tossing papers and computer crap here and there, he digs and digs in a freakish, manic manner. His stomach drops. He starts to think he might not find what he needs. He has to find the instructions he wrote down. The instructions, more like the map, to his emergency-out option.

In disgust, he flings his laptop across the room, letting it skid-spin across the floor. He wraps his face in his hands, dropping to the floor in a heap. Panic is setting in. It's all hitting him at once. The glow of Sean is fading into the distance and the reality of what he's done is landing, punching at his insides.

Sean's face flashes into his head.

That smile.

The spark in those eyes.

Remo calms. His heartbeat returns to a normal pace. His mind slides into place, allowing his thoughts to clear. Remo bolts up, racing toward the bathroom. He lifts the lid to the tank, sliding it to the sink. Inside the toilet is a blue waterproof pouch taped inside the cool waters of the American Standard. He rips the pack off, opening it as fast as he can. With a massive exhale he removes a piece of paper from the pack.

It's a crudely drawn map with a list of instructions.

Remo's head floods with ideas. New hope. Fresh possibilities.

Maybe he can survive this.

Maybe.

As he stumbles back into the bedroom, he eyes the pile of clothes dumped on the bed.

Remo wonders, *where the fuck is my suitcase?*

3

L ester's body shakes and rattles along with the movements of the subway car.

His arms are wrapped around the suitcase he stole from Remo's closet. He lost the bat somewhere along the way, but Lester still has the important things he took from Remo's homes in New York and the Hamptons. Still has the butcher knife and the black plastic bag. Lester leans over, checks the plastic bag stuffed inside the suitcase.

The bag is important to Lester.

It contains Dutch Mashburn's head.

It's become a bit of a nasty habit for Lester, him checking the head every hour or so. He's not completely sure why he does it, either. He's stopped himself a couple of times, but sometimes he checks it without knowing he's even doing it. Like some people might nervously check their phones all the time or play with a scab. Perhaps he wants to make sure Dutch is dead. Needs to be reassured on a consistent basis. The world is a much better place without Dutch in it, that much Lester does know.

Lester is on his way back to New York City.

He believes his work is not done.

And he cannot leave with his work left undone.

He originally came to New York to save Remo. From the Mashburns, and from himself. Lester believes Remo to be a good man who needs a better man to lead him down the correct path. The path of the Lord. He is also troubled with the company Remo seems to keep.

Namely, this man called Hollis.

This Hollis is a man of violence. Lester knows it. He knows the look. It's in the eyes. The eyes tell you everything, and if you know what to look for, the eyes will spill out every damn thing you need to know about a person. The eyes Hollis has in his head scream that this is a man capable of unspeakable things.

Horrible, horrible things.

Of course, so is Lester, but that doesn't concern him at the moment.

Lester knows how to control his horrible, unspeakable side, or at least he'd like to think he does.

If Lester is to truly save Remo, then Remo cannot keep time with a man like Hollis. All of this is why Lester, former criminal, current man of the Lord, is riding on a subway dressed in a three thousand dollar suit he borrowed from Remo's closet, Bible in hand, with a suitcase containing a large butcher knife and a severed head.

4

The cab drops Remo off outside Chuck's Liquor Palace.

He just dropped off Alex's brother, Jasper, in New Jersey in an alley behind the Jiggle Queen. Jasper wanted to meet some criminals so he could do some kind of bullshit movie. A documentary, Remo thinks. Whatever. So Remo set up a meet so Jasper could try and do just that. Remo thinks it's an insane idea, but the man's money was green so, ya know, Remo's sure it'll be fine. Remo giggles to himself as he counts the ten grand Jasper paid him. A Hollywood guy mixing it up with criminals is genuinely dangerous.

However, all of this gives Remo another idea. As he cuts through the aisles containing bottle after bottle that line Chuck's Liquor Palace, Remo massages an idea. The idea movie-boy Jasper had. The core of the idea has some similarities to that of Remo's with the Mashburns. The idea of wanting to use information he holds in order to achieve another goal. Jasper the movie-boy's goals are different perhaps, but the main focus is the same. This idea actually piggy-backs Remo's reasons for double-crossing the Mashburns in the first place. When that moment of clarity hit Remo, it was like a freight train. Remo realized he held information that could stop some bad people from doing harm. He didn't want to sit around watching human garbage get away with hurting people.

It was really that simple.

Remo is–sorry, *was*—the best criminal defense attorney in NYC. He had an amazing list of horrible people who made up his client list. Horrible people Remo defended and won acquittals for on a routine basis.

Until the Mashburn case.

That case was different.

Very different.

Or maybe Remo was different when it hit his desk. It was after Sean was born. Regardless, Remo reviewed the case and the things the Mashburns and their crew did and something clicked. They took down a bank. Not incredibly uncommon or wretched in comparison to all the evil in the world. Remo's seen a ton of evil.

It was the way they did it.

The inhuman disregard for life.

Violent, deep wrongness.

They got their money. They didn't need to kill anyone in the bank. But boy did they. They executed every man, woman and, yes, child in that bank. Remo saw the security camera footage. Something unhinged inside his brain at that moment. Hit him between the eyes like a sledgehammer. Everything he thought he knew got turned around that day. He actually stopped and thought about people. Thought about the people being harmed by his clients. He thought of the son he had. The son he had never met. All of this swirled like a cement mixer inside Remo's jumbled head, leading him to a big decision that day. One that would change him.

Forever.

Remo decided this had to end.

He gave over everything he had on the Mashburn case to the Assistant DA. Big-ass box of evidence. Then later Remo dug up the money the Mashburns stole from the bank and gave it to charity.

Most of it.

A large percentage of it.

Come on, it was a lot of money.

Lester was part of the Mashburn crew at that time. He was the muscle. The driver. He wasn't in the bank and didn't kill anyone, on that day at least, but that day turned Lester too. Changed him. He decided things needed some change as well. The events of that day led Lester to the Lord while he was in prison. Remo wasn't willing to go that far.

Where all this plays into Remo's current state of mind is that he still doesn't like the idea these bad, bad people are out in the world and they're getting away with it all. It pisses off most people, but Remo knows he's in a different position than most people. More to the point, Remo actually knows who these bad, bad people are, and where they are.

He picks up a bottle of Johnnie Blue from the shelf.

Stops. Makes it two.

The singular idea circling round and round Remo's head is a simple one, but a difficult one to answer—*how do I stop these horrible people from doing horrible things?*

Remo spent the night at a shit motel down the street from Chuck's Liquor Palace. Before he left his place last night, he balled up all his clothes and what else he could salvage from the wreckage and dumped it into the middle of his bed. Then he wrapped the sheets around the pile and carried it out of his building, hobo-style. He carved through the onlookers and reporters in the lobby. Gave them a nice photo op, to be sure, then traveled off to the shit hotel and drank himself to sleep.

Which is why he's here now at Chuck's.

He's bone-dry.

After Remo pays for the booze, Chuck, who's working the counter, thumbs toward the back of his palace. No words spoken, none needed. It's obvious they've done this before. Often.

Stepping outside the back of Chuck's Palace and into a dirty alley, Remo looks left then right, then whistles loudly. Cats scatter. A home-less woman tells him to *shut the fuck up*. After a moment or two, out steps a young man in his early twenties. Looks like he doesn't make it out much. Hair looks like it was combed with a pillow and the bags under his eyes have bags. He hands Remo a paper bag from a pharmacy. Remo inspects the bag's contents.

"The hell is this?" asks Remo.

"Adderall. Nobody works Ritalin anymore. That's old, first generation shit."

"I like the old shit."

"Get with the times, man. Shit works the same, just an upgrade."

"Don't want a fucking upgrade, man. Didn't request a fucking upgrade. I want what I want."

"It's what I got. Give *you're welcome* a try next time."

Remo grunts then peels off some bills from the stack he got off movie-boy Jasper.

Adderall Boy's face lights up off the stack. "Wow, you see your pimp today?"

Remo turns, heads back into Chuck's. He slides into a filthy-ass bathroom. Closing the multi-stained toilet lid he takes a seat, cracks the cap and chugs some Johnnie greatness. Through his one open eye he catches a flash of a glance of himself in the cracked mirror. It's not pretty and he knows it. He just doesn't care.

Chugs harder.

Points to himself.

He starts nodding his head, as if this bottle is the correct answer to a question nobody is asking.

Yanking the bottle from his lips, letting a little bit spill on his tattered-ass suit jacket, he checks his eyes in the mirror. Needs something. Pulling the bottle of Adderall from the pharmacy bag, he pops a couple in his mouth and chases them down with Johnnie.

Satisfied with this little tune-up, he closes his eyes, leans against the questionable wall and lets the world slide together. Lets his brain come back online. Things slosh, collide, split apart and form again. For the first time in days a wave of relaxation washes over him. It's not a pure form of relaxation. More muted, but it's welcome in any form given Remo's recent history. He feels himself come down. His heart finding a normal beat. For a brief moment he's able to forget about his situation and just be. Doesn't last long. Like a lightning strike across his mind's eye he sees the Mashburns shooting everybody at the bank. The grainy security footage plays in his head like watching it for the first time.

His eyes spring open.

He pulls out the folded piece of paper that contains the instructions on where to find his *In Case of Emergency* pack. Remo knows what's in that pack, and its contents will help him to be on his way. He checks his watch, checks the instructions—he can still pick up the pack and make it to his showdown with Detective Harris at the police station.

He smiles big.

As fucked up as it is, it's all coming together Remo-style.

He thinks of Sean.

Knows he can still do some good.

Remo points, nodding at the mirror one more time.

5

T he water in the pool is cold as shit.

You'd think an indoor pool would be heated for fuck's sake. Before jumping in, Remo stripped bare-ass naked. His Kiton suit is balled up in a chair with his dress socks stuffed into the toes of his slick, black Salvatore Ferragamos.

He feels his balls shrivel up into sad raisin-like nibblets.

He hears the screams from the old ladies.

Their water aerobics class has been suddenly cut short by a former big-time attorney diving into their pool with his dork swinging. Well, at the very least, it gives a slight sway.

Remo thrusts his arms in and out as hard as he can. Cutting the water. Swimming deeper and deeper like a madman to the bottom. Desperately trying to reach the floor of the deep end. He's got a Phillips screwdriver in one hand and it's hurting his ability to carve through the water like the aqua god he knows he is, but there's no other way to do this fucking thing. He curses himself for setting up the emergency pack like this. It seemed like genius at the time. Of course, at the time he was hammered out of his skull and on the downside of a two-week bender with a couple of women from Australia who dealt in the white powder game.

Good times.

After much effort, he reaches the drain cover. Manages to get one screw off before having to make a panic swim back up for air. He takes a big suck of oxygen, hears someone call him an *asshole*, then plunges back down toward the drain. This time he gets all the screws, pulls off the cover, and removes a gold key.

Exploding to the surface, Remo gasps hard, sucking in as much air as he can. He thinks he's going to die. He hasn't held his breath that long since he went down on that muscle-bound Russian lady during the Cunnilingus Incident of 2007. Holding on to the side of the pool, he can hear the insults and squawking of his new pool friends. As he pulls himself out of the pool, he realizes he's now standing in front of a pack of very angry older women. Dripping. Naked. He says nothing, allowing silence to fill the room.

He lets them stare at his member.

He simply holds his hand out, waiting.

One woman smiles big, blows him a kiss and tosses him a towel.

Remo cracks a grin, snatching the towel from the air with a snap and a wink. *Remo's still the goods, baby.*

6

The booming beat rattles Remo's teeth.

Still damp from his little dip, he stands in front of a massive brick wall across town from the pool. He clears some dirt and grime from the wall with his fingers, then tears away at strips of dark tape and removes a large sheet of cardboard. After he's finished, he can make out a clear indention in the wall. A tall rectangle. The outline of an entrance. An entrance not known by most. Remo knows that once the club inside reaches capacity someone from the place comes out and seals it up so no unwelcome guests try to join the party. Creates exclusivity to the joint, and people dig that shit.

Once this happens, you got to have a special key to get in.

Remo tosses the tape and cardboard aside. The doorway towers over him, almost mocking him and his desire to enter. Dark, gunmetal gray. There's a large goat head made of steel that stares back at him with the blackest of eyes. Inside there are the sounds of a raging party going on. Sounds like a helluva time. Muffled yelps and whoops mixed between the pounding of hip-hop thumps. He can barely make out a woman repeatedly yelling out, "Fuck yeah."

Remo leans down, getting eye to eye with the goat.

He cocks his head.

Remo thumbs the goat's nose.

He pulls out the key he retrieved from the bottom of the pool and inserts it perfectly into the goat's mouth. With a twist of the key the door creeps open on its own. The door clears a path, revealing a vision of beautiful chaos in motion. Gorgeous bodies grind and gyrate to the music blasting from an unseen sound system. The place has a high-end, trying-to-be-shitty industrial vibe going on. Nice, but not too nice. Just enough grit to be cool, but not gross. The floor is an old-school, dark hardwood with imperfections gouged and carved into it. A DJ bounces on the stage, his six-foot-plus frame silhouetted by a wall of light.

Remo stands in the doorway with his high-dollar suit that looks like hell and his moist, mussed-up hair. Looks as if he was buried alive at the bottom of a lake and has recently crawled out looking for revenge. He's painfully out of place. This is a room for the young and cool. For hot men and women with more disposable income than brain cells. One might feel self-conscious in a place like this, but not Remo. Oh no.

He owns the fucking joint.

He adjusts his collar, scans the room and says, "Excuse me, good people."

Nobody pays attention.

"Hello," he says louder.

It's like he's not even there.

He pulls his Glock from his jacket, raises it high above his head and fires a round into the ceiling.

Everything and everyone in the room freezes.

Music stops.

Gorgeous bodies become still.

"My name is Remo Cobb. This is my place. Now, in an orderly fashion, please get the fuck out."

A massive ceiling fan crashes to the floor in front of him.

Not part of Remo's plan, but he thinks the fan drop added a nice exclamation point on the thing.

IN MINUTES the place is cleared out.

The DJ shuts the door and turns back to Remo, who's helping himself to a drink at the bar.

"Wish I'd known you were stopping by, man," the DJ says. "You never come here. Usually meet you at the Chinese joint."

"Came in once, remember?"

The DJ looks away. "I do."

"It was a problem, remember?"

"It was."

Remo remembers the lawsuits that stemmed from his last visit. The hospital stay. The time in a walking boot and the court-*suggested* counseling. It got ugly, man.

"Anyway, I didn't want to be able to just drop in. Just wanted the money that came off this place without having to police my self-control. It's not the greatest system, but it's a system."

"Still, I could have put something nice together for you if I'd known you were coming."

"Yeah, well, didn't know I needed to."

"What's up?"

"You like this place?"

"What? The club? Of course. It's a fucking gold mine for me and—"

"Want to buy it?"

The DJ stares at him, not sure what Remo's game is. Guy like Remo always has his game on. Remo's been good to him, but still, Remo isn't the kinda dude you trust.

"Not feelin' you," the DJ says.

"I'm having some personal issues, as well as a few legal and existential things I'm working through at the moment. I need to cut loose of some tangible items. This place being one of them. Not to mention, there's a good chance it might be taken away from me anyway."

"Yeah, I heard some heavy shit went down."

"Heavy shit indeed," Remo says. He downs his drink and moves closer to the DJ. "What do you have on you?"

The DJ blinks.

"Money. How much money do you have on you? You had to have a decent take up there tonight."

The DJ digs in his pockets, pulling out a wad of cash. Picks through the crumpled bills, a mix of tens, twenties, a Benjamin or two. "Maybe five or six hundred."

"Sold." Remo pulls a bottle of Johnnie from the bar and snatches the money from the DJ's hand.

The DJ laughs in disbelief.

"Now. Let's go in the office over there, have a drink. I'll sign the papers over to you, and then I need a few minutes alone."

"Yeah. Fuck, yeah. Anything you need. Thank you. This is amaz—"

"Is that axe still in the office?"

7

Remo uses his tie to wipe the sweat from his brow.

He brings the axe up over his head, slamming it down hard on the floor with a *thunk*. *Thunk* after *thunk* the hardwood splits and splinters, breaking off into flying pieces with each whack of the axe. Remo has been working the floor by himself like a deranged woodsman for the last hour and he's tired as hell. Soreness already setting in. He stops only long enough for a slug of Johnnie here and there. He looks to his watch. He's only got a little over an hour until his sit-down with the NYPD.

He chops and hacks away at the floor, landing the axe to the hardwood over and over again. The pain in his back and shoulders is excruciating. His muscles burn. Arms shake and vibrate. He swings harder. Faster. Face red. Snot slinging. Veins popping. A man possessed.

The axe lands with a teeth-rattling clank.

A spark fires off. Remo's eyes go wide.

He's hit metal.

Remo exhales huge, tosses the axe aside.

Dropping to his knees, he pulls and yanks with all he's got at a body-sized steel box that's stuck down in a hole in the floor. It's almost like he's dragging a coffin out from the ground. It takes everything he has left in him as he grunts and spits, working, wiggling the box up to the surface. With a final pull the box comes free, sliding through the debris onto what's left of the dance floor. Remo looks like he could puke all over the box.

He almost does.

There's a lock on the box.

"Shit."

He pats himself down, looking for a key he knows damn well he doesn't have. Thinks about pulling his gun out and shooting the damn lock off, but remembers the contents of the box and thinks better of it. He also remembers those old commercials where a lock gets shot but doesn't open. Giving the lock a hopeless tug, Remo falls back to the floor, taking a slug from his bottle.

Think.

Where the hell is that key?

His brain slides into place.

He knows where it is and it sucks.

"Shit."

8

The White Swallow is a little dead at this time of day, but there's still a reasonably sized crowd huddled at the bar.

Remo doesn't hate gays, he knows many, but he's still uncomfortable being with them and he's not sure why. So it's understandable that he's very uncomfortable being in an establishment like The White Swallow. Perhaps it's a holdover from his generation, or perhaps it's his old Texas upbringing in Cut N' Shoot. His daddy used to routinely come home from a card game drunk as hell and call Remo a *fag* or *faggot* for any variety of reasons. The reasons would stem from not taking out the trash on time to giving the old man the wrong look at the wrong time. Those and anything in between would earn a homophobic slur along with a punch or kick. People who know Remo know this about him, which is why this was a perfect place for Remo to hide something.

Rather genius when you boil it all down.

Regardless of the reasons, Remo is uneasy walking through The White Swallow en route to the bathroom. Wait. There's more to it than that. Something else is bothering Remo about being here. He can't remember what it is, but there's some serious ball of worry churning round and round in his stomach. How can his body know and fear something and his brain not have a single clue?

A chair slams into the back of his head.

Remo is launched forward, sent skidding face-first on the polished concrete floor. He flips end over end, spinning around while holding the back of his head. He looks up, fighting to find normal.

It's not here.

Not located at The Swallow.

A chair comes down hard. The legs create a small holding cell of sorts, pinning his shoulders and neck to the floor. Remo struggles briefly before realizing it's a useless exercise.

"What in the fuck, man?" Remo says.

A large wall of muscle takes a seat on the chair, now making it completely impossible for Remo to escape. Remo's eyes pop as recognition slaps him in the brain.

"Okay. Look, Mad Love, I know I owe. How much?" Remo spits out.

Mad Love simply stares down at him, picking his teeth with a toothpick. His arms are the size of thighs. His lime green T-shirt looks as if it could rip any second.

"What's the number?"

Mad Love thinks for a second while looking to the ceiling, then holds up five fingers.

"Five? That's bullshit. More like two, at best."

Mad Love chomps the toothpick between his back teeth, holds up six fingers.

"Okay. I get it. You feel that some time has passed, juice needs to be charged, and I know I've been difficult to locate—"

Seven fingers.

"Stop. Shit, motherfucker. Let me up and I'll pay you right now."

Mad Love cocks his head, birdlike. The toothpick cracks.

"Seriously. I've got it."

Mad Love gets up, removes the chair from Remo's throat, but still holds it in one fist, ready to knock the piss out of Remo if need be.

Remo stands up and pulls the envelope he got from Jasper out from his jacket. He counts out seven grand. "Still think it was bullshit that you pulled a flush that night. Granted, it was three years ago, I should move on, but you had to be a cheating little bitch. Right—"

The chair swings, knocking Remo sideways, flailing into a booth with a yelp. Remo feels his brain slosh, along with the rest of his internal organs. The impact of the chair might have literally knocked the piss out of him.

Mad Love walks over calmly and yanks the envelope from Remo's hand.

"Oh come on. That's ten damn grand. Leave me a crumb or two."

Mad Love picks through the bills and flips a single hundred-dollar bill Remo's way before walking out the door.

"Thanks," Remo mutters as he pushes himself up.

He almost passes out. His sight clouds with spots. Shaking his head violently from side to side to find his focus, he struggles to remember why the hell he came into this dump to begin with.

The bathroom.

Walking into the single-serve crapper, Remo immediately starts feeling his way behind the tank with his fingers. Panic starts to fire through him. He can't find it. His hand slaps around the back but comes up empty. He tries to jam his head between the wall and the toilet but it won't fit. He's pissed at himself for putting the key here in the first place. *Dumbass. You watched The Godfather one too many times.* After a minute or two of near hysteria, his hands frantically searching, he finds something.

A smile spreads over his busted-up face.

With a rip of tape Remo brings his hand around, holding a tiny key.

Checks his watch. It's going to be tight as hell, but he can still make it for his meeting.

A meeting with the cops.

A meeting where the main topic of conversation will be his downfall.

This time, Remo does puke.

All over himself.

9

The lock clicks open.

Remo holds his breath.

With a loud creak and some muscle strain, the metal coffin of a box opens.

Remo exhales for what seems like an hour. Relief surges through every inch of him. Inside the box is what he's been looking for. There's really not much in there, considering how big the box is, but what's in there is what is going to save Remo's moist, broken ass. He takes a pull of Johnnie while sitting on the chopped up club floor, staring at the contents. Inside the box is a brown leather overnight bag that contains the following:

Two bottles of Johnnie Blue.

And, the most important item: a portable hard drive.

Remo had every intention of putting more in the box, like money and car keys, but never got around to it. The hard drive is really all that matters, but a thinking man might have stocked an emergency pack slightly better. Remo takes a mental inventory of what's on the drive. There are about fifty gigs of documents, pics, videos and other sordid forms of digitally incriminating goodness contained on that drive. It's all there. Every bit of info in existence on every asshole criminal Remo has ever defended or come in contact with. Addresses of safe houses, aliases, detailed outlines of operations, networks, bank account numbers, and everything else a criminal can think of. All of it collected over years by him and his law firm.

A treasure chest of criminal information.

Remo created and stashed the box right after he had his moment of clarity with the Mashburn case. He wanted a life raft if the ship went down. Needed a lighthouse if (or when) a category five hurricane blew in. A survival kit with the words *in case of emergency break glass*. Or, in Remo's twisted mind, a box buried under an underground dance den with access via secret-goat-door entrance opened by a key hidden in a public pool, the survival kit key taped to the back of a crapper at The White Swallow.

It seemed reasonable at the time.

Regardless. There is a need for the contents of that box.

A need has indeed come to be, and brother...

This is one motherfucker of an emergency.

10

Remo falls into a yellow cab with the leather bag.

He clasps the bag tightly to his side, using his elbow like a vice grip.

"Nineteenth Precinct, East 67th," Remo tells the driver.

"You are covered in vomit, sir," the driver says.

"No shit."

The door opens.

A fist flies in, crunching Remo's jaw. Remo's head is sent bouncing off the far window like a racquetball. As his face springs back, the fist gives him another smack.

The door closes. A new passenger has arrived.

"You are such an asshole," Hollis says.

"East 67th?" asks the cab driver.

Hollis grunts.

The cab pulls away from the curb like it was shot from a cannon. Remo peels himself off the backseat, rubs his throbbing jaw and tries to believe what his eyes are telling him. It's Hollis and he's sitting next to him in this cab. Remo truly never thought he'd see this man again. Not after last time. Not after the shootout at the Hamptons.

"Hollis, dude," Remo says with glee. He's actually happy to see him.

Another punch.

Remo's head bounces off the window again.

The driver doesn't even look back. Too busy on his phone.

"They left, you know? My family, they packed up. They're gone," Hollis says, looking out the window. "Because of you. They left because of the shitshow you created. Cops came to my house. Threatened me. Threatened her. Now, she and my children are gone."

Remo pulls himself up in the seat next to Hollis. They stare out their respective windows, watching the city roll by. Remo's face swells. Stings like a bastard. He's taken quite a beating today. Not to mention the beating he took in the Hamptons a couple of days ago. His brief hospital stay helped, but he hasn't healed from all of that fun yet. Not by a long shot.

Remo tries to speak, but his mouth isn't working. That last pop from Hollis might have unhinged his jaw a bit. Remo rubs his face, making sure it's all there. He's not completely sure how the cops got to Hollis. Anything is possible. This is a new little wrinkle Remo was not aware of. He'll have to think about it, but later. Right now his friend, a professional killer, is highly pissed off at him.

He gives his face one last rub, resets, then says, "I'm sorry, Hollis."

Silence in the cab. Only the sounds of the city outside seep in. Remo can hear Hollis breathe. It's a slow, deep sort of breath. One of a person who's pissed off and thinking very hard about why he's pissed off. Remo braces himself for another punch that he's sure is coming his way.

"Yeah, I'm sure you're sorry as hell," Hollis says, buried in his own thoughts.

Remo knows he's right. About it all being his fault. Can't argue it. Remo begged Hollis to help him with the Mashburns when he visited Hollis at his home in the burbs. Practically guilted the man into it. Make no mistake, without Hollis's help Remo would be dead as Dillinger. No question about that. Hollis is the toughest person Remo has ever known. The things he's seen and heard about the hitman, it's a scary-ass resume for sure. A killer in every sense of the word. A professional killer with a family he loves and would burn down the entire city to protect. Now they've left him. His wife went bye-bye in order to protect their children.

Now, this man who saved his ass is broken.

All because of Remo.

Remo looks to his leather bag on the floor of the cab.

"I've got a plan, if that helps," he says. "In that bag is something that could get us to free and clear."

Hollis says nothing, still lost inside his head, staring out the window.

"No, really. I think I can get this mess cleared up. You gotta believe me, I had no idea they were going after you and the family."

"Yeah."

"I didn't. Really."

"Yeah."

"Dammit. It's true. I would never put your family at risk—"

Remo's cell goes off. He glances to the screen. It's Anna, his ex-wife.

"Shit." Remo turns to Hollis. "I gotta take this."

"Yeah."

Remo's eyes roll. He's got sympathy for the man, but Hollis's little pity party is starting to get old.

"Anna?"

"Hey. Look, I fought even calling you, but Sean wanted to see if you're okay."

Remo's busted-up face lights up. "He did? That's great."

"Yes, Remo, it's great that our son is wondering if you're okay after seeing on TV that his father was knee-deep in a bloodbath. It's simply fucking fantastic."

"Okay, fine. Does he want to talk?"

"He does, but he's not here." Anna sighs. "Remo, try to grasp what I'm about to say. This... situation is a lot for a little boy to take in. You. Meeting you. What's going on with you. To be honest, it's a lot for me."

"Anna—"

"Shut up and listen. He wants to get to know you. Of course he does." She sounds as if she's working it out as she speaks. "It's probably not horrible if he actually knows his father. Even if it is you. In a limited, monitored capacity of course. Very limited. As in not much. Tiny amount is best."

Her end of the call goes quiet. Remo's not sure what he's supposed to do here. "Let me know when I can speak."

"Shut. Up. I need to think about this, okay? I just— I don't know the best way to go with this."

Remo's stomach flutters. This is what he wanted all along, even if he didn't know it. His brain didn't connect the dots before, but this is what he was really going for when he got involved with all the unfortunate business with the Mashburns. Before, he only thought he wanted to meet Sean before he died, but what he really wants is to be a part of his son's life. If only a small part.

He wants to be a dad.

He realizes he'll never be a dad in the traditional sense. That ship has sailed, and let's be honest, Remo ain't the sort. Not to mention, Anna would rather drink gasoline and shove a match up her ass than reconcile with Remo. Regardless of all of this, Remo can't help but smile.

He looks to Hollis.

He's not smiling.

He's broken. Broken because of Remo. Remo's smile fades.

"You listening to me? Asshole, hello?" says Anna.

"Of course. Take all the time you need to think about it. I'm open to whatever you want to do."

Anna goes silent. She's not sure what to do with an agreeable, rational Remo. "Okay," she says, and hangs up.

Remo pockets his phone while fighting to control his happiness. He's practically bouncing in the seat. Remo's learned over the years that irrational exuberance can lead to some hairy-assed issues. His mom died when he was young and his father wasn't a big fan of showing his happy side, at least not in front of Remo. Dad was more than happy to show his pissed-off, drunken-rage side, however. Yet, despite this, Remo can't help but smile wide. He looks to his bag again. His plan B. His emergency pack and, brother, this is an emergency. Breaking the damn glass on this thing is the only plan. It's flimsy, this little hope of his, this plan Remo is cooking up for his meeting with the cops, but this shit has to work. Now more than ever.

For Remo.

For Hollis.

For Sean.

R emo sits staring into the abyss.

Staring at Detective Harris.

They are on opposite sides of a beaten-to-hell metal table in a room located at the back of the 19th Precinct. Not an attractive room by any stretch. Not supposed to be. Movies and TV have captured its essence pretty well actually. Neutral-colored, bare walls. Nothing to write home about and not a room you'd like to hang out in. Damn bleak. No conversation starters in here. Nothing to distract the occupants from the task at hand, and that task is the cops extracting from your head what you know as quickly as possible.

To be clear, Remo and Harris hate each other.

Not a garden-variety hate either. Not a casual misunderstanding or an argument over blah blah. This is the sort of hate that bubbles and builds over years and years. Years and years of Remo setting criminals free. Criminals Harris and his fellow officers worked damn hard to apprehend. Some of the worst scum New York has ever produced and Harris knows this slick-as-shit lawyer has made a mountain of money defending them.

Remo doesn't have a real reason to hate Harris. He simply hates Harris because Harris hates him. Perhaps not the healthiest way to live, but it's what keeps a guy like Remo plowing through this thing called life. He feeds off the hate of others, thus feeding his own hate and propelling him headlong into questionable decisions at a blinding rate of speed. Again, not recommended, but it's better than living a passionless life. At least that's how Remo sees it.

There's a shit-ton of history between these two and none of it is good. Remo has a convenient way of forgetting history as it happens. More efficient than therapy. Harris, however, digs his fingernails into history and holds on for dear life. Like clinging to the rim before the big flush. It's all he's got. Strangely, the hate is also what keeps a guy like Harris plowing through as well.

But that's all history.

Today they are in the here and now.

The right now.

The two men sit staring at one another without saying a single word. They've been like this for a solid hour. Seriously, a whole hour. Two stubborn assholes sitting eyeballing the hell out of each other. Hate flung back and forth without a word spoken. Remo is screaming inside. Not showing it, but this whole thing is killing him. The silence is making his skin crawl. He wants to get to his plan and get the hell on with his life. He knows this whole unfortunate mess can be cleared up lickety-split if Harris will tap out of prick mode long enough to hear him out.

"Fuck this," Remo mutters to himself, hits reset then throws a toothy grin at Harris. "How ya been, brutha?"

Harris picks his teeth with his thumbnail, sucking in whatever he just jarred loose.

"Last time I saw you I almost got killed. If memory serves," Remo says.

"Which time?"

"Pardon?"

"Which time you almost got killed? I saw you at the Chinese joint after your boy, Lester, got shot up and you hit the floor like a pussy. That was kinda cool, by the way. Actually, the last time I saw you wasn't that long ago. It was in the hospital after you almost bought it in the Hamptons. Some pissed off, piece-of-shit clients you fucked over stopped by to execute your sorry fucking ass. So, I'll ask again: which time are you talking about?"

Now Remo picks his teeth with his thumb. "Doesn't matter."

"No, it does not." Harris goes back to staring.

Remo raps his fingers on the table. He was hoping the booze would even him out, but he's still jumpy. Hollis, along with Remo's brown leather bag from the club floor, is waiting for Remo at a bar not far from here. He trusts Hollis with it. Not because Remo has any kind of deep trust in his fellow man. It's more because he explained his plan to Hollis and Hollis doesn't really have a choice other than to wait and see how this shakes out. Self-preservation. That much Remo trusts.

Remo raps the table faster. The beat he's playing might be Metallica.

"Please stop that shit," Harris says.

"Are we waiting for something?"

"We are."

"What, exactly? Love to get the hell on with this."

Harris clears his throat then smiles big. "The CIA wants a word."

"CIA?"

"Yup. They're kinda dicks about things. If memory serves."

"What do they want?"

"Seems you've stepped in it, Slick."

"Perhaps I did." Remo takes a moment, then says, "Or did they think you'd fuck everything up?"

Harris's stare changes ever so slightly. There's a flash to his eyes. Only a flicker, not much of anything most people would notice, but it's enough for a guy like Remo to dig his claws into.

"Holy shit. That's it. You and your merry little band of dumbshits can't be trusted with the Hamptons shootout. Lots of media on it. Very high profile, right? Needs to done correctly, as in really correctly. That's it, right?"

Remo keeps hammering away at the red-faced, shaking-with-anger Harris.

"Big, bad Detective Harris and his NYPD blue balls can't be trusted to handle something as open and shut as a luxury neighborhood bloodbath. Damn, that's gotta sting."

A man standing behind Remo says, "You're incorrect, Remo."

Harris face turns white as he whispers, "Agent Cormack."

Remo turns, finding Cormack leaning in the doorway. Dark suit. Short, tight hair. Fit as fuck with blue eyes that carve through you. A special agent man right out of central casting.

"Not correct at all. Is it, Detective Harris?" Cormack asks.

Remo looks to Harris. The good detective acts as if his mom just came home early and caught him jerking off. He curls up into a ball of confusion. A frozen-faced, twisted mix of terror and shame. He's no longer the tough New York cop from a few moments ago. No, not even close. Remo has never seen anything like it. He'd take some joy in watching Harris sweat like this if it wasn't for the fact he's more than a little concerned that the CIA is involved in this whole mess. Given that the CIA's primary area of focus is foreign threats and Remo's primary area of focus is domestic assholes, Remo is his own private ball of confusion. This is something he did not plan for.

Never occurred to him.

Why would it?

"Why does the CIA give two shits about me?" Remo asks.

Cormack shrugs off the question as he steps into the room. He pauses, then leans down so he can speak into Remo's ear. "Let's talk. Doesn't have to be a big thing. I want you to be comfortable. We'll head over to your favorite Chinese place. Cool with you?"

Remo turns to face Cormack.

"*Yes* is the word you're hunting for, Remo."

Remo nods.

Cormack nods.

Remo swallows hard.

Cormack pokes Remo on the nose while making a *boop* sound.

Remo needs a drink.

12

The Asian waitress drops off a mug of coffee, along with a big-as-your-face plate of chicken fried rice.

Remo and CIA Agent Cormack sit at Remo's favorite table. The one three tables down from the entrance and three up from the back of the restaurant. It has a big, nice window that looks out upon the buzzing streets of the city. A front-row seat to the twirling soup of humanity that is New York. Remo comes here most nights to get away. To think. To step out of whatever mood-altering sandbox he's been playing in that day. Watching people out the window calms him, much like watching the ocean calms other people. There's something about watching them all move to a path and rhythm only known by them. Driven by meeting a friend, a hot date, late for whatever, an important appointment with who knows. Got to get home to the kid. Got to get to the store. Get to work. Get a job. Get home before they pass out face-first in the gutter.

Endless possibilities.

Remo watches them all. Watches them move through their lives, all through his window to the world. A window that has been recently replaced by the restaurant. A window that a troubled member of the Mashburns known as Chicken Wing shot out while

Remo sat at this very table enjoying the same meal with another man. A man named Lester. During that meal, Remo dove from the booth, hit the floor—as Detective Harris mentioned—and Lester was the one who caught the bad side of that deal. He took a bullet, or was it bullets?

Remo was positive Lester was dead that day.

He wasn't.

"Eat up, man. My treat," Cormack says.

Remo can only look at his steaming plate of rice with chunks of chicken fighting for real estate along with cubes of carrots and the tiny peas. He is hungry, but doesn't want to give any power to Cormack. If Remo took a bite right now, that would come off as Remo taking orders. Putting Cormack in the position of giving orders and Remo in the position of taking them. In Remo's world this is also known as bending over and letting them do what they want with you. Of course there's little doubt Cormack holds every ounce of power in this situation, but Remo would rather not make it so damn obvious, or bend over for Cormack's wants and desires.

"Here." Cormack pulls a small flask from his jacket and pours some familiar brown liquor into Remo's coffee. "That's better. Johnnie Walker Blue, correct?"

Remo wants to jump out of his skin.

1. That is exactly how Remo likes his coffee. Looks soooo good.

2. How does this prick know this?

3. Fuck. Fuck. Fuckity. Fuck. Fuck.

Cormack picks up a spoon and stirs Remo's coffee. "Now, I'm a *cards on the table* kind of dude. I own your buddy, Detective Harris. I'm sure you know this already, but in case you don't, he's in one hell of a mess." Cormack taps the coffee off the spoon using the edge of the cup, then wipes the spoon down with a red napkin. "Not an original story—cop with a gambling debt, hooker troubles, you know the sort. And I've got him on all of it. Could have buried him deep. Could have taken down half his department, but I didn't. Didn't want that. I wanted to trade up. You know why?"

Remo's stomach drops through the floor.

It's the look on Cormack's face.

This guy is in complete control and he knows it. Remo knows the feeling and the look that comes along with it. A feeling that comes from absolute confidence. The look Cormack has right now and the feeling that's more than likely surging through him is one Remo's experienced many, many times. In interrogation rooms. In courtrooms. Bars. Bedrooms. It's a feeling like you've got a bomb in your back pocket that only you know about, and you're just waiting to shove it up someone's ass.

Remo picks up his coffee, taking a long sip, trying hard not to show his shaking hands.

"Don't know?" Cormack asks. "Give up?"

Remo gives a single nod.

"I traded up for you. You, Remo. That has to make you feel special, correct?"

"Special?" asks Remo.

"Yes."

"Not correct."

"Yeah, I gave up all the things I could've done to Harris and his people, and it would have been a blast, to be sure, but I passed all that up to get here. To this place here and now to get to you."

Now Remo eats his rice. Feels like a last-supper type of thing now.

"Now. You're thinking, what's he got? What's this CIA a-hole holding? I'll tell you. I'll lay down my cards for you to look at. Nothing to hide, Remo. Does that interest you?"

Remo drinks some more from his juiced-up coffee mug. His brain spins. Flips. Catches fire. He's still got his emergency pack. His hard drive. His own smart bomb that'll get him out of this. Remo just needs to keep this ego-driven, civil servant fuckstick talking. Let him rant and give up everything. Then Remo will rain down some wrath-of-God-level shit matched by no man.

"I'll help you out, Remo. I'll keep talking and give up all I've got so you can have time to think. I know that's what you're doing. It's the smart way to play this, and you're a smart dude. I like that about you.

The more I talk, the more I give, the more time you get to think and counterattack what I've got. I went to law school too."

Remo runs his tongue across his teeth and leans back into the booth.

"This is fun." Cormack smiles. "Okay. What I've got is video of you and your friend Hollis at multiple stoplights, at a gun store trying out several guns and working over a firing range like weekend warriors in training, and then I've got you buying mattresses and tootling down the aisles of Home Depot."

Remo glances to the door, thinks of running away.

"All of the items in those videos? From the gun store, the mattresses and the cart full of crap you guys bought at Home Depot? I say crap and items—right now they're considered 'evidence.' All of that matches the items-slash-evidence found in the house in the Hamptons. The house that was covered in blood and bodies. Blood and bodies of your clients in a house you own."

Remo thinks of jamming his fork into Cormack's eye.

Cormack slides Remo's knife and fork away and over to his side of the table. "All of that suggests you knew what was going down. Prepared for something, perhaps set a trap. Perhaps premeditated murder. Who knows, but you could make an argument, correct?"

Remo wishes Chicken Wing would come back and shoot him.

"You take all that and mix in the possibility that you threw your case against the Mashburns. Ya know, the same Mashburns who were found shot all to hell in your Hamptons getaway? Plus, oh yeah, your friend Hollis is a known hitman. You can see how this doesn't look great for you. Or Hollis."

Remo's eyes go wide. Now the CIA is threatening Hollis. It's one thing to go after Remo like this, but Hollis has already been through enough because of him. Now Cormack is the one being silent. Waiting. Waiting for Remo's move.

Remo coughs. "I have something, too."

"Do tell."

"I need to know we can talk."

"We are talking."

"Need to know we can talk a deal. A real deal, not some reduced blah blah horseshit. A deal where me and Hollis walk with hands clean."

"Your and Hollis's hands will never be clean. You know that. I can't help you with that, not in a spiritual or moral sense. I can put on my listening ears and hear what you have to say, and if what you have to say is worth anything, then I'll consider almost anything."

"It's worth quite a bit."

"Sounds fantastic."

"It is."

"Can't wait."

Remo takes a gulp of coffee, takes in a deep breath and says, "I've got a hard drive that contains extensive evidence that can put away every client I or my firm has ever worked for."

Cormack simply blinks.

He doesn't even bother changing his expression.

PART II

SOMETHING DRASTIC

13

Remo stares back at Cormack.

The man hasn't said anything for at least a full minute. Remo can't tell if this is good or bad, but he won't give Cormack the satisfaction of asking. He'll sit here a fucking week if he has to.

"That it?" Cormack asks.

"It's a lot."

"It is, no doubt, but it's pretty useless to me."

Remo feels his guts crank. "Useless?"

"Remo, you know damn well I can't use anything from you in court."

"I have everything. Bank accounts. Safe houses. Names and addresses of girlfriends, of boy toys, of everything these fuckers are involved in. All you have to do is say you uncovered it at the house in the Hamptons."

"All good stuff. And you'll probably need it all."

Remo stops, leans forward, doesn't like what he just heard.

Cormack pours another snort of Blue into Remo's coffee. "That's right. *You* will need them."

"*You* might need to clarify that."

"I will. It's great you and I are on the same page. I was thinking more or less the same thing you were, only with a slightly different twist. When I heard you fucked over the Mashburns and that you gave away the money to charity, most of it at least, I was inspired."

Remo looks away, a little sheepish.

"It gave me an idea. That the biggest asshole defense attorney in New York, a guy who has access to the dirty deeds of so many other assholes, can be very, very helpful to me. Especially if that asshole defense attorney has had a crisis of conscience, has struggled with the morality of his work."

"Where is this going?"

"You're going to use what you know, what's on that hard drive and whatever else you've got, to help me take care of some very bad guys and gals."

Remo laughs.

Cormack laughs harder.

Remo tries to top the intensity and volume of Cormack's laughter.

The restaurant looks on with great discomfort.

Cormack goes louder and harder.

It's getting ridiculous.

They wind down to a stop.

"How?" asks Remo.

"How what?"

"I don't understand what you want me to do."

"Simple, really. You are going to continue what you started with the Mashburns. You're going to help rid the earth of horrible people."

Remo rules out the idea Cormack is a mind reader and read his thoughts earlier about doing that very thing. It was fine when it was Remo's idea. When it was Remo's choice. But this is fucked up.

"I'm sorry, I should have been more clear. That Mashburn thing was a onetime deal," Remo says.

"Nope."

"I'm not a trained killer."

"Easy now. Didn't say anything about killing, but if some dead bad guys pop up I won't hate you for it."

"You're insane."

"Nope. I'm not."

"How do you propose I do this?"

"I'm not going to tell you your business, Remo. Get creative. You might start with Hollis though. He's a five-star badass from what I understand."

"We're not the fucking Avengers."

"Of course not, that would be ridiculous. Love those movies though. No, you just need to figure out how to keep doing what you started. How to keep doing good." Cormack picks up the check and slides out from the booth. "I gotta bounce, man. I've enjoyed this, but I want to make sure I leave you with a clear understanding of what we've been talking about here. You will do this, or I will bury you and Hollis under a prison of my choosing. Got it?"

Remo nods.

"Good." Cormack makes it about two steps then snaps his fingers, spinning around. "Oh, one last thing. Mr. Crow."

"What about him?"

"He's a client of yours, and a disease. I'd like you to remove him from circulation."

14

R emo walks into the joint where Hollis sits waiting.

Hollis sits at the bar about halfway through a beer that's larger than his shoe. An empty shot glass also rests in front of him with a mangled lime laid out like a twisted body thrown from a car. He glances up to Remo. He can see it all over him. Hollis doesn't like it, and he doesn't want to hear Remo's bullshit.

"Fuck," Hollis says.

Remo takes a stool next to him, taking note of his brown leather bag resting on the other stool. He motions to the bartender to set them up with another round.

"It's not that bad."

"You're so full of shit," Hollis says.

"Okay, fine. We're fucked."

"Which prison are we going to?"

"Not prison I'm concerned with."

"Oh? Firing squad?"

"Kinda."

This catches Hollis's attention.

The bartender delivers two fresh beers and two tequila shots with salt and lime. Remo holds up a finger, requesting a moment from

Hollis. He raises his shot, clinks it with the one waiting for Hollis. Hollis glances to Remo, trying to guess where this conversation is going. Deciding that's a fool's errand, Hollis picks up his shot with a nod as the two old *friends* throw them back at the same time. Like synchronized swimming for the drunk and despondent. After destroying his lime, Remo empties his beer in three gulps.

"We have to *take down* some bad guys," Remo says.

"Define *take down*." Hollis pauses. "Better define *bad guys,* too."

"Bad gals, too."

"Need a definition there, too."

"I'm a little fuzzy on both, to be honest. CIA is involved however—"

"I'm sorry, CIA? We going after terrorists?"

"There's this agent named Cormack. Real fuckin' ballbuster. This guy, this fucking guy didn't want my hard drive but wants us to use the info on it and whatever else we've got to..." Looks skyward, searching for the words. "Let me make sure I say this right, *to take Mr. Crow out of circulation*."

"What the hell does that even mean?"

"You're the slick-ass hitman, was hoping you knew that type of talk."

"He wants us to hunt and kill Crow?"

"That's what was implied. He never really said kill anybody."

Now Hollis empties his beer in a minimal amount of gulps. Remo gives an air circle to the bartender for another round. They sit with their thoughts churning, both pretending to watch volleyball on ESPN.

"I'm running," says Hollis.

"It's the CIA, man."

"Outrun them before."

"Not like this."

"Why *not like this*?"

"They've got video. Video of you, with me, loading up for war right before the Hamptons, and they found it all after we ran the hell away. That's why they went to your wife and kids, I'm guessing. More of a message to you. They want you to know they will hunt you and your family down."

Bartender delivers the new round. Hollis takes his shot alone this time then grunts out, "Fucking hate you."

"Fine."

"This is all your fucking fault. I had to rush through shit to keep your sorry ass alive. If I had time I would have planned this out the right way. I was forced into being sloppy because of your dumbass, and now I'm fucked. Completely fucked because of you."

"I feel horrible."

"You don't feel shit."

Remo shrugs, then throws back his shot.

The two *friends* drain their beers in perfect harmony without bothering to look at each other. Remo knows Hollis doesn't have any great options with this situation. None that are realistic at least. Technically Hollis doesn't even exist. He's a ghost. The life he's been living is a complete fabrication. His neighbors know him as Bob. Bob plays golf, grills his special pork chops on Saturday, goes to church and helps out at the kids' school whenever needed. Hollis, however, kills people all over the world for a price. A steep price. He's got the dual life thing down cold. Dead-solid perfect. Only problem is that because Bob isn't truly real, everything that *is* real is in his wife's name. The house. The bank and brokerage accounts. Credit cards. All of it. She's real. Real as shit and she's really pissed with Hollis. So pissed she took it all and went gone baby gone leaving Bob/Hollis with three hundred twenty-six dollars and a budding depression that's teetering on an institutional-grade mindfuck.

"I should just shoot you. Dump your carcass. Leave town immediately. Boom, problem solved," Hollis says.

"Those are options, I guess."

"Yes, yes they are."

"And?"

"Nothing is off the table."

"I'm here all day."

A man steps up behind them and speaks. "Excuse me. This seat taken?"

Remo turns. "No..."

Lester cocks his head and gives Remo a finger-curl wave.

Hi.

15

Remo falls off his stool.

Ass hits the tile.

Hollis fires off his stool, sending it slamming into the bar, bouncing off about a foot and a half. He's on his feet, ready to roll. In the blink of an eye Hollis is in beast mode, ready to take Lester's head off. A highly trained instrument of mayhem that's itching to release.

Lester widens his stance, squares his shoulders, but doesn't look all that concerned. Lester lacks Hollis's skills, but he's no stranger to violence. He might not know advanced combat tactics or the sweet, subtle art of hand-to-hand, but Lester has been fighting his whole life. In the streets, in the prisons and everywhere else he's ever been. A lifetime of self-taught survival training that's provided a lifetime scars to prove it.

Remo fumbles getting to feet. His face is a mangled mess of freshly-made confusion and pain. The fall from the stool really hurt his ass, but Lester standing here is almost as painful.

"Lester. What the hell are you doing here?" asks Remo.

"Felt like I was needed after all that unfortunate business at your beach home." He looks to Hollis. "It's this one, really. He was with you, right? There's something about him. Something ugly."

"Did he really just call me ugly?" Hollis asks.

"Not your appearance, friend." Lester smiles. "It's all in your eyes. There's violence behind them. More like your soul that's in disrepair. Much like our mutual friend here, Remo. You need some light too." Lester takes a step closer to Hollis. "Do you wish Remo harm?"

"Of course I do. Everyone who's ever met him wishes him harm."

Lester can't help but chuckle at that one. It's the truth that makes it funny.

Remo waves his hands at Hollis, trying to get his attention. Trying to let him know Lester is a delicate touch and to stop rolling down whatever road Hollis is about to roll down. These are difficult concepts to get across with a simple hand wave, but it doesn't stop Remo from giving it a shot. He adds a whistle to the mix. Doesn't work.

Lester steps even closer to Hollis, just shy of nose to nose. "Tell me I'm wrong about you. Tell me I'm imagining the things I see when I look at you, because I don't think I am."

"No, I think you're seeing me just fine."

Remo attempts to worm his way between them but fails miserably. He jams a hand between them in a feeble attempt to separate the two war machines. Nothing. They don't move, not an inch. Remo tries with two hands. Nothing. It's as if he's trying to separate two trucks that are parked too close together.

Remo rubs his face in a quick, frantic motion. Completely frustrated, Remo resets, takes a deep breath. "How about a drink, Lester? On me. On your old buddy Remo." Looks Lester up and down. "Is that my fucking suit?" He glances to Lester's side. "My suitcase too? Damn it, man."

Lester doesn't bother looking Remo's way. His focus is squarely on Hollis and Hollis is zeroed in on Lester. Hollis has already decided how he's going to kill him. Using previsualization, Hollis has already mapped it all out. He'll start with snapping Lester's right kneecap with his heel then put Lester on the floor with a tomahawk elbow strike to the nose. Once he's down, Hollis will stomp his nuts then finish God Boy off with a snap of the neck.

Lester hasn't mapped it out, but he knows that he'd enjoy making Hollis bleed. Some screaming and begging might be nice as well.

Two warriors toe to toe.

Neither one backing down.

Both prepared to destroy.

Remo knows what these men are capable of. He's seen them both in action, seen them both when they are on fire, and it scares the shit out of him. As much as he'd love to witness this clash of the titans, Remo knows a public bloodbath isn't going to help anyone. They will either both be dead, one of them will be dead and the other will be dying, or worse. In Remo's mind, the worst-case scenario is Remo dying while trying to stop them from killing each other. Also, there's a far-greater-than-zero chance the cops would end up being called, if they haven't been contacted already. There's no upside here. No one is going to win this thing.

"Look, people—friends. We can't do this. We need to stick together," Remo says. His words don't seem to land with either of them. Remo works another angle. "We, the three of us, have some common ground here," Remo presses. "You're fucked up with Jesus, you're fucked up with family shit, and I'm just fucked up. We're the same, when you think about it."

Not even a glance.

This unresponsive behavior upsets Remo more than anything. He thought that last one was a pretty good line.

There's a wave of coldness that seems to slide across Hollis's eyes. Remo's seen it before, and it wasn't a good thing. Looking to Lester, Remo sees nothing. Blank, dark eyes that simply do not care about what happens to him or to Hollis.

This is about to go off. Remo has to do something.

Something drastic.

Something to defuse the situation and give him a chance to talk some sense into these two masters of disaster. Remo holds his breath, then does that *something*.

Remo jams his hands down their pants.

One down the front of Lester's, one down the front of Hollis's.

Remo grabs ahold of their balls, hanging on for dear life. Using the hardest grip he can, Remo clamps his right hand on Hollis's jewels and uses his left to take hold of Lester's hairy set of pills. As if milking two cows at the same time.

Both Lester's and Hollis's eyes pop wide.

Bulge huge.

There's some coughing. Red faces. Lip biting. Teeth grinding. After the initial wave of shock and nausea passes, they both look to Remo, who stands there holding on as if he were competing in a psychopath rodeo.

Remo gives his best apologetic tone. "Look. I'm sorry. I need to talk to both of you like civilized human—"

Lester and Hollis both whip guns out.

Hollis jams the barrel of his gun into Remo's right eye. Lester takes the left. Remo still holds on to his boys' balls. He can feel them there, he just can't see what he's doing with guns blocking his field of vision.

"Okay," Remo says, "I know this is awkward for all of us, but let's think this through."

"Let. Go. Of my balls," Hollis says.

"Yes, Remo. Stop doing that," Lester says.

The bar has already cleared out. Remo's more than fairly sure the bartender has called the cops by now.

He swallows hard. "Look. Let's think, talk it out together. We are in a public place. There are men with guns drawn and balls are in custody. The cops will be here any second. What exactly are we going to tell them?"

Lester and Hollis glance to one another.

Both their faces red as hell.

Sweat drips.

"Think, boys. How does getting arrested right now help any of us?" Remo hopes his words are taking hold this time. He can't see, so he can't get a read on their faces. Can only hope that self nut-love and common sense can cut through the anger of two violent-as-hell men.

Lester removes his gun.

Hollis follows suit.

Remo blinks his vision clear, then releases their sacks.

16

R emo washes his hands.

He decided to make an upgrade on his living arrangements. He's moved on to the Essex House located Midtown across from the park. It was a bit of a gamble, using his Amex to get the room, considering there's a chance the powers that be had frozen his account, but once it cleared he asked for a penthouse that had a nice view of the city he loves. Considering he might be dead or in prison soon, he figured why not live a little?

Besides, he wanted a nice place to have a meeting.

A meeting of dangerous minds.

Lester and Hollis are seated on a plush couch looking out over Central Park. Hollis holds a glass of vodka on the rocks. Lester holds his leather-bound Bible and a bottle of whiskey. Neither one looking at the other. Eyes forward. Still not happy.

Still considering killing one another.

Remo steps out from the bathroom, wiping his hands dry with a hotel towel. He stands behind them and can only see the backs of their heads, but he can feel the anger radiating from the couch.

He takes a moment to look out the window, soaking in the view. *It really is a great park,* he thinks. Massive, sprawling, peppered with every walk of life imaginable, coming from everywhere possible. Life-long New Yorkers, tourists, immigrants fleeing a third world shithole, transplants fleeing a small-town US shithole, and whatever else you can think of. Most chasing a dream or just looking for a better life. Remo's thoughts drift to Sean and Anna.

Are they out there right now?

In the park, enjoying the day?

Remo hopes so.

He hopes Sean is running and playing with all he has. Hopes Sean will play as long and as hard as he can, because one day that will stop. One day Sean will be an adult with adult problems and all the horrible shit that goes along with it. He will more than likely never have to deal with the issues his father has had to work through. At least Remo hopes to hell he won't.

Remo hopes Sean will never have to grab two killers by the balls.

"You might have pulled one loose," Hollis says, rubbing himself.

Remo smirks, then pours himself a glass of water. He needs to lay off the sauce, at least for a bit. He does need to focus, however. He pops a pill. Taking a seat in a cushy-ass chair across from the couch, Remo looks over his people. His new team. His new marriage, of sorts.

Lester, Hollis and Remo.

For better or worse.

"How the fuck did we end up here?" Remo asks.

"You're an asshole, that's how," says Hollis.

"He's not wrong, actually." Lester nods while rubbing his Bible. "You are the link to both of us and you being, pardon the expression, an *asshole* is the reason I'm here. Solid. Can't argue with it, man."

Hollis and Lester share a nod, perhaps common ground.

"Okay, regardless." Remo stands, pacing back and forth in front of the window. "We share a problem. Right?"

"Yeah. You," Hollis says.

Lester nods.

"What I mean is regardless of how or why we got here, we have the same problem and that problem is the CIA, the cops and whatever the fuck else wants to own us." Remo turns to Lester. "You might still be able to bolt, man. Cormack didn't say anything about you."

Lester cocks his head. "Cormack? What's a Cormack?"

Hollis leans over. "CIA dude that has a hard-on for Remo."

Lester nods, then motions for Remo to continue.

Remo goes on. "You can probably break free of us and whatever shit we're knee-deep into."

"I came back to help you, Remo," Lester says. "I made a decision to save you and you are far, far from saved. The Lord placed me with you. Twice now. I see that now more than ever."

Hollis looks over at Lester's suitcase, noticing something.

"Lester. Man, come on."

"Remo, you did an amazing thing for me. You saved me much in the same way. Even if you didn't realize you were doing it. You risked everything with the Mashburns. You put me, and them, in prison. Forced me to take moment. A cleansing moment. In the process you set me free. Don't you see that? Can't you see that is something I can't simply walk away from?"

"I guess, but shit, dude."

Hollis squints, trying to get a better look at the suitcase. There's something that looks a lot like hair peeking out from the zipper of Lester's, really Remo's, suitcase. He gets up, walking toward it while Remo and Lester continue their conversation.

"*You guess*?" Lester says. "That's what is so endearing about you, Remo. You don't even know the good in you. I know what people say about you, and perhaps it's all true, but I see the light in you, and brother, it's bright."

Hollis reaches the suitcase.

"And if you don't realize that light that's inside you, if you don't know that about yourself, that's okay. I see it. The Lord sees it. So if you don't mind, I'd like to stay and help you through this fucked up shit."

Remo feels his eyes water a bit. He's hit with an odd moment of emotion, hearing Lester's words. The fact Lester would pledge his life, not to get all *Lord of the Rings* with this, but in a way Lester is pledging his sword for Remo, is damn touching.

Remo extends his hand to Lester.

Lester grabs it and brings Remo in tight for a massive, bone-crushing hug.

All air escapes Remo's body as Lester squeezes tighter and tighter. Lester speaks into Remo's ear. "I'm not going anywhere, brother. We'll get through this, okay?"

Remo grunts out, "Okay."

"What. The. Fuck?" Hollis barks.

Lester releases Remo. They turn to find Hollis holding Dutch Mashburn's severed head in the air by the hair. Hollis's eyes are wide as plates, looking directly at Remo.

Remo has nothing to say. With his mouth wide open, his eyes slip over to Lester.

Lester shrugs.

"Lester, amigo. We need to lose that head," Remo says.

"I disagree."

"Lester. Dump Dutch's melon."

Dejected, Lester snatches the head from Hollis's grip. With the head swinging by his hip, Lester looks around, then drops it in a trash can next to the desk by the window.

Hollis is in complete disbelief. He runs his hand through his hair. "You can't put it in the trash." He spins toward Remo. "Who the fuck is this guy?"

"Lester, he's right. This room is in my name. Someone might notice a severed head in the trash."

"Then what?" asks Lester.

Remo looks out the window. He presses his forehead against the glass, looking out toward the park, letting the coolness of the window offer some form of comfort in this moment of madness.

Lester's confused. "We can't throw it out that way. Window doesn't open."

Hollis rolls his eyes.

Remo continues to watch the park, wishing he was there and not here. Wishing he was actually anywhere but here. He pivots his face toward Lester, keeping his forehead on the glass. "No, man. We'll go down to the park and find a dumpster or something. They find severed shit in the park all the time."

"Fine, fuck it," Lester says in a huff, jamming Dutch's head back into the suitcase. There's an ear still sticking out.

"Oh for fuck's sake." Hollis moves Lester out of the way, stuffing the head deep into the suitcase himself.

Lester shoves Hollis away from the suitcase.

Hollis shoves Lester back. Looks like two school kids seconds away from a slap fight.

"Hey," Remo barks. "Want me to start snagging nuts?"

The two stop like brothers scolded by a fed-up parent.

"Good. Lets dump that nasty-ass head and figure out how to get un-fucked."

17

L ester shoves his arm shoulder-deep into a Central Park trash can.

Remo and Hollis stand in front of him, attempting to shield Lester from view.

Hollis is quiet, casting a silent stare across the park.

Remo's mind cranks at a thousand thoughts per second.

Lester hums a church hymn.

"Got it yet, God Boy?" asks Hollis.

Lester ignores the jab as he pushes Dutch's head farther and farther into the can. Through the half-eaten hot dogs and ice treats. Past the bags of dog shit, the discarded napkins and the pounds of city waste.

Remo thinks of Crow.

Mr. Crow. Cormack's target.

Remo's client.

A former client who lives the good life of a NYC crime god. Crow enjoys two things, really. Money and his little side hobby of murdering prostitutes. Crow was Remo's client for years, one of his first actually. He started out as a small-time enforcer who rose fast, mainly by killing his competition, and later branched off into his own thing. Not as a drug kingpin, although he had some dealings in pills and powder, unavoidable given his line of work. No, Crow made his mark off running girls and gambling dens of sin. He saw those businesses as a safer way to go. Crow knew he could still make a good living, a very good living, running poker and blackjack tables around the city and providing perks for the players without the ugliness that can come from the drug trade. The perks for the players were girls and the aforementioned pills and powder. He probably could have done all this without a ton of legal issues if it weren't for his unfortunate habit.

Crow enjoys killing people.

Women in particular.

Namely, the women he employs.

Remo feels a wave of nausea pass over him as he calculates the number of times he was able to successfully help Crow out of trouble. The number of women who died, killed by Crow, and how Remo made any form of justice for those crimes disappear. This is what Remo was trying to work out in his damaged brain before all this Cormack shit came into play. This is exactly the type of shit that pushed him to do what he did with the Mashburns.

Remo's guilt, the heaviness of it.

That's it, thinks Remo, that's really what this is all about. That's what set this whole damn shitshow in motion. Remo's guilt is what is powering all of this and he's got tons of it. He turns his head and watches as Lester disposes of Dutch Mashburn's head. Remo's own head fumbles around the truth. The idea that his choice of profession has set him on this path. Perhaps sending him on a path that now has him standing in Central Park watching Lester jam a former client's head into a trash can. Perhaps this was something destined to be. Remo's not a deeply religious person, he'll leave all that shit to Lester, but Remo's thinking is skimming around the edges of predestination and the like.

Is this why Remo is here?

I'd like you to remove him from circulation.

That's what Cormack said.

Is Remo the instrument to undo the wrongs?

"There," Lester says, arm covered to the shoulder in the New York filth. "Bastard's skull is way down in there."

Hollis rolls his eyes.

Remo smiles and looks over at Hollis and Lester. They can do this, he thinks. They can remove Crow from circulation and get clear of Cormack. Remo can be rid of the guilt he's been dragging around because of the Mashburns and Crow. There are many others Remo has helped get away with horrible things, but he's convinced his guilt will subside once Crow is done. The Mashburns and Crow will equal two wrongs undone. Two wrongs make a right, or some shit like that.

"What's our move?" asks Hollis.

Remo continues to smile and stare at them while his mind works it all the way through. Maybe he can write a tell-all book or hit the lecture circuit or teach or whatever. Find a new way to make a living once this is all over. He snickers to himself as he runs over the possibilities of a life post-guilt.

Lester and Hollis look to one another. *Remo's gone bye-bye.*

Remo can find a better way to make a living and maybe, just maybe, he can have a life with Sean. Anna will never come around, that ship has sailed. She has an immeasurable amount of hate for Remo that cannot be overcome. He realizes that and has made peace with it, but Sean? Maybe there can be more. Before all of this went down, all Remo wanted was to meet his son. It's what got him through the ordeal with the Mashburns. Hell, it's what made Remo start the ordeal with the Mashburns.

Now?

Now that he's met Sean, Remo wants more.

"Asshole?" Hollis says.

If taking down Crow will give him that chance, a chance with Sean, a chance to be some form of a father, then Crow needs to be removed.

Remo eyes Hollis and Lester.

Lester blinks, scraping some NYC goo from his arm.

Hollis raises his hands. "Well? What the fuck?"

"We're going to remove Mr. Crow from circulation and get our lives back."

Lester loves this idea. The excitement in his eyes is undeniable. There's an almost visible electric bounce ricocheting inside of him.

Hollis's assessment leans more to the unsure side of things. He knows Remo and knows no matter what Remo is saying, or the reasons he's saying it, there will be blood. Lots of blood. More than likely some of it will be Hollis's.

"You got a plan?" asks Hollis.

"No."

"The Lord has a plan," Lester says, showing his Bible.

Hollis shakes his head.

Remo grins. *Classic Lester.* "I think you're right, Lester."

"Okay." Hollis takes a deep breath. "How does the good Lord want us to remove Mr. Crow?"

"Don't be a dick," says Lester.

"It's a valid fucking question," Hollis says.

"I understand, but there's a certain tone you're using and I don't like it."

"Tone? Fuck my tone."

"See. That. That right there. That's the tone and it's offensive."

"You just shoved a man's head into a trash can."

"So?"

Remo steps in. "Gentlemen, we have to find a way to work together on this thing of ours. All three of us have to get this done. I can't do it alone and you both have your own reasons for doing this. We can all get clear and get where we want to go, but only if we don't tear each other apart."

Hollis and Lester glance at one another, but only a glance. They know Remo's right.

Lester extends his hand to Hollis.

Hollis looks at his filthy, head-dumping paw. "Not a chance in hell, but I accept what you're trying to do with that there."

"Gotta give me something," Lester says.

Hollis thinks, then gives him a half-hearted military-style salute.

Lester's eyes slip to Remo. *Really?*

Remo nods and salutes him as well.

Lester sighs and returns the gesture.

18

"We need to pull our money together," Remo says.

"Fuck you," says Hollis.

"Don't have any money. Not my thing. Material needs are for shit," Lester says, watching the lights blink and ding as the elevator climbs.

Remo realizes he jumped the conversation a bit. In his mind, they had already all agreed to team up in an alliance and go after Crow and end this thing. Meaning that they had all agreed to what needed to be done. Meaning that shit costs money and Remo ain't picking up the tab on all that shit.

He'll take the hit on this hotel room, that was his decision, Remo gets that, but everything else is going to cost. They'll need guns, for starters. They'll also need transportation, be it cabs, airfare or whatever. They might want to eat somewhere along the way. Might have to grease some palms for information. There's a lot of shit, man.

Remo opens his mouth, about to explain.

Hollis sticks a wad of cash into Remo's chest.

Remo catches it before it hits the floor. With a quick count it looks to be maybe a couple a hundred and change. Remo appreciates the gesture, but knows that isn't going to get this crew very far. That combined with what Remo has might get them through Crow, but after that, who knows.

There's no *going away* money.

No *starting over* money.

No *fuck you* money.

It may not seem like it, but a guy like Remo plays life like a game of chess. Thinking several moves ahead. Now, just because he's thinking of moves ahead of time does not mean the moves he's thinking of making are the best or the safest. The moves are almost never cloaked in morality—God knows that's not the case—but nonetheless he's always thinking ahead, and what he's thinking now is...

"We'll have to rob Crow too."

Ding.

The doors open to their hotel floor.

Remo steps out, leaving Lester and Hollis with his words hanging in the elevator like an unspeakable fart.

19

Remo heads straight to the bar in their hotel suite.

Lester and Hollis take a seat on the couch. The room has been cleaned and looks great. This is why Remo wanted a nice room to call their command center, and now that the issue of Dutch's severed head has been resolved they can sit down and figure this the hell out in a civilized manner.

"You want to explain?" asks Hollis.

Remo drops the cash Hollis gave him onto the glass table then begins pulling the cash from his pants and suit jacket pockets, letting the bills fall to the table. It's a fair amount of money. You'd be happy to win that pile in Vegas. But it's not all that impressive if you go big-picture and Remo knows it.

"That's it," Remo says, takes a gulp of Blue. "That's all we've got to go to war with Crow. My credit cards will be frozen any second now, and soon as they are they'll toss our asses the fuck out of this room."

"We should order some food," says Lester with a childish giggle.

Remo snaps his fingers and points to Lester. *Good idea.*

Lester finds the black leather menu by a glass lamp and begins to look it over.

"Order a shitload," Hollis adds. "A last-supper-style thing and some shit we can pack up and take with us."

Remo points to Hollis. *Now we're thinking.*

"So what are you thinking with Crow?" asks Hollis.

Remo pulls a laptop from his brown bag, along with the hard drive. While powering up, he plugs in the drive, letting everything boot and buzz. Remo takes another swig of Blue, letting the burn work its way down. Hollis gestures to pass the glass over. Remo thumbs toward the bar. *Get your own.* Hollis snatches the glass from his hand and drains it.

"Dick." Remo gets up and heads back to the bar, pours himself another. "Crow runs some big-money, exclusive poker games around Midtown." He brings the bottle over to the couch and refills the glass Hollis stole. "Lots of cash at these things. What I'm thinking, to answer your question, is take down one of those and pick up some folding money and maybe get some info."

"Maybe use it to set something else up," Hollis adds.

"What do you mean?"

Lester picks up the phone and begins ordering up the food.

Hollis continues. "I mean maybe we make it the beginning of a bigger plan. Maybe we hit a game and make it look like someone else did it. Flush out Crow. Get him on his heels, then smoke his ass."

Remo thinks on that.

It's raw, this plan, but it's forming. He likes it. He clinks his glass with Hollis. The laptop is booted up and running. Remo begins opening files and sorting through docs, scanned info and images. He turns the screen, allowing Hollis get a good look.

"Yes, that'll be all. Thank you," Lester says, hanging up and standing. "I'm going to take a shit."

"I'll alert the media," Remo says.

Lester heads down the hall to the bathroom.

Remo points to the screen. "That one. That game's been rolling strong for years. His biggest one."

"Pick a different one."

"Why?"

"Don't want to go big first time out. We want to get his attention, not declare war. We save the big one."

"Okay, I'm going to value your opinion on this here, but we might not get a choice on what we hit."

"Value. Yes, that's the right word. You 'value' my opinion."

"Don't have to be a dick about it."

"Oh, but I do."

There's a knock at the door. A woman's voice calls out from behind the door. "Room service."

Remo looks to Hollis. *That was quick.*

Hollis pulls his gun and rushes to check the peephole. A young woman dressed in hotel garb stands outside with a cart. Hollis nods to Remo but takes a place by the door with his gun at the ready. Remo flips the bolt and opens the door.

"Anywhere?" the woman asks, strolling in, pushing a cart that holds a silver dome.

"Over there by the couch is good," says Remo.

Hollis watches her. There's something off, but he can't place it. She doesn't move like a luxury hotel employee. Her walk. It's almost arrogant. Ballsy. There's a look to her too. It's unpolished. Her eyes are wild. Everything about her screams *proceed with caution.*

Hollis re-grips his gun, never taking his eyes off of her.

The woman follows Remo's request and leaves the cart next to the couch. With a wink and smile she exits, quietly shutting the door behind her.

Hollis checks the peephole. "Something's not right."

"What?" asks Remo.

Hollis moves over to the cart.

Lester comes back from the bathroom. "Grub's here?"

Hollis removes the silver dome.

Dutch's head rests on a silver platter.

20

"Well, that's just fucking fantastic," Remo says.

"Not what I ordered," Lester says, placing the dome back.

Hollis stares. Blinking. Thinking.

Remo starts pacing. His anxiety can be measured by the speed of his speech and the wild, frantic motion of his hands. "What in the fuck is that doing back here? Is it some kind of message from some kind of motherfucking asshole? One of those sleep-with-the-fishes mafia motherfucking messages that requires de-fucking-coding. Huh? Anybody got an answer on this one?"

"Remo—" Lester says.

"What's the message sent when someone delivers the head of a dude that you just shoved in a trash can less than an hour ago? Love to hear it. Maybe someone thought we lost it and wanted to return it. Wonderful. Humanity lives."

Lester thinks of saying something, but stops himself.

Remo continues to work the carpet.

Hollis thinks, says, "Let's do the math. Your CIA boy maybe? Wants us to know he's got eyes on us?" He looks to Remo. No answer, only a blank stare. "Remo," Hollis snaps.

Remo stops his pacing long enough to suck down some Johnnie Blue. "Sorry, needed to drink."

"You've had your drink. Now, would Cormack do this?"

Remo ponders. "I don't know who else would."

"I don't either." Hollis turns to Lester. "You got any thoughts on the subject?"

"None other than, 'I'm still hungry.' I'm also annoyed we have to dump Dutch's head again. So, yeah, the combination of those is causing me to get upset. That's what I know."

Hollis can't help but bust a snort-laugh.

Remo follows with a childlike giggle.

Lester doesn't think it's funny. At all. As he's clearly stated, he's annoyed and hungry.

Remo and Hollis are now in a full-on roaring laughing fit. Hollis holds on to the wall for support while Remo falls on the couch. It's the absolute ridiculousness of their situation that's got ahold of them. The acceptance of being completely fucked has washed over them and all they have left to do is laugh. This acceptance hasn't reached Lester. "Why are you laughing?"

Remo barely gets out, "It's better than crying."

Hollis snorts. "We're so fucked."

"I know," Remo roars.

Lester snickers. The sound of others laughing is infectious. He begins to break up, as much as a man like Lester can. He leans forward, looking at the cart. There's a small wadded up napkin. Lester can make out the colors of a fast-food logo. His eyes go wide for a split-second. He gets control of himself, making sure the other two didn't see him. He carefully removes the napkin.

Hollis and Remo continue with the giggle fest.

Lester opens the napkin. "Shit."

"What?" asks Remo.

Lester quickly shoves the napkin deep into his pocket, then lifts the dome from over Dutch Mashburn's head.

"What are you doing?" Remo asks.

Lester picks up the head by the hair and jams it back into his rolling suitcase. "We can't leave it here."

"So we're going to keep it like a good luck charm?"

"Did I miss the good luck?" Hollis asks, wiping a tear from his eye.

A knock at the door.

Hollis pulls his gun. Lester pulls out the butcher knife from the suitcase.

Remo checks the peephole, pauses, then turns to Lester. "How much damn food did you order, man?"

21

M r. Crow lives life like a Bond villain.

He enjoys dressing in the finest of clothes at all times. He carries a deep belief that the clothes do indeed make the man. At the moment, the clothes making Crow a man come in the form of a Kiton navy blue tuxedo. His dark hair is perfect, not a single one out of place. His appearance is a constant state of groomed.

His steady state?

Perfection.

His profession?

A career criminal of means.

Crow makes his daily bread off the weakness of others, no matter the sin. He's used all seven of those deadlies to pad his accounts, but the two main sins Crow's businesses focus on are greed and lust. He's found these to be the easiest to profit from. The simplest of mouse traps to build, but only if you know how to work the buttons right.

He's managed over the years to boil it all down into a profit center that scratches people's itches in a very efficient and profitable manner. If you go to a Crow establishment you know what you'll get. First you have to be invited, but if you do get the invite you'll get a world-class experience consisting of high-class gambling and girls. He added men to the mix a couple of years ago. The rise in the net worth of women and gay men in the city wasn't lost on Crow, and if you're going to grow your business you need to pivot with the times. He's reluctant to add trannies to the mix, but if there's a transgender whale who wants to pay to play, Crow will consider anything.

Crow's big problem?

It's a problem Remo has helped him with from time to time.

Crow enjoys killing.

Women in particular.

The working ladies of his parties to be even more specific.

Matter of fact, he's just killed one now.

There's a few drops of her blood sprayed upon his fine navy blue tux and across his face. Crow stands over her body as a neon sign blinks purple behind him. Even during the day it creates a brightly colored pulse to the otherwise depressing room of hers.

Crow holds a blood-soaked ballpoint pen in one hand.

His phone in the other, poised to call someone for some assistance.

He pauses, letting his eyes scan over his work. Allows his drumming heartbeat to wind down to a normal resting rate. The young blonde's mouth is still open, shock frozen on her face. Eyes wide open, looking for answers. For logic. For hope.

There will be none for her.

Those things ended a week and a half ago when she first met Crow.

She just didn't know it then.

She does now.

Crow leans down to the blonde, plays with her hair a bit, then softly says, "I'm going to find someone to come in here and take care of your mess." He wipes his face with a handkerchief, smearing the blood even more across his face. He locates a dirty mirror in the tiny bathroom. "I am sorry. It's sad you had to pull it out of me, but you did, didn't you?" He moves back into the room, standing over her.

"You said the shit you said and now look at you. You had to go and make it this way. Didn't you, darling?"

Blood pumps from her neck.

Crow moves his foot to avoid it getting on his shoes.

"Gotta run now." Crow sighs big. "Sorry you fucked up."

His phone buzzes. "Yeah." Listens, then, "Okay. Table's good? Right? Good. Send a car." He almost hangs up but stops. "Hey, send some fresh clothes. Another Kiton. Black, pink tie."

Stepping over her body, he drops the pen on her stomach before walking out the door.

Crow walks down the hall with a slight strut in his step. He heads down the barely-lit hallway, passing a man laid out by a door sleeping one off, a stray cat licking his face. Noises from the walls thump and pound. Roars of arguments, of way-too-loud TVs and the muted sounds of abuse in its various forms.

Crow taps his phone, then scrolls down to a name.

A contact.

REMO.

22

Remo, Lester and Hollis are sprawled out in the hotel room. Looks like they just took down a combination of Thanksgiving and a chili cook-off, and when they finished with that they requested a Vegas brunch buffet to top it off. Lester is laid out on the couch with his pants button popped open. Hollis can't breathe. Remo can only stare out the window from his position lying down on the couch. He'd suck his thumb if was alone. No one has said a word for at least fifteen, maybe twenty minutes, which is some form of record with Remo.

Dirty plates and bowls litter the luxury room, along with food-caked utensils scattered around various tables and such. There's a soup spoon on the floor, buffalo wing stuck to the window and half a cake in the bathtub. Remo saw it when he took a piss. Didn't think to question it, but he did grab a piece with his free hand.

Remo's phone buzzes a few feet from him on the floor.

"Guh," Remo grunts.

The phone isn't that far away, but it's far enough to require some effort, and that's effort Remo would rather not expend at the moment.

Buzzes more.

"Get it, dammit," says Hollis. "It's pissing me off."

Remo pushes himself off the couch as if he was rising from a hospital bed after a long coma. Without looking at the screen he grabs the phone and slides his stuffed body down to the floor.

"Who is it?" Hollis asks.

Lester snores.

Remo cracks open one eye, making out the C, then the R. Both eyes fly open. Now they are completely wide and they can't believe what the hell they are seeing.

"It's fucking Crow," he says.

Lester stirs awake. "Answer it."

"Yeah, what the hell? Take the damn call," Hollis says.

Remo sucks in some air.

Closes his eyes tight.

Taps, then says, "Hello."

"Remo," Crow says. Remo hears a car door close. The engine fires up. "Need a little something from you."

"Crow?"

"Don't start, Remo. Don't start with your shit because I don't give a shit. What I do give a shit about is finding someone to assist me with a matter of mine. A matter that you can and will handle for me. A matter that I pay a rather large retainer to be handled by you and the pricks you work for."

Remo's mind goes nuclear. A mushroom cloud plumes inside his skull. He remembers the Crow cases. He's been so consumed with his own shit that he's almost forgotten who and what Crow is. Off the tone in his voice, the way Crow's talking, Remo knows what has happened. He's killed another one. Crow, probably minutes ago, ended the life of another woman. Heat rushes to Remo's face as if someone cranked the room up to a hundred. He feels his hands shake.

Hollis looks to Lester. Something's up with Remo. It's all over him. This is something they haven't seen out of Remo and they're not sure they like it. Remo is on the floor with his eyes closed. If they didn't know better, they'd think he was praying.

"You still there, Remo? I need. I need, man. I need your help, again," Crow says.

Remo tries to count the number of times he's had this conversation with Crow. The number of times they've talked like this, because that would equal the number of women Crow's killed. And if you're keeping score at home, that would also equal the number of times Remo has helped Crow get away with it.

Is it double digits?

"Remo?"

It can't be in the teens, can it? Bet it fucking is. This human garbage has killed so many he can't count them all. Can't count how many times he's helped this bucket of shit walk away free from murder.

"Remo, take an address. Fix this shit."

Hollis and Lester stand up, their eyes dead on Remo. They don't know what to do. The man they seek is on the phone. A strange, and possibly fortunate, twist of fate, and Remo seems to be melting down. If there's one thing these two know about Remo it's that Remo doesn't drop the ball. Remo is never sick at sea.

Hollis snaps his fingers. Not even sure why he did it.

Remo's head makes a quick jerk in his direction. They lock eyes. Remo looks to Lester, who's gripping his prized Bible. Lester's gaze does not waver. Does not break. He does not blink or look away. His face is stone. It is as if he's saying everything, while offering up nothing. Remo isn't let off the hook with an encouraging nod or a look of sympathy. Not from Lester at least. Lester wants Remo to get there by himself. Wants Remo to make the right decision on his own. And if Remo doesn't, Lester might kill him.

Crow says, "Listen, motherfucker. You'd better get on this shit directly."

Remo looks to his new partners in crime and echoes the words he said to Crow about a week ago. "I can ease your troubled mind and heal your heavy heart."

"Fuck you, Remo. I'll meet you at your office in one hour," Crow says.

"No. Not there," Remo spits out in a panic. "I'll text a new place."

"Why?"

"The office is not a good place to talk."

"Again I'll ask you, *why*?"

"There's been some leaks. I don't trust it. Most of us are taking meetings off campus until things get patched up."

There's a pause on Crow's side of the conversation. Lester and Hollis share a look. Remo grips the phone tighter, rocking back and forth on the floor. If Crow goes to the office they are fucked and this opportunity will go away with the wind.

"Okay. Whatever. Meet me at my Hell's Kitchen place in an hour. Nobody's leaking shit there."

"Much appreciated." Remo half-smiles to Lester and Hollis as he lays down the phone. "I think we've got something."

PART III

HE WILL DIE AS HE LIVED

23

Remo, Hollis and Lester push out through the revolving doors of the Essex House, storming their way down West 59th.

Moving with purpose, like men on a mission. They wrapped up a discussion with a vague outline of a plan only moments ago. One that includes Remo taking advantage of this meeting. This sit-down.

This takedown.

They agree they might not get another shot at this. All that talk about which place to take down first and the money they'd get is over. Things change quickly in this life, so they need to be happy with whatever money they can get, if any, as long as they get their man. The main goal, meaning the goal of saving their asses, is to get to Crow. Of course, Lester isn't really in as deep as the other two. Remo lied to him a second ago, telling him that if Cormack had the head sent over, then he was on to Lester as well. *Lie* is strong word. Remo figures it's very possible, so in Remo's mind that's as good as the truth, not to mention Lester is a killing machine on a mission from God. That fact can come in handy if played correctly, and Remo is considered the motherfucking Jimmy Page of playing criminals.

"We'll need shotguns," Hollis says.

Lester nods, pulling the suitcase behind him.

"Need, or want?" asks Remo.

"Need, without question. Well, depends on the setup of the room."

"I've never been to this place."

"Based on the other places you showed me on that hard drive? Shotguns."

Remo doesn't know what they need. Only thing he knows is that they need Crow to go away and they were handed a gift by him calling. He also knows they need to get on with this thing before whoever dropped off that head decides to escalate things.

"Whatever. I don't care about the hardware, I just want to know if we can do this," Remo says.

After Remo hung up with Crow, Hollis explained that he's got a guy not too far from Crow's Hell's Kitchen money game who can hook them up with some tools, but it'll cost them. They worked out the finances. It's not great, but they can get armed to an acceptable level. That's not the problem. The bitch is they need to stop and get a change of clothes if they're going to have a chance of doing this thing right.

According to Remo's files, Crow's setup isn't the kind of thing you can just storm into with guns blazing. Oh no, no, no. Crow's a psychopath and royal motherfucker, but not an idiot. There are check points, access points and space between the entrance and where the party is. Meaning where Crow will be and, not to mention, where the money is.

Also, Crow is expecting his high-priced, attack-dog fixer of an attorney to show up. Not a hobo offering up five-dollar hand jobs plus gratuity. Remo needs to look the part. He needs to look like the guy Crow knows and hates, but needs dearly. Remo's suit is a wreck and Lester's (Remo's to be accurate) needs some freshening up. It's unclear when all of them will go in or how, so it's necessary for all of them to look like they belong at one of Crow's parties. So, logic suggests they need to spend some coin to fit in with the Midtown whales.

Remo luckily has a tailor not far from here. He works out of a shop at The Plaza, but he's not cheap, and considering this is going to be an extreme rush job the odds are this will be the biggest bill Remo's ever seen out of Mario the tailor. All of this is to say that once they get their shit together they aren't going to have much cash left. Not to mention that Remo's credit cards might get frozen any second, and they might not have a hotel room to come back to either.

So this thing, this Crow party takedown, better fucking work, because there's a good chance they will be penniless and homeless once it's over. Regardless of Cormack's agenda, they know they need to pick up a few dollars with this deal. Appeasing their new master in the CIA is still priority one, but what good is your freedom if you're just going to die the streets with no money? Remo's no animal. He's a man of comfort, and by God he's going to get those comforts back no matter the risks. Crow's party is a big first step. A step toward being free, clear and finding some scratch to build a life off of. Remo keeps thinking of Sean. One step at a time. If he can do this, maybe he can pull together a normal life and be some form of father to his son. It's possible. Maybe.

He has to live through his meeting with Crow first, of course.

That much is understood.

Remo stuffed as many of the to-go containers from room service as he could into his brown leather bag. It's flung over his shoulder and stinks of cheese and pork, but it's full of the stuff that's going to keep them alive. Food and evidence. Well, it *was* evidence. Now it's research. There was more room in Lester's suitcase, but Remo didn't want to put any of the food in that rolling disaster. The food's all closed up in the containers, but the idea of having your food anywhere near a severed head is a little gross. Even for this crew.

Time is short.

Divide and conquer.

Remo and Lester cross the street, heading toward The Plaza for some fine-ass threads. Hollis hangs a right, heading off to find his people and some proper instruments of mayhem.

"Shotguns, motherfuckers," Hollis mutters as he walks away, disappearing as if swallowed whole by the walking masses of New York.

24

The suit fits like a dream.

Remo immediately feels like a new man. Actually, the fine threads make him feel like his old self. It's a warm tingle of a feeling, like he was slipping back into character. The second Mario slid the jacket on it was as if a switch flipped and Remo the Wealthy-as-Hell Defender of Assholes was back online. Back in the game and reporting for duty.

He runs his fingers along the sleeves. Feels good. Nice. Feels right. Gray pinstripes with a purple tie and a classic stark, crisp white shirt. His black shoes shine like fucking mirrors. Remo never knew it, but the clothes actually do make the man.

Lester could give two shits.

He likes his suit. It's fine, or least that's what he told Remo, but his character didn't change. At all. The threads feel nice and all, but his focus is the same as it was a few minutes ago. Killing some folks to help out Remo and maybe himself, if Lester allowed himself to think about himself. The self-love thing is not exactly Christlike as far as Lester sees it, but he acknowledges the limitations God placed on people, so he deals with it best he can. It comes and goes. Selfless to selfish. It's a struggle for every man, he knows, but he tries hard to suppress that shit. In regard to the suit, Lester is more concerned with things like: how easy is it to get his gun out and put a bullet in a motherfucker? What's it going to be like, running in this monkey outfit? There are some other hot-button topics on Lester's mind, like punching, kicking, gouging and stabbing, but gunplay is numero uno.

Remo catches Lester practicing violence in his new suit while looking in the full-length mirror. They got Hollis an off-the-rack job based on the size he gave Remo. Hopefully it fits. Remo guesses it doesn't really matter, but there's this part of him that hopes Hollis likes it. The way you give a buddy a gift and want them to show some appreciation for the thought. Remo has already played the scene out in his head. *Just shine it on and act like you like it, Hollis. For fuck's sake.*

Remo adjusts his tie in the mirror next to Lester, who's practicing strangling an invisible man. He's really getting into it, too. Lester's face is red. Veins in his neck are plumping up. Mario watches while attempting not to show on his face that his brain is screaming out *what the fuck?*

"We'll take 'em, Mario. All three," Remo says.

"Of course. I'll have them cleaned for you," Mario says, rushing to his side.

"No need, Mario." Remo hands him a stack of cash. "We'll be wearing them out."

Mario is confused. *This isn't the fucking Gap, man.*

Lester snatches up a fistful of candy from a crystal dish. "These free?"

Mario nods.

Remo feels an unexpected wave of emotion rush over him as he looks to Mario. "We've known each other a long time."

Mario nods.

It hits Remo.

Just now.

Surprising it wasn't until now that Remo thought of this.

He realizes he hasn't had time to think, but still, he should have had a slightly better handle on this situation. He hasn't been able to let his mind take a beat and think things through. Life has been a little hectic today. There's that, the constant pills and booze, but regardless, Remo should have at least thought about this before now.

Looking at Mario's round face, Remo has realized he may never be here again. He may never go anywhere he used to go only days ago. His old life is quite possibly gone forever. It's not just Mario, although he's very fond of the man. It's all of it. The whole thing. His whole life in New York. Where he lives. The routine of his life and the life he's lived being the biggest, baddest defense attorney in New York is quite possibly over. It was a damn fine routine.

Was being the correct word.

Tears begin to form in the corners of Remo's eyes. He places a hand on Mario's shoulder and squeezes. Perhaps a little too hard.

Mario is even more confused now than ever.

Lester practices stomping the invisible man's head.

Remo's life is in the process of changing forever, and for the first time in a long time he has no clue what's up next for him. No idea what the universe has up its sleeve. His former life was insane, no doubt, but there was a rhythm to it. A steady beat to the crazy. If you took a step back and looked at it in its entirety it all made some form of sense. At least it did to Remo. There was a sequence to life he could count on. Money, booze, pills, sex, self-loathing—these were the things Remo could rely on day in and day out.

Now?

He's got nothing.

Nada. Zip. He has no idea how he's going to earn a living, let alone how he's going to live. Where the next bottle of pills is going to come from. When he is going to get laid next. This new moment of clarity is almost as sharp and penetrating as the one that hit him when he first decided he should double-cross the Mashburns. It was so clear then. Simple. So easy. It was the right thing to do and Remo knew it. He didn't fight it. Little did Remo know when he made that quick, snap decision he was pushing reset on his entire life. The good and the bad.

"I'm sorry," Remo says, moist eyes looking deep into the shit-brown of Mario's. Mario gives a nervous smile, wishing he was anywhere but here.

Lester has the invisible man in a headlock.

Remo puts both hands on Mario's shoulders as the tears stream down his face. "I've got to go now. Thank you for everything."

Mario hands him a receipt.

25

The three men cut through the crowded streets like candidates for masters of the universe.

They are not tough-talking MBA pussies working a Wall Street desk.

Not at all.

These men are pissed and they are here to end someone's time on this planet.

They are here to kill a man named Mr. Crow.

They have no idea what to really expect in there. Remo has never met Crow at his place before. Their meetings have always been in the safety of a conference room at Remo's firm. He's heard the stories from Crow and others about what goes on at these places. He's seen some pictures here and there, but being there in the flesh is a much different type of deal. Reality can be a bit more complex.

From the outside the place looks peaceful enough. It's just a metal door at the bottom of a nondescript building located on the edge of Hell's Kitchen. There's an Asian noodle joint. A hipster coffee place on the corner. The city moves and buzzes around here as it does everywhere else. Busy New Yorkers move past them as if they were three simple little stones in a river. Flowing around them. Most of them annoyed, as if Remo, Lester and Hollis were intentionally keeping them from something important.

Hollis hate-watches a hipster yapping on his phone through some headphones.

Lester hates New York. Makes him itchy.

Remo checks his watch.

It's time.

Remo wants to vomit violently.

"You'd think this kinda shit would get easier," he says.

"It doesn't." Hollis puts a hand on Remo's shoulder. "Don't fuck it up."

Hollis slips off in the other direction, putting some distance between him, Lester and Remo. Lester raises his Bible, placing it next to Remo's head. "This is why I came back. You know that, right?"

Remo shakes his head no.

"You remember when I sat down with you at the Chinese place?"

"Before you got shot to shit?"

"Yes."

"I recall, yes."

"The reason I came then is the same reason I'm back now. I'm here to save you. Physically mainly, because you keep dicking around with dangerous people, but you need spiritual saving as well. You've done the hard part, Remo. You made a decision to undo the evil you helped inject into the world. That's the path you chose. Like it or not."

"You coming, Jesus freak?" Hollis calls out from across the street.

Lester gives him the finger then turns back to Remo. "This is just the beginning."

"Beginning? Thinking it's lookin' more like the end."

Lester gets closer, locking eyes, about a half-inch from Remo's nose. "No, friend. This place you're standing? That door over there? Crow? This is the start of something. A revolutionary war that you started. We can wage it together."

Remo is now even more terrified.

Lester giggles like a child with an ice cream cone as he bounces off, leaving Remo and heading toward Hollis across the street.

Remo watches them walk farther and farther down the street. He knows they are taking their place. This was part of the half-assed plan they had. Them heading to their starting blocks for this little project that's about to go down at Crow's. Never in a million years did Remo think he would see those two people, his clients technically, together in the same place at the same time, let alone walking and talking together, involved in a plan, with Remo, to remove Crow, another client, from the earth at the request of the CIA.

It's a lot to stomach.

Much too much to take in.

Remo pops a pill, chasing it down with his flask of some Johnnie Blue.

He shuts his eyes, squeezing them tight. So tight he sees spots.

His big brain works his new world over. Turning it over and over and over again. Taking in all the angles of the situation and the endless possibilities of what he's about to do. Most of the possible outcomes he comes up with end with him being skinned alive and fed to stray cats. This is the spiral of bad things. If a person of Remo's intelligence is allowed to think for too long, then the darkness is going to eventually creep in. He shakes his head hard in an attempt to reset. Restart his thinking.

He thinks of Sean at the end of his hospital bed.

The smile on that kid's face.

Skinny elbows propping up his glowing face. The sound of his laugh.

Remo's eyes snap open.

He charges toward the door that'll lead him where he wants to go.

Hopefully to Sean and not down the path of getting Remo obliterated.

"Hug a nut, Crow."

26

The room is devoid of natural light.

Almost like a luxury bomb shelter.

The place probably had windows at one time, but they have been bricked over and painted long ago. Smooth jazz tickles the eardrums. There's a surprising hint of freshness to the air as well. The place actually smells like a four-star hotel. Remo is in a smaller room, a security post of sorts, that's off the main room. He can only make out parts of the larger room through a small square window located on a stainless steel door in front of him. Remo gets pushed through the metal detectors and patted down by several pairs of large, thick hands. He's fairly sure what's happening is bordering on sexual assault. A hand cups his nuts. A thumb grazes the cusp of his anus.

"Is this absolutely fucking necessary?" Remo asks Crow as his phone and wallet are removed from his pockets.

"Yup," Crow replies with a smirk. "Everybody goes through it. It's for everybody's safety and enjoyment." He looks Remo up and down. "New suit?"

"Yeah, got it today."

"Mario?"

"There anybody else?"

"No, there is not."

The wall of muscle shoves Remo forward, nodding to Crow that he's clean. Remo turns around and considers calling them cunts, but thinks better of it. This is not the time or the place for that kind of talk. Besides, these men are the size of grizzly bears and, also, if all goes well, Lester and Hollis will execute the lot of them soon enough.

"This way," Crow says, showing him toward the door that leads into the main room.

Remo steps through, holds his breath as he crosses the threshold.

It's a large dark room, lit just enough to see what you need to see. The jazz is only slightly louder as the waves of sound slide over the room, providing a mellow, chilled soundtrack to the place. It's like a high-end bar in a swank part of town. At the far end of the room is a towering monument of a bar made of sheets of glass and bottles of booze. It reaches from floor to ceiling. Has to be at least twenty-plus feet high. There are two bartenders on duty. One flips drinks around like a pro and the other is climbing a ladder to reach the good stuff up top.

Remo, a bit of an expert in gentlemen's clubs, quickly notices this place resembles some of the nicer titty joints he's visited over the years. Subtle differences, but there are some. There's no stage, no hip-hop cranked to brain-thumping levels, but there are young, attractive women slinking about the place dressed to seduce and titillate. One by one Remo watches them parade across the room, then take a seat in the laps of men. The women are all fully clothed, but Remo notices that in the short time he's been here, after some forced laughter and playful flicks of the hair, he's seen at least two women lead men into other rooms. Upon closer inspection, there are rooms located on the sides of this room. A row of what seems like smaller rooms on the right and left of where Remo and Crow are standing. An Asian beauty leads a potbellied fifty-something into one of the rooms a few feet to the right of Remo.

The men are a mix of old and new money. No telling how many are in the smaller rooms, but Remo counts ten sitting at the tables and booths of the main bar. He knew Crow ran some prostitution, but didn't know about this club in particular. Remo thought Crow's main vocational interest was gambling, but there is not a single poker or blackjack table anywhere he can see. There's also no sign of drugs. From afar it simply seems like a high-end whorehouse on the edge of Hell's Kitchen.

Crow kisses the hand of a tall brunette. She smiles.

Remo wants to tell her to run away as fast as she can.

"There somewhere we can talk?" he asks Crow.

Crow smiles to the brunette and waves her off. He shows Remo to a large, circular booth in the back corner. It's the only table where no one else is seated. Remo quickly surmises this must be Crow's understood office space. His floating work area.

"Drink?" Crow offers.

"Johnnie—"

"Blue, neat." A leggy redhead finishes his sentence, handing him a glass with a soul-melting smile. She slinks off before Remo can thank her.

"Nice place," Remo says, looking around, trying to understand where the exits are. It's something he's become accustomed to doing when he walks into a room. He always wants to know how to get out. In his line of work, you never know what will happen in a room. As far as he can tell there's only the one way in and out, the way he came in originally, but he knows there has to be some way to get out in the back.

"This can't be it. More in the back?" Remo says, hoping Crow will help him with the layout.

"There's more," Crow says, sipping a vodka martini. "I'll give you a tour after we talk a bit."

"Sounds wonderful. Now, who did you kill this time?"

"Easy, friend-o. Need a little loving before you shove it in."

"Well, *friend-o*, that's why I'm fucking here, right? Or did you plan on taking me into one of those little side rooms for a tussle?"

Remo notices there's a female client being led by a chiseled, Latin model of a man. He's never seen a woman smile so big as she brings the bottle of Red along with her and slaps his ass with her free hand.

In the short amount of time Remo's sat there with Crow he's noticed the place has cleared out. There's nobody else sitting in the main room except for Crow and Remo. A goon of a man, also about the size of a bear, steps over to the table and whispers into Crow's ear. Crow nods, then waves him off.

"I need to have you clean up something for me," Crow says to Remo.

Remo tries not to be a dick but he can't take it. "What the fuck is wrong with you? I mean seriously."

"What?"

"Every damn time I talk to you you've killed some poor woman who trusted you. Why? Why do you need to do that, you fucked-up piece of shit?"

Remo realizes that might have come across a little strong.

Crow drinks his drink with a puzzled look on his face, looking as if his loyal dog has learned to talk.

"Tell me you've got a condition. Tell me it's something rare. Something way the fuck out there. Something so complicated, such a mental shitshow, that nobody can even vaguely diagnose the sewer you've got flowing between your ears."

Crow blinks, drinks, pulls out a pen and scribbles something on a scrap of paper.

"Is it as simple as you get off to it?" Remo asks. "That it? It's just about feeling sexy, sexy. Being a normal scumbag pimp isn't enough for you to get the juice flowing. You have to kill someone. Tell me that's not it. Tell me you're not a garden-variety TV bad guy. Say it ain't so, because that's just fucking sad, man."

Crow places a gun on the table, sips some more of his martini, and folds the scrap of paper into a neat little note.

"Done?" he asks, slips the folded note to Remo.

As Crow slides the note over to him, Remo wishes Hollis and Lester would hurry the fuck up. He knows the damn plan, knows they aren't coming in for another ten minutes, but he really wants to see Crow's brains blown out.

Soon.

Like now.

Remo has never liked Crow, even from day one he hated the prick, but now, after all he knows about him, he can't even bear being in the same room with the guy. Disgusted to breathe the same air as Crow. Remo can't even find the strength to hide the contempt on his face as he opens Crow's note.

Scribbled across the paper are two simple words.

I KNOW.

27

H ollis and Lester stand in a nasty-ass alley.

Sporadic waves of people move past the two open ends of the alley, with the occasional pedestrian strolling through, looking to cut some time off their journey. At the moment, a homeless man is pushing a baby stroller filled with cans past them while murdering a Lady Gaga song at the top of his lungs.

Hollis checks the two sawed-off shotguns he's got stuffed into a green Nike bag along with some boxes of shells, then checks the Glock tucked inside his shoulder holster. Lester slides his Bible into his roller suitcase, then looks to his cracked Timex that's barely ticking. It's off by twenty-three minutes, but Lester knows this and makes the mental calculation each time he looks at it. Material things don't interest him, and the idea of shopping for a new watch doesn't really appeal to him either. He'd rather just work the math.

They look to one another, then look away.

Nothing to do now but wait and they know it.

The silence is deafening. Uncomfortable.

Damn uncomfortable.

This is a first for these two guys. The first time these two have been alone together and the conversation is not flowing.

Not at all.

Even though they have several things they need to discuss. Like, say, how they plan on doing this gun-blazing thing they are about to run face-first into. They've only thinly talked through the details, which is to say they've decided they are going to kill anyone who causes them a problem. Hollis is usually much more prepared—it's what he does, meticulous with the details of every job—but this time he has more or less resigned himself to a *grip it and rip it* philosophy. Hollis's recent personal and legal issues have caused him to relax his standards to a lower level than usual. Besides, he doesn't have much to go on anyway. Remo didn't know the layout. They assumed Crow's people would take his phone and check him when he went into the place. It was the protocol of all Crow's other establishments, so what the hell are they supposed to do?

Spend hours banging their heads against the wall? Waste a ton of time building a sound strategy?

No point.

Nope.

Tearing in with guns blazing was the best they had to go on. Rather than tell Remo that he had no idea what to do, Hollis made up some bullshit about waiting twenty minutes so Remo can get Crow and his people relaxed. Soften them up, make them comfortable. Hollis figured that line of crap beat the hell out of no plan at all. He also noticed Remo was becoming a bit fragile about this thing, so Hollis decided he really needed Remo to be Remo and not some quivering scoop of jelly. Still, as true as all this is, Hollis is uncomfortable about the wall of silence between him and his new partner, Lester. If you're going into a battle with someone, you'd like to think they care if you live or die. At the minimum.

"You like TV?" Hollis asks Lester.

"I like it, don't watch it."

"Oh, right, the religious thing?"

"No, I can separate entertainment from my faith. It's more that lately I've either been incarcerated or in a hospital or on the run from people trying to put me in the hospital, jail or the grave."

"Got it."

More creeping silence.

They check their watches.

Lester does the time-math and opens his mouth, about to say something, but thinks better of it. He wants to be better acquainted, too. They don't have to be best boys or anything, but he knows the value of working with a tight crew. He's seen a lot of jobs go shithouse when the men involved didn't trust or hated one another. Honor among thieves is rare, which is why he's known a lot of people in the joint who either lack honor themselves or got pig-fucked by some honorless asshole.

Deciding to bail on the *how's the family* small talk, Lester keeps his mouth shut. He remembers hearing Hollis saying something about how Remo has ruined all of that for him. Lester thinks it's probably best not to bring that shit up minutes before they're supposed to go storming in to save him.

"How long have you known Remo?" asks Lester.

"Too fucking—" Hollis pauses mid-sentence.

Something catches his eye.

A blur coming in fast, ripping down the alley hard as hell.

He pushes Lester clear at the last second. A 2x4 cracks Hollis in the face. The thick whack knocks him back, stumbling into a brick wall. Lester looks up in time to get the same weapon of wood slapped to his forehead followed by a hurricane-spin whack to the side of his head. The moves of this wood-wielding villain are like mini lightning strikes. Fast. Powerful. Relentless. Lester spins around helpless, tripping over his own feet, dumping himself into a swamp-like puddle in the middle of the nasty-ass alley.

Hollis pulls his shoulder Glock.

The end of the 2x4 jams hard into his ribs. Again and again, cracking his bones with rapid-fire speed. Air escapes his body in a flash. His teeth chomp down on his tongue as the 2x4 whips under his chin with mind-numbing force. Hollis falls back, bouncing off the bricks.

His sight blurs.

Head buzzes.

Through all of it, Hollis thinks that he might recognize their attacker.

He watches the alley warrior drop a wad of paper on Lester's busted-up face. Looks like a wadded up napkin. A fast-food napkin. Hollis realizes he's seen this person before. Recently as a matter of fact. He can't get his mouth to move or his body to react fast enough, but he's damn certain he knows this person. All he can do is watch the woman sprint away out the alley like a nimble, lost deer disappearing into the city. He staggers over to Lester. His eyes are shut, he's breathing, but not moving or responding to anything. Hollis shakes him hard, trying to get him to come around.

Hollis slaps him.

"Lester," he yells in his face.

Nothing. Lester is out like a light.

"Fuck," Hollis says, leaning back in the alley.

His mind floats back to the woman who beat their asses moments ago.

It's her.

It's the same woman from hotel room service.

The one who returned Dutch's head to them on a platter.

"What the fuck is her problem?"

28

I know.

I know is what Crow's little note said.

Troubling.

This could mean all kinds of shit.

Big question is: what exactly does Crow know?

Remo runs through the possibilities. Does Crow know about Hollis and Lester about to storm in blasting like the Wild Bunch? About Cormack? What exactly does this asshole know? There's only one way to find out, thinks Remo. Of course, he only has a split-second to form a question that'll keep him alive, but at the same time make everything seem like no matter what Crow knows, *that* knowledge is all bullshit and Remo is Crow's boy. Like he always was and always will be.

Remo decides to go with...

"Wow. I am over-fucking-whelmed. What in the fuck do you think you fucking know?"

Remo lets that float over the conversation.

Crow leans back, studying Remo. Eyes scanning him up and down. Remo can see his mind crank. There's some serious calculations going on in there. Crow licks his lips, then snaps his fingers.

Two of his bear-sized goons step up, moving closer to the booth as casually as a lazy waiter. The smooth jazz still plays, but the place feels like it's suddenly gone deadly silent. Air in the room is now incredibly tight. Crow leans in close, allowing his stare to bore through Remo. He gently raps his fingers on the grip of his gun that waits patiently on the table. Remo feels his heart bounce up into his sinuses. Not knowing what's about to happen with a guy like Crow is not comforting.

"What went down in the Hamptons, Remo?" Crow finally asks.

"Why? What did you hear?"

"Things."

"Things like what? You heard I got into a shootout with some dissatisfied clients. Is that what you know so much about?"

"That, plus a little more."

Remo feels some relief. If all Crow knows about is the Mashburn showdown, he can wiggle out of that. Explain it away as a misunderstanding among irrational people. That'll work. Yeah. Maybe. The problem now is that *a little more* line of bullshit Crow added on the end there. Remo needs to know what else Crow is hanging on to. What else is drifting around in this psycho's skull.

"Well, don't play hard to get. Stick it in. What else ya got?" Remo asks.

Crow sips his drink. Raps his fingers on his gun.

Remo fights to keep his eyes from bugging out. *Where. The. Fuck. Are Lester and Hollis?* Remo wants to check his watch so bad he can taste it.

"You don't think that's enough?" Crow asks.

"It's a lot, to be sure, but I thought you found out I fucked your sister."

Crow cocks his head. Remo has decided to play this angle, regretting it a bit at the moment, but deciding it was all he really had. Jokes work most times.

This isn't one of them.

Crow looks like he swallowed a bug.

"I didn't fuck her," Remo says. "She's a lady. Only heavy petting, and by heavy petting I mean oral, and by oral I mean blowjobs, and by blowjobs I mean a lot of—"

Crow slams his palm down on the table. His gun and drink jump up off the wood. Remo saves his Johnnie before it dumps over. He chugs it down as if it was his last. Just might be.

"You know what else I know, Remo? I know you don't have a law firm anymore. I know you're not lawyer. Not anymore."

"Well shit."

"So if you're not a lawyer, and that seems to be the case, then the big question is what in the name of sweet fuck are you doing here?"

"Missed you?"

Crow looks to his bear-goons. They move toward Remo like he's a sugar-coated slab of meat as they put their paws on him.

"Oh come the fuck on, man. This isn't right. You and me got history. I came here for a business opportunity."

"Bullshit," says Crow.

"Okay fine. I've got nothing. I was going to tell you about all that unpleasant shit. I was. I need your help, man. I need help to get back on my feet."

Crow snaps his fingers.

The bear-goons pull Remo by the arms, dragging him out from the booth kicking and screaming. They yank him up upright and drop him on his feet facing Crow. Crow slides out from the booth, adjusts his suit, finishes the last drop of his martini. "I do have an opening. A business opportunity."

Remo does not like the look on his face, or his tone for that matter.

Not one bit.

"You a gambling man, Remo Cobb?"

29

Remo is dragged past the towering bar into the darkness. Legs and arms flailing like a pissed off two-year-old. The bear-goons manhandle Remo into the back of the place through a set of dark curtains. A light flicks on.

Remo gets shoved through the entrance of a six-inch thick metal door that resembles the entrance to a bank vault. The inside of this new room looks and feels a lot like a high-end poker room. All dark save for a few well-placed single bulbs that hang from the ceiling by black cords. There's another well-stocked bar along the far wall with some long, plush purple couches positioned around a stainless steel table that seats four. The couches and table are empty at the moment. The chairs at the table are pushed out, as if awaiting guests.

The smooth jazz that filled the other room is gone.

This room is quiet. A vacuum. As if shut off from the world.

Remo makes a note that two more bear-goons man both sides of the entrance. Their suit jackets bulge from their shoulder holsters. Once Crow enters the room the vault-like door is closed and locked by another bear-goon cranking a wheel.

Remo can feel his luck drain out from his ass as he watches the wheel turn. With each crank his hope gets smaller and smaller. The muscles in his face sag. He chews the inside of his cheek. Stomach twists in knots knowing there's no way in hell Lester and Hollis are busting through that thing. Hollis and Lester are good, but cracking a door like that and taking down Crow and his team of bear-goons is not damn likely.

"Any chance I can go to the bathroom?" Remo asks.

"None," Crow replies.

"Need to drop a deuce."

"Might not be a problem for long."

Remo doesn't have time to process Crow's statement. Out from the darkness step the men and women Remo saw earlier in the other room. The ones who went into the smaller rooms and the ones who showed them the way. Remo notices that all of them have a bit of a post-coitus glow about them as they pass under the lights. Some more than others. The pros seem to be shining it on with fake signs of how amazing it was.

Remo knows the look.

The men and women take their places on the purple couches that circle the lone table, creating an audience of sorts. They sit and wait. Their faces seem solemn in nature. Almost respectful, as if they were attending an event that required much respect. No one says a word. Eyes forward. Mouths shut. It's as if everyone knows what's up except for Remo.

Remo's heart pounds.

His breathing becomes minimal. Short, quick. In and out and only as needed. Teeth grinding while trying to control the fear spiking higher and higher with each passing second.

Crow watches Remo squirm. He loves it. He smiles, then nods to someone out of view. From the darkness steps a dapper man dressed in a classic tux with a red rose pinned in his lapel. His jet-black hair is slicked back and he looks like he lives at a gym and has an everlasting tan. Holding an envelope in one hand, he holds a leather box balanced on his fingertips with the other. Treating the box as a special thing. He presents the box to the crowd for a viewing.

Remo looks over the faces of the crowd seated on the couches.

There's a mix of wide eyes, nods and an *ooooh* or two. A few members of the crowd clap. A couple of others whoop and laugh. This is what they've been waiting for. Whatever the hell this guy and his damn box are up to is what they came here to see. The side room sex was an extra. A bonus. Make no mistake that this, this thing here in this room with all the theatrics, is the main event these people came for. The Dapper Man sets the leather box down in the center of the table, directly under the light. Stepping back, he addresses the room like the master of ceremonies that he is.

"Welcome. We have a great evening planned for you. Have you enjoyed yourselves so far?"

The room breaks into applause. A few of the ladies in the room lay big kisses on their *dates*. They mess with their hair and give them loving, false as hell, but nonetheless warm looks. The woman client slaps her Latin boy toy and spits in his face.

"Well, I hope you have. That's what we do here. A full experience taking you from one end of the spectrum to the other. An experience of extremes in a short amount of time." He pauses. "You've enjoyed the rush of pleasure. Have you not?"

More from the crowd.

"Now comes the rush of risk." He pauses for dramatic effect. "A rush that can only come from taking a true risk. You all have money. Great success. Merely gambling money provides a bit of an uptick in heartbeats, right? But not like this." He points to a few in the group. "Some of you have been fortunate enough to be repeat guests. Congratulations, truly. That's impressive. Impressive that you're back, but more impressive that you wanted to do it again." He raises a drink. "Salute."

Remo watches the room in disbelief. *What the hell is happening here?*

The Dapper Man downs his drink and hands the empty glass to a bear-goon. He looks out over the group. Waits, then steps to the table. Remo finds it hard to find air, as if it's been sucked out of the room. There's an intensity that fills the area. It can be felt. In your stomach. On your skin. It's as if the scientific makeup of the room has actually changed. There's a clear moment where time has hit pause. Time has simply stopped as the room waits for the Dapper Man to reach the table. He places his hand on the box, then looks over the group.

"He's good. He's milking the moment," Crow whispers to Remo. "Watch."

The Dapper Man opens the box.

Remo wilts.

Crow laughs.

The group erupts with excitement.

The box holds a gun.

30

The chrome revolver shines under the light like a diamond in a goat's ass.

Sitting, resting in its velvet bed inside the box, the gun lies waiting for an outcome.

Remo can guess what that might be.

What outcome Crow has in mind.

The Dapper Man turns to Remo and offers him a chair. "We have a special guest. A first-timer who is eager to compete this evening."

"You could've let me get laid first," Remo says.

Crow shrugs. *Sorry.*

Remo looks to the bear-goons, who are seconds away from *placing* Remo in that chair. Accepting his limited options, Remo takes a seat at the table. The group cheers him on. A bartender sets another Johnnie Blue in front of him. At least Crow was good enough to give him that, thinks Remo. The Dapper Man calls up another two from the crowd. Two men. One in his sixties, a man made of old Manhattan wealth that seems to ooze from his pores. His suit is crafted in the finest of quality, but dated in style. He removes a cigar from inside his jacket and lays it on the table in front of him. The second man represents new money. Thirties, yoga-fit, with jeans that equal a Lexus payment.

Remo's eyes scan over the two of them. They carry very different exteriors, but both seem to have the same tangled ball of emotions underneath. There's a mix of fear, regret and a sense of *how the hell do I get out of this* trapped bouncing behind their eyes.

The Dapper Man removes the gun from the box and holds it above his head, presenting it to the room in a samurai-like fashion. The box is quickly removed from the table by the bartender. Everything is orchestrated. Every single one of Crow's staff seems to have a purpose, and they all have their timing down. Even the Dapper Man seems to be operating off a script. Remo's fairly sure he saw Crow's lips move while the Dapper Man delivered his "pleasure and extremes" speech. Remo can't help but wonder when they practiced all this. Is there a team meeting before they open? Are there training classes for new hires?

"You know the name of this game," the Dapper Man says.

The room explodes into roaring applause.

He removes a single golden bullet from his jacket. Again holding it up for the room to see. The light bounces off the shine of the polished tip. The crowd's applause grows even louder. The Dapper Man makes sure Remo sees it before he opens the cylinder. As he slips the bullet into the gun he says, "A lethal game of chance."

Two of the bear-goons walk through the room, making sure to stop at the guests seated on the couches, accepting their cash as if working the offering plates at a church. Another set of bear-goons make quick taps on iPads, taking notes as they accept the money. Remo can't believe it. They're taking bets. This shouldn't be a surprise to Remo, but it is. He truly can't believe this happening. That human beings are gambling on Russian roulette and, more to the point, that he's in the middle of it.

An aging millionaire seated on a couch across the table from Remo whispers into a young girl's ear. She nuzzles close to his cheek, whispers and points at Remo. He nods, then hands over a stack of cash, pointing his boney finger at Remo as well. He's putting his money on Remo per the young lady on his lap. Remo can't help but feel appreciative. Ya know, because they believe in him?

The young girl blows Remo a kiss.

Remo stares at her blankly. For a second he thinks about using his hand and tongue to act out a blowjob in response to her, but he lacks the conviction at the moment.

"All bets are in," says the Dapper Man. "No more bets." He waves his arm about the room and looks over the people seated at the table. The contestants of the game. Never allowing his world-class showmanship slip, not for a second, he raises the gun up over his head again.

He spins the chamber.

A hush falls over the room.

The group watches, on the edges of their seats.

Remo glances to his watch. It's past the time. Hollis and Lester should fucking be here by now.

Where the hell are they?

What the fuck, man?

They're not coming.

The Dapper Man slaps the cylinder in place. "Six chambers. One bullet. This gun is maintained and weighted perfectly, so there is precisely a one in six chance of a player drawing a loaded chamber."

He lays the gun down in the center of the table and stands to the side, looking to Crow. Waiting for the signal to start the game.

Remo turns to Crow, who still stands near the vault-like door, surrounded by bear-goons. Remo's thoughts slide, surprisingly, to his father. To how his old man died. Not exactly like this, but it was similar. The old man died in a shootout during a card game in Texas. He caught a hanger off his deal, revealing he was cheating like a bastard. The old man died facedown on the table after a couple of bullet blasts blew a hole in his chest the size of a pizza. It occurs to Remo he might very well bite it in a similar way. Different game. Poker versus Russian roulette. Bullet to the head versus the chest, but the result will be the same. Dead via gun. Facedown on a table. Remo thinks of his son and wonders if he'll have the same memory of his father. Will

Sean ever know Remo died this way? Will Sean even know Remo is dead at all?

The Dapper Man waits for Crow.

Crow smiles big and nods at Remo, his new favorite player.

"Whichever player the barrel stops on starts us off tonight," the Dapper Man says, flipping the gun around with his finger.

The gun spins.

Round.

Round.

Round and...

31

R emo places the gun to his head.

His heart beats faster than a vibrator stuck on eleven. His fear is ratcheted up so high he doesn't even feel it, so damn intense it seems like it's not even present. There's a buzz that started in his stomach and has now taken over his entire body, a feeling Remo has never known before. He's been afraid before, sure, but this is a different brand of fucked up. Different from anything he's dealt with up until today. Different from any courtroom. Different from anything with the Mashburns. Way different. The thought of knowing you might kill yourself without wanting to kill yourself is a damn odd thing to get your mind around. However, Remo knows damn well that if he doesn't pull this trigger he's a dead man anyway. Crow will see to that for sure.

Remo turns toward Crow.

That smug fuck.

Standing there in his suit in complete control of this whole thing. The murderer who will continue to get away with it. At least he won't have Remo around to help him anymore. That is what passes for comfort at a moment like this. Remo's trembling hand holds the barrel of the gun to his temple.

Crow raises his drink, saluting Remo with a wink.

Remo makes a decision in that moment. In that moment he decides he's not going to give this dickhead the satisfaction of knowing his fear. Remo will not show him how damn terrified he truly is. No way he'll let Crow think he's won. Nope. If Remo is to die right here, tonight, then he will go out on his own terms and in his own way.

He will die as he's lived.

Like a complete asshole.

Remo downs his Blue then throws the glass directly at Crow's head.

Crow drops down as the glass barely sails over his skull, shattering on impact with the vault door. Shards of glass fall, bouncing off the floor. There are a few gasps, along with open mouths, across the room. Crow whips his head back around to Remo, who's shooting him the finger with his free hand, gun still held to his head with the other.

Remo looks Crow dead in the eye and pulls the trigger.

Click.

Half the crowd goes wild. The other half is pissed.

Count Crow as one of the pissed.

"Somebody bring me a bottle." Remo slams down the gun. "I can do this all night, motherfuckers."

32

A nother dead millionaire gets dragged away with half a head missing.

That makes six now.

The bear-goons move quickly to clear the remains as fast as they can. Remo drinks directly from the bottle now. He's been at this awhile, and is getting pretty lit at this point. The last time around he stuck the barrel up his nose and pulled the trigger.

Remo thinks this must be what it's like when Jordan or LeBron slip into a zone. When no matter what kind of shot they throw up it goes in, hitting nothing but net. The hoop becomes the size of a swimming pool. They simply cannot miss. Only difference here is Remo doesn't want to shoot and certainly doesn't want to hit anything. He gets that, but the principle is the same.

Crow burns by the door.

Face red.

Fists and teeth clinched tight.

With every click Remo draws from the gun Crow can feel himself dying inside. That, along with the fact Remo is now singing Toto's "Africa" at the top of his lungs. Despite all of Crow's anger, the group is enjoying themselves. Money is changing hands and more and more people are putting their money on Remo. He's the people's champion, until he gets a loaded chamber at least.

Remo, now completely hammered, pauses his signing only long enough to do the fake blowjob thing toward the girl who originally whispered about betting on (or against) him. It's tasteless, to be sure, but even more so now, since the same guy she was sitting on a while ago is now being dragged off with half his head gone. Hers is not a sentimental business, but still, she'd rather not see the old guy killed in front of her.

The Dapper Man calls over two more players, who cautiously take their seats at the table next to Remo. They are much more nervous than the previous contestants. Egos gone. Bravado is a memory. Remo is on a heater of a streak and nobody in that room wants to go head to head with this guy.

One of them is the lone female player. Mid-forties and the owner of a successful clothing line. She started with nothing and clawed her way to the top, but the top can be boring once you get there. She gave up the drugs years ago and has nothing left to prove in business. She also got rid of her husband around the same time she gave up drugs and now focuses on herself, and brother, she gets bored easily. At the moment, however, she really wishes she'd picked another way to scratch that itch. Should have just paid to fuck the Latin kid rather than fuck with all this gun shit.

Remo senses her terror. She's not up for this. He knows they're all grownups here, but still, he feels a little sorry for her. He's not sure if that's sexist or not. He didn't give two shits about the men who stepped up to the table, blew their heads off and got dragged away. Should he feel empathy for her and not for them? It's a troubling question for the drunk-as-fuck Remo Cobb. Whatever the social or political right and wrong of the thing is, Remo decides communication is the key.

"This looked more fun from the cheap seats, didn't it?" Remo asks her.

She nods.

"Want a drink?" He tries to hand her the bottle. "It helps a lot."

She waves it off.

The Dapper Man spins the gun. Her eyes bulge.

"You sure?" Remo asks, offering her the bottle again.

She takes it this time. The barrel points her way. She chugs. Remo watches her hands shake. A tear falls.

"Let her out," Remo says to Crow.

"What did you say?" Crow asks.

"Fine, fuck it, I'm a sexist dickhead, but she's not into this game. Not her thing. You've got her money. She's not going to talk, she can't; she's a witness to all of this and will go to jail. Let her out of her turn."

Under normal circumstances she'd be hostile as hell about Remo's obvious *big man* bullshit taking place here. All that *oh the little lady can't handle it* shit she's had climb her way over the years. But at this particular moment she's more than happy to let Remo be an asshole. She'll happily tap out of this game and play the poor, terrified vagina card.

About time it paid off.

"I'm not into this shit either," the other man at the table says, thumbing toward Remo. "Not against that one."

Crow watches the room. The rest of the people seem to agree. He sees the nods. The blank stares. The mood has shifted dramatically. The rest of them have finally put themselves in that seat and they want nothing to do with it. Nobody here wants to go up against Remo. Understandable. They've sat there and watched six people's heads explode while playing against him. They may not be a superstitious crowd, but after a while you start to believe it's just Remo's night.

Remo smiles big as shit at Crow.

A self-satisfied grin that comes from pissing all over someone's big plan.

Crow comes close to letting his rage get the best of him. He lets the hostility rise up, lets it cloud his thoughts, lets it muddy the waters. He thinks of grabbing a gun and blowing Remo's brains out himself, but doesn't. He thinks of instructing one of his bear-goons to drag Remo outside and beat him to death, but he doesn't. No, Crow is a pro. He decides to take lemons and make himself a big-ass pitcher of lemonade.

"New game," Crow announces as he walks over to the table, picking up the gun. He opens the cylinder and slides in two more bullets. "Three bullets total. One player. New odds."

The crowd perks up.

"Fuck," Remo says.

Crow motions to the woman and man seated at the table to take a seat on the couch. The woman tips the bottle at Remo as she slinks off, chugging some more. She could have at least left the bottle, Remo thinks. He did kinda save her life. Where's the fucking gratitude in the world?

Now it's Remo against three bullets.

"Clear the books, taking new bets," Crow calls out.

There's a new shot of energy to the room. A new buzz of excitement as money changes hands. Remo watches it all. Watching this new level of inhumanity in these people is leaving him numb. It was there before, sure, but at least then they had a share in the risk. They could catch a bullet in the skull just as easily as Remo. Now they are basically looking to profit off a forced suicide.

Are you entertained?

Crow shoves the revolver into Remo's hand. "If you're thinking about taking that piece, pointing it at me and squeezing the trigger until you put a bullet in the chamber, don't. My boys will cut you down before you get a single shot off."

He pats Remo on the shoulder as he turns and walks back over to his spot by the vault door. Nestled between his trusty bear-goons.

The sudden change in the house rules of the game has removed some of his scotch high, but make no mistake, Remo is still drunk. He starts to laugh uncontrollably. Shaking. A hard laugh that starts with a chuckle and snort but grows into an intense silence. His mouth and eyes wide open. The gun quivers back and forth in his hand. Tears roll down his face. Remo can't decide if this is truly funny or a full-blown mental meltdown. Crow and the crowd watch, not sure what to do with this. They look to one another. Remo pulls himself together, waves the gun around. Everyone ducks.

"Let's get this over with, okay people?" he says, standing up.

Remo puts the gun to his head.

In his mind he can see the bullet leave the chamber.

"This what we all want here tonight?"

He hopes Sean will understand his father someday.

Remo pulls the trigger.

Click.

He snorts a laugh, dropping the gun to his side, then quickly raises the gun back up stabbing himself in the temple with the barrel.

"Wait," yells Crow. "They have to place their bets." He motions for the Dapper Man to stop him.

The Dapper Man grabs Remo's hand, trying to pull the gun away. Remo fights him by yanking the gun back. They both have their hands locked around the gun as they sway side to side, moving in a circle.

Spit flies from the Dapper Man's mouth as he pulls at the gun with all he has. "Give me the damn gun."

"Go fuck yourself, slick."

"Slick?"

Blam.

The back of the Dapper Man's head explodes.

A collective gasp from the room. Wide-eyed stares all around.

Pin-drop silence.

Dapper Man's body slumps to the floor.

Remo shrugs.

The ceiling above the table cracks then crumbles down. Chunks of plaster drop at first. A muted pop sound echoes, then another. A large section of the ceiling the size of a piano comes crashing down, showering the floor with debris.

Remo wastes no time analyzing the situation. He rips the six-shooter from the Dapper Man's dead hand. Spinning around he turns the gun on Crow, squeezing the trigger.

He feels an unsatisfying *click*.

"Fuck me," Remo barks.

People scatter away from the couches like roaches when the lights come on. Hollis drops down onto the table, blasting his sawed-off as he lands. The rhythmic pumps burst, cutting up bear-goons left and right. Blood and meat pop and spread across the vault-like door as the bodies drop like oversized sacks of dirt. Crow dives clear, lead peppering the air his face occupied a split-second ago.

Remo runs at Crow with all he has. Releases a primal scream, putting his shoulder down. Crow pivots like a matador. Remo misses his mark, slamming face-first into the vault door, his cheek slip-sliding across the slick, fresh bear-goon blood.

Crow hauls ass toward the back.

Hollis blasts away at Crow as he races by, exploding couch cushions, tables and walls along the way. Crow grabs a guest by the suit jacket, pulling him along, using him as a human shield. The guest takes a shot in the chest. A red burst sprays the air as Crow releases his jacket, dumping the deadweight to the floor. Hollis pumps, blasts again. A bear-goon is blown back over the bar. Crow bolts out a door that was previously hidden by the darkness. A door-sized shaft of light cuts through the room, revealing gun smoke spiraling upward, along with the aftermath of sudden mayhem. Screams roar. Guests trample over other guests. Blood pools on the floor.

Remo gets to his feet, charging hard at the door after Crow. He pushes a guest to the floor on his way out, manages to put an elbow into the woman who stole his bottle, putting a little extra humph on it.

Hollis jumps down from the table. He has his Nike bag over his shoulder. Digging into the bag he pulls out his second sawed-off. "Remo."

As Remo turns Hollis tosses him the shotgun. Remo wants to lay into Hollis's ass about being late more than anything, but even Remo knows now is not the time. Hollis showed up. Remo is alive and that's what matters. Later, at a time of his choosing, Remo will tear him a fresh one.

Remo and Hollis burst out of Crow's place, spilling into the streets of New York. Remo fights to get his vision right after coming out of the dark room and stumbling into the blinding light of day. He bounces off a light post and a few not-so-understanding New Yorkers. His face is smeared with bear-goon blood, he's drunk as a motherfucker, carrying a sawed-off shotgun, but that doesn't mean a damn thing to Remo. He has one thing on his hammered mind, and that thing is killing Crow.

Hollis is running beside Remo, with Crow up ahead by a few car lengths. Remo raises his sawed-off one-handed while running at top speed down the busy street. There's a scream behind him. Hollis quickly reaches over, shoving the gun down. Not a great idea to fire a shotgun while burning ass down a busy city street. Many reasons. Too many to cover now.

Hollis and Remo push harder. Legs churn. Thighs burn. Lungs pumping acid. They're gaining on him.

There's a busy intersection up ahead.

They know they need to get him before he crosses. High odds of losing him in that mess.

Crow cuts and weaves between the throngs of people packed along the street. Remo and Hollis follow with relentless determination. Crow flies across the street. Remo hits the curb, about to jump across as Hollis grabs him by the collar, pulling him back. A massive city bus rips down the street, almost taking Remo's nose with it.

A split-second after the bus blazes past, Hollis and Remo take off as if a starter's pistol fired. Their heads whip around, looking for Crow. He could have gone in any direction. Panic starts to set in.

"Over there," Hollis says.

Crow has put some distance between them, but they can still see him cutting through the crowded streets up ahead.

They push harder.

Sirens wail behind them.

Hollis looks back. Cops are back there, coming fast.

"Running out of time," Hollis yells at Remo.

Remo doesn't care. He pumps his legs harder and harder. Crow is putting some distance between them. He can taste killing him.

Remo's not a murderer, but he could really get into killing a piece of shit like Crow. Many people could.

Sirens get louder. Closer.

Crow races across another clogged street.

Remo and Hollis are on him, in pursuit like focused blood-hounds, but Crow is getting farther and farther away.

"Shit," Hollis spits.

Sirens wail a few blocks back.

Remo feels hope slip. They're going to lose him. After all this, he's going to get away with it.

Again.

Lester slams Crow hard to street.

Hollis and Remo can't believe what they're seeing. From out of nowhere, Lester wraps his tatted-up arms around Crow's ribs planting him to the concrete. A full-on, brutal NFL sack. Crow's head bounces off the sidewalk, leaving a blood spot. Lester pins Crow's arms down with his knees and begins beating him mercilessly with his prison-tested fists. Thick thumps of skin beating skin. Cracks. Crunches of skull. Blood spurts. A crowd builds up, surrounding them.

Hollis and Remo reach the crowd. Hollis pulls Lester off of what's left of Crow. Lester screams and spits like a wild dog having his bone taken away. This is the dark side of Lester. The side that deserved to go to prison. The side you don't want to be on the wrong end of. The side that cut off Dutch's head.

Lester catches his breath and notices the blood on Remo's face. Touching him, he says, "You okay?"

Sirens are even closer now.

"Fantastic," says Remo. "We gotta get gone."

The three partners-in-mayhem burn ass away from the scene. Lester leads them right, then left then down an alley. Lester's suitcase sits near the back of a restaurant. Lester grabs the handle as they race by, pulling it along behind him. The wheels skip, barely touching the ground.

Up ahead a white van screeches to a stop, closing off the exit to the alley.

They spin around. Another van cuts off the other end of the alley.

They're completely boxed in.

Hollis jams more shells into his shotgun.

Remo readies his with a pump.

Lester pulls a butcher knife from the suitcase with one hand and rips his Glock loose from his shoulder holster with the other.

They stand ready to face whatever special brand of asshole is about to come at them. United. Strong. A force that will not go quietly into that good or any other fucking night.

Fssst. A whisper-zip cuts through the air.

A tiny red dart lands in Hollis's neck with a thunk. His legs fold out from under him immediately, as if his legs gave up upon impact. Another dart sticks into Lester's neck. He pulls it out, tosses it aside, makes it two steps with his weapons raised. He screams, almost barks at them.

Fsst. Fsst. Double darts. Red blurs. One to the neck, one to the forehead.

Lester folds.

"Fuck this shit," Remo says, running full-throttle with his shotgun raised, screaming at the top of his lungs like an insane warrior from days past.

Fsst.

Remo's world goes black.

Insane warrior down.

33

Remo sits at the end of a long table made of polished stone. He holds the guest of honor position in the middle of an exclusive private dining room. A little-known room located at the back of his favorite steak house. This room is reserved at a steep price, and is only for the special, elite folks of the city. You don't hear people talk about it and it is not offered to many.

Seated along both sides of the table are people Remo knows well.

To his right sits Hollis, Lester and the Mashburn brothers, whose names, in order of age and importance, are Dutch, Ferris and Chicken Wing. Dutch is the only one at the table without a head. It is, however, placed with care in front of Dutch, next to the butter plate but far enough away from the food that nobody gets too uncomfortable.

Nobody seems to care, not that kind of crowd, but you never know.

On the left side sit Detective Harris, what's left of Crow, the Dapper Man with a massive hole in his head, and big, bad CIA man Cormack.

At the far end of the table, directly across from Remo, is his son Sean, who is sitting in Remo's ex-wife Anna's lap.

All of the dinner guests look on, staring at Remo with glazed, emotionless eyes, but with smiles plastered wide as sunrises. It's as if they have all been heavily sedated, or possibly lobotomized, recently. They are all silently watching Remo eat. Not a word spoken or blink made as they watch on, soaking in the vision of Remo taking down the feast laid out in front of him. A feast fit for a king. A thick, perfect medium-rare filet is placed in front of him, along with the following: a loaded baked potato, a big-ass Caesar salad, thinly cut french fries, a plate of chicken fried rice the size of his face, a gorgeous apple pie, and a bottle of mother's milk—Johnnie Blue.

Remo swallows the last chunk of steak, wipes the red juice from his lips and washes it all away with a sip of Blue.

He looks to his guests. They still sit silently smiling his way. Remo sighs a massive sigh, shrugs his shoulders, then pushes away from the table.

As if on cue, Sean slips off his mother's lap and opens the door that provides an exit out the private room. Remo steps away from the table and pats his son's head as he passes through the door. The rest of the table stands and follows him out single file. Dutch brings his head.

Outside, the sun shines bright with clouds rolling across the bluest of skies. Remo takes his place in front of a red brick wall. He holds a glass of Johnnie Blue in his hand, taking a gulp as he turns around.

He's now facing a firing squad made up solely of his dinner guests.

They're all there, most with weapons pointed directly at him, but their smiles are long gone. They hold a variety of weapons. Mostly handguns, a shotgun or two, with the notable exceptions being Dutch, who has a WWII flamethrower, and Crow, who holds some Chinese throwing stars.

Anna and Sean are unarmed, but watch on.

Remo looks to Sean.

The little boy raises his thumb.

Remo exhales and smiles.

Sean turns his thumb down.

Remo nods and closes his eyes tight.

34

Remo's head feels like the inside of a used diaper.

Forcing his lids open, he only finds more darkness before him. Hints and rumors of light peak out via slits and slants but only at the margins of his vision. More like the light is along the bottom and sides of something. Actually, it's exactly like light is working its way through the cracks of something that's over Remo's head.

"Hello?" he says.

"Hello," says Hollis.

"Hello," says Lester.

"Hello, gentlemen," Cormack says.

Remo trembles like a bomb went off inside his chest. An anger-shake shudders from the tips of his toes to the top of his cloaked head. He tries to get whatever's covering his head off but realizes his arms are bound behind him. His feet are strapped to the chair he's sitting in. He's guessing zip ties. It's embarrassing to admit he knows what they feel like, but he can't help but admire the quality of the material. Nothing but the best for the CIA.

"Can you take this fucking thing off my head?" Remo asks.

There's a long pause.

"Are you shitting me? You need me to say please?"

Another long, drawn out pause.

Without warning, the bag is ripped away, blasting blinding light into his face. With one eye open and one closed tight, Remo looks around, seeing that Lester and Hollis are also both zip-tied to chairs next to him. As he adjusts to the light, he can see they are in a small room in what looks like a modest home. Walls painted in accessible beige. Shit pictures on the walls and blackout curtains pulled closed on the windows. No telling if it's night or day, let alone what day it is. There's a high-intensity light shining on each of them like they were being interviewed on a TV show. Remo, Lester and Hollis can safely assume they are no longer in NYC based on the fact there is no street noise. There's no noise at all. There is a dead silence all around. No cars. No talking. Not even a damn cricket.

Cormack leans in the doorway dressed in his standard navy blue CIA garb. The expression on his face can be described as expressionless. He's neither happy, sad, nor angry. He is simply there. Shifting slightly to the left, Cormack now leans on the other side of the door. He clucks his tongue, raises his eyebrows, then holds his hands out as if looking for questions from his captive audience.

"Where would you like to start?" Cormack asks.

Remo, Hollis and Lester look to one another. *This guy, this fucking guy.*

"How about kick it off with *what the fuck, man*?" Remo says. "Or, *where the fuck are we?* Perhaps, *what was the fucking deal with those fucking darts* and, last but not least, *what in the fuck are you doing with us tied up like a trio of fucking fuckheads*?"

"Your buddy bashed Crow's skull in on the streets of New York."

"So?" Lester asks.

"Yeah, so what? It's done," Hollis says.

"We did the thing, we took out Crow," Remo says.

Cormack clucks his tongue again. He looks to the ceiling for some form of divine strength. "How are we supposed to question Crow now? Huh? He's barely alive in a hospital room and if he does pull through he'll more than likely only be able to urinate blood and meow answers."

"Sounds like a *you* problem," Hollis says.

Lester nods.

"Look. If you wanted this handled a certain way, Cormack, perhaps you should have been a little more specific with your instructions," Remo says.

"Now I know," Cormack replies. "I'll make sure this next one is explained in much, much more detail."

Silent pause in the room. Looks between Remo and his partners in crime fire off. Confusion circling the three of them.

"Next one?" Remo asks.

"Yes," Cormack says. "Meaning the one after the one you just did. Specific enough?"

"Wasn't the deal, man," Remo says, gritting his teeth.

"Did you think there was a deal? That's adorable. There is not. The only deal is you do what I want until I say we are done or you're dead. Does that provide the clarity you boys seek?" Cormack turns, leaving the room.

Remo feels himself deflating.

As if his bones and muscles have been nullified by Cormack, and he could simply spill out onto the floor into a puddle of goo. Any hope Remo had of being a normal person or a somewhat normal father to Sean is slipping through his fingers.

Perhaps gone.

Forever.

Cormack stops after a few steps then turns back to the room. "Okay. That wasn't completely fair, what I just did there a second ago. Sorry. Let me reset, okay? This next one, the one you boys are going to do, it's a big one. To be honest it's the one I really brought you in to accomplish, Remo. Oh, big thanks by the way for bringing in Lester. I hoped you would, but it really brings this thing together."

Lester stares.

The old Lester would gut Cormack right here and now without a hint of hesitation. Actually, the new Lester is considering it.

"You clowns left a hell of a mess to clean up in New York, but don't worry, I'll take care of it. It'll give Detective Harris something to do," Cormack says, then snaps his fingers as if he remembered something. "I've got some cash and prepaid credit cards for you, along with the clothes and weapons you'll need. You know, a good faith measure to show we're all one team." Cormack extends a hand, showing someone in. "My new friend will fill you in. I gotta bounce."

Cormack leaves.

As he clears the doorway, in walks a woman dressed in jeans and a torn man's dress shirt that hangs on her two sizes too large. She wears no shoes, nails firing off neon green.

It's the woman from the hotel.

The one who brought back Dutch's head.

The one who attacked Lester and Hollis in the alley.

The one who keeps dropping off fast-food napkins.

Hollis's and Lester's eyes bug out.

"Get that woman the hell away from me, man," Hollis says, trying to squirm away while still in a chair that's bolted to the floor.

Lester just stares at her with eyes wide as pies.

Remo looks to them, then to her. "Wait. I know you?"

She smiles sweetly, twisting her hair around her finger. "I'm Cloris." She waves to Lester like a schoolgirl with a massive crush. "Cloris Mashburn."

Remo and Hollis whip their heads around to Lester.

Lester looks like he's just been kicked in the balls. Twice.

"Mashburn?" Remo asks.

Cloris giggles, twisting her hair tighter. "As in Ferris, Chicken Wing and poor Dutch. Ya know? The head I delivered back to you. Those Mashburns. I'm the sister. Nice to meet you all." She looks to Lester. "You want to tell them what else, Buttercup?"

Remo's eyes slip to Hollis. *Buttercup?*

Lester shakes his head violently, like a toddler who doesn't want to admit he spilled grape juice on the new carpet.

Remo and Hollis are all ears, jaws on the floor.

"Lester and me, we're sweeties. As in engaged," she says, showing off her ring. "We're a bona fide thing."

REMO WENT WILD

REMO COBB # 3

PART I

BECAUSE OF HER VAGINA

C loris Mashburn is a train wreck of a woman.

Her face is a wadded-up ball of worry and rage as she peeks out over the rocky ridge. Something over there is troubling her deeply. Her stomach does flips while she sits looking down toward the base of a hill near Diablo Range, New Mexico. Her face flashes red. Teeth grind. Eyes laser-focused.

She can only watch as a house burns.

Her house.

Well, at least the house she shared with her three brothers and her lover.

There were a couple of other people who came in and out of the house, but it was always her, her brothers and the love of her life. The Mashburns were planning a series of robberies, so of course there were various goons and crime boys that came and went as the days passed. It was pretty common.

Cloris fell somewhere in the middle of the Mashburn family— wedged between Ferris and Chicken Wing, but younger than Dutch. Regardless of pecking order, they treated her like she was an infant. Always the little sister, no matter that she's older than Chicken Wing (one year) and only slightly younger than Ferris (one year.)

She accepted that it was because of her vagina, but didn't like it.

She's a solid decade (or more) younger than her lover—well, fiancé—Lester. Lester became a part of the Mashburn crew about six months ago, or was it a year now? Cloris can't remember. What she can remember is how much she cares for that man. A big, strong, mean man who loves hard and doesn't mind going down on her. That's pretty much what Cloris had been looking for during her tumultuous twenty-five years on this earth.

Lester reminds her of her father. Ain't that the way? Aside from the going down on her bit. Let's not be gross. The way she sees it, most girls/women she's known have either been searching for their dads or for someone who will piss their dads off. Cloris had no intention of pissing off Daddy Mashburn.

That would be stupid.

Very stupid.

Daddy Mashburn, known as Big Daddy Mashburn in most criminal circles and to the law, isn't in the burning house, but Dutch, Ferris, Chicken Wing and Lester certainly are.

Cloris went on a walk to clear her head after a fight with Chicken Wing. Nothing serious. The usual. Chicken Wing was being a complete fucking dick to her and Lester. Lester took his bullshit in stride, but it upset Cloris. Strike that. It really pissed her off. She used to drag it out for days, would not let it go.

Lester took her aside one day, told her to just take a deep breath and walk away. Cloris found that odd, because she'd watched Lester beat the ever-loving shit out of more than a few people for talking shit. But she took what he said to heart and started following his words, not his actions.

This is why she's perched on this ridge, in the dirt, watching the house burn while the cops trade gunfire back and forth with her brothers and Lester. She should be in there blasting away, fighting alongside her people. She should be down there doing the thing.

She sucks in a deep breath. The head honcho cop calls out to his squad to stop firing. The pops and rat-a-tats of gunfire slow to a trickle, then a stop, with the last sound of a shotgun blast echoing, trailing off into the mountains.

The house still burns.

Flames lick the sky.

Everyone goes quiet.

Only the crackle of wood burning. The whisper of wind.

The door bursts open. Smoke spills out, twisting into the wind. The cops' tension ratchets up, their weapons ready, tracking on the door and what might come out. Every muscle in Cloris pulls wire-tight. She breathes in slowly and deeply, but exhales hard through her nose. Seconds pass like hours to her.

Dutch and Lester fall out through the smoke, landing in the dirt.

The cops rush in, jamming knees in their backs and planting hands on their heads, pushing their skulls into the ground.

Every molecule in Cloris is dying to run rip-shit down that ridge and do damage. Those fuckers shouldn't even think about touching them. She yearns to claw the eyes from those cops' fat skulls. Not so much for what they're doing to Dutch, more for them manhandling her man. Her Lester.

She bites her lip.

Her eyes pop.

Her face shakes.

"Get up slowly," a man says in a very cop-like voice.

The voice is behind her. She can't see the man's face, but she knows it's a cop. She's been around enough of them. A criminal with any kind of ear can tell just by the tone and the words chosen. Without allowing another second to pass she spins on the ball of one foot, letting lose a whip-strike with her other leg. Cuts the much larger man's legs out from under him. He drops down hard to the ground before he can even realize what's happened. As he lands with a thud his training kicks in.

He levels his weapon on her.

She kicks his gun hand away.

Cloris scampers with a quick grab, picks up a rock the size of a baseball and hurls a fastball strike to his face. His nose explodes. She grabs a bigger rock with both hands, kneels over him and slams the rock down like a prehistoric warrior.

The rock goes up then crashes down.

Over and over again.

Until she feels the fight is done.

"Not doing that," Cloris tells her father.

"Honey, Ferris and Chicken Wing, they're gone. Dutch and Lester are tagged, going inside as we speak." Daddy Mashburn stuffs cash and whatever else he can find into a trash bag. "Time to regroup, rebuild and rise up later down the road."

A ragtag group of criminals enter and leave the room, moving as fast as they can down the hall and in and out of rooms. Most of them covered in tats. Most of them armed. All of them carrying trash bags of money. They are in a safe house that's buzzing like a hornet's nest. The place is located in a town only a few miles from where the other house burned down to the ground. Daddy Mashburn has several of these places scattered around New Mexico. He's been working hard to put together a better situation, a more permanent, secure command center. A single compound for his operations. It is so damn close to being ready, but shit keeps getting interrupted.

"Only a matter of time before they find this place. Everyone's going to separate and we'll meet up at the new place."

"Is it ready?" Cloris asks.

"Real close. Damn close. The timing is actually not bad. Far from perfect, but the new place is going to rock and roll. Boost us into second level type shit." He pauses, pinches the bridge of his nose. "Kills me to lose the boys, it does, haven't had proper time to process the loss." He releases his fingers and stares deep into a crack in the wall, letting his mind unspool. He feels Cloris watching him. Snakes his head left and right, then says, "This is the life we signed up for."

He turns, facing Cloris. The look on his daughter's face freezes his heart. She's hurting. He knows it. She's pissed. He knows that too. He also knows his little girl, and his little girl will go full-on war machine at the flick of a switch. It's in her blood. Long family history of flick-switch war machines.

It's all in her eyes.

She's already gone.

That switch has done been flipped.

He takes her face into his thick hands, holding it like an egg. "Honey, Lester doesn't want you locked in some cage. He wants you to be free. He'd say the same if he was standing here."

Daddy Mashburn is a massive man. A physically imposing presence. Shoulders of a linebacker. He keeps his scalp free from hair, shaving it daily. His skin is also clean from tats. Thinks they are a silly game for the younger crop coming up now. Tagging themselves. Using them as ego-boosting signs of criminal allegiance or accomplishments. Making it easier for the cops to identify you. Young bucks using skin art to signal how many murders they've performed, like they were WWII fighter pilots marking their planes with the number of kills. He understands the need to put up a badass front. It keeps lesser fools at bay. But it also invites bigger badasses to take a swing and, oh yeah, makes the cops fully aware you've killed people.

Daddy Mashburn doesn't get it.

So damn silly.

His daughter feels differently. She'd tat up every centimeter of skin if she'd let herself. Use her body to scream out, release to the world what's been wanting to bust and spill out from her volcano mind. Unload what she feels. What she loves and what she hates. Her vanity keeps all that off her neck and face. There's a line for her and it stops at the collar of most shirts. Pretty much every other part of her is spoken for and covered in ink. She respects her dad's thoughts on the subject, which is why she always wears long-sleeved shirts around him.

Cloris looks into her daddy's eyes as her mind chews on what he said to her a few seconds ago. What he said about coming with him. She translates her father's words through her own filter. She hears it as him telling her to *play it safe. Do the smart thing. Give up. Stand down, little girl.*

She kisses him on the cheek.

Tells him softly, sweetly into his ear, "Fuck off, Daddy. I'm getting Lester back."

IT'S BEEN A STRUGGLE.

Tracking down all the leads that lead nowhere. False info. Wrong turns. Glimmers of hope that flash and burn bright as the sun only to have them extinguished by the cold, hard realities of the truth. It's been a long, hard slog hunting and searching, day after day. Scraps of information keep her going. Burning love keeps her putting one foot in front of the other. Today, however, it's finally paying off. All the shit she's shifted through, all the doors she's kicked in, all the ass she's beaten down, and telling her big, scary father to fuck off has brought her here. Through it all she made it here. To this place.

They were here, she thinks.

All of them.

In the Hamptons.

She missed them by a few minutes, maybe seconds.

Here at the Hamptons home of one Remo Cobb there was a fight. A big and bad one. Cloris tours what's left of the lawyer's place like she was a prospective buyer at an open house in a war zone. She's on the second floor inspecting the blown-out windows, the chunks of wall removed by bullets and shell casings scattered across the floor like confetti. Out the window she can see damaged trees and crude holes in the lawn churned up by gunfire.

Downstairs is where the real bloodbath must have taken place. The front door is a disaster. There's blood everywhere. Bodies dropped here and there. Most of them she doesn't recognize. Men who look like people she could have known. They look like the hard, rough crime boys who have surrounded Cloris her whole life, but she can't place any of these particular ones.

She stops.

There's one she does know.

Her brother Ferris is dead as Dillinger on the floor in front of her. She looks at the recent ice cream scoop-style wounds on his body. The gunshot wounds are past their prime, but they still produce an unmistakable level of nasty.

Her eyes moisten. She allows a single tear, but no more.

She follows a blood trail down the hall to a room. It's a study or an office of some kind, or at least it used to be. The door is busted all to hell. There's an overturned desk with large gashes removed by gun blasts. There's a blood-soaked knife on the floor. A half a thug laid out on the floor and another dead brother. Chicken Wing is stretched in a death spread, his upper body made up mainly of barely-held-together pulpy bits.

This time there are no tears.

A brief, shooting star of emotion that burned out before it started.

Barely a glance, then Cloris spits on Chicken Wing's lifeless face as she leaves the room.

Out in the back of the house is the strangest of sights. Yes, there is more blood and gunfire damage, but there's something new out here. Something strange. A headless body. Dutch's headless body, she's sure of it. She'd know his tats anywhere. This was her last brother. Much older brother. She doesn't offer up tears or spit for Dutch, because she never really knew him that well. Large age difference and all. She is somewhat curious as to where his head is, however.

The fact that Dutch, Ferris and Chicken Wing are here offers some clarity. They're dead, but they are here nonetheless, and it does confirm some ideas, while raising some new questions. The rumor was that Ferris and Chicken Wing survived the New Mexico shootout and were running with Dutch. Seems those rumors were true. Obviously the stories about Dutch busting out of prison are now confirmed to be accurate. Also a rumor about Lester being out as well. No signs of that, although the headless Dutch is possibly Lester's work. She's seen him do it in the past. Still, you can never be sure in this life.

There was also a rumor they were searching for their lost money. Which brings Cloris to some new questions.

Where does this lawyer, this Remo, fit in to all this? And, actually the only question that truly matters -- where is my Lester?

Her intense focus while searching the house has left her unaware of the sirens that have been screaming her way. Her moment of deep, questioning, analytical thought has left her in the incredibly vulnerable position of being alone in the middle of a crime scene. The lone living soul in a massacre.

Police cars skid in.

Doors fly open, then slam shut. Guns are drawn.

Cloris is told to get down on the ground.

She wishes she had a rock.

~

CLORIS SITS IN A CRAMPED CELL.

Stinks of sweat and lost hope.

They've moved her twice. While she was staying in the first cell she beat the piss out of a drunk Hamptons millionaire who thought he'd have a grab at her tits. He'll be eating out of a tube for the foreseeable future. In the second cell she almost escaped by pulling off an almost impossible gymnast-style move up and over a guard who underestimated her abilities. Now, she's alone in a cell that's all hers to enjoy. A cell in the city so nice they named it twice. She's done New York many times, but not like this. Much different NYC experience behind bars and under lock and key. Her mouth is dry from screaming. Her face radiates heat from fighting back anger-tears.

She's been here for hours.

A little confused that she's not sitting at Rikers.

This place is different. She can't put her finger on it, but it is different.

She's not happy, but what the hell is she going to do about it? She chews a nail and lets the anger burn. Lets her imagination roll.

Allows it to run down some dark corridors, thinking of all the possibilities of what's going on with her Lester.

Is he alive? Is he hurt? Is he fucking someone?

"Hello, Cloris."

She snaps loose from her thoughts. Looking up, she finds a man right out of central casting standing outside her cell.

Dark, navy blue suit.

Perfect government hair.

Hard government eyes.

CIA man Cormac smiles.

2

Remo and Hollis are motionless, like statues held hostage.
They alternate their stares between Cloris and Lester while sitting zip-tied to chairs bolted to the floor. This woman just dropped one helluva bomb. Her announcement: that her and Lester were engaged.

Sorry, *a bona fide thing*.

This flies in the face of everything Remo and Hollis thought they knew about their new partner in crime. This isn't the Lester they know. The Lester they thought they knew. Lester, man of the Lord and violent avenger of whatever he feels like. That's their boy. Now what? He's a man with an emotional attachment? The pieces don't fit no matter how hard you try to jam them together.

"I'm sorry," says Remo, "you two are scheduled to be married?"

"Haven't set a date," Cloris chirps. "That shit takes time, ya know?"

Lester stares out into the void, wishing he were anywhere but here, hoping for a rescue that isn't coming.

"I have questions." Remo turns to Hollis. "You mind if I take the lead?"

Hollis shakes his head, unable to form his own questions.

"Shoot, counselor," Cloris says.

"One. Can you cut us free? Two... well, let's start with one."

Cloris cocks her head. "Later on one. Let's talk more, see how two goes."

"Okay. Two. How much do you know about your brothers?"

"A lot. They're dead. Found them at your house."

Remo sucks in a breath, glances to Hollis and Lester, then asks, "And Dutch?"

"I know you still have his head. It's in the other room, actually."

"Sorry, I should have been more clear. Do you know how it was removed?"

"Guessing someone in this room is responsible."

"And how do you feel about that?"

"Doesn't make me happy, but I'm willing to let it go."

Lester squirms.

"Big of you," Remo says.

"I think so. That all, counselor?"

"I have several questions about Cormac and you, but I'm assuming you two have a whole presentation of sorts on that."

"Something like that." Cloris smiles, giving her hair a twist. "I've got a question before I cut you boys loose. If that's okay?"

"Shoot," Remo says.

"Not for you." She turns to Lester. "Did you leave me, or did you just get caught up in all the stuff with my brothers and they wouldn't just let us live our lives together, even though you asked and pleaded repeatedly, but they were assholes not capable of understanding love, so consumed with their own bullshit that they told you 'no' so you felt trapped like a caged animal and didn't feel like you could come find me no matter how much you wanted to?"

Remo processes her question as fast as he can.

She gave him a lot there to work with.

She doesn't know everything. That much is clear. She doesn't know Lester split from her brothers. Doesn't know Lester never said a word about her, or the fact he's gone full-on saved by the Lord. She also doesn't know that Lester cut off Dutch's head. More importantly, Cormac didn't tell her everything.

Or...

Cormac did tell her everything and she's testing Lester right now, and if he gives the wrong answer she's going to cover all three of them in gasoline and light them on fire. She might feed them their own dicks first.

Remo's and Hollis's eyes slide over toward Lester. There's a lot riding on his answer and they're not exactly sure what the right answer is. They hope like holy hell he does.

Cloris looks to Lester with eyebrows raised, running her tongue over her teeth waiting for his response. It better be good.

Damn good.

Lester clears his throat, pauses, then says, "Buttercup, I didn't know what to do. You know Dutch, he didn't want to hear a damn thing about me and you being together. Only had money on his mind."

Cloris's eyes soften, moisture forming in the corners.

"I tried. I did," Lester says.

Cloris wraps her arms around his neck, squeezing him tight.

Remo and Hollis exhale—thank God that worked. That was like watching a bomb being defused with the seconds ticking closer and closer to zero.

She weeps uncontrollably, trembling as she lets go of everything she's been holding onto these long, long days. Days and nights of crushing uncertainty. The searching. The hunting for her man and the truth. All the anxious churning in her stomach surrounding her and Lester. The not knowing what was true and what was bullshit. The rumors she's heard. The ugly rumors she never trusted.

That's all gone bye-bye. Removed by Lester's well-chosen words. Washed away by a tsunami of joy. Lester and Cloris are together and that's all that matters. They are back to being a bona-fucking-fide thing and the man she loves has told her everything she's been dying to hear.

Lester looks over to Remo and Hollis as Cloris sobs uncontrollably all over his shoulder. They give a thumbs-up, best they can at least with their hands bound, and plaster on over-the-top, massive smiles. *Way to go, bro.*

Lester mouths, *Help me.*

3

Remo twists his feet, first right then left, shakes his legs and squeezes his fists.

Working to get the feeling back into his wrists and hands after being bound by the tight-as-shit zip ties. His lower extremities are beginning to show signs of returning blood flow and his toes have stopped with their annoying throbbing. Lester and Hollis are up and free and rubbing the hell out of their wrists and ankles as well, just with less bitching than Remo.

Remo's head is still spinning from all that has happened in the last few days. It's a lot to take in, but there's no time to dwell on Russian roulette betting or the disaster in the streets of New York with Mr. Crow or the fact the CIA is fucking with him and his boys.

It's the CIA thing that's really eating at Remo.

Why them? Why the CIA? What's the international angle? Is there an international angle?

It has to be Remo's old clients. Maybe they have some global money-laundering ties or they funded some south-of-the-border cartel operations here and there. He'd heard that Crow dabbled in gunrunning for a blink of time, but he'd never heard anything vaguely global going on with the Mashburns. They are straight-up, good ole American crime boys. At least Remo thinks so. There's a gnawing, growing list of Cormac-related questions.

Why did Cormac go after Cloris?

Can anything Cormac said be trusted?

Doubtful.

Cormac said <u>this</u> is the one job he really wanted Remo for.

Why?

"Why?" Remo asks Cloris.

She's hanging all over Lester, trying to snuggle as close as she can with him. Lester is fighting her while trying hard not to show that he's fighting her. It's a delicate balance. Requires touch. Just like a teenager who doesn't know how to tell his girlfriend it's all over and he'd rather see other people. This situation is slightly more complicated of course, more life and death, but confused teenager is the look Lester's sporting at the moment and Cloris is completely oblivious to the vibe her dear sweet Lester is putting off.

Remo resets and tries again. "Cloris."

Nothing but more awkward hugs and shifts.

Lester taps her on the shoulder and points to Remo.

"What?" Cloris asks with a bit of bite.

"Why?" Remo asks.

"*Why* what?"

"Why us? Why now? Why you? Why does Cormac want us all together?"

"Oh." She plays with Lester's hair. "Daddy has a house not far from here. There's some other guys there too. Friends. Hired hands. Ya know, some sluggers, some battle boys. Cormac wants us to go in and kill 'em all."

"One more time?" Hollis chimes in.

"Simple. The four of us need to figure out a way to go into the house and kill everybody in there. More of a compound, really. Daddy's been working on the place for a while. *Kill 'em all.* Those were Cormac's words, not mine." Cloris takes in their blank stares. "We made a deal. Kill them. That was the deal. Simple shit really. Where did I lose you?"

Lester slips off to the side of Cloris, attempting to put a little space between them. "We're not a death squad."

Cloris giggles. "Since when?"

Lester opens his mouth to respond, but thinks better of it.

"Can we see the rest of the house?" Remo moves to the door. "Perhaps tell us where we are exactly? Last time I was conscious I was in an alley in New York."

Cloris takes Lester by the hand and bounces past Remo, leading the group into the living room. The décor is full-on mountain getaway cabin. Wood, wood and more wood. A fish on the wall and lots of bear art. Cloris escorts Lester to a plush-ish leather couch that's way past its prime. As they sink into the cushions Cloris wraps herself around Lester like a snake. Hollis and Remo look out the window. It's a gorgeous view of nature's glory. Trees and green in every direction with the bluest of skies peeking through. Mountains on the edges of their sight rest in the background. A running stream rolls not far from the front of the house. If they listen closely they can hear the water rumble and ramble. Remo isn't sure where this is, but it sure as shit ain't New York.

Remo points out the window, his face resembling a question mark.

"New Mexico. Pretty, right?" says Cloris.

On the floor in front of the fireplace is everything Cormac promised. Some rolls of cash, a small stack of prepaid credit cards, three separate piles of clothes and enough firepower to invade a tiny nation.

Remo and Hollis look over the spread. Lester tries to get up from the couch and join them, but is pulled back down by Cloris. She continues clawing at his hair. Can't take her eyes off of him.

The weapons are neatly laid out in sets of four. Four Glocks, four modified ARs and four pistol-grip assault shotguns. Boxes of shells, bullets and magazines are piled up with each set. There's also a convenient stack of Kevlar vests next to the clothing. Remo nudges his expert, Hollis, for an assessment of the weapons buffet.

"That'll do some damage," Hollis says. "Might be great. Might be shit. Depends on what we're walking into."

"Cloris, any idea when we are supposed to do all this killing you speak of?" Remo asks.

"Didn't get a specific time, but he did say *within a reasonable time-frame*." Cloris points toward the back of the house. "He's outside if you want to follow up."

Remo looks to Hollis then the back of the house. "He's fucking still here?"

"Yup," Cloris chirps.

Remo storms past the couch with Hollis close behind.

Cloris bounces up from the couch, dragging Lester by the hand toward a bedroom at the back of the house.

"Let's get the first one out of the way," Cloris says.

"Cloris..." Lester says.

"Don't worry. No worries if you blow one quick, I get it."

"No, I'm different now."

Cloris cocks her head.

"I changed in prison."

"You like dick now?"

"No."

"Can only do doggie? Had a friend who had a fella that got locked down in Huntsville and when he got out he could only do her doggie. Called her Bobby when he came. It'll be a transition, but I'm cool with it."

"No." Lester places his hands on the sides of her face. "I'm with the Lord now. I'm saved."

Cloris squints, scrunching up her nose.

"You know, God? That sort of thing," Lester says.

"That mean we can't fuck?"

"Yes."

"But you still kill people?"

"Yes, but only—"

"Is sex worse than violence?"

"Yes. No. Not necessarily. You're missing the—"

"Your rules are confusing, but this is how I see it. We're engaged, we should be married by now, which I think is enough gray area for us to go get weird for a few minutes."

She looks into his eyes, flicks her upper lip with her tongue and unbuttons the top two buttons of her shirt. Lester can't help but sneak a peek. It's been a while.

"How about this? No actual sex," Cloris purrs. "You use that magic tongue of yours and I'll take care of you too. Deal?"

Lester's breathing quickens.

Memories of the hot nights spent with Cloris bounce around his skull like a horny Ping-Pong ball.

His shoulders drop.

His will wilts.

She leads him by the hand into the room.

4

Remo storms out of the house.

The cool, crisp mountain air hits his face and wraps around his body, giving him a refreshing blast of lovely. No matter how pissed he is, Remo can't help but love it. Actual fresh air can have a magical effect on a person. He didn't realize how much of a city boy he'd become over the years. Country-born and -bred, but the years of New York have changed him without a doubt. He hasn't felt the healing power of open, pure air in a long, long time.

It's nice, but there's no time to linger over this shit. He's heading straight toward a man who needs to answer a few of Remo's questions. Right the fuck now. He feels his anger fire up from his stomach to his face. Even the nice as hell mountain air can't cool off his rage.

Cormac sits on the hood of a white Chevy Yukon smoking a cigarette. This also pisses Remo off. This asshole is running Remo's life as if Remo were attached to strings and now, now this fucking dickhole is actually smoking in the mountains. Dicking up the nice, clean mountain air Remo was enjoying.

The balls on this guy.

"What special breed of a fucking fuckstick are you?" Remo asks.

Cormac blows a smoke ring up into the air.

Remo watches the ring break and dissolve into nothing. He takes a beat, resets and says, "You don't come off as a smoker."

"Watch porn too. We all got our stuff, Remo," Cormac says, then licks his fingers. "You seem unhappy. How can I make you happy?" Cormac holds Remo's eyes as he snuffs out the cigarette, crushing the tip by rubbing the lit end between his thumb and index finger.

The not so subtle symbolism isn't lost on Remo.

"So what? We're a bloodthirsty boy band now?" Remo asks.

"Look, if labels help you and your team, fine, but let's be clear on something. You started this thing. That's right, you. You set it all in motion the second you turned on the Mashburns. All of that—them, the money, prison, the little war in the Hamptons—that's on you and *that* has led us to here."

"Never once did I think this was what I was doing."

"Your intentions are irrelevant. Cute, but irrelevant. What is relevant is what's actually happening, and what's happening is you need to do something for me and your country."

Hollis steps up fast. Remo has no idea how long he's been there, but the look on his face has Remo thinking he's heard a lot. He looks Cormac in the eye and asks, "We waving flags now?"

"You're a former military man. Read all about you." Cormac smiles. "You're a bad man who's killed a lot of bad people. A lot of them not fans of the US."

"This ain't quite the same. Fairly sure you know that."

"Why? These people we're talking about, the ones hunkered down at Camp Mashburn, are indeed enemies of this country. And"—Cormac stabs a finger into Remo's chest—"this is an excellent chance to finish them off. Put a cherry on top of the fine work you started."

Remo's mouth goes dry.

All the memories of the Mashburns flood his brain like a dam busting wide open.

Their vicious nature. Their insanity.

All the blood. The pain. The fear.

From behind Remo a loud spank echoes, followed by a quick, sharp yelp.

Remo and Hollis look back to the house then return to Cormac.

"What about Cloris?" Remo asks. "She get to be the surviving Mashburn in all this?"

Cormac clucks his tongue and looks to the house. "That, sir, is up to you. She's here to help you without getting you killed. Think of her as a key to the front door. She's the only link to them and the best way inside."

"You can't just send in your own squad of CIA murder boys? You got plenty," Hollis says.

"We do. You're right. But we'd have to go in with force. Gun blazing kind of deal and we'd win, eventually. We did that very thing here in the mountains not that long ago." Cormac looks to Remo. "You remember, right? That's when we got Dutch and your pal, Lester. Thought we killed Ferris and Chicken Wing. We were wrong, but you two took care of that later in the Hamptons. Didn't you?"

Remo nods.

Hollis nods.

Cormac gives them a finger gun with a wink. "Good work, boys. The problem was that during our little firefight here in New Mexico we lost a lot of good people. And by *we* I mean law enforcement. CIA was nowhere near that mess. So the burning question is why put good women and men in danger when I've got you."

Remo studies Cormac. He's become really good at reading people over the years. The problem here is Cormac is a master at giving up nothing. Cormac has had the jump on Remo since the day they met. Remo couldn't find a crack in his bullshit. A first for Remo, but now he has a read on something. He senses something is locked up behind those eyes of Cormac. He just needs to wiggle it free.

"You don't know where they are," Remo asks, "do you? I mean you know they are in this state, but you have no idea where or how many of them there are. Am I right, buddy?"

Cormac smiles, impressed with Remo. He's rarely surprised, but

Remo has made a career out of surprising a lot of people. Remo keeps unspooling his thoughts while trying to read Cormac's eyes.

"Cloris didn't tell you everything, or rather, not much of anything," Remo says. "She traded up to get to Lester and now it's time for her to pay up by getting us into the Mashburn compound."

Cormac shrugs without confirming or denying anything. He motions for Remo to come over to him. With great reluctance Remo moves toward the Yukon, standing in front of Cormac.

"Remo, man," Cormac says low so only they can hear, "I know you don't have any reason to trust me."

"Nope."

"No reason to believe anything I tell you."

"You're right, and I do not."

"Do you really have a choice though?"

Remo stares back at him, burning. His insides on fire because Cormac is right and not having a choice is not a place Remo likes to hang out. Hollis, not liking the vibe, begins to move their way. Remo holds out a hand, requesting a moment. Hollis stands down.

"Trust me or not, I'm being straight with you here," Cormac continues. "After all this Mashburn unpleasantness is over with you will be free and clear. Can't promise that you'll ever get your life back. You probably won't. Certainly never be the same. I can't promise your kid will love you forever either, but what I can promise you is a chance for you to find out."

Remo looks anywhere but Cormac's eyes. Trying to find a clear thought.

"You do this thing and you're good with me. No strings. All done," Cormac says, holding out a hand. "Cool?"

Remo eyes the extended hand that's hanging, waiting for a confirmation shake. He's made a lot of deals with the devil. At times, he's been the devil. He takes a moment to try and read Cormac one more time. Straining to use all his powers, his gifts, all the ability he's developed over the years to break down the human race into simple, digestible pieces. Even with all of that, Remo is still not sure with

Cormac. This CIA man is good. Real good. He's also right. Remo has no choice but to trust him.

Remo shakes his hand.

"Good," Cormac says, then holds up a finger like he forgot something. He raises his finger up into the air and swirls it three times.

From the trees, from out of nowhere, four men appear.

Remo jump-bounces back. He'd almost screamed but he stopped himself.

Hollis simply sets his feet and balls up his fists.

The four men are in full-on tactical gear. Dressed in black. Helmets, vests, guns strapped on and hard, lifeless eyes that dig into your soul. They surround Cormac as he slides off the hood of the Yukon.

"I recognize there's a chance the Mashburn place might have anywhere between two and two hundred armed, mean and nasty people inside. As you stated correctly before, I really don't know. Not sure Cloris does either." Cormac motions around him. "This, these people here, this is your backup. Your nuclear option. If things get too hot you call them in, but not until you get inside and have eyes on the man affectionately known as Big Daddy Mashburn."

"And how do we contact these pretty little kill boys? Do I do that cute finger swirl thing?" Remo rubs his face as the uncomfortable rush that comes from a sudden spike in blood pressure takes hold of him.

"We'll get you set up with communications," Cormac says.

Hollis stares. Blinks. Rolls his eyes.

Remo wants to throw up.

"What could go wrong?" Cormac says with a cluck of his tongue.

Cloris and Lester exit the house in a post-orgasm stumble. Both of sport head of hair that resemble bird's nests. Lipstick smeared across Lester's blank face. Massive, toothy smiles on hers.

"S'up, fellas?" Cloris asks.

5

"What in the name of good fuck is the plan?" Remo asks.

He receives little in response. Maybe a glance, a flash of eyes, but certainly nothing that would be considered a response. The four of them are now back in the living room staring at the buffet of weapons and clothes laid out on the floor. Hollis begins inspecting the guns one by one. Cloris holds onto Lester tight. Lester stares out into the void. Lost as hell. He enjoyed the pleasure bounce earlier, but the glow has faded back to the realities of the situation.

Remo slips off from the group and heads back outside. The porch creaks and moans as he steps across wood that has been battered by the elements over the years. He takes a seat in an old rocking chair that offers one helluva view.

He uses that view to help his head spill out the events of the day. Watching the wilderness before him helps soothe the shittiness in a way. Makes it all seem not so bad. Remo knows he's fucked, but a nice view coupled with a nice breeze can fool the shit out of you if you'll just let it.

Before Cormac left he gave Remo a device he can use to *communicate* with the CIA murder goons/kill squad/nuclear option. It's a small, tiny-ass thing that he could crack between his fingers. There's a small pull-strip adhesive so it'll stick to something. Cormac recommended somewhere safe, like on his person or on the side or underneath of an object that won't see much action. Once the device breaks, it will send a signal to the kill squad they can zero in on, and they will come riding in with guns blazing. He was told they will not respond unless Remo is inside and they have *reasonable confidence* Remo has *viable intelligence.*

Remo made a joke about his LSAT scores.

Get it? Viable intelligence? LSAT?

The joke didn't land with Cormac. Or the kill squad.

Humorless fucks.

Once they are inside the Mashburn place and they know the layout and an approximate number of bad guys and have put eyes on Big Daddy Mashburn, then Remo is to break the device and say the words *burn it down.*

Remo asked if he could spice it up with "Burn this motherfucker down" or "Let's light this bitch the fuck up." He received blank stares, a couple of blinks and a snort in return, then was told they will only respond to the agreed upon verbiage.

No vision among these people.

Fuckers.

Burn it down is just a little dramatic, he thought, perhaps a touch macho, but he was in no position to question what his personal CIA attack team wanted to use as a safety phrase. If *burn it down* gets them to their happy place, then so be it.

Remo's got bigger issues at the moment.

Management issues.

The management issue facing Remo right now is how the hell he's going to bring together the shit show that is currently his team. A team he never asked for. A team he did not recruit. A team of people that has killed more people than french fries. These people are not only his team now. It's more serious than that—this group of whackos will have a lot to do with Remo's survival. Meaning, they will also play a huge part in helping Remo get out of this mess. Remo still holds onto hope that Cormac will make good on his promise of getting Remo free and clear once this is all over. Getting Remo back to some form of a normal life.

A life with his son. Just a good, normal life.

There's still hope.

You lose hope, you lose everything.

Remo is still a realist, however. He knows that *normal* has been lit on fire and thrown out a window, but he does hope he can find some way to become a functioning member of society. It won't be conventional, to be damn sure, but Remo knows he can work it out. Find a way to make it all come together. That's what he does.

He figures shit the fuck out.

He only needs Cormac to do what he says he's going to do. Unfortunately it's a major piece of the puzzle, and not one Remo can control or really count on. Cormac kinda said the same shit before that last little thing with Mr. Crow, yet somehow, after Remo took care of Crow—well, Lester and Hollis played a role—but after that Crow thing was resolved Remo ended up tied to a chair with a bag over his head in New Mexico.

Trust in Cormac is some thin crust-style shit, at best.

Unfortunately, trust and hope in hopelessly untrustworthy people is territory Remo is all too familiar with.

And Remo is back where he was before he came outside.

Completely fucked with limited, shit options.

Hollis takes a seat in an old, busted-up rocking chair next to Remo. He says nothing, looking out over the trees watching the branches sway slightly, the peacefulness of the place taking him by the hand. Hollis closes his eyes, lets the moment breathe, forgets all the shit the man next to him has put him through. Sets aside all the shit this man is going to put him through in the future. The very near future. He should snap Remo's neck, kill the other two inside, take the money on the living room floor and take off to find his wife and kids. Wherever they are. Hollis smiles. He maps out the whole thing in his mind, playing a movie only he can see. A movie where he's free of these people and living happily ever after with his family. A life he should be enjoying right now. A life interrupted by Remo.

"What you think?" Remo asks.

"Shut the fuck up before I snap your neck, is what I think."

Remo nods then closes his eyes as well.

They'll talk later.

6

Cloris serves up a large, steaming plate of chicken pepperoni.

She smiles at Lester as she places the plate in the center of table, carefully placing the serving spoon and fork on either side.

It's Lester's favorite.

Cloris knows it.

Lester knows it.

"What is it?" asks Remo.

"Chicken pepperoni," Cloris says, setting down the Caesar salad. "It's Italian-ish. Dig in and chill out."

The plate looks magnificent. A mouthwatering, bubbling red sauce covering a pile of perfectly breaded chicken breasts with mozzarella and thick slices of pepperoni spilling out from the sides, and it's all sitting upon a mountain of cloud-like pasta.

Lester watches her serve his friends like a perfect little hostess. He's not sure he's met this woman before. She plates Remo first, then Hollis, letting Lester watch. Letting the sight and smells of his favorite meal wash over him. Cloris knows this guy and she knows a little sexual release and a good meal will bust him wide open.

Confusion streams, swirls inside Lester's brain. He wants to jump up from the table, run screaming into the mountains and never come back. He wants nothing more than to leave this woman, this house, this situation as fast as he can, but he knows damn well he cannot.

That fact sticks in his brain like a pitchfork.

In a way, he's already tried.

Sort of already tried to leave.

It's not like he was trying to work a fake death or anything. He just used the shootout and jail as a convenient way of getting out from under a relationship he felt should have ended a while back. It happens all the time. Not like this, of course, but relationships do end. People break up. No big deal. Lester's situation was complicated by the fact she's the boss's daughter and, oh yeah, the boss is a crime boss and, oh yeah, the daughter has a bit of a temper and carries a prominent violent streak.

"This is pretty fucking good," Remo says with mouth stuffed, red sauce dripped on his chin and pasta snaking up to his lips.

"Thank you, Remo," she says.

"And she cooks too," Hollis says with a *complete prick* grin to Lester.

Hollis cuts a big bite of chicken with just the right amount of cheese and pepperoni and swirls a healthy amount of spaghetti onto his fork. He snickers to himself, taking some pride in his little dig at Lester—it's fun for Hollis to fuck with Lester. Then he notices the death stare firing off from across the table.

Cloris grips her knife with eyes locked in on Hollis. It's as if the temperature in the room dropped thirty degrees. Her stare bores into Hollis.

Hollis chews slowly, assessing the situation. He holds his knife as well.

Remo and Lester both take note of this potential problem.

"He didn't mean anything," Lester says. "He was making a joke. Busting balls."

"That it?" Cloris asks Hollis. "You being funny?"

Hollis swallows. He'd rather not get into a thing with her. He's fought women before, really tough women that almost killed him, and he's pretty sure Cloris falls into that category, but he also doesn't want to back down and let Cloris think she's running this thing, or running him for that matter.

"Just having a little fun with Lester, that's all. We've been through a lot together. That okay by you?"

"You think a woman's place is in the kitchen?" Cloris asks. "That the kinda joke you're making, funny man?"

Remo wipes his mouth, not liking the mood of the table. "Okay, okay, people. It's been a rough few days for everybody. Let's press reset and enjoy this great dinner Cloris put together."

"No, I don't think a woman's place is in the kitchen. My wife was an attorney before she decided to give up her practice and stay home with the kids. I think a woman's place is wherever she wants to be. Same as a man. If a woman wants to be a CEO, a housewife or give handjobs for crack in Central Park that's her call and nobody, regardless of genitalia, should tell her otherwise. That make sense or should I talk slower for you?" Hollis says.

"Can we just enjoy the fucking chicken?" Remo asks.

Cloris slices the air with knife toward Remo. "Suck it, counselor." She points the knife back to Hollis. "Since you're so fuckin' in tune with the vagina movement, what's the joke? What's so goddamn funny about me making dinner?"

Lester's and Remo's eyebrows rise without allowing eye contact to happen. Both hoping the conversation will simply run out of gas on its own.

"Look, if you're going to jam me into an answer, I'll oblige," Hollis says, pointing his knife to Lester then back to her. "The joke I was making with Lester was based on the fact he's been a little, I don't know, off since you showed up. That's really it, Cloris. Has jack shit to do with your kitchen wizardry or what's between your legs."

Cloris leans back, stabs a pepperoni with her knife and gnaws at it while thinking over what Hollis just said. The gears behind her eyes crank as her teeth gnash. She simply does not like this guy.

Something in Hollis has clicked. Somewhere in his head he's made the transition from just wanting to get along to wanting to push some buttons and see where this goes. See where she'll go. Hollis needs to know who he's about to go to war with.

"Looking back now, your little drop-ins in New York," Hollis continues, "you dropping fast-food napkins. You knew what the hell was going on."

Lester swallows then says, "I suspected it."

"First time we fucked was in a burger joint bathroom," Cloris says. "It was dirty-sexy-brilliant."

"Buttercup," Lester says. "Not helpful."

"It was magic," she says. "Eat."

"Perhaps you should have made burgers then," Hollis says.

Cloris cocks her head, eyes again boring into Hollis.

Lester and Remo look down. Eyes only at their plates, while shoveling in food as fast as they can. As if the secret code to getting the hell out of this meal is written at the bottom of the plate.

The silence is deafening.

Forks scrape plates. Chewing. Stares hold, break, then fire off again.

The room is an ever-expanding balloon of tension with everyone sitting on edge watching, waiting for it to explode.

Cloris tears off some bread, chews, sits watching Hollis.

She's boiling inside.

Hollis glances up to her, smiles, then looks back down to his plate. He cuts another big bite and says, "I don't know about the bathroom sex, but I must say, the chicken is fantastic."

Cloris launches herself up and over the table.

Hollis catches her in mid-air and the force sends them falling back in his chair. They slam to the hardwood floor. The chair cracks in two. There's a dull thud of meat hitting wood. A crunch of bone. Plates fly. Glasses dump. Salad goes airborne.

Cloris and Hollis roll over and over. A tumbleweed of violence. Muscles tight. Veins pop. Faces red. Each holds the other's knife at bay. Spit flies from Cloris's mouth as she screams, barking in tongues. Hollis is fighting to play defense, but Cloris's anger is fueling a level of attack strength he wasn't expecting.

Lester and Remo throw their chairs back from the table, but neither has any idea what to do or how to stop this. They pivot on the balls of their feet, dancing a dance of uncertain steps. Both think of jumping in, but stop as Cloris's and Hollis's knife blades slash back and forth. Remo and Lester end up simply standing there with faces slack, jaws dropped.

"People," Remo says without a clue. "What the fuck?"

Lester eyes the floor. He picks up a piece of chicken by the broken chair and starts chomping it down. It helps him think.

Cloris and Hollis fire straight up, springing to their feet. Squaring off like gladiators. Hollis grabs a chair using it to hold off Cloris as she swipes and stabs her steak knife wildly. Hollis the lion tamer works the chair, sticking and jabbing the legs at Cloris. Sweat drips as he attempts to back her into a corner of the room. He's working it slow as he can, an inch at a time, backing her up a little here and a little there. So subtle she doesn't notice what's happening.

Remo follows them with Lester behind him, still taking down the chicken.

"Cloris," Remo barks, "let's take a breath and figure this the hell out. We need each other, remember?"

Cloris glances to Remo, kicks at Hollis. "Then tell your boy to stand the fuck down."

"Hollis?" asks Remo.

"Tell her to stop trying to gut me and I'll consider it."

"Can't promise that," Cloris says.

Cloris sees a flash of a moment. A wrinkle of an opening. Hollis has let his focus slip to Remo for just a blink, but long enough for her. She kicks the chair hard to left and pounces like an animal. She slams into Hollis like a hard-hitting battle ram, sending them both smashing back down to the floor. Both lose hold of their knives upon impact sending them sliding across the floor. Wailing like a child torn from the wild, she grips Hollis by the ears, slamming his head down on the wood floor.

Hollis's sight flashes white, but he pulls himself back in. He fires a leg straight up, almost getting it up over her face and down her body.

She wiggles left and right like a world-class cage fighter, avoiding getting caught in his vice leg grip. She rips a lighting punch. He whips his head right, clear from the strike. Her fist cracks into the wood. Her bones crunch. Biting down on her lip she sticks a fist to his nose with other hand.

Remo can't believe his eyes.

Hollis is losing.

She tags him again in the face.

From the corner of her vision she spies one of the knives. Its slide was stopped by Lester's suitcase against the wall. Diving free from Hollis, she grabs the knife and spins back around, landing on her knees. Cloris grips the knife with both hands, raising it high up over her head, about to jam it down into Hollis's chest.

A thick slab of chicken pepperoni slaps her in the face.

Lester dive-tackles her away from Hollis pinning her down on the floor.

"Breathe," Lester tells her with his large hands holding her down. "You need to breathe and chill, Cloris."

She fights it.

"Do it." He presses. His face hard but calm.

Cloris sucks in and out through her teeth. Her skin is bright red. A single stream of blood snakes down her cheek. Lester can see her pulse bump inside the veins of her neck. Her eyes are locked onto his. Like a semi-crazy Lamaze coach, Lester is actually bringing her down to a normal level by his presence and the sound of his voice.

"Breathe."

She obeys.

Remo helps Hollis up to his feet. Hollis will never admit it, but Remo can see the man is shaken. A warrior like Hollis can't afford to admit when he's been beaten. Challenged, sure, but never acknowledge a defeat. That's the kind of thing that can dig into the skull of a man like Hollis. He needs to believe he can walk into anything and kill everyone. Hollis knows it. Remo knows it. Remo also knows he needs his boy's shit wire tight. He needs Hollis firing on all confidence cylinders. He needs his killing machine humming. A good leader knows exactly what to say to his or her people at moments like this.

"She fucked you up, man," Remo says.

Remo is a horrific leader.

Hollis simply glances his way, then kicks him in the balls.

Remo folds like a dish towel then drops to the floor. First to his knees and then full-on fetal.

Hollis quietly seethes. He sees Lester's roller suitcase from New York against the wall. He steps over Remo and rushes over to it. Hollis unzips the top and pulls out Dutch's severed head by the hair. He holds it up for all to see.

"See this? This is what your sweetie did to your brother," Hollis yells.

He turns slightly and punts the head like a football. Dutch's head sails awkwardly across the room, crashing through the window. Glass falls, bouncing off the wood floor like a spilled bag of jelly beans.

Remo watches through his broken-ball tears.

Lester shakes his head.

"Fine! He was a fuckin' asshole anyway!" Cloris screams, then she sweetly turns to Lester. "I forgive you. You did what you had to do, I'm sure of it."

Hollis rolls his eyes.

Lester can only stare at her, taking in the crazy as he has her pinned on the floor, the slab of chicken pepperoni still plastered to the side of her face.

Remo grunts, holding his nuts.

Tomorrow they're going to storm Camp Mashburn.

Go team.

7

Remo sits beside his son Sean in front of a crackling campfire.

Roasting marshmallows, telling ghost stories and loving it. The smiles are big. The night sky is deep and dark. The laughs are huge. This is what Remo wanted for his life. This is what Remo hoped he'd get when he double-crossed the Mashburns in the first place. He didn't know it at the time, but this is what he was doing. This was the goal. His brain was taking him to this, even if he didn't realize it at the time. His body and soul were working to get to this place without his day-to-day lizard brain putting it all together for him.

Perhaps there could have been easier ways to get here.

Perhaps if Remo was in his right mind, sans the booze and drugs, he would have come up with a stronger plan than pissing off homicidal maniacs, but he didn't and here we are.

Remo has never done things in a straight line.

Never the easy path.

What's the fun in that?

"Thanks, Daddy," says Sean. He gives a smile that melts Remo's heart upon impact.

Remo feels his eyes swell, water building up, about to bust open floodgates. He puts an arm around his boy and holds on tight. These are the moments that make it okay. That make the shittiness of the world and people in it bearable.

"Time to go," Anna says.

Remo's heart freezes.

He turns around to find his ex-wife walking out from the thick, dark forest behind them. She's wearing the dress she wore on their wedding day. White. Flowing. Gorgeous as she ever was, but her face is twisted and wracked with emotion. She's here to do something she doesn't want to do, but has to. A mother who knows that parenting isn't always smiles and giggles. She's here with a job to do.

"I'm sorry," she says, "but Sean needs to leave."

"What? Why?" Remo asks, stumbling as he stands up. "We're just getting started."

Anna shrugs her shoulders.

"Sorry, Daddy," Sean says. "Should have fucking started sooner, prick."

Sean punches Remo in the gut then takes his mother's hand, storming off into the woods.

Remo holds his stomach, mouth wide in complete shock.

There's a rumbling sound behind him. Something primal.

Remo whips back around. There's a wave, a mass of movement coming at him. Charging. Their speed is relentless. Hundreds of them. An army of headless men running at him holding crude weapons made of bone and rock. All covered, caked in dirt and blood.

Remo closes his eyes.

Accepts his fate.

8

R emo jolts awake.

He finds himself laid out on the couch with the chilly night mountain air whistling through the busted-out window. Releasing a huge sigh, Remo sees his breath exit his lungs, circling and twirling into the air, creating a spirit-like shape above him. His brain starts to unwind, watching his spirit-breath dissipate into nothingness. That dream he just shook loose from twists inside his head like a fat worm working its way around his very thoughts. He shakes his head hard, as if his brain were an Etch A Sketch. His thoughts shift to tomorrow, or today; he has no idea what time it is, or the date for that matter.

What the hell is he going to do?

Can Cloris deliver? Can she get them into Camp Mashburn?

Are they walking into certain death?

Will Cormac fuck him over no matter what happens?

Should he jump and run right now, take his chances and hope like hell that Sean and Anna will take him in?

"We're in trouble," Lester says.

Remo jumps-bounces up into a seated position and yelps, "What the fuck, man?"

Lester shushes him, pointing to the back rooms.

"What the fuck, man?" Remo whisper-barks.

"She's crazy."

"No shit."

"She'll kill us all."

"So you're saying you don't trust her."

"I trust her to be her."

"What the hell does that even mean?"

"If she wants something, she cannot be stopped, but what she wants can change dramatically with little or no notice or reason."

Remo thinks on that one. His mind gnaws it, chews away at it. He's dealt with many members of the criminal element, most of them less than sane, and he has known a few people who fit exactly what Lester has just described. One thing is certain: things rarely end well with that sort of folk.

"Well, what should we do, Lester? I'm asking because I really don't know. We don't have a strong play here. Not much in the way of a choice that I can see. Cormac more than likely has people watching us right now. If we don't go after the Mashburn place, we're fucked. Fucked hard. Not the beautiful, 'sweet act of love' kind of fucked."

Now Lester chews on that one.

Remo watches him sitting in the darkness. He's never seen Lester like this. Conflicted. Unsure. Off-kilter and all bunched up over another human being. Lester has come to Remo in several forms. Hard-as-hell criminal. A killer. A savior. A friend, of sorts. But never as a man busted up by a woman.

"If you want to run, I get it," Remo says. "I've had some women that have made me want to cut and run. There's probably more than one woman who would say the same about me. Of course, never had one who could take down a highly functional hit man, but that shit's neither here nor there."

Lester looks to the ceiling and closes his eyes. Remo sees him begin to mumble to himself in the moonlight.

"What's that, friend?" Remo asks.

Lester continues his chat with himself.

Remo snaps his fingers at him, trying to get his attention.

Lester opens one eye, looking in his direction, then shuts it immediately, going back to his conversation.

Remo is getting pissed here. It's a little rude, this thing Lester's doing. He can feel his anxiety rising until he realizes something.

The man is praying.

"Oh. I'll shut the fuck up. Sorry, man," Remo says.

Remo tries not to stare, but he really doesn't know what to do with this. It's quiet in the house, save for the slight whisper coming from Lester's chat with the Lord and the wind kicking up through the shattered window caused by the Dutch head-punt earlier. Remo has nothing to do. It's making him uncomfortable. As if he's a third wheel. He folds then unfolds his hands. He looks around the room three, four times. Finally he lies down, staring at the ceiling. For a moment he considers praying himself. It's been a while.

A long while.

He was raised in Texas, and church was a big thing in his neighborhood, even though most of the people he knew growing up weren't exactly strict followers of the Bible. Not outside the walls of church at least. They sang the songs and recited the words they were told to recite, but once they left the building they went back to doing whatever the fuck they wanted. Mainly being self-serving assholes.

His father was a perfect example.

The man drank and fucked everything he could. He beat his kid and gambled like a son of a bitch. But, by God, he was at church every Sunday morning singing his balls off. Maybe it was his only redeeming quality. Maybe the old man was just hedging his bets on the whole heaven gamble. The big dice roll in the sky. Remo has his guesses, but he'll never really know. The old man didn't discuss much of anything when it came to his philosophy on life, let alone his thoughts on the afterlife. Lester seems to have a better a handle on the religion side of the equation. Maybe the man and/or woman upstairs can provide some light on the situation they're in. Perhaps a conversation with the Lord will allow Lester to loosen up his thoughts and allow him to come up with something that will help them.

Can't fucking hurt, thinks Remo.

"I have an idea," Lester says.

Remo sits up, all ears. The Lord did give him something.

"We need to kill her," Lester says. "You know, before she does us."

Remo blinks, then lies back down.

9

No one says a word at breakfast.

Only the sound of forks scraping plates. The occasional cough.

Little eye contact.

Lester says grace.

Cloris sits stone-faced, burning a spot on the table with her stare.

Remo thinks he should have run, but enjoys the food.

Hollis made eggs and bacon.

10

Everyone sits in silence in the living room.

Except for the brief conversation between Lester and Remo, and then Lester and the Lord, literally no one has said a word since the Chicken Pepperoni Incident. Inside, Remo is burning. He can't take it. He knows what's at stake and he can't let this stubborn pride, whateverthefuck wall of immeasurable bullshit, stand in the way of him getting clear with Cormac. Even if Cormac is completely full of shit and will never let him go.

Hope.

Hope is all he's got.

All that's left.

It's not great, can't sink your teeth into it, it's not what Remo wants, but it's where he is in his life. Hope that a son of a bitch CIA man will deliver on what he said he'd do.

Remo thinks he had stronger odds playing Russian roulette at Crow's.

Remo remembers something Chicken Wing told him once. Something Chicken Wing's older brother Dutch told him. He said, "We are the sum of our mistakes." At this particular moment Remo can't argue with that statement or the mathematics of it. The math on Remo has brought him to this place, without question. Here, now, in this room with these people at this moment in time.

Not much sense in fighting it, Remo decides.

Gotta roll with it, baby.

Remo clears his throat. "Okay. I'm not going to rehash what happened. I hope we can agree that shit was unfortunate, right?"

He looks around the room. He gets nothing verbal in the way of confirmation. Only tops of heads bobbing. Slightly. He'll take it.

"Look, we have to work together. Don't have a choice. None. The CIA doesn't give a single damn about our conflicts. They want us to go after the Mashburn place. Period. I don't like it. I don't want to do it. But it's what we've been tasked with, and dammit, if this is what we've got to do to get free then, dearest motherfuckers, that's what we're gonna do."

Heads pick up a bit.

Remo stands and continues. "Not the time for bullshit. Now, I have no idea what is waiting for us out there at this Camp Mashburn. I don't." Remo's feeling it now as he moves around the room. "We could be stepping face-first into a sausage grinder. But what I do know is that we are tough people. A real squad of badass individuals. Badasses capable of some badass shit, and together we can rain down some serious damn damage."

All eyes on Remo now.

"Most of us in this room have killed some of those piece of shit Mashburns." Remo pauses. "Sorry, Cloris."

Cloris shrugs. *No problema.*

Hollis grins.

Lester nods like he's gobbling up Remo's sermon with a fork.

"We've got tools on the floor and work to be done. Hard work, no question, but I have no doubt in my mind that we can put our bullshit in the rearview and end these motherfuckers. Am I right?"

Nods from his people.

"We got this?"

Hollis stands.

Lester follows.

They all look to Cloris. The only one left seated. She crunches some bacon she brought in from the kitchen.

"I've gone to war with these guys. I trust them with my life," Remo says, speaking directly to Cloris. "I'm going to extend that trust to you. Will you help us do this thing?"

Cloris's eyes slip over to her fiancé.

At first glance it seems she's looking to him for some form of confirmation. To the uneducated, it seems as if she's seeking some sign of what to do from her man, but Remo picks up on something else. He knows that look. It can be easily misinterpreted, but Remo sees right through it. Cloris doesn't need a damn thing from Lester in the way of confirmation. No. She's not looking for direction from her man, she's reading him. She's studying Lester. Picking his body language, his eyes, his expression apart to see if this is the same guy she fell in love with or if he's something else. Something she wants or doesn't want. Remo thinks of what Lester said last night.

About killing her.

About her killing all of them.

Did she stay up all night thinking about similar things?

Is she losing trust in Lester, or is Lester the only thing she does trust?

There's a lot going on behind those eyes of hers and Remo would be a fool to think he can decode it all, let alone trust any of it. Cloris isn't someone who's an easy read and Remo, despite all of his faults, is not a fool. Immature, impulsive and a complete asshole, but foolish Remo is not.

Cloris allows a smirk to break as she stands. "Let's do some work, bitches."

She extends a hand to Hollis. They shake with smiles. Somewhat guarded, fake, plastered-on smiles, but smiles nonetheless. She then hugs Lester, squeezing as tight as she can. Remo watches, letting his shoulders ease down, allowing his body to exhale. It might not all be honest, but it's better than a knife fight.

"Great. Great," Remo repeats, trying to convince himself everything is going to be fine.

Peace among the team.

For the moment at least.

11

The team of four stands in the living room, locked and loaded.

Ready to fight a war.

They are riddled with questions and they have little in the way of answers, but being armed seems to soothe some of the doubt. Glocks are tucked in shoulder holsters. Pistol-grip assault shotguns are slung over their backs. Kevlar vests strapped on tight and ARs placed in hand. Bullets, shells and magazines have been evenly distributed and secured.

Remo looks around to his team. He'll think of them as a team for lack of a better name, but he realizes they are far from united. The term *team* works better than thinking of them as Remo's Fun Bunch Death Squad That Can Barely Stand One Another. He did, briefly, think about giving them a proper name for the sake of unity. Maybe the War Eagles or Death from Above or simply Bad Motherfuckers, but nothing was gaining any traction in his mind, and he didn't see the need to put it up for a vote and muddy the already murky-as-fuck waters.

This isn't that type of deal.

There are no cheerleaders here.

No rah-rah shit up in here.

This is a team of rough and tumble folks who don't trust one another and, under any other circumstances, would rather kill each other than work together. Save, of course, for Cloris and Lester, but even those two might kill one another if this situation tilts a certain way. There are a lot of *ifs* floating around. Lester without question would off Cloris and even stated it as such. Remo isn't so sure about Cloris. She's the wild card. Love 'em, or kill 'em all? She might indeed murder every single one of them and grind their bones to toothpicks.

Who knows?

Not knowing is part of the journey, right?

"Fuck," Remo whispers to himself.

The only positive thing here is the fact everyone wants the same thing. There is a single want and need shared by all.

A common goal.

It's the one true binding agent of any team that's worth a shit.

For this team the common goal is plain, old-fashioned self-preservation. Self-preservation is stronger than oak, tougher than steel, and by God self-preservation is what is going to keep this ultra-psychotic, powder keg of unstable death machines in line. That can and should be enough to unite them.

At least that's what Remo is going with.

"All dressed up and nowhere to go," Remo jokes.

No one is laughing or smiling. Only blank looks and blinks fire off from his fully-armed traveling companions.

"We have somewhere to go," Cloris says with bite.

"Yeah. Really?" Hollis snaps.

"What do you mean, Remo?" asks Lester.

"It was a joke, people. An expression. I fucking know we fucking have somewhere to go. What I'm saying is I don't know where we are going dressed like we're going to attack Tony Montana's mountain getaway."

"Well, why didn't you just say that?" Cloris says, again with bite.

"Yeah, what's with the bullshit?" Hollis snaps.

"It's just kind of confusing. Can you say what you mean next time, Remo?" asks Lester.

Remo shakes his head, watching the other three exit the house onto the porch. A new concern spikes up from his anus, rocketing toward his mind. Has the common ground among them changed? Has it? It can't be. Nah, things can't go like that so quickly. Can it? Has the new true binding agent for this team become mocking Remo?

No.

This will not do.

Not by a damn sight.

As much as Remo wants the team to come together, being a dick to Remo, the leader, even if no one other than Remo has decided Remo is the leader, will not do. Being a dick to Remo is no way to start this adventure. It's damned divisive. Not binding at all.

"Fuck," Remo whispers to himself.

He stops cold.

Another thought slaps him. This one is more troubling than the previous thought. Much more disturbing than the notion that his new team—that's right, HIS team—is bonding over being unbridled dicks to him.

No. This new thought is worse.

Much worse.

This new thought needs to be resolved. As in now.

Remo sets down the AR and removes his shotgun, then staggers around the room like a frightened boy searching for his lost woobie. His mind fires off the most horrific of ideas. Panic rolling in like the strongest of tides. Hands shake. Head quakes. He flings couch cushions across the room. Shoves the coffee table aside. This thought that just occurred to Remo, but it's growing like an unstoppable tumor and it's the type of idea that can, and will, bury a man like Remo.

Catastrophic, if it is proven to be reality.

This can't be happening.

Remo fling-tosses the bearskin against the wall.

Good God no.

He races to the kitchen, throwing open cabinets left and right.

Swings the refrigerator door open wide, letting it slam against the wall.

Sweat begins to bead along his forehead. His heart rate is redlining. His hands shake more and more as an emotional earthquake shutters and rumbles inside of him. His back hits the kitchen wall. Sliding down to the floor, his eyes glaze over, forming lifeless pinholes looking out into the void. A thousand-yard stare sets in. Face a statue of fear.

Hollis steps in, taking note of Remo's feeble, fragile state. He starts to say something, stops, swallows, winces, then asks, "You okay, man?"

Remo mouths some words but no sound comes out.

"What?" Hollis asks.

More inaudible sounds from Remo.

Hollis leans down, getting closer.

"Where's the Johnnie Blue?" Remo says, grabbing Hollis by the collar. "Where's the Blue and the fucking Adderall?"

PART II

HIS SUFFERING IS THE KEY

12

Hollis helps Remo out the door and onto the porch, carrying him like a wounded soldier.

He sets him down in the rocking chair, letting him sink into the old, worn wood. Rocking gently back and forth, Remo's stare out into nothingness looks like that of a mental patient. The mountain air feels nice. There's a part of Remo that acknowledges it, but he's still melting down inside and that cannot be derailed by the niceties provided by Mother Nature.

"He gonna make it?" Cloris asks.

Hollis shrugs, then steps back inside to grab Remo's guns.

Lester takes a knee next to Remo as if he were consoling a dying man bound to a wheelchair. He touches his friend's hand and says, "It's all a bit much, isn't it? I know you're not a church man, but I find strength in the words." He pulls his Bible from his pack then thumbs to a certain spot. "Here. You'll dig this one." He reads, "Even though I walk through the darkest valley, I will fear no evil, for you are with me. Your rod and your staff, they comfort me."

Nothing from Remo.

Cloris can't believe what she's seeing.

She's watching her man, her master of disaster, quoting scripture in a caring, moving way. More to the point, he's quoting the word of the Lord in a caring, moving way toward the attorney who fucked him over and killed her brothers.

"Your rod and your staff, asshole," Hollis says, dropping the AR and shotgun on Remo's lap.

"What happened?" asks Lester.

"CIA doesn't supply booze and pills," Hollis says.

"Ooooo." Cloris sucks in through her teeth. "That fuckin' sucks, bro."

Lester thumbs through the pages, finding another verse. "Watch and pray so that you will not fall into temptation. The spirit is willing, but the flesh is weak."

Remo's eyes slip over to Lester.

"I think it's working," Lester says.

Remo's lips part. He whispers, "Lester?"

"Yes, Remo."

"Kill me."

"No, Remo."

"You told me once you were on a mission of mercy."

"I did and I am."

"Then I'm asking for you to shoot me. Now."

"Not what I meant."

"Then fuck the fuck off."

Cloris leans in and slaps the shit out of Remo.

Spit flies. Remo's lips immediately swell as the side of his face throbs. He can feel the heat of his skin trying to work itself back to normal. Cloris grabs Remo by the face, twisting it left and right, up and down, all while holding eye contact.

"I've got no scripture for you, jerkoff. No words of wisdom, comfort or salvation." Cloris moves in even closer to Remo's face, their noses almost touching. "What I've got, all I've got, is a job to do, and you're a part of that job. A big part. I can't do it without you, Remo. *We* can't do it without you."

Remo glances to Lester and Hollis, looking for their assistance.

There is none.

They stand a healthy distance away, both sharing a look of understood helplessness. As if watching the final minutes of a game where the score is 58 to 10. It's over, but it's not.

Cloris yanks Remo's face back over to hers. "You say these are your friends, then be one for fuck's sake. You say you love your son..."

Something inside Remo comes unhinged.

Like a lightning strike went off inside him.

He slaps her hands back and stands, letting the guns slip to the porch but staying in her face. His eyes locked on hers. Burning. Neither backing down.

"That's got nothing to do with you," Remo says.

"It's got everything to do with—"

"No. You don't talk about my son. Got shit to do with you."

"Good. So you do care about something. One thing, at least. Me? My one thing?" She looks over at Lester. "That's mine." She scrunches her nose at Hollis. "Fuck that guy."

Hollis puts his hands up. *What did I do?*

Cloris turns back to Remo. "You done with the alcoholic self-pity bit?" She raises her eyebrows and nods, trying to draw a confirmation from Remo.

He closes his eyes, then nods.

Cloris smiles. She bends down to the porch, thumps Remo's pecker with a flick of her finger, then picks up his guns and hands them to him. Remo takes the guns, ignores the pecker thump best he can, and tries to forget about his chemical needs.

Cloris steps back, points out in the distance like she's calling her shot. She's pointing toward a road that leads like a winding serpent into the mountains. There's a black Yukon parked at the base of the road. She turns back, checking out the faces of the team, smiles and shows them the keys in her hand.

They all share eyes.

Undefined looks flickering back and forth between them.

The same questions rip through all three of them: *How long did she have keys to that thing? What else is she not telling them? And, of course, what the fuck?*

Cloris steps off the porch, letting her foot crunch into the gravel and dirt. She slinks toward the Yukon like a heavily armed goddess of war. Hollis shrugs. Lester chews the inside of his cheek. Remo feels like he's falling off a cliff. His stomach drops. He feels sick as hell. Fresh out of good options, they each fall in behind her one by one, walking a line toward the Yukon. Not a word spoken. None needed.

They have reached a silent understanding.

We need her.

She's trouble.

We're fucked.

13

"Now that we're all friendly," Remo says, "could you please enlighten me as to what in the good fuck we're marching into?"

They've been huffing it up this road for some time now. To be fair, it turned into a dirt path a long time ago, and the team is starting to show signs of fatigue. They ditched the Yukon after the road narrowed and changed to dirt, rock and brush. Cloris said something about needing to be on foot for this part. Since then she's been leading them upward and onward as if she's heading toward the new gold rush. Pausing only briefly to grab ahold of Lester's hand occasionally. Thankfully, the temperature has been doing them a huge favor by not opening up the whoop-ass, but the sun has been shining down hard like God's spotlight for the hour or so they've been walking.

They've remained in silence for most of the trip. This journey into the heart of darkness. This team. This fellowship of questionable people. None of them felt the need to communicate during the drive up, and no one thought it was a great idea to ask questions when Cloris threw the Yukon in park behind some trees and led them up and into this insanely steep motherfucker of a path.

Remo, having endured the early stages of all sorts of withdrawal, is currently dealing with his own personal hell, and isn't enjoying this experience.

Not one damn bit.

The lack of booze and pills is not helping his mood or his ability to tackle a difficult physical activity with a smile. The shakes stopped about ten minutes ago, but he's sure they will be back with a vengeance. Sweat pours from his pores. It coats his skin and stings his eyes, no matter the cool mountain breeze. He can feel the red veins plumping up along his eyes. There's this unnerving sensation, as if ants are crawling all over the rest of him. Wiggling. Dancing. Having a little ant orgy. It escalates. The nonexistent ant horde sex party takes things up a notch. It's as if the ants got bored with doing each other and called in some fleas and ticks to spice things up a bit.

His left ear has clogged up as if someone jammed a doorstop inside it.

His mouth is dry as a drum.

His feet are swelling up to Hobbit-style proportions.

All of this is to say that Remo is not happy.

He's done. Done with this passive-aggressive silent treatment.

Done with playing nice. Just flat-out over the whole fucking thing.

"Cloris, I was addressing you with that question just a second ago. You. I was asking you. In case you were wondering," Remo says, pressing his agenda again. "Should I repeat it? Ask in a different way? More profanity perhaps? Less? Draw some pictures?"

Cloris tries to ignore him, but Lester can tell she's showing signs of breaking down. Remo has a way of doing that to people. Even people as tough to crack as Cloris.

"Cloris? I'm back here." Remo continues to dig at her.

She breathes deeply, bringing in long pulls of air through her nose. Her eyes burn. She feels her shoulders tense. Her body tightens.

"Cloris, no really, I'd like a word."

Cloris seethes.

"Perhaps I should bark or grunt in an attempt to mimic the native tongue of your fucked-up people."

Cloris spins around like an anger-fueled top. She jams her 9 mm between Remo's teeth. Her eyes pop wide. Crazy-person bulging. She breathes deeply in and out through her nose as she presses the gun deeper down Remo's throat. He starts to gag. Lester tries to pull her back. She slaps him back with a free hand.

Hollis pulls his gun, leveling it on her face.

Cloris shoots Hollis the finger then pushes her gun down harder. Deeper down Remo's throat.

He gags. His eyes water.

Cloris giggles.

Her face drops as she feels cold steel pressed against her temple.

Turning slightly, she finds Lester is holding his gun against her head. She can't believe it. Her expression flashes to that of a lost woman. Betrayal washes over her. Betrayed by the man she loves.

"I'm sorry, Buttercup," Lester says. "Need you to remove that gun from his mouth."

"Why?" she asks softly.

"I'm here to save him."

Cloris's eyes drift. It's hitting her now. She finally sees what she thought wasn't so. She wasn't sure before, maybe didn't want to truly consider it as a possibility. But now, with a gun to her head, she has no choice but to deal with the idea as a full-fledged reality.

Has she really lost him?

Is that possible?

This is not the man she knew. Clearly. Something has shifted him into this thing she can't understand. This... whatever he is now. This imposter posing like her Lester. She looks to Remo.

Remo winks at her.

He did this, she thinks. Not sure how, but she knows this lawyer, this fucker is responsible. The thought of pulling the trigger and blowing Remo's face away just on principle flashes across her mind, but she thinks better of it. Cloris removes her gun from his mouth, wipes the spit across Remo's chest, then returns it to its holster.

Lester lowers his weapon.

Hollis follows suit.

Everyone breathes normally again.

Remo can't help but smile. Feel a little giddy. His small victory.

The team is his again.

"We've got a little ways to go, but we're not that far," Cloris says with her head down. "There's a place up the road we can regroup, talk and form a plan or whatever." She looks up to Remo. "You asked what we are marching into?"

Remo nods, still grinning.

"Not sure. Never been inside. Daddy has been putting that place together for some time. A compound of sorts. A command center." Cloris locks into Remo's eyes. "You, Remo, you're our way in. They want you to die and die horribly for what you've done. What you did to my brothers and, more importantly, with the money. Cormac knew this, and that's why he came at you. You see, your suffering is the key to unlock the front door."

Remo swallows hard.

Cloris turns around, heading back up the path. "Come on now."

Hollis shrugs.

Lester puts a hand on Remo's shoulder. "It'll be fine."

Remo wishes the team would go back to not talking.

14

The team sits on some large rocks overlooking a mountain view.

The vastness.

The scope.

The overwhelming sight of blue skies, rolling clouds, forests of trees spanning up and around the towering monuments of former volcanic activity. Millions of years of nature's effort, front and center. It's a gorgeous sight to soak in, even for this crew.

Cloris sits perched on a massive stone with her eyes closed, letting the sun work its touch over her face. The winds gently run their fingers through her hair. A woman at complete peace. Lost in the moment. Letting her thoughts and concerns float and drift away. Lester watches her. Hard to get his read on the situation. He admires the Lord's wonderful canvas too, but Lester is still troubled by one of the Lord's children. One of the Lord's bat-shit crazy children. The one he's convinced will try to kill them all.

Hollis gets up, unzips and begins pissing on a tree.

The peacefulness of the surroundings do not match what's churning around inside Remo. In addition to really, really wanting a drink, he has Cloris's last statement rattling around in his skull.

"His suffering is the key."

That's what that woman actually said.

Remo watches her. Like Lester, but in a different way. He's trying to decode. Seems like he's spending a lot of time recently trying to crack this Cloris. She talked about Cormac using Remo for this. Using him to pull this team together, even if Remo didn't know he was doing it.

What the hell is the deal with Cormac?

Why is the CIA all over us?

Remo can think of several things, but nothing concrete. Earlier he thought it was only Crow back in NYC. He'd heard Crow had some dealings with gunrunners. Some international money laundering stuff. Nothing too insane, but maybe enough to get the CIA involved.

Maybe.

But not at this level. Not to this extent.

No way.

Cormac brought in a group of civilians to kill people. That's more than a garden-variety crime boy dipping his wick in international waters. Crow, at the max, was a mid-level crime lord with a fraction of his business overseas.

The Mashburns?

Are the Mashburns what Cormac has such a hard-on for?

Remo thinks hard. Punching and pulling away at the cobwebs of his mind. Moving old furniture and boxes out of the way in the dusty attic of his memory. He tries to remember if there was anything in the Mashburns' files that would bring in the CIA. Anything in their history that would bring in this brand of high heat.

Nope.

Nothing.

The Mashburns were all about smash-and-grab jobs. Banks. Armored car takedowns. They'd work over some drug dealers here and there. Move some powder. Roll a stash house. He heard about Chicken Wing going apeshit at a strip joint once. Dutch put a bouncer at a biker bar in a coma, while Ferris lit a bartender on fire. All crimes, sure, but nothing on a global scale. No immediate, external threat or clear and present danger to the security of these United States.

Maybe that's what's going on at this compound.

Maybe there's some big-time, big-money, international crime shit going on in there, and the Mashburn brothers and Cloris were on the outside of it all. Daddy Mashburn knew not to involve those wild cards in his bigger plans. They would only fuck things up, and Daddy Mashburn didn't want any of that.

Maybe this Daddy Mashburn is a global crime lord who slipped under the radar. The white whale of the law enforcement community. People like Cormac have been on him for years, but could never get their hands on him. Chasing. Fighting. Scouring the earth to find a way to bring this mastermind to justice, and now Remo is the key to making America safe again. That's right, Remo-Captain-Mother-Fucking-America-Cobb is here to make things right. Sleep safe kids. Remo's got this.

Remo stands up on top of his rock, letting the wind's fingers work through his hair.

His chest out.

He wishes he had a cape.

"You're so fucked," Hollis says, shaking his dick then zipping his fly. "These whacky psycho bastards are going to eat your liver, shit it out and feed it back to you."

Remo sits back down.

Thinks. Rubs his face.

Fuck.

Resets and reassesses the situation.

Remo scrambles up from his rock and hauls ass into the woods.

15

"Do we have a plan?" Remo asks as he picks a twig out from of his ear.

Cloris and the rest of the team side-eye a pissed off glance his way as they gather their weapons. None of them are happy with Remo at the moment. None of them wanted to drop everything and chase him out into the wild. He didn't make if very far, but still, it was an energy burn, and once they got to him he had a pretty embarrassing meltdown. There weren't any tears, but there was screaming, random profanity and panic.

Lots of panic.

Okay, fine, there were tears.

A lot of them.

Snot, too.

Cloris dove-tackled him to the ground after Remo made it about twenty yards or so into the thick trees. They rolled, tumbled and fought. Well, Remo tried to fight. He swung hard. Made it look good for a second or two. Then Cloris punched him in the nose. Only once. The fight ended shortly after it started. Lester then picked him up and carried him back down to where they were sitting. Hollis called

Remo a dumbass and mumbled something about fucking hating him.

Remo recognized that he panicked. He even apologized, which is something he doesn't do on a regular basis, and said he was fine now. Just a momentary lapse of reason. *It will never happen again*, he said. He explained that it's been a rough few days, plus him giving up the booze and the pills has caused him to not be himself. He said he won't do it again, won't even think about doing it again, and that they could count on it. Trust him. Take it to the bank. Remo is solid.

Then he ran like a child toward the woods, his arms flailing.

That time Hollis put out his forearm and clotheslined Remo in the throat, putting him on his back before he could make it very far.

Cloris appreciated that.

They are now all seated back on their respective rocks. Back to letting the wind's fingers work their hair. This time Hollis and Remo share a rock. Just in case.

"Because if we've got one, I'd love to hear it. Your plan," Remo says, picking a bug out of his shirt. "I mean some plan other than my suffering being the main focus of it."

"It's only fair," Lester says to Cloris. "Not only to Remo, but to all of us to know what you're thinking, here."

"Yeah," Hollis says. "We need to know what you know."

Cloris lets her eyes glide over all of them. Taking in each of their faces. She sighs, letting her shoulders drop. "I don't know much," she says. "I know Daddy's been working on this for a while. I know there are probably a lot of tough boys up in there, and I know they'll want Remo. Like in a bad kind of way."

"You're his daughter," Remo says. "Why can't you just walk in there and talk to these animals?"

"Because I left when Daddy probably needed me the most. The cops were all over us. His boys slipped up. Couple dead and one headed to prison, or so we thought," Cloris explains. "Also, I told him to fuck off the last time we spoke."

"Oh, good," Remo says.

"Smart," Hollis says.

Lester thinks it's better to stay out of this.

"Never heard anything about Daddy Mashburn while I was on the brothers' case," Remo says. "Never saw a file or any kind of record or any mention of him."

"He's never been caught," Cloris says.

"Never? How's that possible?" Remo asks.

"He's pretty good at shit," she says.

"Also means he doesn't leave loose ends," Hollis says, thinking out loud. "Witnesses get gone quick. He keeps his people close and kills the ones he thinks might turn and, oh yeah, he hides in the mountains like a frightened little bitch."

"Daddy doesn't hide," Cloris fires back.

Hollis nods, letting it go. He's learning how to talk to her. Picking up on where to go and where not to. He looks to Remo. Remo picks up on it too.

"So, Cloris, what *is* your plan?" Remo asks again. "Please share. I'm guessing you need me as a peace offering of sorts. That the thing?"

Cloris nods.

"That's how I'm the key to the front door?"

She nods again.

"Then what?" Remo asks.

She shrugs.

Remo shrugs back, mocking her.

She shrugs again with a *fuck you* smile this time.

"Really," Remo says, "that's what you've got? Well fuck me all over the place. That is some amazing shit you've got there."

Lester puts a calming hand on Remo. Cloris giggles.

"Well," Hollis chimes in, "how far out can they see us? I mean do they know we're here?"

She shrugs.

"Can you join the fucking conversation?" Remo asks.

"I don't know," Cloris says. "Daddy's not a huge technology guy, but he's got people who are. I picked this spot to hang because I thought it was far enough out. Based on what I know about the old place, this was a good distance away. By at least a couple hundred yards or so."

Lester looks around. "Good tree coverage too. Not sure he's got the tech to see us here."

"Okay," Hollis starts up again. "Let's assume they don't have eyes on us. Our best bet is to have you take Remo in. A peace offering from his daughter. You've been away and you were an ungrateful child, but you're back with a prize. A gift for Daddy. You're offering up that slimy, piece of shit dickhole who killed your brothers."

"Easy now," Remo says.

Cloris is all ears, liking what she's hearing.

Lester leans in, digging what Hollis is laying down.

"Once you're in," Hollis says, "Lester and I will give it ten minutes and come in with guns blazing."

Silent beat. The breeze blows.

Cloris scrunches her nose. "That it?"

"Yeah, that's it," Hollis says with a look of pride.

"Kinda lean, don't ya think?" she says.

"Not much of plan," Lester says.

"I've heard this plan," Remo says. "It's the same bullshit plan you had with Crow in New York, and you didn't fucking show. I almost got killed. Shit, man. I almost killed myself for fuck's sake."

"It was a good plan then, and it's a good plan now. Daddy Mashburn's people are going to search you, just like at Crow's, so you can't contact us and tell us where to go or what the situation is. Not to mention," Hollis says, tilting his head toward Cloris, "she's the one who fucked the Crow thing all up."

Lester nods.

"Me?" Cloris chirps.

"Yes, you. You beat the piss out of me and your boy with a two by four and left us facedown in an alley right before we were headed in to save this fucking prick."

Remo holds his hands out. *What the fuck, man?*

"How in the hell was I supposed to know that shit?" she says.

"Well, she's here now at least, and she can't fuck this one up," Lester says, pauses, then, "yet."

Cloris fires him a look. Lester shuts down, realizing his stupidity. He goes with the proven method of slumping over with eyes looking toward the ground.

"Seven," Remo says. "Seven minutes."

"Why seven?" Cloris asks.

"Better than ten," Remo says.

"Why not six or eight?" she asks.

"Don't be stupid," Remo says.

Lester puts a hand out, holding back Cloris.

"Fine. Fuck it," Hollis says. "Seven minutes and we'll come in."

Hollis looks around the circle. Slowly the nods roll in, one by one. They are all in, more or less. The team of four sits in silence. Each of them staring out over the mountain view. Just as gorgeous as it was before they started this conversation, before Remo tried to haul ass away, but it doesn't have the same feeling as it did a few minutes ago. A bird soars. The breeze blows. The sun shines down on them.

"You better fucking show this time," Remo mutters.

"Don't doubt my shit, fuckhead," Hollis says.

More silence.

Cloris holds Lester's hand. He lets her. He tries to not like it. Cloris shares a flash of eyes with him. Sparks a dangerous thought. A feeling. A feeling that there's still a place for her in there somewhere. Something inside Lester still wants her. Wants this. Remo sees all this. Lester senses Remo's questioning look and drops her hand.

Cloris rolls her eyes. *Why is this so damn difficult?*

"What about the kill squad?" Lester asks. "What about Cormac's people?"

Cloris is pissed about the hand dropping but lets it go, for the moment.

"I can't signal them in until I know where Daddy Mashburn is," Remo says. "They gave me this thing." He pulls a tiny device from his chest pocket. "I'm going to hide it under my ball sack."

Cloris winces in disgust, like she swallowed a bug.

"Oh, excuse me, *delicate flower*," Remo snips. "Why don't you try fucking the faith out of Lester again."

Cloris pops up. Lester holds her back, again. He knows if she wanted to she could easily bust through is arm block. She sits back down, but still pissed.

"When I find him," Remo continues, now speaking directly at Cloris, "I remove the device from under my sweaty beanbag and crack it open. That will send a signal out and then they come riding in like cowboys from hell."

"Okay. So what if you see him in the first minute?" Hollis asks.

"What?" Remo fires back.

"Well, if the kill squad comes riding in, " Hollis says, "should we still wait ten—"

"Seven," Remo says.

"Sorry, seven. Should we still wait seven minutes?"

Remo leans back on that one. The rest of the team share looks. None of them know. Not for sure.

"How about this." Remo stands. "Seven minutes unless you hear some serious shit going down."

"Do I get a definition of *serious shit*?" Hollis asks.

"Yeah, that one's a little vague," Cloris says.

"Yeah," Lester adds.

"Gunshots," Remo says. "If you hear gunshots you should engage."

"As in multiple?" Hollis ask.

"No, one, motherfucker," Remo barks. "You hear one gunshot you need to storm in directly."

Hollis thinks, then looks over, raising his eyebrows to Lester as if silently asking, *You cool with this?* Lester puts his hands up, nodding as if to say, *Sure, fuck it.*

They both look to Remo and give him the nod.

Remo gives a half-smirk to Cloris. It's still his team, dammit.

Cloris throws him a stare that would kill a thousand people in their tracks. Hollis and Lester start packing up their weapons, not paying attention to the little moment Remo and Cloris are having between them.

Remo sits, frozen off Cloris's crazed expression.

Cloris swipes her finger across her throat and blows him a kiss.

Remo swallows and remembers a fact he'd forgotten. Something he should never forget. He's a complete asshole and he cannot, will not, allow a Mashburn to out asshole him.

He stands, unzips, drops his pants, raises his ball sack ever so slightly then sticks the CIA device safely underneath his boys. All this with a goofy-as-hell smile plastered on his face, never allowing his eye contact with Cloris to break.

Her expression fades. Chin drops. Her eyes burn.

"Remo, dude." Hollis sighs. "Enough with the balls."

16

Cloris and Remo push their way up a steep incline.

The area is thick with trees and brush. The rocky ground makes for tricky travel, seconds away from turning an ankle or landing face-first in the dirt.

Feels like it's hard to find enough air to suck in.

Their lungs burn. Hurts to breathe.

The dirt path that once resembled a road disappeared about an hour ago. It's been straight slogging up through the wild ever since. Cloris removed Remo's guns and handed them off to Lester and Hollis to hang on to. An armed Remo doesn't fit the narrative. Besides, she likes him feeling defenseless as hell. Makes her happy.

Their thighs burn. Calves balled up hard like concrete. Remo's limbs feel the spike of pain much more than hers. She's got younger muscles and joints and probably, even though he'd never admit it, she is simply a better athlete. One thing they share is the shortness of breath. The higher altitude, along with the physical demands of huffing it up the mountain, is wearing them both down fast. Their labored breath plumes out in front of their mouths. Each one is harder and harder to draw in and out. The temperature seems to have dropped dramatically since they started this climb.

The good news?

Remo has long forgotten about his alcohol and pill withdrawal issues. That time has passed. It's hard now for him to separate the physical pain caused by this little adventure and the longing for booze and big pharma. Everything hurts. Life is simply one big ball of hurt. His limbs, his lungs, his brain and pounding heart are all demanding his attention and sympathy, regardless of the cause.

"How much more of this shit?" Remo asks.

"Not much," Cloris says. "I think."

"There has to be another way up here. A road or something. This is insane."

"Nope. No other way."

"This sucks."

"Think it sucks now, wait 'til we get there."

That shut Remo up. He had almost forgotten for a minute where they were headed. Truth is, this isn't much fun for her either, but she'll never let Remo know how much she's hurting too. Fuck that. She'd rather die before admitting weakness to this man. This *lawyer.*

She places a hand on a tree, feeling for something in the bark. Looking up and around, there's something she recognizes. The place, the compound, it's close. So close. She stares up along a row of trees, then looks behind her, and then up ahead again. Yeah, she knows it's not far now. Cloris stops Remo and pulls out a set of zip tie handcuffs. Remo's eyes pop wide.

"Fuck. That," he says.

"Got to, bro."

"No, *bro*, ya really don't."

"Think. Am I really supposed to make them believe I've tracked you down and dragged you in from New York without any kind of restraint? You think that tells a convincing story? Oh yeah..."

She punches Remo in the nose, then the eye, and then the nose again. Remo stumbles back holding his swelling face. Blood slipping through his fingers.

"What the fuck, lady!" Remo yelps.

"Gotta look good. Look like you put up a fight."

"Couldn't try convincing them with your words? Fuck!" he says, struggling to hold back his beaten-down man-tears.

She rolls her eyes. *This fucking guy's killing me.*

She wishes Lester were here with her now. He'd talk some sense into this asshole. This asshole *lawyer.* Lester and Hollis are staying back a bit, letting Cloris and Remo make their way, and then advancing forward bit by bit so they don't trigger any attention. According to the finer points of the plan, Lester and Hollis have stopped a ways back. Out of sight. Keeping a safe distance from where Cloris thinks the compound is located.

"Trust, Remo. Trust me," Cloris says, holding out the zip ties. "This is all about trust. You trusting me, and them trusting that I'm doing what I tell them I'm doing."

Remo listens, but doesn't offer up his hands for the ties either.

"If they don't believe our story, then this thing is over before it starts. They will kill us both," she says.

"You think they'd kill you too?"

"It's a strong possibility. They'll kick the shit out of me and throw me in a hole at the minimum."

She takes his hands in hers and speaks softly. "This is it. Up there not much farther is a house, perhaps a fortress, full of people who want to pull you to pieces. If you bolt, the CIA will pull you to pieces. The only thing stopping both of those things from happening is me and the two guys back there."

Remo knows damn well she's right. He hates it, but knows everything she's saying is true. Trusting is not something that comes easily to a man like Remo. In his defense, he hasn't had much reason to trust anyone, given the company he's kept. Certainly no reason to trust this woman, but he knows he really has no choice.

He gives a defeated nod, offering up his wrists to her.

Cloris mouths a silent *thank you* then slips the zip ties over his wrists, securing them tightly. "Used to use these all the time on Lester, " she says, then spanks Remo's ass hard as she can. "Before he found Jesus and shit."

Remo swallows hard, pushing some blood down his throat.

He remembers Lester's concerns about Cloris killing all of them. There's this look in her eyes. It comes and goes. Hard to tell what triggers it exactly. There have been times when the trigger was obvious. When she wanted to kill Hollis at dinner that look in her eyes made perfect sense, but it's here now too. Like it's this wandering wave of whacko that comes and goes with the wind. Sometimes it makes some sense, but most of the time it's just plain fucking whacko for the sake of being whacko. Remo wonders if there's a way to harness that power. To bottle up her whacko and release it when necessary, like popping a bottle of bubbly on special occasions. He wonders if Lester knows that's not possible. Maybe he's tried. Remo wonders if this is why Lester thinks she will kill them all. Then realizes how pointless it is to wonder while being zip-tied by a crazy person.

"Shit," Remo mutters to himself.

Cloris grabs him by the cuffs and leads Remo upward and onward. This is the hardest part of their trip. Remo is completely relying on Cloris to help him balance and move. He can barely use his upper body and certainly can't use his hands because of the zip ties. Didn't think it was possible, but it seems as if the terrain has actually gotten steeper and more challenging. Harder and harder to churn their thighs upward and onward. They huff and puff for maybe twenty more minutes and then Remo stops.

His feet stick in the ground like a statue.

He sees it.

Up just above a ridge of rocks and behind some trees is a fence. A big one. A seven-foot high fence made of steel with razor wire protecting its top. Cloris stops as well, but her awe has more of a sense of appreciation to it than Remo's *what the fuck* expression. This is the first time she's seen it too. The first time she's seen it as a fully realized thing. Her daddy had talked and talked about it. It was a dream of his to construct a command center in the mountains. Cloris thought her daddy had watched too many Bond movies and wanted an evil lair. Maybe she was right, but it is a sight to see in the flesh. She can't help but be taken aback by the reality of her daddy's vision sitting in front of her.

To the uninformed, it looks like a really nice mountain getaway for the rich and famous. Maybe a lodge of sorts. Wood and stone accent the walls and the roof appears to be made of metal. Of course the razor wire on top of the fence takes some of the homeness off of the place, but it does have an "upscale cabin out in the woods" vibe to it. The fence seems to be a box, with the edges cutting back toward the east and west. What Cloris and Remo are standing in front of seems to be the main entrance of the place, measuring about half a football field wide.

From the angle they are standing at they can see the upper portion of the place. The second floor. Might even be the third. They can't see it all because of the fence, but the place does seem huge. As if a mansion had been dropped by helicopter on the side of the mountain.

Remo sees a beefy bastard with a sniper rifle on the deck.

Jumping back, Remo tries to hide behind a tree.

Cloris sees the beefy sniper too. She smiles and turns to Remo. "Oh, that's Ronnie. He's cool. Worked for Daddy for years. Just stick with me and he shouldn't put a bullet in your skull."

There's a flurry of crunches on the ground. Whiffs of tree limbs.

They both freeze, stopping dead in their tracks.

Feels like the sounds are rushing toward them from all directions. Something or someone is moving their way fast.

No time to run or hide. The sounds are closing in. Rolling on top of them.

Before Remo can process exactly what's happening, a blur of humanity blankets them, surrounding them in a circle. Guns, too many to count, leveled at their heads. A shotgun barrel rests on Remo's nose.

The silence booms.

Time crawls.

Seconds seem like hours.

A bird chirps.

A massive man with head void of hair moves in, parting the gun-toting crowd that has wrapped around Remo and Cloris.

Cloris giggles. "Hi, Daddy."

PART III

BEFORE THE MONSTER RIPS YOU APART

17

H ollis and Lester have taken positions among the trees.

Lester is hidden behind a wide spruce.

Hollis has climbed up the same tree, perching himself on a large limb with an ideal sightline. Reminds him of the old days. He's taken the lives of several people while perched like a bird on a limb. Using the scope on his AR as a telescope of sorts, he scans the area straight ahead of him. He's been watching Cloris and Remo best he can through the foliage and wilderness. Seconds ago he witnessed them get bum-rushed by a pack of heavily armed bad guys. There was one, bigger than the rest, who was clearly in charge. Hollis is guessing that is none other than Daddy Mashburn.

Hollis thinks of taking a shot and ending this thing.

Drop Daddy Mashburn right here. Right now.

Places his finger on the trigger, truly considering removing the proverbial head of the snake.

He stops.

He's never fired this particular gun before. Even though he's very familiar with ARs, you never know a weapon until you dance with it a bit. He also knows the odds of pulling off a perfect headshot a hundred-plus yards away through heavy foliage, mountain air and a touch of wind with an unfamiliar assault rifle is a dicey proposition at best.

So he removes his finger from the trigger.

Takes a deep breath, then waves down to Lester, giving him a thumbs-up.

Lester nods and immediately starts his watch's timer to count-down from seven minutes to zero. He returns the thumbs-up to Hollis.

Hollis goes back to watching Cloris and Remo. They are now being lead through the steel gates of the compound. It only opens up a crack for them, just enough for everybody to slip inside the walls. It wasn't much information, but certainly enough for Hollis to under-stand this wasn't going to be easy. A seven-foot steel fence with razor wire and a steel gate that more than likely has some armed dickheads behind it is a challenge. Also, that pack of bad guys knew Cloris and Remo were there, so they have some kind of sensors or surveillance around the place.

Not the toughest test Hollis has faced, but it's a challenge none-theless. He immediately starts making some calculations in his battle-brain about the equipment he and Lester have. They have guns, of course, and some explosives. He tries to determine if the charges they have are enough to blow the gate. Of course this doesn't solve the problem of what's behind the gate.

Are there two dozen dickheads in there, or two hundred?

Will the gates fall and Lester and Hollis be met by a wave of bullets?

Will Hollis ever see his wife and kids again?

Hollis shakes his head hard, trying to clear that shit out.

No time to think of them.

Not now.

Cormac slipped him a note when Remo wasn't looking. Hollis hasn't told any of the team about it. Remo would go apeshit. He thinks he's the leader. Don't make Hollis laugh. Hollis has struggled with keeping the Cormac note from them since the second it was handed to him. He doesn't like secrets among his team. For many reasons, Hollis is still a man of his word, and believes in being straight with people, especially those he's going to war with. To be clear, for better or worse Lester, Cloris and Remo qualify. They are a team. *Dammit.*

Also, Hollis doesn't know if he can trust Cormac in any way, shape or form. Hollis wanted to talk to Remo privately, because Remo seems to be the one who's had the most face time with Cormac. Hollis respects Remo's ability to read people, even though he's been off recently, and Hollis knows Remo to be sharp when playing the people game. There just hasn't been much time for a one-on-one, private conversation.

The note from Cormac simply said: *Kill Daddy Mashburn = Hollis gets his family back.*

Hollis deeply wants this to be true. It's hard for your logical brain to overpower your emotions. He'd kill Daddy Mashburn and a thousand others like him if he could go back. Turn back the clock. Go back to the life he had only a few days ago. A life with his wife and kids. A normal, good life. A life like before Remo came to his door. A life void of Remo? A man can dream.

Fucking Remo.

Hollis continues scanning the area, then stops cold.

Through his scope he sees something.

He has another man in his sights.

Another man with a scope. A beefy bastard. A sniper pointing a McMillan TAC-50 directly at him. Hollis knows this gun too.

Very familiar with it.

"That's disappointing," Hollis whispers.

18

Remo and Cloris are escorted into the compound by Daddy Mashburn and his armed friends.

The gate rolls to a close behind them with a clank of steel that leaves a bone-chilling sound rattling around in Remo's ears. His heart pounds, but he keeps his eyes glued on Cloris. He wants to take in her every move. Wants to know exactly how she acts around these people. Around her father. Her facial expressions. The tone in her voice. These are the things that will help Remo form a moderately informed decision about her.

Is she nervous?

Relaxed, like there's nothing wrong?

More to the point, is she full of shit and playing all of them—Remo, Hollis, Cormac, even Lester? Is her relationship with Daddy Mashburn really strained, or was that all prefabricated bullshit? Perhaps Cormac and Cloris are playing Daddy and the whole fucking lot of them. The possible combinations of mindfucks Cloris is capable of right now is reaching lotto levels.

Cloris blows Remo a kiss.

Remo's butt puckers.

"You did it, honey," Daddy Mashburn says, giving his special girl a big, special hug. A tear rolls down his smiling face. "You really did it. You found this piece of shit legal eagle cocksucker." Daddy Mashburn jams his sausage finger into Remo's chest. "You have no idea how long I'm going to take killing you."

Remo's stomach drops.

Daddy Mashburn hugs Cloris again. Squeezes her even harder this time.

Remo reaches for his balls. Under his balls, to be exact.

A gunshot cracks from above.

19

The tree explodes above Hollis's head.

He jumped a fraction of a second before the .50 caliber round turned the upper section of the tree into toothpicks. Tumbling, twisting, crashing, Hollis absorbs every thwap and whip of the limbs on the way down. He hits the open air, freefalling down, down and down.

Hollis thinks of his family again.

What he wouldn't give to get back to them.

Fucking Remo.

As he float-tumbles toward the ground, he shakes Remo from his head and decides now is the perfect time to think of his family. He'd like to have some pleasant thoughts before his body makes impact with the hard earth below him.

He had a fall like this in Hong Kong a few years ago. No trees, but he hit the street hard from roughly the same height. He managed to peel himself off the concrete and kill four people with a fork, but he spent the better part of six months laid up in a hospital afterward. He was younger then. Healed faster then. A man north of forty doesn't snap back that way anymore.

This is going suck so bad, he thinks.

He's fairly sure Cloris fucked them all over.

He whispers an apology to his wife and kids.

Lester catches Hollis, or at least tries to. More like he slows him down slightly by breaking his high-speed tumble to the ground. Hollis slams into Lester like a piano dropped from a building. Lester's knees buckle under the crushing force and weight of Hollis, sending them both down hard to the dirt like a couple two-hundred-pound sacks of sod. It's not pretty. A salad of legs, elbows and arms without grace or a hint of fun, but Hollis is alive and relatively okay. It was painful to be sure, and he'll feel it more tomorrow or later today, but the results of the fall would have been far worse had Lester not been there for him.

As Hollis lies there on top of Lester with his eyes looking skyward, his mind slams into place. He realizes quickly the reality of Lester being there for him. Something very clear hits Hollis like a baseball bat to the face.

Lester risked himself to help Hollis.

This is not something to take lightly.

Hollis and Lester were moments away from killing one another just a few days ago. There was no trust. No bond. No way the two of them even liked one another. Couldn't even hold a simple conversation. But still, Lester risked his well-being to save him.

Hollis knows this is on him.

Knows damn well he should have checked for snipers.

It's the first thing he should have done. He underestimated the enemy and that's a sin that cannot be forgiven where Hollis is from. He's better than that. He let the shitstorm he's currently in with Remo and company cloud his training and experience. He let all the things that have happen with Crow and Cormac, the Mashburns and Cloris, and, yes, fucking Remo, stop him from being what he is—a weapon. A trained man of murder. A certified badass.

Right now, he's a stack of meat and bone laid out on top of a criminal man of the Lord. He allowed all the crazy get the best of him. He allowed a crazy woman to get the upper hand. Both at the house last night and just now. He let the sadness over his family dull his edge.

He let the outside world creep into his battle-brain and that shit has to stop. Right fucking now.

Lester grunts something.

"Thank you," Hollis says, almost too quiet to hear.

Lester grunts something that could be *you're welcome.*

"I gotta say two things before I get off of you," Hollis says. "First, I was wrong. You're good people."

Another grunt.

"Second, I think your girl is going to fuck us over."

Silence.

Another gunshot crack sounds from above taking more of the tree apart. Bark and chunks of wood rain down all over them. Hollis rolls, pulling Lester along with him. A massive hunk of tree stabs into the ground where they were lying a half-second ago. Sticks in the ground looking a lot like a wooden tombstone.

Hollis and Lester are now face-to-face. Eyes locked. Goofy grins spread across their faces. It's as if they just communicated telepathically. Something just occurred to them at the exact same time.

"That was two shots," Lester says.

Hollis nods. "Yes, yes it was."

"We were supposed to go in after one."

"We're late."

Lester's eyes flare. "Let's go kill some bad guys."

20

A second shot rips, echoing from above.

Remo continues to finger-dig under his balls looking for the device Cormac gave him. It's difficult, given that his hands are cuffed with zip ties, but the CIA death squad is very much needed right now, and their presence would be deeply appreciated.

"You said you would grab the asshole attorney and you did it," Daddy Mashburn says, beaming with pride. "Now, I assume Ronnie is hammering away at some people who tailed you."

His expression slams to ice cold. Takes Cloris off guard.

"People you let track you," he says. "Let track you to here."

His face goes hard. Angry. Blood boiling under the skin.

"Here. You know what this place means to me. How hard I've worked."

Cloris recoils a bit, a child being scolded by her father. Her chin quivers as she says, "I didn't see anybody—"

Daddy Mashburn slaps her to the ground.

Remo takes note while fidgeting with his nuts. Perhaps she didn't fuck them all over. It's possible she's playing a different game.

What the hell is she doing?

Is she playing us or is she playing Daddy?

The CIA?

Or all of us?

Cloris's face bounces off the dirt. Had to hurt like hell, but she manages a smile along with a wink that only Remo can see. *That wasn't a mistake. She knowingly did something, but again, what the hell is she doing?* Remo thinks. He's highly confused by what's going on with Cloris right now, but not half as confused as he is with the fact he can't find that goddamn thing under his hairy beanbag.

"Find who her dumb ass led to us and put 'em in the ground," Daddy Mashburn barks to his boys, then looks down to his daughter. "Thanks for the lawyer, but you're truly a fucking disappointment."

Daddy Mashburn and the others scatter with weapons ready. Two know to stay behind and keep watch on Cloris and Remo. They take positions standing over Cloris with eyes on Remo. They don't know what to make of Remo. They simply watch as he has his cuffed hands jammed down his pants.

"Jesus, man," one of Mashburn's boys says. "Show some class."

Cloris springs up with a tactical SOG knife gripped in her fist. She whips around like a spinning ball of whirling violence that just got her string pulled. Slits both of their throats wide open in one single rip of the blade. Their bodies flop to the ground, necks spitting crimson, dropped and bleeding out in a blink of an eye.

Remo freezes at the sight of it. Stuck on pause.

"Well, get the damn thing already," she says, nodding to his balls.

Remo snaps back to reality. He's getting better with the all the blood, guts and blinding violence being played out in front of him, but it still takes him a second to get unstuck from the sight of it. He goes back to searching his undercarriage. Same results. It's very frustrating. He's doing the best he can, dammit. The zip ties are cutting into him, not to mention his focus has been slowed by all the pumping, spilling blood in front of him. He feels his sweaty boys slip and slide between his struggling digits. Gliding over the tips of his fingers.

"I... I..." he stammers. "My balls. My fingers. I fucking..."

Cloris rolls her eyes.

Pussy.

Wasting no time, she drops to her knees, unzips his pants, and shoves his balls hard upward like she was stowing a carry-on in an overhead bin. It takes a second, but she zeroes in and yanks the device from Remo's trembling crotch. The adhesive gives a rip taking a bit of skin and hair with it. Upon under-nut-release, Remo buckles over. Spins twice then topples over like a bowling pin, landing with his face a few inches from the gushing, recently cut throats.

Cloris closes her eyes. Thinks of Lester.

Whispers a quick prayer. Been a long time, but she thinks she did it right.

She snaps the CIA device in half. With her eyes still closed, as clearly and calmly as can be, she says, "Burn it down," into a tiny round black thing inside the snapped device.

"Come on in, boys," Cloris says as her eyes pop wide open. "Come kill Daddy so I don't have to."

Through the pain Remo recognizes the crazed look in her eyes.

"Fuck me," he whispers.

21

L ester and Hollis move quickly up the mountain.

They try to exercise as much caution as they can manage without reducing the speed of their charge. Lester follows Hollis's lead. He's learning from Hollis. He studies his moves. Hollis makes subtle tilts, takes smooth angles and does not waste movements. These are moves a highly trained killer makes.

Lester is not too proud to learn from others. He would usually charge face-first into this type of situation with guns blazing like he was shoved right into *The Wild Bunch*. Hollis has done that before, but only as a last resort.

Hollis is moving forward, claiming territory inch by inch with his AR scanning the area. He takes a position behind the largest tree he can find.

He nods for Lester.

Lester mimics the move, but passes Hollis, taking a tree about ten yards farther up ahead. They are trying to scan and clear chunks of the landscape while pushing their way toward the compound. As if the two of them were carving up the mountain into manageable bite-size pieces. They can somewhat safely assume the danger is in front of them, so their zone of bad shit is minimized somewhat.

Hollis spins out from the tree as Lester stops. Something catches his eye up ahead. A movement. A sound. Hollis takes his position behind a tree directly next to Lester. Hollis points up ahead. Lester nods then raises his AR along with Hollis. In almost perfect harmony they look through their scopes, pointing in the same direction—the front of the compound.

There's a sound of rolling wheels along metal. They see the gate opening.

Four, armed, tatted-up crime boys rush out.

A large, bald man steps out behind them.

Tilting up, they see the beefy bastard sniper above. Hollis lines him up about to take him out, but stops. The sniper is turning away from their direction. He takes aim to the west side of the compound. Something new has his attention.

Tilting down, Hollis sees the CIA kill squad securing explosive charges to the west-side wall, moments away from breaching the compound.

A wave of rapid-fire bullets carves up the bark and ground around Hollis and Lester. They spin hard back behind their respective trees. They share a glance. Amid the punishing firepower, the two men who were forced into teamwork, wedged into respect, and jammed into a friendship look to one another. This is it. This is their world. It's not a pretty or perfect or a clean place to live. It's more of the dirty, ugly and shitty variety, but it's a world they've learned to excel in.

They nod.

They spin.

They open fire.

22

G unfire erupts beyond the wall.

Cloris and Remo turn to one another. Eyes wide. Mouths open.

It's starting. They both think of Lester and Hollis out there in the woods.

The west wall explodes.

The CIA kill squad storms in, draped all in black. Every muscle attached to every member has an assignment. A task. Not a single move wasted. Not a breath taken in without a plan. One member of the squad ever so slightly turns upward and fires two controlled bursts of three rounds apiece.

The beefy bastard sniper slumps, falls, then lands to the ground in a broken, bloody mess.

The four-member kill squad rushes in with amazing efficiency toward Cloris and Remo. Like a small pack of highly disciplined wolves. Scanning up, down and around the compound while moving in a spread out, yet still tight formation.

Remo lets his shoulders relax. He feels a huge weight being lifted off his chest. This is almost over. There are a lot of loose ends, and he has to trust somebody he can't trust, meaning

Cormac, but this feels like hope to him, or least a mutated version of it. Hope that he can get out from under this thing. He can leave this all far behind if he can only stay alive. There's hope.

Hope he can have a life with Sean in it.

The kill squad circles Cloris and Remo with one of them, the leader, moving close to Remo, conversation close, but still scanning the area with his HK416 held tight.

"Daddy Mashburn?" the kill squad leader asks Remo.

"He went out the gate," Remo says. "But I have a question."

The leader, completely ignoring Remo, gives a hand motion to his squad. They roll like water, moving on toward the gate. Remo grabs the leader's arm. The leader lands a quick, lightning elbow strike to Remo's nose then jams his HK onto Remo's forehead. The nose strike restarts the blood flow from the tag to the nose he took earlier from Cloris.

"Wait. Shit, man," Remo says, spitting blood but still holding on to his arm. "Tell me. What does the CIA want with me?"

The leader shakes his arm loose.

Remo, despite his better judgment, grabs his arm again. This time he dodges the elbow jab. "Ha, motherfucker."

Two other kill squad members slam him to the ground, putting gun barrels on him.

"He does that again? Shoot him," the leader says.

"Tell me, dammit. What the hell does the CIA want with me? Is it global? Guns? Money laundering? What? What the fuck?" Remo pleads, nearing a breakdown. "Just tell me. I want out. I want a normal, real life."

The leader starts to move away.

"Please. How do I get free of Cormac? For my son."

"You never get free of that guy," the leader says as he storms away with the rest of the squad following close behind him.

Cloris helps Remo to his feet. She wipes the blood off her SOG blade with his sleeve. That hope Remo was feeling has emptied. Spilled out into the bloody dirt. His face is void. As if he were a robot that had simply been turned off. Cloris looks into his eyes. She waves her hand back and forth in front of them.

Nothing.

She tries again, using both hands.

Nothing.

She slaps him as hard as she can.

Non-responsive.

She runs her tongue over her teeth and says, "Not the time for this shit, man." She points toward the gate as the kill squad charges hard toward it. "We need to fucking engage. Like now."

Remo's eyes drill a hole into a space in the universe that only he can see.

Cloris picks up a Glock off a dead body and jams it into Remo's hand. She cuts his zip tie cuffs free. Remo lets the gun slip and fall from his fingers.

"Suit yourself," Cloris says as she steps away, "but I promise the one sure way to never see your son again is for you to die."

The gunfire outside the walls rages on.

Cloris's words hang in the air. Remo can almost see them typed out in front of him, as if they were in a cartoon comic book bubble pointing from her lips. He knows she's right.

He digs deep. Real deep. Pushing all his self-pity aside, and there's a lot, he starts to move. He'll get back to it later, he's sure.

"Wait," Remo says, moving towards the Glock. "Need a little something."

Cloris grins.

An engine roars.

Remo stands straight up.

Their heads whip toward the sound coming from the east side of the compound. The kill squad leader holds up his fist and turns, facing the east side along with the rest of his team. The roaring engine has their undivided attention.

Cloris grabs Remo by the arm as his fingers fumble and miss picking up the Glock off the ground. Pulling Remo along, they round the corner of the compound where they can see another gate on the east side. A gate that's open. One they didn't realize was there before. One that connects to a driveway. A driveway that is filling with large SUVs—four of them to be exact—and one of them is tearing ass their way.

"Fucking told you there was another way here," Remo says, "*La La, there's no other way.*"

"Shut your hole." Cloris says.

The SUV screams toward them at ramming speed.

23

Lester and Hollis wage war like the lords of murder and mayhem they are.

Their weapons blaze. Breathe fire. Puke bullets. They blast in spits and starts then release steady, seamless streams of lead. A sporadic, unpredictable rhythm with no end in sight.

They give 'em some hell.

They get some more in return.

Daddy Mashburn's crew isn't backing down. Not by a damn sight. They return fire. Pounding guns explode into the trees without a clear target in mind. To them it's about creating an uncomfortable place to hide. They know that time is on their side. If they keep up the relentless pressure, whoever's out there will eventually wilt or get dead.

However, these time-honored strategies are not currently working.

Whoever is out in the woods today is more skilled than what Daddy Mashburn's crew is used to.

More dangerous.

Mashburn tells his people to follow their guns.

They'll spot the flash of an AR barrel. They'll see it then shift their blasts to another tree like tracking a traveling firefly. Then a Glock will pop from another. Then another and another. It's as if Daddy Mashburn's crew were fighting a hundred of them.

"It's insane," one of them tells Daddy Mashburn.

Daddy Mashburn is no stranger to a gunfight, but this feels different. He's not seen one like this. A man next to him takes a slug to the shoulder, spins, then grits his teeth and keeps on it. Then another man takes a pop to the forehead. He gets spun, but doesn't keep on it. At all. No. His eyes go blank and his body flies back as if the ghost of Bruce Lee clicked him in the forehead. Daddy Mashburn can see this fight is wearing down his boys. Only a matter of time before the bodies start piling up.

Hollis and Lester keep one thing constant.

Constant movement in one direction.

24

They keep the pressure up with the blasting, pounding guns, continuing to get closer to the compound. Fighting for every step. Earning every step. Killing for a foot. Spilling blood while gaining ground inch by inch. When this started there were five of them out there, counting Daddy Mashburn. Hollis knows he put one of them down with a headshot. He saw the red plume behind the head and the body flop to the dirt.

Lester knows he put a bullet in one, but he's fairly sure it was only a shoulder. He feels his rage building. Simmering to the top. That thing. That little gift from God that makes him shift from green to red. From the calm, thoughtful man of the Lord to someone—sorry, scratch that, some *thing*—that wouldn't think twice about cutting off a man's head. Type of man who would smash another man's head into the streets of New York over and over again. His focus has reached second-level type stuff. His breathing is deep. Slow. Sucking in and out between gnashed teeth. He's already decided what he's going to do if he is blessed enough to get his hands on one of these mother-fuckers, and God fucking help them if they lay a finger on Remo or...

Cloris.

What? Lester thinks. Did her name just slip in there? It did.

Lester's head caves in. A mental collapse he wasn't counting on. Not at all. In the heat of battle, did his prehistoric mind just pull up Cloris on his list of people to save? People to protect? Not that she needs protection. She's a badass. It's more like she needs protection from herself. Nonetheless, what the fuck is her name doing popping up in his head like that?

Out of the corner of his eye, Hollis sees his war-buddy has lowered his gun. Lester's eyes are drifting. Far-off gaze taking hold.

"What the fuck, man?" Hollis says. "Get in the game."

It's as if the world has turned into a silent, slow-motion movie for Lester. He sees everything, but it's slowed down to a crawl and someone hit the mute button on the remote. A tree will explode and the bark will separate into the air, splitting into splinters of fragments before his very eyes. He can almost see the bullets in mid-air.

Is his feeling for this woman short-circuiting his brain?

Is this what a breakdown feels like?

The timing is piss-poor, but Lester is accepting it.

"Oh, Lord," Lester says, looking toward the sky, "help me."

Hollis is not in the acceptance phase of things. He grabs Lester by the vest and shakes him hard, slamming his body against the tree. Screams into his face, but Lester can't hear him. His senses still dulled by his mental vacation from the situation. Hollis's lips move but Lester can't make out what he's saying. Hollis keeps screaming the same thing over and over again. The words are coming in a little bit better each time Hollis screams it.

Slowly Lester hears an *R*.

Hollis is encouraged by an ever-so-slight sign of recognition from Lester. He keeps up the screaming as the bullets whiz by. He knows this little pause has cost them a shit-ton of momentum.

Emo comes through to Lester's ears. He perks up. He's coming back online.

Again Hollis screams.

"Remo will die."

Lester's eyes go wide.

"Remo will die if we don't stop them," Hollis screams one last time.

Lester tosses Hollis aside and puts multiple bullets into the face of a man charging around a tree.

Hollis can't help but smile.

25

The Tahoe mows down the CIA kill squad.

Two go airborne. Shoot straight up on impact, bounce over the top of the roaring machine and stick a broken-ankle landing on the other side in a heap of bone and flesh.

Another one is stuck to the grill. Planted like a meaty hood ornament.

The leader dropped to the ground at the last second, thinking there was a chance he could slide under as the Tahoe passed. Instead he caught a bumper to his temple and is currently caught on the rear axle being dragged like a large, muscular rag doll.

The Tahoe skids to a stop. Dirt swirls and plumes. The passenger door flings open. Out steps a Hispanic mountain of a man. Tall as a tower. His muscles have muscles. He grips a 9 mm in his meaty paw. The CIA man on the hood twitches.

The Hispanic mountain puts a bullet in his skull.

Twitching ends.

He turns to Cloris and Remo, studying them. He's not shooting or rushing toward them. He's assessing. Remo and Cloris have no idea what to make of this. Their CIA lifeline just got run over and these people don't seem to be on the same page as the folks waging war outside the gates with Hollis and Lester.

Cloris's face scrunches as she fights to process. She doesn't recognize this guy, or the Tahoes. Sure, she's been away awhile, but not that long. Not to mention, Daddy Mashburn has always been a bit of racist, and would never consider working with Mexicans.

Remo decides "defiant prick" is the way to go with this. It's his steady state, his go-to move, and a strategy that has gotten him this far in life. So, logic suggests one should dance with who brought you here.

"Excuse me, fuck-o," Remo calls out. "Those guys were with us."

Cloris grabs his arm, shaking her head *NO* violently. *Something's not right with this shit here.*

Remo shrugs her off. He's been here before. He's got this.

"You?" the Hispanic Mountain asks, still eyeballing the fuck out of them. "You Remo?"

"I am." Remo nods. "Who the in the good fuck might you be?"

The Hispanic Mountain whistles.

All the Tahoe doors open and four more mountains from Mexico pour out. All big as shit. All just as mean. All armed with guns. Except one. There's one mountain now moving directly toward Remo and Cloris. He has a large axe in one hand and chains wrapped around his other thick fist.

Cloris readies her gun.

Remo squints. *This is new.*

The original Hispanic Mountain gives a hand sign to the other two Tahoes sitting in the driveway on the east side of the compound. One Tahoe's engine fires up and it begins heading toward them, while the other stays, taking a position blocking the back gate.

Remo and Cloris take a step back.

"What's up, Pedro?" Remo says, swallowing hard. Eyes fixed on the axe and chains. "Take a wrong turn at Albuquerque?"

"We were handed simple instructions," Axe and Chains says. "Find Remo and make it hurt."

26

Hollis slips around a tree.

This guy didn't even see his death coming, Hollis thinks, right before he fires a blast into the back of the guy's head. As the body falls away, Hollis can see across from him that Lester is holding another by the hair, bashing his head into a tree.

Hollis does the math.

Multiple dead. One wounded. One Daddy Mashburn left.

They are only about fifteen, twenty yards away from the front gate of the compound. The firing has stopped. The woods are actually quiet now. Hollis had been so busy unleashing nasty moves he hadn't noticed the silence.

"What the hell?" Hollis says to himself.

He turns and finds Lester is now stomping his boot heel into the face of another one of Mashburn's crew.

New math.

Only Daddy Mashburn is left.

Hollis hasn't seen him since this fight started. He's kinda hard to miss, too. Big, bald dude running around in the woods sort of sticks out among the foliage, and also doesn't move all that quiet among the brush.

The sound of an engine roars beyond the gate.

Dull thumps of metal colliding with something.

Hollis counts four.

Still no gunshots.

Lester moves over next to Hollis. He wipes some blood from his forehead, picks a clump of something from his sleeve then points up ahead.

Daddy Mashburn is standing in front of the gate, but he's not paying attention to them. He has his back turned to them. Turning back to Hollis and Lester, he makes eye contact and raises his empty hands. A show of good faith. He's not looking to fight, at least not now. Hollis doesn't trust it. Lester certainly doesn't trust it, given the history he has with this man. They both level their guns on him as they move forward. Daddy Mashburn points inside the gates, signals for them to be quiet, and then motions for them to join him, all with his hands open and empty.

A single gunshot rings out beyond the wall.

Hollis and Lester move up quickly with guns on Daddy Mashburn. Hollis makes quick scans left, right and up. Trusts nothing, ever, and won't ever trust a Mashburn, but at the moment he really is out of trustworthy options.

They reach Daddy Mashburn. Hollis places the barrel of his gun on his neck. If he so much as looks at them the wrong way Hollis is going to spray him all over that gate.

Daddy Mashburn simply points through a crack in the gate.

Before Hollis and Lester can even steal a look they hear Remo say, "Excuse me, fuck-o..."

27

A xe and Chains stalks toward Cloris and Remo.

He actually moves past Cloris, heading straight toward Remo.

"We got no beef with you. Only want that one," the lead Hispanic Mountain says to her.

She holds her gun on Axe and Chains as he passes, then rotates her aim to the rest of the Hispanic mountains, attempting to hold them at bay.

"That one you can have," Cloris says.

Remo holds his arms out. *What the fuck?*

He backs up as Axe and Chains gets closer and closer. Remo looks behind him. He's being moved, backed up toward the wall. Seconds away from being backed into it and completely trapped. Axe and Chains lets the chains clink and drop down to the ground, still holding the end with his thick-ass fist. Remo does the only thing an honorable man can do at a moment like this.

He kicks him in the balls.

It does nothing.

Remo kicks his junk again, then again, harder, but still nothing.

The axe rises.

Remo thinks of that Glock Cloris handed him.

The one he dropped. The one over there. He hates how stupid he is sometimes.

The chains come at him. A hard swing clinking, cutting through the air whips toward Remo's head. He ducks. If he moved a hair less the chains would have taken his head clean off.

The axe chops down. Remo dives.

It thunks into the ground an inch from where he was standing. Would have cut him clean in half. Axe and Chains resets, pulling the axe from the ground and cocking back his chains. He stands over Remo.

Remo lies frozen. Fear has removed his ability to do anything. He doesn't scream, fight or even consider being an asshole. This is Remo shutting down.

This is Remo understanding this is game over.

Three shots rip up the back of Axe and Chains.

The pops start between his shoulder blades, working up to the back of his head. He falls face-first into the wall with his forehead sliding down from the lubrication provided from the exit wound.

Remo twists away, jumping to his feet.

Game back on.

It's as if his brain had taken a break for a moment. A defense mechanism he supposes, but he's back. Just needed a second. A new battle is raging in front of him. He must have blocked this all out as well while he was accepting his own death.

He sees the bodies.

The blood.

The muzzle flashes are fast as Hollis and Daddy Mashburn blast away at a Tahoe that's speeding toward them. Holes carve up the hood and pop the windshield as it rambles closer and closer.

All Remo can think is, *When did they all become buddy-buddy?*

Remo then sees Lester on top of the Hispanic Mountain. His knees pinning him down as Lester pounds away at his skull with the butt of his AR.

Remo sees Cloris too. She's unloading her Glock at the speeding

Tahoe, taking a position next to her daddy with Hollis on the other side. She slams in a fresh seventeen rounds.

What the fuck did I miss? thinks Remo.

His mind clicks as he watches the mayhem unfold in front of him. Cloris. The woman who only seconds ago let Axe and Chains pass her by and said something about "fuck Remo." He's paraphrasing, but that's pretty much how it went down. He didn't miss that shit.

Remo picks up the axe and moves toward them. He limps and drags himself forward. Must have fucked up his leg somewhere in all this mess. Hard to pinpoint when exactly, but he's got a limp to be sure.

The remaining friends of Hispanic Mountain by the back gate have engaged, joining the fight as well. They open fire from across the compound.

Remo feels himself slipping away. He's never come to this place in his mind before. Maybe this is how Lester feels sometimes. This redline of rage. Remo gets it now. He feels completely okay with cutting off someone's head at the moment. It's a comforting idea, if Remo's honest. The idea of killing Cloris is very comforting.

The battle at the Hamptons didn't trigger this.

The Russian roulette at Crow's place didn't bring him to this point in his life.

No, this desire is purely vengeance-based, and it's a new one for Remo.

He drags the axe behind him like a deranged serial killer, limping slowly toward her. He leans down and picks up the Glock on the ground, tucking it behind his back. He might use that later, but not now.

No.

She gets the axe.

Remo doesn't know what her game is, but he knows for damn certain it doesn't involve Remo living happily ever after.

The Tahoe swerves. A bullet-riddled body spills and falls from the driver's side, rolling in the dirt. The driverless Tahoe cuts harder now with no one at the wheel. The large SUV cuts hard toward the wall, slamming into the metal then bouncing backward a foot and a half.

Remo is getting closer.

Closer to Cloris.

She's completely unaware, as she keeps alternating her blasts between the recently-crashed Tahoe and the other crew parked by the east gate. She has no idea what's headed toward her. Unaware that Remo and his axe are coming for her.

A man flings open a rear door of the crashed Tahoe. He slides out, only to be cut up like Sonny C in *Part I*. Once he flops, Hollis, Daddy Mashburn and Cloris turn their attention fully on the group down by the east gate. Hollis uses controlled bursts, whereas Daddy Mashburn and Cloris scream and wail, firing at will without control or thought.

Remo pushes forward step by step.

The gunfire booms.

He's a few feet away from Cloris.

He raises the axe above his head.

"Remo!" Lester calls out. "Don't."

Remo tilts his attention to him.

A large foot slams into Remo's gut, sending him flying backward with the axe still in hand. Daddy Mashburn just kicked the shit out of him, almost literally, and is storming his way. Protecting his daughter with a vengeance. Nobody raises an axe to his little girl, and certainly not the fucking lawyer who killed his sons. Daddy Mashburn's sight has blurred to white as the rage has taken hold of him. He charges toward Remo with the speed and force of a man on fire.

Remo tries to use the axe handle to help himself up, but slips and falls back to the ground. The axe slips from his grip.

Daddy Mashburn shoves it away with one foot and in a single motion stomps his other foot down on Remo's chest. The pain is sharp. Immediate. All air leaves Remo's body. Daddy Mashburn's foot lifts up and slams down again and again and again.

Vision is leaving Remo. Leaving fast. The world blurs.

Daddy Mashburn picks Remo up by the collar, holding him up off the ground. He wants Remo to see what's coming.

"You killed my sons," he barks through grinding teeth.

Remo feels around behind his back for the Glock. It's not there. His fingers fumble, panic-searching for something that's simply not there. Out of the corner of his eye he sees the gun on the ground next to him. *Fuuuuuck.*

Remo knows he's left with the only weapon he has available. His constant, never-ending arsenal. His weapon of choice.

Being a complete asshole.

"I did," Remo says. "Had some help, but yes, I did kill them and guess what, big boy? I. Fucking. Liked. It."

Daddy Mashburn head-butts him. Remo's nose splits just shy of exploding. After the beatings he's taken today, one would think there wouldn't be any blood left in his face, but oh yes, there is. Blood pours down his mouth and chin. Remo fights passing out, pulling out a smile.

"Your sons died like a pack of cunts. Ya know that, Daddy-O? They cried and bitched and bitched and cried. Oh, and the begging. Holy fucking shit the begging. You would have been sooooo embarrassed."

Something breaks behind Daddy Mashburn's eyes. Snaps. He has wanted to find this man, this Remo Cobb, ever since he heard what he did to his boys. What he did to his family. And now he has him in his hands and he is going to fuck this boy up something ferocious.

Remo closes his eyes in anticipation of what is about to come his way.

He feels his body fall. The drop. The weightlessness. He feels the impact with the ground. Fucking hurts, but he's alive. He cracks one eye open.

Standing above him is a headless Daddy Mashburn.

His massive body is there, but his head is gone.

His neck stump spits blood out in short then longer bursts, firing up into the air like a busted sprinkler. After a second or two his body falls away revealing Cloris holding the axe with both hands. Her body is fully twisted around as if she just took a major-league swing.

Remo sees Daddy Mashburn's head roll past his Glock.

Lester steps next to her, places a hand on her shoulder and carefully removes the axe from her fingers. She's shaken. Her breathing is erratic. Her face drained of color, turning her white as a sheet.

"What the fuck is wrong with you people?" Remo yells. "With the heads and the cutting and the chopping of heads?" He gets up, holding his gushing nose. "Seriously, what the fuck?"

Remo notices the gunfire has stopped. With a quick glance he sees the eastside gate is littered with several motionless bodies, along with a Tahoe pocked to hell with gashes and holes.

Cloris looks up to Lester.

She wraps her fingers in his. He lets her.

She's searching for something. Hunting for an answer that's locked inside his head. One that only he can open up and share with her. He looks down to her. His face is unreadable. A typical expression for Lester. Always seconds away from spirituality or brutality. The switch flips both ways, but it is hard to know which way until it goes.

Hollis moves to them with his AR on Cloris. He saw what she did with Remo. How she let Axe and Chains move past her toward him, and what she said. Hollis is the one who ripped three shots into Axe and Chains. He also saw what she did to Daddy Mashburn. That one has Remo and Hollis both puzzled as shit. Her actions don't match clear motives.

The thought occurs to Remo that she doesn't have any.

Chaos motivates her. She simply operates from minute to minute and her reasons sixty seconds ago may or may not apply to the current sixty seconds.

This scares the shit out of Remo.

Hollis too, which is why he has his AR leveled on her at the moment.

Lester glances to Hollis. "Put it down."

"She almost got Remo killed," Hollis says. "She was going to let it happen, man. You and I both saw the whole damn thing."

"It's true. She fucking did, man," Remo says.

Lester's eyes bounce between the three of them. To Hollis, to Cloris, then to Remo. Remo. His reason for being here. The reason he came back. The one asshole who needed saving. His eyes slip back over to Cloris. He has loved the woman, and probably still does. He looks at her as if trying to read her soul. As if he could.

She tries to explain herself without saying a word. Tries to let her eyes, her lips, her face tell him everything he needs to know. That she is still the woman he loves and needs. It's still just Cloris, despite all the crazy, and they can be together and be happy as hell. It's a lot get out with just a look, so she decides to throw some words onto the fire.

"I knew he wouldn't do it," she says. "I knew the axe and chain guy wouldn't do it."

"How in the fuck did you know that?" Remo says.

"It was soooo obvious," she says, leaving that impenetrable argument to stand. She lets silence wash over the conversation, hoping everyone will move on.

Remo is not moving on.

"Well, that clears everything up," Remo says. "Can't even begin to argue with that. Don't worry about it. We're cool."

"She *did* kill Daddy Mashburn," Lester adds. "Right before he was going to kill you."

"I know, right?" Remo says. "It's a real head-scratcher with her. I do not get what the hell is going on with this one." He turns and asks, "Hollis? Thoughts?"

"I don't trust anything about her. She's completely out of control." Hollis re-grips his AR. "She can make some damn fine chicken, but shit, she's a whacko."

Cloris's veins pop.

Hollis smiles big. Blows her a kiss. He's testing her.

She becomes unhinged inside. She's failing the test.

Cloris jumps at Hollis. It's all Lester can do to hold her back. Like a rabid beast going after fresh meat.

"See?" Hollis says. "See that shit?"

"Stop," Lester says.

"You know it's true," Hollis says. "She would kill us all and you fucking know it, man."

Lester's expression hardens. Hollis sees what's happening. So does Remo and he hates it.

"I know you care about her," Hollis says to Lester, "but she's no good, man. We can't count on anything about her."

"Stop," Lester says again.

"We just watched her cut her father's head off, for fuck's sake," Hollis insists.

Lester struggles holding her back. He's losing his grip. She's reached a new, higher level of pissed off. She's lost the ability to form a complete word in English, let alone a sentence. She's barking, hissing in a jumbled form of rage-speak. Eyes bulging. Face fire-engine red.

"I know," Lester says, fighting to hold on. "I know what you're saying—"

She breaks loose from Lester, tearing ass toward Hollis. Hollis fires a single shot. Tags her in the shoulder. It barely slows her down. She springs from her feet, launching into Hollis like she was shot from a cannon. They tumble to the ground much like they did back at the house.

Spit flies.

Fists. Elbows. Palms of hands.

Hollis lands a punch.

Cloris bites his neck then chomps on his ear.

Lester dives into the fray. His arms tugging at the sporadic movements of angry people bent on murder. Hands fumbling and slipping away as he tries to pull them apart, but he can't. They are both strong as hell and burning on high-octane, rage-fueled hate.

A gun goes off. Lester feels the air zip by his face. He has no idea who triggered the shot, since they both have guns raised. Both of them fighting to angle a kill shot on the other. Lester goes from green to red. Flips to instinct rather than thought. He plows headfirst into the tumbling mass of violent humanity.

Remo can only stand on the sidelines, holding his bleeding nose.

He picks up the Glock, tucking it under his shirt. Just in case.

He watches as his *team* dissolves in front of him. Even in the middle of this chaos in the mountains, he feels the twinge of failure. Failed leadership. Remo feels he was a good leader, at least he tried, but his rule was set up to fail, considering the players he was given. No matter if this is the truth or not, it does comfort Remo. It's not really his fault. Not entirely. The coach always takes the blame.

It happens.

Remo is solid as a leader.

He's snapped free from his thoughts when the cold barrel of a gun presses hard against his temple. A hand grabs his shoulder tightly.

"We gotta bounce, Remo," Cormac says.

28

Remo sees Cormac.

Can't believe it.

Not sure what it means, but Cormac is sure as shit here and standing next to him with a gun pressed to his head. Cormac pulls at him. Tugs his arm hard with the gun still planted, digging into his temple. Cormac is manhandling Remo away toward the east gate.

Away from his companions.

Away from his team.

Away from his friends. Well, Cloris is hard to put in the "friend" bucket, but she's what passes for friendship these days. At least for Remo.

Remo doesn't even bother fighting it. *What's the point?* Something has shut down inside of him. As if the *We're Open* sign on his front window has been turned around and now reads *Fucking Done*. Resignation is taking hold, and Remo may even like it.

As he's moved away he watches them fight. They are really going at it. Cloris, Lester and Hollis locked in battle. Remo can't help but try to place odds on the thing. Logic suggests Hollis, given his training and experience, will take this thing in the end, but Lester could easily come out on top with his maniac switch flipped on. And Cloris? Shit, Cloris could kill them both and then go have pizza and watch a movie and not think twice about the whole thing.

Remo's mind wanders further.

Fumbling.

Tumbling.

Farther and farther down a dark twirl of memories tangled with emotional knots he'd rather not unspool. The losses he's piled up recently. The loss of it all. He never dealt with the loss of his New York life. His job. His status. Certainly didn't get to deal with the upside of meeting his son, which made up for all the other losses. For a fraction of a sliver of a moment in time Remo understood that *happy* thing people talk about so much. At least he felt it once before he bit the big one. That much he can be thankful for.

He can almost feel himself peeling away from the here and now.

His mind lifting up, not accepting what's happening.

He thinks of his dream about Sean in the woods and Anna taking him away. Then the angry, headless hordes coming at him. He shook awake before they got to him, as you do in dreams but don't get to in real life.

You wake up from falling right before you make impact.

Before the monster rips you apart.

Something inside you jolts awake during the ones that scare the shit out of you. Then you sit up in bed wondering what the hell that was all about.

Now that he's wide awake, living in this meat grinder of a life, he lets that dream play out in his broken mind as he's leaving his friends behind. He goes back to those woods at night. Next to the campfire watching his son and ex-wife move away from him. He sees the headless hordes rambling toward him with their crude weapons made of bone. He imagines they get hold of him, tearing away at his flesh with their bare hands. Yanking it all clean from the bones. Hacking away at him. He imagines himself screaming in terror. Face twisted in indescribable pain.

No.

Scratch that.

He imagines himself standing there with a blank expression plastered on his face. Serene. Eyes glazed over with zero sign of emotion or thought. Mouth closed with an ever so slight smirk planted on his lips.

A look of complete understanding regarding his position in life.

Pure acceptance.

Acceptance that world had finally eaten him alive.

29

A firm hand slaps the shit out of Remo's face.

Cormac's hand.

Remo snaps to.

He'd let his head drift a bit. Checked out of the here and now, perhaps letting denial take him by the hand and lead him to a place where this disaster he's in isn't truly his life. A dream that this isn't the world he's living in. Where he's not riding in a beaten-down Chevy truck that CIA dickhole Cormac explained earlier that he stole. They are roaring at an unsafe speed through the narrow, winding mountain roads of New Mexico. Remo peeks over the side of the road. They are way the hell up and it's a steep dive down the side of the mountain.

The last he saw Hollis, Cloris and Lester they were engaged in a vicious display of hand-to-hand combat at the Mashburn compound. Dead bodies were scattered about the place, including a headless Daddy Mashburn. Remo thinks he's come a long way only to get back where he started from—another home littered with the dead, another headless Mashburn.

The more things change, the more they stay the same.

There are a couple of new wrinkles this time. One in particular strikes Remo at the moment.

There's a car following them.

Cormac hasn't said it, but Remo can tell. Cormac is nervous. Twitchy. Not the cold, in control, calm Lord of the CIA Remo has come to know and hate. This Cormac speaks in spits and starts. Can't form a clear, complete sentence. He clutches his gun in a shaky hand, turning around constantly checking on the car that's on them.

Cormac told Remo earlier that they had to leave the compound. Sorry, he said they needed to *bounce*. Told Remo at gunpoint to be exact, then led Remo to this truck. A rusted, used-to-be-red Chevy that still runs like a mad beast of a V8 machine. Cormac fights to control the car. Driving like a crazy person. Hands gripping the wheel so tight his knuckles pop then fade to white. Doing everything he can to take the truck on turns well beyond the recommended speed limit. Cormac and Remo sway and bounce around inside the truck's cab like dice thrown on a craps table.

"Get off me, motherfucker," Cormac says to the rearview mirror.

"Perhaps he doesn't like you," Remo says, digging his fingertips into the dashboard for dear life.

"Perhaps, but I know he doesn't like you," Cormac says.

"Doesn't rule a lot of people out."

"Look, I screwed this up. I know I did, but it is what it is and we're going to work through it all."

"You're going to need to clarify."

"Well." Cormac takes a moment, looks back, looks to Remo and then spills it. "I might have let it leak what you did with the Mashburn case."

Remo blinks.

"You know, " Cormac explains, "that you stole the Mashburns' money and framed them and then killed them."

"When you say *might have* and *leaked*..."

"Let's say a lot. Leaked to everybody, actually. All your clients, I mean. And your former clients did not respond well to this news. A few of the larger ones have brought in some hired hands to remove you."

Remo's mind slides in and out of place. That's what was up with the Hispanic Mountain and friends. They were with the Diaz brothers. He thought he recognized the one, but it was hard to place him through the fog of fear. They had nothing to do with Daddy Mashburn and everything to do with Remo. Remo can think of several past clients who might call in a hard-hitting crew like that if they thought Remo was doing them wrong. If Cormac somehow confirmed that Remo fucked over the Mashburns then, well, that would definitely trigger some calls.

But that's only one.

There are dozens who could, would and probably *did* make some calls.

"When I say they hired hands to *remove you*, you know I mean *kill you*, right?"

"I get it," Remo says. "Is that who's behind us?"

Cormac nods, checking his mirrors again.

Remo should be more concerned than he is. He's uncomfortable with how well he's taking this. Uncomfortable with how comfortable he's becoming with folks trying to kill him. Maybe he's simply getting used to constantly being the target of killers and thieves. He's not proud of it, but it's where his head is. His big brain keeps flipping through the hows and whys of the situation in an attempt to construct a way out. He keeps fumbling around one question as they continue to slip and slide along the truck's bench seat. A question that has been eating at him ever since Cormac came into his life.

"Why the CIA?" Remo asks. "Why were you so damned interested in me and my clients to begin with? International gunrunning? Global money laundering schemes? What? What was it?"

Cormac looks to Remo then back to the road. There's an almost-shame wave that spreads over his face. He starts to speak, stops, tries again, thinks, and then says, "It's not what you think."

"Okay. Explain. Talk to me like I was five," Remo says.

"There was a bartender you used to date not long ago," Cormac says. "She left you, said you were an asshole and you didn't respect her."

Remo hangs on to the dashboard again as they almost slide off the road and over into the abyss. He regroups and thinks. He tries to think of a woman who meets that description. It's difficult, given the number of candidates. More than a few who consider him an asshole.

Then one comes to mind.

He thinks of the woman he faked an orgasm with. The one who worked at the hipster bar. The one he bought the boob job for a while back. He remembers respect wasn't really held on either side, but lets that part go.

"Okay..." Remo says.

"Well, she's my sister. She came over to my house in tears and wanted me to do something to you. Wanted me to dig into your life and find something to squeeze. I checked you out and found out there was probably some tax stuff I could hand to the IRS, but then you did the Mashburn thing in the Hamptons and I realized I could use you to take care of some other stuff."

"Wait. Let me get this straight," Remo says, rubbing his temples. "I pissed off your sister and you figured out a way to use the shit out of me?"

"Started that way. Then I kept digging and digging and the layers kept piling on. There was Hollis and Lester and then Cloris and it all fell into place. I could create a great little task force of convenience that I could leverage."

"When was it going to end?" Remo asks.

Cormac checks behind him, ignoring the question. They've reached the bottom of the mountain and are moving through a small town. Remo looks back and sees there are now two cars on them.

Remo remembers the Glock. He makes a quick feel in the front of his pants. It's still there. In the middle of all the craziness, Cormac didn't pat him down.

"There's a safe house up here," Cormac says. "We can stop there. I can talk to these guys behind us."

"When, fucker?" Remo barks. "When was all this going to end? What was your plan?"

"There wasn't a specific finish date." Cormac swallows hard. "It was over when you were dead or no longer of use to me."

Remo looks out the window, watching the brown and tan of the New Mexico town pass by. He feels foolish. Stupid for thinking he had a chance to be with his son. He let the illusion of hope cloud what he knew about life. The knowledge that we're all fucked no matter what we do. He can feel himself dissolve inside, letting all the hope that had built up inside of him drain out into the floorboard of this piece of shit truck.

He presses pause on his pity party for one.

One simple truth clicks as they make a turn, leaving the town and moving out toward wide-open nothingness. There's a single home on a plot of land in the distance. Remo knows that must be where they are headed. Out of the way. Somewhat secluded. The simple truth Remo unearthed is now confirmed.

"The people coming after me now," Remo says, "they got to you first, didn't they? Me, Hollis, Lester and Cloris, we're an off-the-books operation. The rest of the CIA, or any law enforcement for that matter, they don't know anything about us. Aside from Detective Harris, the way you got to me. And he's dirty as fuck, so he's not going to say shit, right?"

Cormac stares at the road and the house up ahead as they drive closer and closer. Remo glances to the rearview. Now three cars are on them and not another soul on the road.

"They got to you. Threatened you with God-knows-what and now you're serving me up on a platter to save your own bitch ass," Remo says. "You can't call in the rest of the CIA, because then they'll know you went off the reservation, all because I pissed off your sister. I bought her tits, for fuck's sake."

Cormac drives off the main road onto the dirt path leading up to the house. He glances back. The three cars are following.

"Tell me I'm wrong," Remo presses. "Lie to me. At least give me that."

"You're right," Cormac finally admits. "I had a few people I called on, the kill squad back there and whatnot, but yeah, overall it's a damn mess."

Cormac jams it in park.

Remo looks back. The three cars will be there in seconds. Cormac clucks his tongue and reaches for his gun. Remo pulls his Glock from under his shirt. Cormac fires a shot as Remo lunges forward slamming into the dash. The back window explodes. Remo twists, firing three blasts. The first blows out the driver's window behind Cormac. The second and third tear apart Cormac's neck and face. His body slumps over, lying on the horn.

The cars are only a few feet from turning into the driveway.

The horn blares.

Remo grabs the keys and pushes Cormac off the horn. He grabs Cormac's gun. He needs all he can get.

Flying from the truck, he stumble-runs to the back of the house, charging hard to the back door as the three cars skid to a stop in the gravel driveway behind the truck.

The back door of the house opens as Remo gets within a foot of it. Another CIA man steps out, armed with an assault rifle.

"Where's Cormac?" the CIA man asks, raising his AR.

Thank God, Remo thinks as he fires a shot, dropping the CIA man. Remo knows he'll need that assault rifle and whatever else he can get off this asshole.

The cars start to unload a mishmash of bad dudes. There's no color coding of race with this crew. No uniforms or matching tats. Simply a pack of mean dudes from every walk of life with guns in hand and murder in their hearts. They explode out from the car doors, ready to rock.

Remo scampers into the house, slamming the door behind him.

He locks it for some reason.

He checks the windows. The bad dudes are surrounding the house. They take positions at every possible angle. He can hear boots and shoes thump and patter down the sides. Remo's been in this situation before. Trapped in a house, pinned down by heavily armed, evil dildos wishing do him harm. Only last time it was in his own home in the Hamptons.

Last time there were fewer bad guys who wanted Remo dead.

Last time he had more guns.

Last time he was a bit of a pussy.

Times have changed.

Remo puts one in the chamber.

30

Remo checks the window.

More of a formality than anything. He knew what he'd see out there, but just needed to see it with his own eyes. They haven't started shooting or busting down the door. At least not yet. That's a good sign.

Maybe.

They have all their guns pointed at the house, scanning the windows and the doors, but they haven't opened up on him. At least not yet. They're waiting for something. *But what?* They know damn well Remo is in here alone. So why not finish this thing? Remo sees another man step out from the last car.

Remo realizes why, now.

A tall, slender man with hair cut close to the skull moves toward the house. He nods as one of the bad dude dildos tells him something. The slender man slides on some shades and moves with the swagger of a man without a care in the world and a dick the size of King Kong. He's dressed in a casual, cool style that cost him thousands. Remo is a little annoyed with the fact that even at a time like this he can calculate the cost of this guy's outfit. Holdover from his former life. *Can't help it,* he tells himself.

Remo knows this guy.

Hates this guy.

Used to have this guy as a client.

Justin Slim. J. Slim they call him. He is a man similar to Hollis. A contract killer, but with only one client, and that client is what has Remo moments away from pissing his pants.

"Remo," J. Slim calls out.

Remo says nothing, checks the AR.

"Remo, I know you can hear me. So I'll keep talking even if you don't return the favor."

J. Slim pauses on the off chance Remo will give up his position and he can go grab a drink and screw a local.

"Ray's not happy, as you can probably guess. Sure you've got a few former clients who feel the same," J. Slim says. "You fucked up, Remo. You really did. I don't know if you did us like you did the Mashburns..."

Remo opens the door a crack and bounces back, hoping he's not cut down by a storm of lead. When the bullets don't fly, he leans by the edge of the door and calls out, "I didn't do shit to Ray or you, motherfucker."

J. Slim cracks a smile. *Ahhh, Remo.* "Yeah, but the problem now is, how can we trust you? I mean every little thing that's gone wrong they can now pin directly on you, right or wrong. You see?"

Remo shuts his eyes tight. *Shit.* Cormac has made Remo the perfect scapegoat for every criminal organization on the planet.

How did the cops find us? Remo.

How did that get so fucked up? Remo.

Who took our fucking money? Remo.

Who did the thing about the thing? Remo.

"What do you do here, Remo? We're outside town, but not that far. If we start blasting it out with you the cops will eventually come and that doesn't do anybody any good. Think about it. You're hunkered down on a property with two dead CIA agents. That won't play well."

Remo bites his lip.

Thinks of Sean.

Thinks of putting a bullet in J. Slim and starting this thing off. If he can drop J. Slim he can start picking off the rest one by one, then jack one of these cars and get gone before the small-town, law-and-order mutts show up for the party. Remo can't believe this is how mutated his thinking has become. He used to think about suit fabric, good scotch and pussy. Now he's plotting mass murder at a CIA safe house, with an escape plan to boot.

Never stop learning, he thinks.

He takes aim on J. Slim's head. Fingers the trigger.

He can envision J. Slim's head bursting like a melon.

"I don't want a bloodbath here, Remo. I don't," J. Slim says, then motions to one of his bad dude dildos. "I can't see a way this ends with you alive, but I can make it as painless as possible."

The bad dude dildo takes something from J. Slim and moves toward the front of the house. Remo watches him holster his gun and walk to the front door. Remo positions himself behind a couch and takes aim at the front door. He waits for the firestorm to come.

It doesn't.

He hears the boots and footsteps patter as they move away from the house, followed by the sound of car doors closing. Out the window Remo watches the cars back up and leave the driveway. Only dirt in the wind.

Remo moves around the house checking all the windows. Looking to make sure there wasn't some dildo left behind to take Remo out when his guard is down. He gives the place a few good scans but doesn't find anyone.

Remo takes a deep breath and opens the front door wider.

Just a crack more, letting him get a peak of what's outside.

The dirt yard is empty. Only a plant that's barely alive and a three-legged dog hobbling down the gravel road barking at him. At his feet on the faded *Welcome Home* mat is an iPad with a Post-it note stuck on the screen.

There's a New York street address printed on the Post-it, along with the words, *Tap then meet us here!*

Remo's stomach drops through the ground before he even taps the screen.

With a single touch of his finger a video image of Sean and Anna playing at a park appears in crystal-clear HD. They are playing at a park Remo knows well. The same park Remo stumbled into after his battle in the Hamptons. Sean is laughing and running. Anna is chasing. Remo can't help but want to smile, but a tear rolls instead.

The camera turns around to face the man who's filming them. Remo doesn't recognize the man, but he knows the look. Sharp-dressed criminal. A high-net-worth asshole who's been upped from street murder boy to Manhattan resident based on his body count. Remo also recognizes the look in his eyes.

This guy is a killer.

This man enjoys the pain of others.

This man waves to the camera.

To Remo.

REMO WENT OFF

REMO COBB # 4

PART I

THE CHAOS OF ALL
THAT SHIT

R emo is one fucked up slab of humanity.

He stares at the iPad for what seems like an hour. He knows it's only a few seconds, a minute tops, but it feels like an eternity. He simply stands there, helpless, watching a glass screen. Watching a killer while that killer watches his family. Remo is armed to the teeth, but powerless to do anything from his current position.

His finger tickles the trigger of his gun.

He allows his tired mind to wander.

A flash of a fantasy zips through his mind. A necessary break from reality. A much-appreciated defense mechanism. This private fantasy moment. The fantasy of pulling the trigger and removing whomever this motherfucker is off the planet. It provides Remo some comfort at least.

He shakes his head hard, trying to get right.

No time for this shit.

Setting the iPad down, he walks the room. With each passing moment, the pace becomes more and more manic. Back and forth. Sideways. Circles. Figure eights. A pause, then quick bursts of steps, then stopping suddenly and leaning against the wall with his head down. He needs a plan, an idea, an idea of a plan of what in the hell he can do make this all better. If only there were a pill to swallow to make this all go away. A button to unfuck himself. A way to undo the good deed of his that started this whole shitshow in the first place.

What was he thinking?

He had a good life.

A great life.

And he dicked it all up when he grew a conscience and decided to double-cross the Mashburn brothers after he saw some security camera footage. A slice of video that changed everything. He'd seen thousands of hours of security camera footage over the years mind you, but this particular footage on this particular day set a fire inside Remo that is currently burning down his life and everyone else's in it.

Remo's eyes blink as if clicking through a presentation.

He throws the Mashburn case.

Mashburns get pissed and come after him.

He gets into a massive bullet-ballet that leaves the Mashburns dead.

Most of them.

CIA gets their hooks into Remo.

They dig in deep by going through Detective Harris of the NYPD, who hates Remo with a passion. CIA boy Cormack—who's dead in a truck outside by the way—puts the screws to Remo and his boys, Hollis and Lester, to do Cormack's dirty work.

This included an unpleasant time with Mr. Crow, and taking down a heavily armed compound in the New Mexico mountains.

After slipping out of that disaster, Remo finds out Cormack put his thumb down on Remo because Remo pissed off Cormack's sister, and now Remo is in a CIA safe house with CIA dead bodies, guns and an iPad showing streaming footage of a psycho asshole eyeballing his family. Well, former family. Anna and he are divorced but he still cares about her, not to mention his son is really the thing that made Remo look at that security footage in a different, more human way to begin with.

Remo's head is a swirling mess of confusion, fear and regret.

No easy answers are coming his way. None out there to be found.

He rubs his gun as if rubbing a lantern in hopes a genie will appear and grant him three wishes. Hell, one good one would be nice. Then it hits him. It's a fragment of an idea at first. In his mind, Remo starts moving, sliding pieces into place. They don't all fit, mind you, but there are at least some pieces to work with. He knows what has to happen. The only shot he's got.

How do you start the million-mile journey?

By taking the first step.

Remo grabs the iPad, the note with the NY address, and a couple of guns and flies out the door. He opens the truck, letting Cormack's lifeless body drop to the driveway. The driver's side is a pulpy, bloody mess, but so is Remo. He can't feel most of his body and he's not completely sure how he's even able to walk. No time for self-examination. He'll go until he can't. Until he collapses or sees a long tunnel with a white light at the end. Remo slides in, literally, and sets his stuff down in the floorboard. As he fires up the engine he catches a glance of himself in the mirror.

It's not good.

Dark bags hang under his bloodshot eyes. Fresh blood is mixed with dried wounds from recent battles. They are a maze of reds and browns, indistinguishable as to where one begins and the next one ends. He can see the crazy in his own eyes. He used to have the calm eyes of an attorney who had the world by the nuts. Now the world has his in a tightly held, unkind grip.

He slaps himself.

Finds a classic rock station on the radio.

Cranks it up and jams the gear in R.

He slams on the brakes as a three-legged dog passes by the back bumper.

Remo hopes like hell he can remember how to get back.

How to get back to the Mashburn compound nestled up in the mountains.

2

Winding up the mountain everything looks the damn same.

Every tree. Every rock. Every twist and turn in the road reveals the same thing. He has no idea where he is going. The trip down the mountain with Cormack was only an hour ago, but it was a blur. Remo had been beaten, shot at and held at gunpoint while CIA man Cormack explained how he'd truly ruined Remo's life. The information came at him a like a sledgehammer. Each word hitting harder than the next. Every syllable explaining how Remo was a dead man. So, Remo wasn't exactly paying attention to the way he came down the mountain.

Maybe he's seen that sign before.

Maybe.

Don't know, not for sure.

All he does know is he needs to go up. The Mashburn compound was up the mountain, so if he heads that way he will at least be moving in the right direction. Blind-ass progress is better than no progress at all.

The serpent-like road dead-ends.

He backs up and takes another route that leads him up.

Up is good, he thinks.

He reaches an RV park. Doesn't remember seeing it before. Wrong way. He hits R again and takes another path that wraps around and up the mountain. It's all too much. He can feel himself coming undone. This needle in the haystack feeling is crushing what's left of his battered, fragile psyche. Every wood house looks the same. Every mountains-vacation family looks the same. Every stone. Every tree. Every hand-carved wooded bear looks the damn same.

Up and up he goes. The old truck pushes farther and farther up the mountain like an aging climber driven beyond reason. Remo's mind is on fire. His thoughts collide, spin, flip then burst into flames. None of his ideas or memories are connecting into anything he can use. He's only processing fear and darkness. There's no great way out of this and he knows it. This will end with people dying. He can only hope it's not Sean and Anna.

He glances to the iPad. Its screen has long since gone dark. He made the wise decision not to look at it while trying to navigate the mountain road. Didn't see the value in it. He is, of course, appreciative that J. Slim and company gave him one with cell service rather than just Wi-Fi, so he can watch wherever he goes. So thoughtful, those folks. He looks to the black screen. Can't help but think about what's going on in the darkness of that glass. Just a harmless advance in tech resting on a seat, but yet it holds all the hopes and fears Remo has.

He can't help himself.

He swipes the screen.

He checks the road. Clear.

The screen lights up. The whacko killer is following Anna and Sean. Now they are on the streets of New York. This is new. It's a jerking, bouncing, camera style footage with the images moving back and forth with his walking, but it's plain to see that he is following them wherever they go.

Remo feels sweat forming on the back of his neck. His mouth goes dry.

He realizes he has to get to New York fast. He has no idea how to get there or what the smartest or best way to do it is, but he cannot continue to watch from afar like this. This is unbearable, and that's probably the point. He realizes that was the plan. He realizes that's what J. Slim and Ray want.

He realizes he hasn't looked at the road in a long time.

Remo looks up.

Locks the brakes.

He sees something strangely familiar. Something he most definitely recognizes. Remo smacks his lips. Blinks. Stares in disbelief. Seems like years ago, but it was actually earlier today when he last saw it.

Cracking a sly grin, Remo points a finger gun at a Yukon parked on the side of the mountain road.

"Gotcha."

3

He, Hollis, Lester and Cloris left the Yukon there not long ago.

Feels like a lifetime ago.

Remo's heart skips a beat or six. He's close. They have to be around here somewhere. His memories flood in fast like a tsunami. All of it. The house. The chicken pepperoni fight between Hollis and Cloris. Cloris and Lester. Cloris and everyone. The chaos of all that shit. The blood. The three of them fighting, arguing while hiking up the mountain.

Remo grinds his teeth. *Holy shit he's close.*

The compound has to be up just a bit farther. Thinking hard, he remembers there was a second driveway that big Mexican Mountain bastard and his angry-ass friends drove into before they started with the shooting and all that shit. There has to be another way up, one he can drive. He doesn't have time to hoof it up the side of the mountain the way he and Cloris did earlier today.

His eyes dart left and right looking for a way. A path. Something that will show him the fastest route to the compound. Out of the corner of his eye he sees something.

It's not a faster route.

Not a road.

Not a path of least resistance.

It's something rolling. Falling. Tumbling down the mountain through the trees. Rumbling awkwardly without much style or sense of direction. Remo looks harder. He makes out a rolling mass of arms and legs. A whirling dervish of fists and feet that starts and stops, then moves down only to stop again. A ball of elbows, anger and red faces locked in hate.

Cloris, Hollis and Lester are fighting like hell, wrapped around each other while falling down the mountain. Remo can't believe what he's seeing. This misplaced tumbleweed of hostility coming his way. He watches as one breaks off from the other two, stumbles, then jumps back in. It's hard to determine who's on whose side. There seems to be no real winners or losers here.

A threesome of violence as opposed to lust.

Remo opens the creaky truck door and steps out. Stops and then grabs a gun. Just in case Cloris is still in the mindset of killing Remo. He walks up cautiously, trying to devise a plan as he moves closer. In very quick order he runs through the possibilities of what he should do here. He could shoot one of them, probably Cloris, but that might set off Lester. He'd rather not hurt any of them. They've been through a lot recently, especially him, Hollis and Lester. Okay, fine, he won't shoot anyone. Unless of course Cloris tries to shoot him. Remo is still on the fence as to what the hell Cloris's big plan is here. She probably doesn't have one. If she does, it probably resets from minute to minute as her crazy-ass mind clicks and clacks its way through life. Her love for Lester seems to be the constant. Her unhealthy, destructive, crazy-as-hell love for Lester.

They've reached a flat part of land. A "landing spot," if you will. They are about thirty feet ahead of Remo, still giving him some room to operate and think. For the first time Remo can make out what's happening.

Hollis swings a backhand toward Cloris.

She ducks and lands a jab to his kidneys. He alters his swing and ends up tagging Lester in the eye. Maybe by mistake, but it doesn't stop Lester from taking a full swing that misses Hollis and crunches Cloris square in the jaw.

Hollis slumps to a knee.

Cloris spins to the ground.

Lester is straight-up staring at Remo. Confusion washes over his dirty, bloody face. He looks back toward the mountain, then to Remo, then to the truck with the cracked windshield, blown-out passenger window and blood slopped everywhere. His eyes move back to Remo.

"How'd you get here, friend?" Lester asks, trying to catch his breath.

"Long story, friend," Remo replies.

"Can't be that long. We just been fighting for an hour or so, tops."

"A lot can happen in an hour."

Lester nods.

Cloris stands up, as does Hollis. They both take defensives stances but don't attack. More out of exhaustion than anything. Rage burns hot and fast, but doesn't last. Not at these levels. Hollis spits out a wad of blood and dirt. Cloris tries to hold Lester's hand. He pulls away. Cloris does her best to hide her hurt, but she sucks at it. Suppressing emotions isn't her strong suit. She twirls her head to pop her aching neck, then crosses her arms, then allows a finger to twirl a strand of hair.

Remo has no idea where to start, but knows he has to. He wanted so badly to be the leader at the beginning of today, and now he knows he has to be a good one if he is going to have any chance of finding Anna and Sean. There's no time to read a best-selling book on management, filled with pyramids and blah-blah about paradigm shifts and top-ten lists of heady horseshit that in the real world equates to blank stares and jokes behind your back at the water cooler. Still, Remo needs to find a way to get these people on board. Needs to find a button to push within them to get these three masters of mayhem up for battle one more time. Perhaps one last time.

Does he go with a big speech?

Honest begging?

Crying?

Remo realizes more than a moment of silence has passed since they stopped beating the piss out of one another. All three of the battered, beaten members of his *team* are looking at him. Waiting. Waiting for something out of Remo. Anything Remo has to offer. They don't have any answers. If they did, they wouldn't have spent their time fight-falling down a mountain. They continue to stare at Remo as their breathing starts to even out.

Remo simply clucks his tongue like Cormack used to do. Well, before Remo blew his brains all over the truck behind him.

"Looks like you've got something on your mind," Hollis says, breaking the silence.

"That I do, Hollis," Remo says, scratching his nuts with his gun. "That I do."

4

emo does his best to explain what in the hell has
happened since they last saw him at the Mashburn
compound.

There's a lot.

More than Remo would like.

He tells them about Cormack and how he fucked all of them over.
Mainly Remo, but they are all involved. CIA man Cormack let it slip
out to the greater part of the US criminal community that Remo
ratted out the Mashburn brothers. He more or less told every thug,
murderer and criminal overlord that Remo threw a case and had the
Mashburns sent to prison. Not to mention Remo also took the Mashburns' money from a bank robbery. Cormack probably left out the
part where Remo gave (most of) it to charity. This info leak thus
started off a shitstorm of other criminals thinking Remo might have
or will do the same to them.

That's what caused the larger issues at the Mashburn compound.
The uninvited guests. The Mexican Mountain and his friends who
stormed in with guns blazing. Remo tables his concerns over Cloris
chopping off her father's head—doesn't see the need to open that can
of worms—but he does talk about killing Cormack and another CIA

agent at the CIA safe house and the little chat he had with J. Slim. Remo even goes as far as to show them the iPad, which now has the psycho watching Anna and Sean's apartment from across the street.

"I know J. Slim," Hollis says. "He's a fucking asshole."

Remo nods in agreement. No need to say more. No need to dig up all that.

"Like to put a bullet or ten into him and Ray." Hollis continues talking, seeming to get more and more worked up with each word. "But since he brought Anna and Sean into this thing of ours, I'll make their deaths slightly less humane."

Remo smiles with appreciation.

He was hoping Hollis would take this point of view. Perhaps managing by doing and saying less is the answer here. Let them fill in the gaps. Let their brains work it through rather than tell them what to think. He turns to Lester and Cloris, but says nothing. There's a sting of silence. The wind blows. The trees shift, limbs swaying in the breeze.

Cloris looks to Lester. Lester looks to Remo.

"I'd like to help you," Lester says. "If you'll still have me."

Remo lets a sigh escape. A wave of relief rolls over him. He knows it's silly to get emotional about a completely insane, Jesus-freak killer choosing to join him on a half-baked mission leading them to almost-certain death, but Remo can't help but get a little choked up.

"Of course," Remo says. "And thank you."

Lester nods.

"You fucking kidding me?" Cloris says.

The silence is back. The wind blows.

"You're more than welcome to join," Remo says through clenched teeth. "Of course we'd need to resolve a few issues beforehand."

"Like?" she says.

"Like, say, I don't know, the fact you tried to kill me about an hour ago."

"That's the past."

"Not very distant past."

"The past nonetheless."

Remo lets it go, clucks his tongue. Now he can't stop doing it.

Cloris takes Lester's face in her hands. "What do you want me to do?" Lester looks down. Cloris raises his face to meet her eyes. "Tell me, baby. What do you want?"

"What I've always wanted," Lester says. "For you to do what makes you happy."

Cloris slaps the shit out of him.

"Just fucking say you don't want me anywhere near you next time," she barks. "Don't be a snatch about it."

Hollis and Remo glance to one another, then let their eyes slide back to the unhappy couple. Lester doesn't even bother touching his pulsing face. He lets it throb and burn, or he doesn't even feel it, given the beatings they've taken and laid down on each other today.

"We can use your help," Remo chimes in, trying to appeal to Cloris. "I. Me. I can use your help."

Cloris lets her death stare whip over from Lester to Remo. She's listening, but there's no telling how she's processing the words that have been spoken to her. There's what's said and then there's the perception of those words, and trying to guess how the words will translate in that meat grinder of a head is a fool's errand.

Remo resets and starts again.

"They have my son and my ex-wife. Anna and Sean have nothing to do with any of this shit," Remo says. "They are completely innocent. Their only mistake was having me in their lives."

"Massive mistake," Cloris says.

Hollis can't help but chuckle. *You ain't kiddin'.*

"Be that as it may, " Remo continues, ignoring their bullshit, "I have to help them. I came back here for your help. I'm asking for your help. I'm willing to go it alone, but I can really use all of you."

Remo knows he's lying a bit. He really only wanted Hollis and Lester, and could give two shits if Cloris joins in or not. Actually, he thinks her leaving would be best, but he doesn't want to further escalate or reignite the violence between the four of them. He knows he needs to make this look good. He decides to add some more shine.

"I'll ask you again." Remo puts his best sincere face on display. "Will you help me—"

"Fuck you," Cloris says. She slaps the shit out of Lester again, kisses him with a sloppy tongue, then stomps his foot and plants a foot into his knee.

As Lester drops to the dirt she storms past Remo, giving him a lightning-fast thump to the nuts as she passes by. Remo buckles. As he twists to the ground he watches her tear off down the mountain in the opposite direction.

Hollis helps Lester up. They share a look, but don't bother speaking. What's the point? They've been through a lot in the last few days. Way too much to discuss. Cloris leaving is just another bullet point in a long list of questionable shit.

Remo sucks in a long breath, letting the queasiness in his stomach subside. Pulling himself upright, he looks to his boys. His brothers-in-arms. His team.

They share odd smiles.

Together again.

For better or worst.

"Okay, Remo," Hollis says, "you got us. What's your master plan?"

Remo starts to cluck his tongue again, but stops himself. He really doesn't know what his plan is, but he's got some fragments of ideas that might work. Anything is possible.

"Please tell us you've got something," Hollis says.

"Yeah, give us something, Remo," Lester says.

Remo holds up a finger. He needs to frame the sketchiness of this thing in a positive way or this new buy-in from them will dissolve rapidly. Words need to be well chosen. Structured properly and delivered with strength.

"We're going to..." Remo pauses. "I don't fucking know, but I've got some ideas."

Hollis and Lester actually seem surprised by his honesty. They were fully expecting layers upon layers of cascading bullshit to come raining down from Remo, but instead they got raw honesty. A new development. They appreciate the break for once. Remo picks up on the vibe and makes another mental managerial note.

Honesty and selective silence.

It works.

Who fucking knew?

5

R emo, Hollis and Lester climb out of the Yukon.

Hollis had pulled up as close to the cabin as he could in case they needed to bounce the hell out of there at a moment's notice. They do a quick sweep around the place taking some quick peeks into the windows with guns drawn. They have no idea how many people really know about this place. Given what Cormack told Remo, it's hard to believe Cormack told anybody. The way Cormack explained it, he had this whole operation with Remo completely off the books and the only people who knew about it were now recently departed, their dead bodies littered in various places in New Mexico.

But.

But, Cormack could have told the world. Anything and everything is a possibility. He could have someone else in the CIA working this thing. Somebody they don't even know about. Not out of the questions at all. There's an off chance Detective Harris from New York might know a little, but Remo doesn't think Cormack would feed that dipshit much info. No upside for Cormack.

Once the place seems clear the three enter through the front door. The place is exactly the way they left it. Some dishes and shit still in the kitchen. The remnants of the chicken pepperoni battle that raged last night. Some stained sheets from Lester and Cloris's little afternoon delight. But that's about it.

They take seats on the couches in the living room. Wasn't much talking on the ride over. The exhaustion of the last couple of days is really hitting them hard. They all needed a minute to reboot. To let the silence heal them a bit. Remo thinks of his lost friends—Johnnie Walker Blue and his pills. Be nice if he could reconnect with them some time soon.

He's pretty sure that time, violence and blood loss have helped him detox, but Remo never asked to detox and was not, and still is not, interested in giving either one of them up. After he gets Anna and Sean safe and sound, the second order of business is to get the pipeline of sauce and pills flowing again.

Remo pulls over checking the iPad. That psycho asshole is still sitting watching the apartment. Remo tries to send mental telepathy their way. *Stay in the apartment and out of sight. Do not let anybody inside. Not without a fight.*

"We going to cut up a plan or not?" Hollis asks, breaking the silence.

"Yeah, what's the word on this thing?" Lester adds.

Remo picks at the corners of an idea he had on the way over. "Hollis, you remember J. Slim having a brother? A little one. A little piece of shit asshole brother?"

Hollis thinks. "Sounds about right. Started with a D or some shit."

"Yeah, D-something."

"David?"

"No."

"Desmond?"

"No."

"Douchebag?"

"Yes, but no."

They pause.

Remo's mind unspools. It's as if the hard drive in his skull is unloading data. He remembers J. Slim and his boss Ray and how they used to do business. J. Slim used to be a contract guy. Freelance killer, a lot like Hollis, which is how Hollis knows him. They traveled in similar circles. Both former military. Both competed for similar work. Then J. Slim went exclusive. Got a retainer, for lack of a better explanation, from a criminal superpower named Ray.

Just Ray.

No cool nickname or badass handle. Simply Ray, and Ray ran shit. He even ran Mr. Crow, and Mr. Crow's operations. Remo remembers Crow for a split second and how Remo, Lester and Hollis almost went down dealing with one of Crow's establishments only a couple of days ago.

Ray has had a paw in a lot of things, but the larger cash cows are drugs, guns and money. No big shocks there, but Remo did hear recently that Ray was big into counterfeiting. Counterfeiting foreign currencies in particular. Harder and harder to bullshit the US paper these days. Ray was working to perfect some of the third world, emerging markets stuff and then convert to dollars. Not a bad plan. Remo pieced this together based on some meetings he had with Ray's associates who came to Remo for legal services over the last year or so.

You see, Ray had Remo on retainer as well. Different from J. Slim, but similar.

All of this is to say Remo knows Ray moves a lot of things around the board. Tons of illegal tonnage pushed, pulled, bought and sold. Drugs, guns, money, both fake and real, and if Remo and his buddies can find a way to disrupt that or, better yet, steal some significant portion of it, then they can use it to leverage a way out for Anna and Sean.

Maybe.

Perhaps.

It's not a plan without risk, but it's the best one Remo has.

Remo explains his thoughts to Lester and Hollis and ties this idea back to that piece of shit, asshole D-something brother of J. Slim. That guy is the way to get in. That guy is the weakest link in a chain that is otherwise strong as hell. If they break D-something wide open, then they've got a chance.

Remo and Hollis know something else.

This D-something motherfucker is a junkie, and a junkie can be squeezed. More to the point, this D-something junkie can be squeezed hard by Hollis and Lester, and will sing like a canary. After the singing ends, Remo can find out where to hit Ray, but first they need to find this guy. Well, first they need to remember the little fucker's name.

"Duffy," Lester says.

Remo stops just short of telling him, *No*. He can't. Hollis and Remo look to one another. That's it. Lester's right.

"Do you know this guy?" Remo asks Lester.

"No," he says.

"Well," Hollis says, "how in the hell—"

"Was thinking of Cloris and I remembered a three-way we had once together and it was with this dude named Duffy." Lester sighs. "This was a while back. It's not your Duffy, because Cloris killed him after we were done. He made a rude comment about her. Something about a nipple. Anyway, that's what made me think of it."

Remo and Hollis blink. That's the most they've heard Lester say at one time.

"Glad I could help," Lester says.

6

It's a long road to NY from NM.

They can do it in a day if they ride hard straight through and if they don't mind destroying a few speed laws along the way. Remo thinks he has a day or so to work with. J. Slim knows damn well he can't roll with a commercial airline back to NYC. Not with the heat that's on him. Even a fucking asshole like him knows how the world works. This is why the psycho on the iPad is simply watching. All these things lead Remo to believe he has some time to get to New York. Also, the psycho on the iPad had held up a piece of paper with a date and time written on it. A time to meet.

It's in two days.

Remo, Lester and Hollis have loaded up the Yukon with the guns and money they took from Cormack. This gives them a somewhat respectable stash of weapons, ammo and cash. They know it's not enough. They know they need things. Things they don't have. They need more money if they are going to go after Ray. On a positive note, they have a good idea where to get some. They've decided to make a quick stop by the Mashburn compound. It's a risky-as-hell move, but they know it will be worth it.

Hopefully.

After much fighting and getting lost trying to find the way up the mountain, they pull up to the back gate. They've made it. They decide that one of them should stay by the Yukon and lay on the horn if any shit comes their way. Hollis draws the short straw and stays behind. Armed to the teeth, of course.

It's very strange being back here, Remo thinks. Granted it's only been about an hour or so, but stepping over the bodies, dodging the blood and all that can mess with a person's head. Even if that person is Remo Cobb.

They also know they have to be quick. There's no telling how fast people will come and check it out or how quickly Johnny Law will work its way up the mountain. They made a shitload of noise during that battle at the compound. Hard to believe it went completely unnoticed, but the isolated location does buy them some time.

Some time. Not an eternity.

The thinking was there might be some money or guns or at least something to eat at the compound that they could use. Money is a cure-all for some of the shit they might encounter and they know damn well they don't have enough of it. As selfish as it sounds, Remo is secretly hoping there's some Johnnie Blue in the compound. He hates himself for even looking, but shit, man, the urge goes bone deep.

Remo wanted Lester to come along with him into the compound on the off chance he might have some familiarity with the place, considering Lester knew Daddy Mashburn better than he and Hollis did. Lester, of course, had no idea where to go once they got inside.

The place is massive in every direction. A truly jaw-dropping home, and it's a little hard to believe the Mashburns put this place together. It's like an upscale ski lodge. Stone fireplace. Ceiling reaching to the heavens. Skylight letting the sun peek in, with rays bouncing off the hardwood floors and polished oak furniture.

They hit the kitchen first. Lester fills a Nike bag with some chips, drinks and shit. There's a fully cooked, five-pound brisket wrapped in foil centered in the fridge like a prized jewel in a museum. Big score. They also snag some potato salad and some forks.

Lester assumes that any money or anything of value would be hidden.

He's right.

Not only hidden, but protected.

There's a side wing to the compound. Just off the back part of the main house. Blacked out windows. Heavy door. Pretty damn obvious. Remo and Lester take positions on either side of the door. They share eyes and make a silent count to three. Remo tries the knob knowing damn well it won't work.

It doesn't.

He looks to his watch. They've been there about five minutes already. They wanted to be in and out in less than ten. Remo looks to Lester. Lester shrugs his shoulders. Remo shrugs his shoulders. He doesn't like being there this long. His look to Lester is almost trying to tell him, *Well, we tried. Let's get the hell out of here.*

Lester gets the signal, doesn't disagree, and he starts backing away.

A blast rips through the door.

Lester and Remo hit the floor face-first.

There's the faint sound of a shotgun pump from the other side of the door before another hole punches through.

Remo covers his head with his hands while turning to Lester. Lester springs up with his gun at the ready. He pushes his back against the wall to the right of the blown-out door. It's now quiet. Smoke from the shotgun blast twists and twirls into the air. Stink of gunpowder fills the room. There's an ever-so-slight rustling sound from inside the room.

"Dammit. Look," Remo calls out to whoever's in the room as he gets up, "we don't want a lot of shit. We just want to get out of here. No harm. No foul."

"Shut the fuck up," Cloris says, strolling out of the room with a bag in her fist and a shotgun leaning against her shoulder. She stops, standing between Remo and Lester. She looks them up and down then tags both of them in the dick with the butt of her shotgun. Remo and Lester drop to their knees.

"You pussies can have what's left," she says as she leaves.

From the ground, Lester and Remo can only watch her leave. She gives them the finger as she slips through the door and out of sight.

Remo has no idea what to say to Lester. Who would at a moment like this? She has punched him, nut thumped him, shot at him and left him all in the same day. This is new territory, even for Remo.

Remo goes with an understanding smile. Always a good move.

"Told you she'd kill us all," Lester says.

7

The longest part of the drive wasn't from New Mexico to New York.

It was when they hit NYC. It was a crawl. Remo kept an eye on the iPad, but to their word J. Slim's boy did not make a move. The connection was sketchy in spots along the trip. When they went dark outside New Mexico Remo's anxiety shot through the roof, but he was able to keep in good contact most of the way.

Oddly enough, there wasn't a whole lot of talk along the way. They took turns driving while at least one of them slept. The weight of the last few days had finally kicked all three of them in the teeth and they needed the time to decompress. As much as they could at least. There was a dicey moment when they thought they were going to get pulled over in Ohio, but thankfully the cop breezed on by.

They managed to get a decent take off the Mashburn compound. A fair amount of cash, and a stockpile of guns and ammo. They took it all, thinking that it might come in handy. You never know, but getting pulled over and explaining to cops why you're traveling with cash and an arsenal might prove challenging.

The ride also gave Remo some time to try and process this plan of theirs. It has holes you could drive a truck through, but it's what they've got to work with. Besides, in all the hours the trip has taken, Remo couldn't pull a more viable plan out of his ass.

Remo isn't completely sure where to find Duffy, but he's got a guess. The Jiggle Queen is a New Jersey strip joint and was a second home for young Duffy, if Remo remembers correctly. Of course Remo has spent some chunks of his life there as well. He tells himself it was all about business, and it was to a certain extent, but Remo enjoyed the flashes of bare skin and the smiles from ladies as much as the next poor slob.

Remo, Hollis and Lester haven't worked out the details yet, but they need to get Duffy to tell them what Ray has going on next. They need him to give up a money drop, a safe house, a card game, anything. Ray's operations are a flowing thing that roll in and out on a daily basis. Multiple moving parts. Things are always in constant motion. Remo needs one of those things. A thing that's got size. A thing that's big enough to get Ray's attention. Something that will hurt if it gets taken down and, oh yeah, they need it to happen today.

They enter the Jiggle Queen. The dark, open room is packed to the gills with desperation, driving beats and surgically enhanced grace twisting and grinding onstage. The air feels sweaty. The floor feels sticky. The money feels dirty. The three cut through the place like men on a mission. They are met by full-frontal nudity and fake smiles, but our boys pay them no mind. Well, not exactly no mind. They steal a quick eyeful, but the point is they don't stop and chat or get a dance for fuck's sake.

Scanning.

Searching.

They split up to cover the place. Remo watches with steely eyes. He takes in every face. Every drunken hope for companionship. Every twenty passed and every set of rolling eyes from the ladies. He glances toward the back.

His eyes pop.

He sees Duffy being led by the hand into a VIP room—the Jiggle Lounge. A separate room in the back for private dances at a price.

Remo twirls his finger in the air, getting Hollis's and Lester's attention. He points to the Jiggle Lounge's closing door.

Hollis and Remo rush in. They leave Lester to stay outside and watch the door. He knows his role here. He's there to grease the bouncers with some flash cash if they come by, and also to keep any pain in the ass horndogs from trying to step in. Lester can use force only if necessary.

Destiny is not happy about her new guests arriving in the lounge. Her faux sweetness dissolves fast the second she sees Remo and Hollis enter. There are rules here, dammit.

"No. No. Fuck no," Destiny spits out in the thickest of Jersey accents. "You motherfuckers step the hell outta this motherfucker here. Not doing some weird group love..." She pauses. Scrunches her nose. "Remo?"

Remo nods. "Hi."

She's not happy to see him. She charges hard at him. Like a pissed off bull. Hollis grabs her by the shoulders, holding her back along with her swinging arms and kicking legs. She screams, but Hollis covers her mouth best he can.

"I know. I know." Remo steps up to her, trying to reason with her. "I don't have time for apologies and all that shit. Let's just say you're not happy with me and I don't remember why."

She screams louder through Hollis's fingers.

Duffy now realizes what's up and starts to move toward the door on the sly.

"Sit the fuck down," Hollis barks.

Duffy complies. His ass lands in a chair fast.

"Good boy." Remo turns his attention back to Destiny. "Go outside. There is a man by the door. He will hand you a stack of cash and you will happily go away from this room and tell no one who's in here. Take the rest of the day off. Enjoy yourself."

She calms a bit. Stops screaming.

Remo nods for Hollis to move his hand.

"Outside? How much?" she asks hard, then shifts to a purr. "Give me a number, hon."

"It's enough," Remo says, hoping that Lester has enough.

"Okay," she says as she kisses Hollis and Remo on the cheek then slinks out of the room like the temptress she was born to be.

As the door shuts, Remo and Hollis turn their attention solely to Duffy. If Duffy could crawl under the dirty, sticky floor he would. He shakes, tremors working overtime from his fingers to his toes. Remo can't tell if this is fear or if the kid needs a taste to get him right.

This reminds Remo of something.

Something important.

He sticks his head outside the door, finding Destiny dancing for Lester. Lester has a hundred folded and stuck between his teeth. Remo starts to comment and/or condemn the both of them, but instead he stays on task.

"Can someone get me a Johnnie Blue?" Remo asks.

He gets blank stares from the two of them. Destiny has her head between her legs looking up at him with a *what the fuck, I'm working here* expression. Remo snatches the hundred from Lester's teeth, hands it to her and points to the bar.

"Johnnie. Blue, please."

Stepping back into the room, Remo shuts the door. The hum of Mötley Crüe is rattling the walls. Remo loves this jam, but fights that shit. He has work to do here. Hollis already has Duffy wrapped into a human pretzel. Remo flips a steel chair around and takes a seat so that he's eye level with Duffy. Remo has seen this scene worked by cops over the years. Now it's his turn to give it whirl.

"Now, Duffy, what should we talk about?" Remo asks.

"What the hell, man?" Duffy spits and sputters. "I didn't do shit to you and this ape prick."

Hollis slaps him.

Not too hard, but hard enough to let Duffy know there's another level he can go to. Remo lets the sting take hold. Wants to make sure Duffy can even feel it and is not completely stoned to the point of numbness. Duffy's twisted expression of sharp pain and annoyance lets Remo know that Duffy is firmly planted in the here and now.

"We don't have a lot of time here," Remo says. "We've come a long way just to see you, my boy."

"Ooooo, to what do I owe the pleasure of your company? I heard you're a dead man," Duffy says.

Hollis slaps him harder, almost knocking him from the chair.

"Probably, but before they get to me I might take some time and watch Hollis hurt you for a while. Give me a little giggle before I get my ticket punched." Remo leans back. "Yeah, let me think on that. It is the little things I'll miss when I'm dead."

As if on cue, Destiny steps in with Remo's Johnnie Blue. She sticks it in his hand.

"No change," she says, leaving.

Remo becomes entranced. Lost while looking into the glass. It really hasn't been that long, but it feels like decades to Remo. He sniffs. The hairs on the back of his neck fire up. He touches his mouth to the edge of the glass, letting the booze touch his lips ever so gently. He pulls back. Taking a moment. Don't rush it, he thinks. Then he tilts the glass back, taking a long pull. It burns the good burn. Remo almost feels himself come back online. His brain slides into place. His soul realigns. Can't help but think of Popeye getting him some spinach. Remo is back, and not a moment too soon.

He forgets that he's not alone in the universe. Turning, he sees both Hollis and Duffy staring at him like he's out of his mind.

"Didn't think that I'd like to have something?" Hollis holds his hands out. "Maybe dear Hollis would like a drink?"

"Yeah, rude motherfucker," Duffy chimes in.

Hollis slaps Duffy again, this time sending him spinning out from the chair. Remo downs the rest of his magical elixir, then slams the empty glass down hard. Making sure he has Duffy's attention, he gets up and helps Duffy back up into his chair. As he does, Remo fixes his shirt, giving Duffy a look of compassion. It's complete bullshit, but Remo couldn't care less. It's all part of the game he's running here.

"Tell him to stand down, man," Duffy says, looking at Hollis with eyes bugging out.

"No, no I'm not going to let Hollis tear you apart," Remo says, petting Duffy's hair. "As entertaining as that would be, I'm going high road with this here. I'm going to let you help us instead."

Duffy adjusts his mouth, working the feeling back to it as Remo walks toward the back corner of the room as if he's pondering something deeply. Duffy doesn't like the sound of this at all. When a man like Remo tracks you down at a strip club in the middle of the day, it's usually not out of kindness. This man wants something, and it's more than likely not something you'd like to give. Duffy shifts in his seat. Waiting like a child for his medicine.

"I need something. A time and a place. I need a time and place of a money thing that J. Slim is doing for Ray," Remo says, moving closer to Duffy as he speaks. The Johnnie Blue is working through his system, healing as it goes. Remo is feeling his superpowers of bullshit returning with a vengeance. "What I want—sorry." He motions to Hollis and then himself. "What we want is for you to give us something we can use. That's all."

Duffy wiggles in his chair. Claws at his wrists and arms.

"I know there's something going on out there. Ray's always got some kind of cash moving around the board. Just tell me what's going on. Today, preferably. Maybe we can help each other."

Duffy's head perks up.

Remo raises his eyebrows while nodding, coaxing it out of him.

"See. I appreciate you working with me on this. Maybe, just maybe, there's something you know about that you'd like a piece of. Something for you." Remo is reading the story that Duffy's weak, pathetic face is telling him. His sagging, tired mug is speaking to Remo loud and clear. The eyes, really. Remo is feeding off the hints his eyes are giving. Remo presses down the gas. "Can't be easy with a brother like J. Slim. Big. Bad. Mean as shit. The money. All the power. All the pussy." Remo looks to the door. "That why you come here so much? You take the few dollars J. Slim gives you and you come here to feel better. Scraps to raise self-esteem. Here they have to respect you, right? It's part of the deal. What you pay a cover charge for."

Duffy looks away. Hollis thinks of slapping him again, but sees that Remo is working him over harder than Hollis ever could.

"What if I offer you a cut of what we take?" Remo nods as Duffy looks his way. "That's it. What if I give you a nice slice for yourself? A little something to go off and do your own thing. Start something new."

Duffy's eyes lock with Remo's. Ding. Ding. Remo has his hooks in deep.

"You'd do that?" Duffy asks.

"Just give me something good and I'm open to all kinds of shit."

"How good?"

"Start talking and I'll let you know when we get to something."

Duffy sticks his tongue in the side of his cheek. Eyes look to the ceiling. Remo knows the first thing Duffy gives him is going to be complete shit. He hopes Hollis is ready to slap the shit out of him when Duffy comes back with whatever weak-ass offer is coming.

"I got one," Duffy says, snapping his fingers. "There's the game he runs on—"

Remo snaps his fingers too.

Hollis slaps the shit out of Duffy. Sends him spinning to the floor again.

"Okay. Okay. Fuck me." Duffy looks for Remo to help him up again.

Remo does not. Remo simply stares back, waiting. Hollis crosses his arms.

"There's a big one," Duffy says. "Tomorrow morning. At an airport."

"Where?" Hollis asks, moving closer.

Duffy cowers. "White Plains, man. Tiny, private airport. Hangar with a strip of land. J. Slim is working an exchange—real dollars for funny money."

Remo looks to Hollis. They know the implication of this. They both know Ray has been working the counterfeit game hard for a while. If they can take this down it'll be US cash and God knows how much fake foreign currencies. This might work.

Could be huge.

Could be enough to move the needle.

Could be enough to make this right and get Anna and Sean out of harm's way.

Remo helps Duffy up and sits him down, flashing kind eyes as he says, "That's a good one, Duffy. We can work you a nice cut off that one."

"You better."

"Now, let's not go that way now. We were doing so well," Remo says, looking to Hollis.

Duffy recoils.

"You got a time?" Remo asks.

"I do."

"And you're sure about this thing?" Hollis says. "If you have us stepping into a shitstorm I will personally gut your weak bitch ass."

"No. It's real. It's huge. So huge..." Duffy trails off.

"What?" Remo asks.

"Might need more people."

Remo and Hollis share a look.

"What do you mean?" Remo asks.

"I mean this is a big fucking deal. There's going to be numbers, guns and muscle. You've got, what? How many of you? I'm a lover not a fighter. There's money to harvest, bro, I swear, but you're walking into a heavily armed situation."

Hollis starts to pace.

"How many of them?" Remo asks.

"Hard to say."

"Fucking guess."

"Ten, twenty."

"Thirty?" Hollis steps up. "Forty? Fifty?"

"It's possible," Duffy says. "Can I get a drink, too?"

"No," Remo says. "How much money?"

"Millions."

"Millions? Millions of real or millions of fake?" Remo asks.

"Both. Shit, man."

Hollis takes Remo aside. He talks clearly and deliberately, making sure each word lands with Remo. "I'm not saying no. You know I'm in,

MIKE MCCRARY

but if this fuckstick is telling the truth, this is one of those things that could start a war."

Remo nods. He knows, but he knows he doesn't have a choice.

"He's not wrong," Hollis says. "We need more people."

Remo turns to Duffy. "You got somebody in mind, don't you? Somebody to bring in."

Duffy grins and nods.

Remo and Hollis do not like the look he's giving.

"Well, who?" Remo asks.

"The Turkovs," Duffy says. "They reached out too. Just yesterday, but they just threatened to kill me. No money like you fine folks. I was actually here with Destiney as a little 'goodbye to the world' party."

"You know these Turkovs?" Remo asks Hollis. Hollis shakes his head no.

"Oh, you'll love them." Duffy laughs. "And they will sure as shit love you."

PART II

EVERYBODY'S COOL UNTIL THEY'RE NOT

8

L uxury by the square foot.

Windows stretch from the polished concrete floors to the ceiling giving a stunning view out onto the Hudson. Remo, Lester and Hollis stand a few feet behind Duffy. Duffy hasn't introduced everyone yet. He only stands, shakes and stares. Actually, he hasn't even spoken yet.

There's a dull thump as a body hits the floor across the room.

They pretend not to notice, but they do.

At a long table sit two Russian kingpins. The before-mentioned Turkovs. Not twins, but close. Big, all business, stone-cold killers. Turkov Brother One sets down his smoking .45, returning to his massive meal while seated next to his brother. Steaming plates of motherland goodness are laid out in front of them. Cabbage rolls, borscht and some shashlik are being destroyed by Turkov Brothers One and Two. Near the table are two well-dressed Russian thugs who try to hide their profession with expensive suits.

A cell buzzes by the borscht. Turkov Brother Two answers. "Yes?"

Remo, Hollis and Lester watch on as the gunshot-riddled body is dragged off by two more thugs using chains while the Turkov phone conversation continues.

"Yes," Brother Two says. "Then correct the problem. You've been a good friend and it is appreciated, but you cannot argue there have been bumps."

Brother One keeps working the food on his plate, stopping only to add, "Fuckin' bumps."

"Be sure your operation works better than your last stray little doggie we just took care of."

"Fuckin' doggie."

A chainsaw starts up in the background. Brother Two ends his call and stabs a chunk of beef with his fork. The brothers don't even pause their chewing as the chainsaw wails going to work in the other room.

To nobody in particular, Brother One says, "Fear and greed are only what moves people. This is why we have plenty of guns and money."

The brothers lock eyes with their guests. Making a point as the noise from the other room changes slightly. It's clear now the sound of the chainsaw has shifted to cutting flesh. The brothers return to their meal. Remo fights not to show his fear. Hollis and Lester are very skilled at either not being afraid at all or masking the hell out of it. Duffy is seconds away from pissing all over himself.

"You," Brother One says, motioning to Duffy. "The fuck you want? You bring friends this time. Why?"

Duffy clears his throat. Stops. Then starts again. He gives the Turkovs a quick, but more or less accurate, explanation of why Remo and company are there. Tells them that they want what the Turkovs want. They want to take down Ray and his White Plains airport operation. He explains who Remo is and how, maybe, they could help.

The chainsaw sound stops.

The Turkovs glance to one another.

"You," Brother One says to Remo. "Step up here."

Remo reluctantly moves up beside Duffy, tries a fake smile.

"Don't do that," Brother One says. "The smile, it's false, fuck that."

Remo's face drops.

"You a lawyer?"

Remo nods.

"I have no use for lawyers. You see we take care of things before there is a need for lawyer."

Brother Two raises his gun and puts two bullets into Duffy's chest.

Duffy spins then drops to the floor.

Remo jumps about a foot and a half. Lester and Hollis don't even blink. The two Russian thugs from before come back to the room with the chains and drag off Duffy's body. Remo's pretty sure he saw one of them roll their eyes, annoyed with the heavy workload.

"You see?" Brother One says. "No need for lawyer. Duffy was a cunt."

"Cunt," Brother Two says, returning to his meal.

"Mr. Turkov, both of you, we can help you," Remo says.

"Explain how you can help," Brother One says.

"We have guns. A lot of them. Clean. All of them. We have no use for them. We will give them to you as a gift." Remo gets nothing from them but dead eyes. "We also have this." He motions for Lester, who steps forward and sets down an envelope of cash. Cash they lifted from the Mashburn compound. Brother Two picks it up, thumbing through the bills.

Remo continues. "Not to mention you get the three of us on the job. Now think about it. That's guns, money and three hitters to help make this a smoother score."

Brother One leans back.

The chainsaw starts up again in the other room.

"Why?" he asks.

"Why what?" Remo asks back.

"Why do you want this so bad? Why so generous, or so desperate?"

"I need J. Slim."

The brothers perk up.

"You can have the take. The US dollars and the foreign funny money. I don't care about it. I need J. Slim alive. That's it. Period."

"Again, why?"

"He has my ex-wife."

"So?"

Remo pauses, thinks of laying on some serious bullshit but thinks better of it. He remembers his moment of honesty with Hollis and Lester. It worked. Worked like a charm. Given that Hollis and Lester probably share some of the same characteristics as these Turkov brothers, Remo thinks a similar tactic might work.

Can't hurt.

He hopes.

He takes a deep breath, swims through the bullshit he had loaded up, then looks deep, digging out the truth.

"And my son."

This stops the Turkovs cold. Their stares harden.

"J. Slim and Ray took my son."

There's a sudden, silent anger that seems to tighten their once blank faces. Remo has no idea what the genesis is, but there is an unmistakable shift in attitude. Maybe they have sons. Maybe they lost sons. Perhaps they are about to have sons or any combination thereof, but the second the word *son* left Remo's lips the mood changed.

The brothers nod together.

Remo looks back to Hollis and Lester. They know the same thing. These mean-ass Russians? They're all in.

Brother One says, "The enemy of my enemy is my friend."

Remo nods. *Indeed.*

The meaty hum of a chainsaw hitting flesh sounds from the next room.

Perhaps Destiny will remember Duffy fondly.

9

Oleg and Poe are two walls of Russian muscle, and they do not speak much.

Hardly at all.

These are the two men the Turkovs assigned/gave to them for assistance. They are big, intimidating and, from what they're told, deadly as hell. Remo unloaded the guns they took off the Mashburn compound along with a healthy sum of cash, as promised. The Turkovs grunted thanks of some sort and offered up these two muscle-bound, trigger-happy Russian death machines.

These fine boys, along with Remo, Lester and Hollis, are in the Yukon and headed to the place Duffy spoke of in White Plains. Hollis drives with Lester riding shotgun, and Remo sits sandwiched between Oleg and Poe in the back. The Turkovs wanted it this way so their people could keep an eye on things, and if something went the wrong way Oleg and Poe could gun down everyone in the car.

Forward-thinking, those Turkovs.

Remo can appreciate that.

Thankfully, Duffy gave the Turkovs all the info about the drop before they shot him in the chest and carved him up into cuts of beef. Truly a rookie move on Duffy's part. Never give up everything before the job. Never tell them that you've told them ALL they need to know. Always leave something, a piece of info, in your back pocket so they don't do to you exactly what they did to Duffy. Sad, but stupid doesn't last long in this business of sin, or any business for that matter, regardless of morality.

There's a small airport near White Plains, New York, with a warehouse or hangar or whatever you want to call it just off the runway. According to the Turkovs it's a private deal. So private and exclusive that only a handful of assholes know about its existence. It's as if a rectangle has been cut out of the trees, and then a tiny airport was dumped in.

The funny money drop is between some asshole criminals, not the Turkovs, and Ray's people. The Turkovs hate everyone involved and would really like it if Remo and company kill everybody there, but they are realistic. They'll settle for the cash, both funny and real, and as many deaths as humanly possible. They are not greedy people.

Remo isn't completely comfortable with the slaughter aspect of the Turkovs' plans, but he'll leave that up to Oleg and Poe. His focus is zeroed in on J. Slim. Remo, Lester and Hollis all know they are to grab him and get him to give up where Sean and Anna are.

That's it.

Simple.

Not easy, but not complicated either.

They may have to become, more or less, bodyguards for J. Slim once the party gets started. Once the bullets start popping and the shells start dropping things can get weird in a hurry. Nobody knows this more than Remo, Lester and Hollis. If J. Slim catches a stray 9mm to the skull, then this whole thing was a waste of time. Once they get to J. Slim they have to go full-on Secret Service and protect him as if the free world depended on him. If J. Slim gets popped, then Anna and Sean are as good as dead.

Even the idea of that twists at Remo's guts. The idea he'd be the cause of that would be the end of Remo. That's it. If that's how this thing plays out, Remo will turn the gun on himself and lullaby his own ass. He's already decided it. Maybe it's the coward's way out, but Remo isn't all that concerned about his legacy at this point.

"Fuck that shit," Remo says to himself.

That isn't going to happen.

He's not a *power of positive thinking* type of dude, but he knows he can't allow the idea of failure to creep into his thinking. If you start thinking that way there's a possibility of you thinking scared. Scared makes you cautious. Makes you second-guess. Makes you waste time with thought and analysis. That fraction of a second you spend on that bullshit might be the difference between success and failure.

Or life and death.

Remo has to already think—sorry, *know*—in his heart that this battle is won and he's done what he had to do. In Remo's mind, the war has already been won. Anna and Sean are safe and everything is okay. Now all he has to do is paint by numbers and get this little exercise done. Lester and Hollis know what to do. Not a concern there. Oleg and Poe look like they've done this sort of thing before and have enjoyed it. Well, as much as they can enjoy anything.

Yeah, Remo and this crew, they're gonna make this shit look easy.

There's no way in hell they're going to storm that airport hangar, get mowed down in seconds flat by a wave of lead. No way Ray's psycho boy in NYC will kill Anna and Sean with a grin on his face.

That can't happen.

Not even possible.

No.

The hell with that shit.

Remo swallows big as the airport appears beyond the trees.

plane cuts through the purple dawn sky.

Remo spots it in the distance, pointing it out to everyone in car as if he were a child seeing a plane for the first time. He's actually bouncing in his seat. The anxiety is getting to him. It's tearing, pulling at him, but he knows he can't let it rip him completely apart. He's been cool up until now, somewhat cool, but the weight of it all is starting to take its toll, and it shows. He's starting to exhibit some cracks. Frayed edges can no longer be hidden by ego and bravado. Lester and Hollis share a look between them, knowing they need to keep an eye on Remo. They are fairly sure he'll pull it together. They've known him to be a gamer recently, but you never know someone's breaking point until it snaps in two.

Everybody's cool until they're not.

Hollis parks the Yukon a safe distance from the airport, but close enough to get a good view of the comings and goings of the place. Lester and Oleg watch through high-powered binoculars. As the plane gets closer and closer to touchdown, they notice something else moving toward the airport. On the ground this time. There are two silver Cadillacs passing through the gates and pulling up to the metal hangar near the runway. Everyone in the car stops. Collective breath held. This is the moment they get some idea of how many people and what kind of firepower they are up against. They all know it.

Four armed goons step out from the Caddies. Armed, but not ridiculous.

"Now we got something," Lester says.

A grunt from Oleg. A collective sigh. They all lock eyes on the runway.

"Where's J. Slim?" Remo asks, his nervous energy lumping up into this throat.

"Don't see 'em yet," Lester says.

"Where the hell is he?"

"Just said I don't see him."

Oleg grunts. So does Poe.

"That's not okay," Remo says.

"What would you like him to do about it?" Hollis chimes in, trying to bring Remo back down to earth. "Dial it down, man."

"I'd like him to tell me that J. Slim is there. I'd love for him to tell me that piece of shit is there, because if he's not then this whole thing is one big motherfucking—"

"Got 'em," Lester says.

Remo turns quickly. Eyes wide. Like a dog that heard a cheese wrapper. He shoves Oleg to the side and plants his face against the glass to get a better view. They all watch J. Slim slip out from the back seat of the last Caddy. He's dressed to the nines, as usual, with his smug confidence front and center, even from this distance. J. Slim nods to his goons. From the trunks, large forty-pound black bags are unloaded, one after the other. The goons snatch them up, loading them into the hangar without a hint of ceremony, all under the watchful eye of J. Slim.

Remo's stare goes in and out of focus, only allowing his eyes leave J. Slim long enough to look to Hollis. They share the briefest of moments. Recognition. A memory shared between them. A memory of J. Slim. A story they both know.

The J. Slim story.

It's a rare thing when someone gets over on Remo and Hollis, but J. Slim is a rare bird indeed.

J. Slim was on a job. On a hit in Singapore.

Hollis was on a job. On a hit in Singapore.

They were both paid handsomely to eliminate a target by two separate parties. One had paid J. Slim and the other paid Hollis. An overlap in killer coverage. Not unheard of, but it doesn't happen very often.

Both of the killers were clients of Remo Cobb, so Remo being Remo, brokered a deal between Hollis and J. Slim that would allow them both to get credit for the kill and get them both paid by their separate parties. Their employers wouldn't care one way or the other. They cared about getting a corpse in return. Dead is dead no matter who does the deed. The idea being that two trained killers working together would almost guarantee a desired result without headaches. That is really what these people wanted in the end. It's not about the money, necessarily, it's about getting this dude done dead without problems. Problems can turn out to be more expensive than hitmen.

Of course, this all went to hell.

J. Slim and Hollis meticulously worked out the details. Combed over every single nuance. Went over the schematics of buildings. Street maps. Layouts of rooms. Weather patterns. They kept spreadsheets of comings and goings. They knew when his kids went to school, when his wife went to work and when he walked the dog. This was designed to be a clean, tight kill. One target. One body. No muss and certainly no fuss.

On the day of the thing J. Slim went in early.

Alone.

He went in without telling Hollis or Remo.

J. Slim went in and murdered everyone in the house. The target, the wife, the kids and the dog. J. Slim said later it was to send a message. A clear message to others that would think about talking to the Feds as the target did.

Hollis beat the shit out of him.

Remo watched. Remo enjoyed watching, because he hated J. Slim just as much as Hollis for what he had done. Their shared hate had nothing to do with the job or the money. Like stated before, both paying parties just wanted the thing done, and then J. Slim went off on his own. He ignored the plan that was tight and clean and humane and didn't involve killing an innocent family. J. Slim did the job via a gas leak and a lit match while they were sleeping.

"No muss. No fuss," said J. Slim

Not how Hollis took it as he beat on J. Slim's face like he was tenderizing a roast. Remo held Hollis' gun and stood back, but was very supportive from the sidelines.

After taking a considerable pounding, J. Slim pulled his emergency blade from his ankle. Gave it a whip-slice. Cut Hollis across the chest, leaving a scar that Hollis still holds. This gave J. Slim enough of a break to escape. He slipped off back to Ray, never to been seen again. That was until J. Slim showed up at a CIA safe house in New Mexico not long ago.

Much to Remo's disgust.

Men like Hollis and Remo have learned to compartmentalize their hate and horror. It's the only way to survive their lines of work. The only way to deal with the ups and downs and the horrific humans they run across. Remo's compartmentalization has sprung some leaks as of late, but he had indeed put his box of J. Slim loathing aside until recently. Seeing him come out of the car in New Mexico opened it up however. Remo can't speak for Hollis, but he would like nothing more than to see a lot of blood loss from J. Slim.

No, Remo is pretty sure he can speak for Hollis on this one.

J. Slim face down in a puddle of his own blood would be agreeable.

That? That they can both get onboard with.

Remo stares out the window, watching J. Slim. Back to the here and now. His mind rolling, racing, ripping through the events that have passed and the moments that are passing before his eyes now. He checks the back. The Yukon is filled with guns.

Tools, Hollis calls them.

Indeed. Work needs to be done.

A lot of people are going to die. Remo is way past the morality of all that. A few days ago death bothered him. Gave him a moment of pause. A few days ago he didn't know what it was like to have your life truly in danger.

Now?

Now having his life on the line is his steady state. A constant, daily activity much like water, air and Johnnie Blue. Actually, now, meaning today, it's worse than that. Remo didn't think it could get worse, but he was wrong. Now, today, his family's lives are on the line, and that is not something Remo will ever get comfortable with. Yes, it's a strained family at best, but it is the only family he knows, and they don't deserve to be in the middle of this jacked-up, Remo-induced shitshow.

He snaps away from the path his brain has taken him on and turns his focus on the task at hand—the runaway, the hangar and the assholes with the Caddies. The bags have been removed and moved into the hangar. One can assume those bags are filled with money of some sort. Who knows how much green is in there? Who knows how much firepower waits in there? Who knows who or what is in that plane?

Hollis looks to Remo, then Lester. The three nod. This is what they do. Friends forged by chaos. Partners who've weathered some choppy-ass seas. Partners in their new, thrown-together startup —Mayhem Inc.

Oleg and Poe grunt while loading up 9mm sidearms, shotguns, assault rifles and strapping on Kevlar vests. Lester and Hollis do the same. Oleg shoves a vest into Remo's chest.

He takes a deep breath.

The plane's wheels touch ground.

Shit just got real, real fast.

11

The nondescript warehouse-looking plane hangar sits among several other run-down storage facilities.

Remo and the rest of Mayhem Inc. are now on foot. They stay slow and low, stopping frequently so they can study the target ahead and pivot to any changes that might pop up.

Like bullets and carnage.

The surrounding trees provide a good amount of cover for them to move in and out, along with some shade from a clear line of sight from the runway. Remo thinks they've come a long way from New Mexico to be right back in the woods about to storm into certain death. This seems to be new for Oleg and Poe. Hiking is not part of their skillset. They lean against trees catching their breath, but remain pissed-off looking and focused on the runway ahead.

Two of J. Slim's goons stand by the doors of the hangar. Watchful faces darting left and right. Suits, shades and guns. They roll the large steel doors open, allowing J. Slim and the rest of the goons to enter. At a quick count, there seems to be four, not counting J. Slim. All with hard looks and armed as hell. Five on five, Remo thinks, maybe another couple on the plane. Element of surprise riding on their side. This they can do without breaking a sweat.

Another Caddy pulls up. Five more armed goons step out.

"Fuck," Remo mutters.

J. Slim motions for his new friends to take positions. He stops just short of entering the hangar as he steals a peek at the plane that's now taxiing in.

Remo's not an expert on aircraft, but he thinks the plane is a Gulfstream G-something. He's flown in a couple of similar-looking jets before. Last-minute trips to Vegas, Aspen, Thailand and every place in between. All with clients. All with criminals, murderers and thieves. Remo guesses that's exactly what's about to stroll out of this Gulfstream G-something, too.

J. Slim waves to the plane as the door opens. He motions for his goons to make a move. A pack of them race over from the side of the hangar towards the plane as it rolls to a stop. The goons position themselves perfectly in line with the opening door of the plane as the stairs begin folding down. A few moments pass. Remo can see J. Slim smiling, but keeping a hand on his gun. Business-friendly without an ounce of trust.

From out of the plane steps what looks to be some muscle from that side of the deal. Eurotrash with a good tailor. All with five o'clock stubble, dark hair, dark complexions and dark, dark souls. Two of them carefully work their way down the stairs with assault rifles held tightly to their chests. They move with purpose, but don't rush, scanning the area while working their way down the stairs toward the hangar. One stays near the doors of the hangar in sight of the plane while the other goes inside.

Remo watches carefully to try and pick up anything they might give him. Some kind of info he can glean from appearances. From their faces. Their eyes.

Nothing.

Expressions? Stone-faced.

Talking? None.

Anything useful? Nope.

After a minute or so one of the Eurotrash muscle boys comes out from the hangar and gives a thumbs-up to the plane. Remo and the rest of his team share eyes, re-grip their guns, then move forward a few feet. They are still about fifty yards from the hangar, but close enough for striking distance.

They stop again, taking a new position behind some trees closer to the hangar. Out from the plane step two more walking slabs of Eurotrash muscle, followed by a three-hundred-pound man in a white suit, black tie, and a Yankees cap, puffing a cigarette like a chimney. Behind him is another batch of muscle. Remo has given up counting the goons and Eurotrash. It's doing more harm to his confidence than good.

"You know him?" Remo whispers to Oleg and Poe.

They shake their heads.

"Never seen Mr. Three Bills around before?" he asks again.

They look annoyed, but still shake their heads.

"You?" Remo asks, looking to Hollis and Lester. "You know Three Bills over there?"

Hollis and Lester both answer the same as Oleg and Poe.

Remo looks hard, trying to place him, but cannot. More than a little odd that no one from this group recognizes this guy. This is a group of people who know more than a few criminals. It's a big country, but a fairly small community, and word gets around. Especially ones who have big money. Three Bills appears to be connected to something. Something big. At least connected to Ray in some way.

Three Bills stops by the stairs and returns J. Slim's wave. He waits as two of his guys come from the back of the plane wheeling out two large silver cases about the size of coffins. Three Bills points them to the hangar. J. Slim watches as the cases are pushed past him and into the hangar. He pats the top of one. It takes a minute or two, but Three Bills eventually reaches J. Slim. They shake hands and enter the hangar together.

Once they are inside, the two goons stationed at the doors roll them shut with a loud, echoing clang. The goons get back into position, waiting outside the doors. Lester points out another two, who are walking around the outside of the hangar, and two Eurotrash muscle boys waiting by the plane.

Remo brings everyone in close. He speaks low, choosing his words carefully, because he knows he doesn't have much time to work with.

"You can murder every motherfucker in there. Do whatever you have to do, but J. Slim lives. Secure him, slap him around, whatever, but I need him with a functioning brain and the ability to speak. Got it?"

He looks around his team, making strong eye contact with each of them. Making sure he's heard loud and clear. There's a long pause, then he gets the response he wants. The nods come in one by one.

"Good. Now, let's see if we can do this without getting our asses shot to hell."

whisper-zip of a bullet slices through the air.

A goon's head explodes.

The body drops.

Another whisper-zip.

A second goon's head explodes. That body drops.

Hollis has fired two bullets, dropped two goons and cleared the entrance for him and his team without a single extra beat of his heart.

Calm.

Cool.

Precise murder.

This is what Hollis does. Lester, Oleg and Poe move fast out from the trees. They hit the Eurotrash muscle hard, moving like lightning. They work their knives to slice the life away from them.

Quiet.

Only the wind.

Airplane is now cleared. Remo stands next to Hollis by a tree just off the runway. Hollis's breathing is slow and steady, tracking the area through his scope. Remo fights his breathing that desperately wants to go apeshit. He works hard, keeping it under wraps, but he has to gasp, wheeze and cry. Hollis waits patiently. He wants the other two goons to round the hangar so he can remove them from the planet just as he did the two by the hangar doors. Lester, Oleg and Poe take cover behind one of the Caddies, checking their weapons. Waiting for Hollis to drop these clowns.

Seconds crawl. Creep. Each one more painful than the next.

Seems like hours.

Unbearable.

The first one comes around the corner, stops and lights a cigarette. The two dead goons with freshly popped skulls are close by, lying not far from his feet. Hollis knows he needs to get a visual on both of them before he can fire. Does him no good to drop one and then have the other go berserk and start yelling, shooting or making phone calls for reinforcements.

Lester sees the other goon. One Hollis and Remo can't see from where they are.

The goon's texting near the back corner of the hangar. The goon with the cigarette is now only a few feet from stumbling over the dead bodies. If he finds them and goes berserk, then this thing gets set off and shit gets much, much more complicated.

Hollis knows it.

Remo knows it.

Everybody knows it.

Remo looks to Lester. Lester can't maneuver to get anywhere near Texting Goon without the other one spotting him. Lester points toward the back corner, letting Remo and Hollis know where Texting Goon is located. Cigarette Goon takes a step forward without looking, his toe barely an inch or two away from the body on the ground.

Remo can feel this whole thing going to hell. In his mind, he can envision everything falling apart and drifting away. The mistakes that can happen when panic and fear set in. The coveted element of surprise can go to shit in a hurry when everyone is armed, dangerous and scared as hell. Bullets fly. People you don't want dead end up dead. Remo can see J. Slim catching a bullet and getting killed before Remo can find out where Anna and Sean are.

He can't let that happen.

That will not happen.

He checks his Glock, thinks, then grabs the Sig Live Free or Die knife off of Hollis's ankle. Hollis looks at him like *what the hell are you doing?* Remo runs hard around the other side of the hangar, away from Cigarette Goon, with his gun in one hand and the knife in the other. Lester and Hollis look to one another with arms out. *What the hell is he doing?*

Hollis returns his focus back on Cigarette Goon. It's a delicate game here. If that goon can clear the corner and get out of sight from Texting Goon then Hollis can take him out. But he can't fire until Cigarette Goon is out of sight, and if Cigarette Goon moves too much farther he'll see the bodies for sure. Hollis tracks his face for two reasons. One, to pull the trigger and remove half of it. Two, to see if his expression changes to something that reads like *holy shit, dead bodies.*

Remo reaches the back of the hangar. He slows to a walk, doing his best to quiet his steps. He can hear a cough from around the corner. Maybe only a few feet from where Remo is standing.

Hollis keeps his finger on the trigger.

Remo inches closer and closer. He pulls the Sig knife back.

Cigarette Goon's toe touches a dead goon's body.

He stops, looks down, then looks up.

"Shit," Hollis whispers to himself.

Hollis drops Cigarette Goon with a zip-shot between the eyes.

Remo rounds the corner, finding Texting Goon, who's no longer texting. He's got his back to Remo looking toward the front of the hangar where his smoking buddy's body just leaned back, straightened, swayed, then slumped to the ground.

"Fuck," Remo says.

It happened so fast.

He can't believe he said it out loud.

He simply let the word slip from his mouth. Texting Goon spins back around to Remo. Remo lunges hard, slamming his hand over the goon's mouth. The second he does it he realizes he should have done something different. Hollis would have just slashed the guy's

throat without thinking about it. Lester would have destroyed him
before he could have turned around in the first place. This is the
difference between Remo and them. Crazy and sane. Killer and not.
Remo is tougher and stronger than he was a few days ago, but he is
not a natural born killer, and if he's being honest, he doesn't want
to be.

Remo manages to cover the goon's mouth, forcing him down to
the ground. He slaps his cell phone away as it buzzes with a new text.
The goon throws a punch, tagging Remo in the nose. A muted
crunch. Remo falls back a bit giving the goon a second of freedom.
The goon flips over, reverse crab-crawling away. Remo leaps forward,
landing on the goon's back and jamming an elbow in his back and a
hand under his chin forcing his mouth closed. Remo whips and
rocks. Rough-riding him like a mechanical bull cranked to intense.
He holds on for dear life, makes it maybe two seconds.

A whisper-zip.

Remo hits the ground face-first. Skids.

The body that was throwing him like a rag doll went completely
limp. In a snap. Just like that. Looking up from the dirt, Remo sees
Hollis and Lester standing at the other end of the hangar.

Hollis lowers his rifle. Lester gives a thumbs-up. Oleg and
Poe stare.

"Fuck," Remo says again. His face throbs. He can feel the blood
dripping from his nose. Hopes the dirt will slow the flow.

Lester helps Remo to his feet, handing him his gear. They each
pull down classic bank robber ski masks and walk toward the
entrance of the hangar. No discussion. The plan is still a green light.
They decided that covering their faces was the best way to go. No
reason to advertise who they are on the off chance that anyone comes
out of this party alive.

Remo and Mayhem Inc. ready themselves at the doors.

Lester carefully places his hands on the door's handle, ready to
slide it open on command. Remo's command. Hollis has slung the
rifle over his back and positioned an AR ready to go. Oleg and Poe
check their sidearms and ankle knives. Remo gives Hollis his Sig

back. The Russians set their ARs as well. Remo, not Hollis's suggestion, will stick with the Glock 9mm. Hollis wanted Remo to go in heavy just like everybody else. Even though Remo had used some heavy tools during the Mashburn ambush at his place in the Hamptons, Remo is more comfortable with the handgun. Not sure why. Feels right.

Remo stands with Hollis on one side with Poe and Oleg behind them and Lester at the door. Hollis went over some sweeping techniques earlier and he hopes to hell that information sunk into these thick, dickhead skulls. He kept it basic, but ya know, it's all about the audience.

Taking a moment of pause, Remo stops to reset. A second to breathe. He hasn't done much of it in the last few minutes. Perhaps it's a mistake to stand here and think about what he's about to do. About what he's about to walk into. All the potential violence that's waiting beyond that door. The amount that will be inflicted on both sides. The blood that will spill and splat. The screams of pain and the ending of life.

Perhaps Remo's got it all wrong.

Perhaps it will go peacefully. Remo can get J. Slim and Oleg and Poe can grab their money and then Remo will find Anna and Sean and everything will be fine. Just fine. Remo knows that's absolute bullshit, but he finds the idea comforting. At least at a time like this. Power of positive thinking. Glass half full and all that.

Hollis looks to the frozen Remo.

Hollis spanks him on the ass. Hard.

Remo snaps back to the here and now.

He smiles, then nods to Lester to open death's damn door.

13

The hangar is empty save for a few long tables with a few more goons stationed at each table.

Next to them are clipboards, paperwork and heavy-duty money counting machines. Bags are systematically emptied on the tables. Goons and Eurotrash take their places watching over as the others pull out stacks and stacks of fresh, shrink-wrapped cash. The goons count and check the contents of the bags under the watchful eyes of J. Slim and Three Bills. Their focus is hard, but they try to hang onto a level of cool. At least J. Slim does. Three Bills gave up on cool a long time ago.

The hangar is silent save for the rhythmic flipping of bills running through counting machines. No one speaks. Moderate eye contact.

Three Bills busts up the quiet by leaning over to J. Slim and saying, "If there's a penny missing, I'm cutting off balls."

J. Slim nods, acknowledging the threat but not necessarily concerned by it. The room goes back to the white noise soundtrack of money counting.

The door gives a clang, then a rattling shudder.

All heads whip around at the same time.

Pause.

Another clang with a shudder of metal. The door shakes harder and harder.

It's stuck.

There's a muffled sound of, "Motherfucker!"

Pause.

The sound of a fist banging on the door from the outside.

Three Bills looks to J. Slim. *You expecting someone?*

He shrugs, then motions to his goons to check the door. All eyes on the front doors with hands on guns and fingers on triggers. The goons pull the doors open, revealing a masked squad. A masked Remo squad armed with enough firepower to take over a small country.

ARs get planted on the goons' heads before they can get off a single shot. The remaining members of the masked crew pour in with military precision. Guns tracking on the goons, Eurotrash, J. Slim and Three Bills.

"Don't move, motherfuckers!" a masked Hollis barks. His voice booms and echoes in the open space.

Remo's the last one through the door. Shoves a goon inside the hangar to the floor, then slides the door shut. Not all the way—doesn't want that embarrassing stuck shit to happen again—but enough to hide a clear view inside. He turns his attention to J. Slim, making sure of where he is at all times.

Poe removes the barrel from one goon's head then cracks his jaw with the butt of his AR, putting him to the floor with a bounce. He zip-ties two goons and removes their guns, sliding them across the floor toward the corner of the hangar.

Remo can't help but be impressed.

Those Russian dudes don't talk much, but they can work a room like a bad bunch of bastards. He'll be sure to let the Turkovs know. Maybe it'll show up on their review.

Hollis works the rest of the room. "Faces on the floor, palms flat." He looks to his watch timer ticking down. "Forty-two seconds."

"Fuck you," Three Bills spits out. "I will kill each and every one of you piece of shit mother—"

Hollis slams his AR into Three Bills's ample stomach then rips the butt up to his chin, leveling all three hundred pounds of him in a split second. The remaining goons and Eurotrash follow orders, going down quickly to the floor with hands flat on the concrete. Oleg and Poe move quickly, securing their hands with flex cuffs, all while removing guns, cells and emergency weapons from ankles. They move with absolute fluidity. Not a single motion wasted, every movement has purpose.

J. Slim still stands.

He burns as he watches these masked men pick up bag after bag. Remo steps over to him, standing a few inches from his face. J. Slim smiles. Remo thinks of blowing his head off. This is the second time in a matter of days he's considered shooting this guy. Once in New Mexico, and now in a secluded airstrip in White Plains, New York. No matter the locale, the desire to blow this fucker's brains out remains strong.

"You are so dead," J. Slim says. "You get me? All of you are ghosts, you just don't know it."

"Shut up, dildo," Remo says through grinding teeth.

J. Slim cocks his head. "Remo?" He smiles bigger now. "That you in there?"

"Fuck."

Remo cracks J. Slim upside the head with the butt of his gun. J. Slim's legs wilt underneath him. He slumps, then falls to the floor in a lump of asshole.

"Oh shit," Remo mutters.

He drops to his knees, trying to wake J. Slim up. In a moment of panic mixed with amped-up hostility he cracked J. Slim in the temple. He just knocked out the one guy he needs in this whole fucking thing. The one person he needs to be upright and speaking. The one who knows where Anna and Sean are located.

"Shit. Fuck. Shit," Remo stammers as he tries to open J. Slim's eyes with his gloved fingers. It's not working. He tries petting his hair. Tries talking sweetly. None of it's working. J. Slim is down. Out cold.

Lester comes over with a money bag thrown over his shoulder. He looks down. "That's not good."

"No shit," Remo says.

"What'd you do?"

"Nothing."

"Nothing?"

"I didn't do shit."

"He just fainted?"

Remo pauses. "Yes."

Lester nods, knowing that's complete bullshit, but lets it go. He bends down and cuffs J. Slim's hands and removes his weapons.

"Just in case he wakes up," he says, with a hint of patronizing.

Oleg and Poe dig through one bag and pull out the multiple shrink-wrapped bricks of various foreign currencies. All fake as hell, but impossible for the naked eye to catch. They both nod. Perhaps they're happy. Perhaps they know the Turkovs will be happy. Who can tell? The two slabs of Russian beef throw the bags over their shoulders. Hollis checks his watch, throwing the last bag over his shoulder. The entire takedown took less than ninety seconds.

Hollis smiles.

Still got it.

He twirls his finger in the air. Poe nods. It's the signal for him to run out and bring the Yukon around so they can load up the bags and get gone. Poe runs hard out the door like a well-trained Labrador.

"There's more cash on the plane," Three Bills says.

"What?" Hollis spins around with his AR pointed down at Three Bills's face.

"Two more bags," Three Bills says, looking up. "Close to two million. Some good going away money. My people will still hunt you down, can't stop that, but that two million out there? That'll help you buy some time. For a bit at least."

Hollis looks to Lester and Remo. Remo is still deeply concerned about the health of J. Slim. He's sitting with J. Slim's head in his lap, petting his hair gently.

"You let me back on that plane," Three Bills says, "and you can have all the money in there."

Lester and Hollis both know that no matter what happens, they need as much money as they can grab. Hollis turns to Oleg.

"Cut it up? Fifty-fifty?" Hollis asks.

Oleg nods, yanking at Three Bills's elbow, working to get him up to his feet.

"I need one of my guys," Three Bills says. "He's the only one who can fly the damn thing."

"Bullshit," Hollis says.

"It's true," Three Bills says, pointing to one of the Eurotrash boys on the floor. "Damn lucky you didn't kill him. He can fly us out. You've taken the guns off us. What's he gonna do?"

Hollis breathes out, then nods.

Lester goes over to Remo and helps him pick up J. Slim. They work his cuffs so they can throw his arms over their shoulders and let his feet drag between them. It's a pretzel of a move, but it's working. Oleg and Hollis move behind with guns tracking Three Bills and his pilot as they all exit the hangar.

Stepping out into the light of day.

Stepping over the dead goons on the ground, they move toward the plane with Three Bills and Eurotrash out front and Hollis and Oleg behind them. Lester and Remo wrestle with the dead weight of the passed-out J. Slim. He's a big guy and he's not helping. Remo hates himself. Hates how stupid he is. He just hopes he didn't catch J. Slim in the one spot of the head that'll turn him into a vegetable or slip into a coma or break his memory. Remo shakes his head, beating himself up on the inside.

Lester sees what Remo is doing to himself. "Not your fault."

"Oh, but it is."

"True, you did this, but this is a fluid fight and things happen. He's still breathing. We simply need to wait."

"You sure?"

Lester thinks for a moment. "No."

Poe pulls up fast in the Yukon. Lester and Remo load J. Slim into the back, along with bags of money and close the back hatch. They turn to watch the others walking toward the plane. Remo scans the area. He can't believe they've done it. They're going to make it. Sure, it's had some snags. Some hiccups here and there, and they still have a ways to go, but this leg of the thing is working.

He reflects on how he got here. Allows himself to take a moment of pride in the fact he's still alive and still has chance. Given the circumstances that's not bad. Many a man would have crawled under a table and cried. Remo smiles. *Who's the man?*

He grabs the iPad, taking the opportunity to check in on Anna and Sean.

There are some new images now. It's no longer the psycho watching and following his ex-wife and son. They are all in the same room now. The iPad has been set up in a dirty, beaten up, slum of a room. It's set up so it has a view of Anna and Sean seated on a filthy couch with the psycho seated next to them.

The psycho smiles and waves. Anna and Sean are scared. Something in Remo unhinges. He feels himself falling away. His helplessness has reached a new and unthinkable level. He grips the iPad hard, screaming into the screen. Lester grabs Remo by the shoulders, trying to control him. Hoping to comfort his friend. Veins in Remo's neck pop. His face rushes to red. He doesn't want to see, but he stares into the screen. They look unharmed, but frightened as hell.

Remo wants to kill these people. He wants to grind their bones and eat their souls. Lester grabs Remo by the face, speaking calmly and directly while looking into his eyes. "We'll get it done."

Remo shakes.

Lester repeats the words. Remo comes down slightly. He nods.

A crack sounds out from the distance. Lester and Remo whip around toward the plane and the group walking toward it.

The Eurotrash pilot's head explodes.

Remo's hand lets the iPad slip from his fingers. A momentary lapse of concentration sends his window to Anna and Sean falling down. The screen cracks upon impact with the runway's blacktop. Through the spiderweb of busted glass Remo sees Sean's terrified face before the screen goes black.

14

Gunfire erupts from every direction. Everyone freezes.

Except Remo.

Remo's sole focus is on the nonresponsive iPad. He's dropped to his knees, holding it as if it was a crying child.

Remo's tongue becomes fat, too big for his mouth. He fumbles around words, stuttering nonsense, only able to get out, "What's happening?" He says it over and over again. Remo is completely stunned, stuck, frozen by the chaos that's swelling up around him. He can't get his mind around the speed with which it happened. How quickly it's all come undone. The relentless, ferocious nature of the deteriorating situation has him floating in a void.

Lester shoves him into the Yukon as Hollis races toward them ducking, weaving, trying to avoid the firepower from an enemy unseen. Poe and Oleg dive in the back. Hollis hits the hood with full force, coming to a stop, spins off, then slides in behind the wheel. Bullets pop and rip. A shot tags the hood. Hollis punches the ignition, slams it in reverse and jams down the pedal. Tires scream as the Yukon flies backward toward the open gate behind them.

"What's happening?" Remo repeats, still clinging to the busted iPad.

Two black sedans move in fast through the gates, headed straight toward them at ramming speed. Unmarked cops or feds, hard to tell. Hollis locks up the breaks. The black sedans stop and men dressed in jeans and T-shirts covered by Kevlar vests pour out from the cars with guns raised and ready.

A stream of bullets knocks the Kevlar dudes down. Holes punch the front of the black sedans.

A driver takes a few in the face through the windshield.

Three Bills is racing toward the Yukon with a full-auto AR, firing wildly at what's left of the black sedans.

"Let me the fuck in," Three Bills yells, pointing his AR at the windshield. "Now, bitches."

More bullets zip from an unseen source.

More black sedans come screaming in from the other direction. Headed right at them. Lester flies out from the Yukon, blasting toward the sedans hauling ass toward them down the runway. He flings open the back door for Three Bills to get in. All three hundred pounds of him jumps in, landing in the laps of Oleg and Poe and on top of Remo, who hadn't had an opportunity to sit up yet.

"Son of bitch," Remo yelps, barely able to breathe, let alone speak.

"Get in the damn car," Hollis yells to Lester.

Lester rips a last stream of suppression fire then hops back in. Hollis turns the wheel hard, slams into D and punches it. Putting the pedal down, the Yukon whips around, pulling hard Gs, heading around the decimated black sedans and out the gate.

Bullets zip and whiz past the window as they pull away.

The black sedans clear the plane, speeding toward the Yukon. More vested men poke out from the windows, blasting away at the Yukon as they give chase.

"Get the fuck off me you fat motherfucker," Remo yells, struggling to get out from under. He wrestles and tugs himself free, gasping for air. The sudden loss of oxygen and fear of being buried alive has hit reset. Remo has put the iPad and the psycho on hold. "Who the hell is that out there?" Remo asks, spinning, looking out the back window, trying to get a look at the sedans running rip-shit after them.

J. Slim jolts up from the back, sitting straight up with his face firing up about an inch from Remo's nose.

Remo shrieks.

Slams the butt of his Glock against the side of J. Slim's head.

J. Slim slumps back down.

"Shit!" Remo yells.

Oleg and Poe wrestle Three Bills's gun away from his sausage fingers.

"Who was on you?" Remo yells at Three Bills.

"Hell if I know," Three Bills says. "Cops, feds ... they're always on us. Fuckin' popular."

The Yukon burns down the winding backcountry road with the sedans a few clicks behind. The engines roar. Tires fight for traction. Hollis's knuckles pop as his fists tighten on the wheel. Oleg and Poe lock and load. Lester, cool. Mad as hell, but cool. Three Bills a hostile mess.

Remo is about to shit himself.

His mind caves in.

Sensory overload crashing, overloading everything in his battle-weary brain. This is when he should consider giving up. They've reached the point when a sane person would let it all go. Simply accept that he gave it all a good try and realize that life wasn't meant to work out for people like him. Oh well, you play the hand you're dealt.

Remo knows that style of thinking won't work here. Not today.

There are other people involved who need him to pull his shit together and figure this all the fuck out. The last look he got at Sean is burned into his brain. Remo can't allow that to be how he remembers his boy. Let that be the image he sees day after day. That will haunt him when he sleeps. When he wakes.

"Fuck that," Remo says. He dumps the clip from his Glock. He's not sure he even fired a shot during all this, but it seems like the thing to do. He jams in a fresh one.

Remo's eyes go wide, almost popping from his head.

Through the front windshield three new black sedans pull up ahead in the middle of the road. They park in a sideways position, blocking the road ahead. T-shirt and vest boys jump out, taking positions behind the cars.

Remo swallows hard.

Poe and Oleg don't even hesitate.

15

Poe and Oleg open up through the front windshield with rapid pops of fire.

Shells fling and bounce off the ceiling and leather of the Yukon. Jumping all around Remo and Three Bills. Hollis, with one hand on the wheel, follows Oleg and Poe's lead, blasting his Glock while slamming down on the gas. The Yukon jerks forward racing headlong toward the barricade like a runaway crazy train.

Up ahead in the middle of the road, the vest boys drop and roll like bowling pins. Some take bullets. Some dive clear. The Yukon plows between the sedans, ramming through, splitting two cars as it mows past. Front end smashed, bumper twisted, the Yukon skids, tilts on two wheels, then finally gains control, landing back down on all four tires, and keeps moving. Slowing down was never considered.

Gunfire from sedans behind them blows out the back window.

Oleg and Poe whip around in a single motion and continue their blasting back toward the enemy behind them. Remo looks back over the seat, checking on J. Slim. He's breathing, but covered in broken glass. Still out cold.

Through the blown-out window it looks like there are more of them now. More sedans have joined the party, also joined by state cruisers with reds blazing, pulsing along the tops of the cars in bars of lights.

Hollis drives like a madman. He reloads, blasting back at the cops and feds while driving with his free hand. Remo's eyes dance, brain clicking at the speed of light. Doesn't participate in the gunplay. His thoughts are torn apart, trying to formulate a plan on what the hell to do.

This was not discussed. This was not mapped out or diagrammed.

Tearing down the road, the Yukon rams headlong toward an entrance to a bridge. Hollis's eyes go wide. He doesn't want to get on that bridge. There's traffic up there. Not crazy, but enough to add to the complications they already have.

He tries to take a hard right to a side road—no dice.

Another black sedan slams into the side of them, forcing them straight ahead. The Yukon and sedan crash sides, ramming back and forth into one another as the Yukon passes any chance to stay off the bridge.

Poe fires into the sedan. The sedan peels off, slamming off the shoulder of the road and barely missing diving down into a ditch. The driver's dead. Head a limp, bloody mess. The remaining vest boy tries to steer from the passenger side, still slamming into the Yukon, coming off and on the road from the shoulder.

One more sedan pulls up alongside the driver's side of the Yukon. Now one on each side. Forcing them on the path onto the bridge. Poe and Oleg exchange fire with the sedans. One vest boy tries to shoot out the tires. Oleg leans out, putting a bullet into his face. Both the black sedans and Yukon ramble on. Bullets flying back and forth. Sounds popping. Steel tearing. All ramming at breakneck speed onto the bridge.

The New Croton Reservoir Bridge.

A steel, through arch bridge over New Croton Reservoir on Taconic State Parkway. It clocks in at seven hundred and fifty-foot-long steel suspended arch trusses with riveted structural steel members. The deck is a cast-in-place concrete deck with a concrete wearing surface. The approaches are enclosed chambers with solid beams. A stretch of steel and rock filled with innocent civilians rolling through their day. Traffic is moderate, but enough, and moves at a decent pace. Commuters, truckers, families all go about their days, completely unaware of what is coming up behind them.

The Yukon screams onto the bridge at high speed, weaving in and out of traffic as if it were standing still. Black sedans on their ass. New York State cruisers follow, though some peel off to block more traffic coming onto the bridge.

Gunfire between the Yukon and pursuers continues. Shells fall from windows, bouncing off the concrete. Innocent drivers lock up brakes and swerve out of the way. Smashing into one another, slamming into the guardrails and spinning to a stop.

The seeds of chaos taking root.

Cars and trucks filled with unsuspecting innocents peel off to the side as the war rages on. The Yukon is almost neck and neck with the cavalry of feds and cops behind them.

Poe and Oleg both fire with reckless abandon.

The feds and cops try to dodge the cascading walls of bullets being thrown down on them while firing back best they can, while trying not to kill civilians. Hollis keeps blasting. Cutting and jerking the wheel, trying to dodge the streaming panic that's sliding and braking along the bridge. The Yukon rams the back edge of the bumper on a Ford F-150. Everyone inside jerks forward then back hard as hell. Oleg sends an errant spray of lead into the air then pulls himself back down, blowing the windshield of a black sedan all to hell.

Screeching tires, crunching metal and the crack of gunfire is mind-numbing. Too much to bear. The F-150 the Yukon clipped begins to spin, locks up its brakes, causing the cars behind to slam into it.

Sparks off a chain reaction of traffic slamming into one another— a five-car pileup and growing by the second. In the wake of the Yukon and the F-150 is nothing but feds and cops. The innocent bystanders have either wrecked a couple hundred feet back or were lucky enough to find safety.

Hollis's eyes pop wide.

An 18-wheeler has jackknifed up ahead, creating a makeshift wall blocking the other end of the bridge. They're unable to see around it. No idea what's on the other side. The Yukon locks up the brakes, skidding to a stop just shy of the disaster ahead of them.

FBI and cops lock up to a tire-shredding stop about a hundred yards behind them.

Battle lines are being drawn.

The feds and cops on one side and Mayhem Inc. on the other, with an 18-wheeler providing a wall of sorts behind them. A pileup of innocent cars in the distance behind the line created by the feds and cops. Civilians bolt from the wreckage. Some bloodied, others only stunned or mildly injured. Several scurry to escape while clawing and climbing as far away as possible.

Oleg and Poe spring out from the Yukon. Guns locked and loaded. Ready for anything and everything. Eyes hard. Thoughts singular, focused, as spit flies from their lips and battle cries rage from their throats.

Remo slips out from the Yukon, trying to fight through the chemical impulses roaring through his veins. He scrambles behind the large SUV. Fear, confusion, fear. Thoughts of his family fly. Sean's face. Anna's looks. His eyes slam shut.

Hollis and Lester fall out, joining him. Watching the insanity of Oleg and Poe. The ruthless, reckless abandon they're operating under. Their bullets land only a few feet from innocent civilians simply trying to escape. Remo feels it in his chest—this isn't right. Not what he wants at all.

"They're out of control," Remo screams, pointing to Oleg and Poe.

Hollis nods.

"They can't carve up innocent people, goddammit. It's all fucked up."

Lester nods.

Remo peeks around the Yukon.

The feds and cops do their best to get out and take a position as bullets fly from the rampaging Oleg and Poe. Three Bills has joined them at the front of the Yukon, blasting away with his AR. A cop takes one in the shoulder. A fed pulls him behind a car, returning fire only to get spun around by another bullet.

Remo looks to the right of where he's crouched. One police cruiser and one unmarked black sedan are trapped in the middle, along with an ambulance, an RV and a Civic on fire. A dead driver slumps out the Civic's window. Flames roar from under the hood. A lone vest boy shot up in the driver side of the unmarked car.

A cop slips out from the car, dodging Oleg's and Poe's gunfire.

They load and unload without hesitation or a hint of compassion.

Remo pulls his Glock. Alternates his aim between Oleg, Poe and Three Bills. Has a perfect shot on them.

No idea what to do.

Take out these guys and end this now or hold back?

Opportunity burns away with every second. Mind fumbles for the right decision. Take the shot or not? He looks to Hollis. He isn't shooting at the cops either. Neither is Lester. This isn't what they signed up for.

Remo looks behind them at the 18-wheeler that has them walled off from the other side of the bridge. He thumbs behind him. "What if we jack another car and haul ass the hell the other way."

Hollis raises his eyebrows. *Maybe.*

Lester shrugs.

Remo ducks and weaves through the gunfire, making it to the edge of the front bumper of the jackknifed 18-wheeler. He can taste the way out of here. Another alternative to dying on a bridge filled full of holes and regret. Gunned down like a dog. As he peeks around the edge his hope dies a sudden, painful death.

The other side of the bridge is a line of police cruisers with red lights pulsing in and out. Cops with shotguns and handguns shielded by a wall of cars, leaning on hoods and trunks with their aim dead on them. They're waiting for the word. The word that'll cut them loose to come storming in.

But who's giving the word?

Remo spins back around the other side of the 18-wheeler. The opportunity he dreamt of is gone before it even started. Remo ducks down as a bullet screams by inches from his head. He ignores the near death.

His face is twisted. He's agonizing. *What the hell does he do now?*

He thinks. His mind on fire. There has to be something. He races back to Hollis and Lester behind the Yukon. They can tell by the look on Remo's face that the way out beyond the 18-wheeler is not a viable option.

The cops and vest boys are outgunned. The trio of madness made up of Oleg, Poe and Three Bills is terrifying, impressive in their ability to lay down wave after wave of punishing firepower.

Remo notices the shooting has almost completely stopped from the side of the bridge beyond the Yukon. He fights to get his bearings back. Steadies his fumbling mind. Looking around, he starts surveying the situation at lightning speed.

His thoughts slam into place.

Remo works his way toward Oleg, Poe and Three Bills, who've now moved up and taken cover behind an abandoned, shot-up Camry. His stomach drops fifty feet. A bad situation looks even worse up close. Oleg and Poe blast at the cops like men possessed. Loving it. Yelling out their disturbing war cry. Three Bills jiggles and bounces like a man made of marshmallow holding a jackhammer.

"Stop with the shooting, dammit," Remo yells at the three of them.

They continue blasting away.

"Hey. Assholes," he screams. "Stop firing your fucking guns."

Still nothing.

Remo, being a master of improv, does what he feels is the correct and only way to go in this particular situation. The only proven method he's seen over the years. He starts kicking these mother-fuckers in the balls.

Starting with Three Bills, then Oleg and last Poe.

One after the other they fold.

The last shot fired by Poe leaves a faint echo in the air. The bridge goes eerily silent. Remo takes this moment of silence to seize an opportunity to get his message across.

"Sorry about the balls, but you were not listening." Remo talks while keeping an eye on the cops and what he now can safely guess are feds. "They will keep sending wave after wave at us until we're either out of bullets or dead. We have to work out a deal with these people."

"Fuck you," Three Bills says through gritted teeth.

Oleg and Poe stare hate-holes into him.

"We. Are. Trapped," Remo says. "I'm going to talk to them. It's the only way we're going to get out of this thing."

Oleg grabs Remo by the throat while shaking his head no.

"Dude. There's not another way," Remo says while gagging. "They've got us totally boxed in."

Hollis and Lester move up next to them while staying low. Remo looks to them, his friends, to help remove this big-ass Russian's hand away from his throat.

They do not. They understand Oleg's point of view.

"Look," Remo says. His speech is strained as his face gets redder and redder. "Let me try at least. If it doesn't work you can always start shooting again."

Oleg lets his eyes slip over to Poe, looking for direction. An opinion from a co-worker. Poe thinks, then nods. Oleg releases Remo's throat, letting him fall back to the concrete of the bridge.

For a fraction of a second Remo gets a gorgeous view of the blue sky. Fluffy clouds roll by as if nothing's wrong. A bird soars by without a care in the world. For this brief sliver of time Remo has disconnected from his current disaster. Allowed himself to leave this place. A micro-vacation from hell. It's nice. He's glad the universe allowed him this moment.

He's rudely snapped out of it by the sound of someone yelling his name.

It's not anyone from his little group here.

Not Hollis or Lester or Three Bills, and certainly not Oleg or Poe.

Remo does, however, recognize the voice.

"Remo! Remo Cobb!" the voice yells again, louder this time.

Remo turns his head. He now realizes that when he fell back from Oleg's grasp he left his head out in the open in full view. Exposed. Free from the cover of the Camry and for all to see from the other side. Across the bridge he sees something. Someone he recognizes. Across the enemy lines is a lone familiar face.

A face Remo does not like.

"Remo!" Detective Harris screams across. He picks up a bullhorn and tries again. "Remo fucking Cobb!"

16

L ast time Remo saw Detective Harris was in New York City.
Last time he saw this guy was when Detective Harris introduced Remo to CIA man Cormack in a bland interrogation room at a police station. Remo was there, or so Remo thought, to talk to Detective Harris about the events that took place at Remo's house in the Hamptons. The events that led to a few dead Mashburn brothers and damn near killed Remo. Remo had no idea what Detective Harris had in mind at the time. Not a clue that he wanted to introduce Cormack into Remo's life.

For those keeping score, CIA man Cormack has spent the last couple of days trying to get Remo and his friends killed. He sent them out on a couple of suicide missions and things eventually ended with Cormack dead, slumped over with half a head, but not before Cormack let the entire criminal underworld know Remo double-crossed the Mashburns. This information has led the criminal underworld to be all over Remo. The most notable is J. Slim, and this is the reason Remo's sitting in the middle of a war zone atop a bridge he can't get off of.

"Remo!" Detective Harris calls out again.

Simple math dictates that Detective Harris directly or indirectly, more than likely directly, tried to get Remo killed and put his ex-wife and son in great danger. Remo feels his blood pressure spike. His face runs hot.

He stands up. He's now out in the open, completely exposed. He closes his eyes tight, expecting the worst. They could gun him down right now. Drop him to the cold concrete, but they don't. Only sound is quiet. The only motion around him is the wind.

Detective Harris and Remo stare at one another. A chunk of open bridge separates them. A pack of armed friends stands ready behind each of them. Harris holds up his hand, letting his friends know to stand down. Remo does the same.

"Fuck that shit," Three Bills says. "Who the fuck made you Chief Dickhead?"

Lester puts him in a headlock and takes his gun away. He nods to Remo, letting him know that all's well.

Harris passes by a burning car as he walks toward the center of the bridge. Remo does the same. Remo takes in a deep breath, trying hard to find some sense of calm in all this madness. He's walking toward a cop who hates him and whom he hates equally. This cop has tried everything over the years to destroy Remo, and Remo has beaten Harris in court time and time again. Usually in a humiliating fashion.

The two get closer and closer. Seconds from meeting together alone, one-on-one, in the middle of the open space on the war-torn bridge. Cars burn around them. Shells and tire marks pepper the concrete floor of the bridge. Remo lets his thoughts bounce around the idea of bashing this asshole's head into the concrete and letting the two sides go into all-out battle mode. Let the guns decide the winner.

Remo reaches Harris.

They stand about a foot away from one another.

Eyes locked.

A lot of history here. None of it good.

Neither says a word for what seems like hours.

"Well?" Harris says.

"That's all you've got, Harris?" Remo raises his eyebrows. "You fucking kidding me?"

"What should I say?"

"I'm not sure, but I need a little more than *well*."

"How the hell did you get into this shitshow?"

"Well, Detective Harris, one might say it's because you sold my pale ass to CIA man Cormack."

Harris looks down at his feet, kicking at a spent shell casing.

"This. All this shit," Remo says. "It's the domino effect of you handing me off to that motherfucker."

"It happens."

"You're such a fucking stupid prick. How did you even find me at that airport?"

"Cormack had me put your name and face out with every officer in the state of New York. Every man and woman around. Every set of eyeballs. Every security camera. Everyone was supposed to be aware if you stepped one toe back into the state of New York. His words."

Remo rolls his eyes. He can't believe this shit. Cormack is killing him from the grave.

"You and your buddies got all the way into the city before I knew about it," Harris says. "Then I had someone tail you to that Jersey titty joint. I could tell something was up."

"Unbelievable."

"Look. Things got a little fucked up. Slightly out of control. I'll admit that."

"Ya think?"

"Cormack has me. Deep. I'm so boxed in with that guy I can't even tell you. What was I supposed to do? He's going to bury me under the prison."

It hits Remo. Harris has no idea that Cormack is dead. He doesn't know that Cormack is missing half his head, laid out in a garage at some not-so-safe house in the middle of nowhere New Mexico. It's as if Remo's head actually makes a *ding* sound.

"What if I can work something out with Cormack?" Remo asks.

"What do you mean?"

"I mean I've got something. A lot of shit's happened since you saw me last."

"Apparently."

"I can control Cormack. I can call the dog off. I can get you well again."

"How?"

"Never mind how. I can guarantee you will never see or hear from Cormack again, but only if you help me out of this little pickle I'm in."

Harris looks around at the pack of killers behind Remo, and then back to his people, who are standing behind him, waiting for his orders. Remo can tell his mind is ripping at a hundred miles a second. Harris has no reason to trust Remo, but the very idea that Remo could help him is enough for Harris's desperate mind to consider the possibly. Lost souls are an easy sell, and Remo knows it. He pushes the pedal down on the conversation.

"I'll be honest, Harris. I have no idea what Cormack has on you, and I don't care. I need to get off this damn bridge." Remo resets, rubs his tongue over his teeth, then starts up again. "I need to get off this damn thing with a couple of people I've got over there. They're nothing to you. You can have the other three. You'll want the other three. They've got some pretty large ties. Could be a very good day for you. Get out from under Cormack and take down a big-ass bust."

Remo can tell he's got hooks deep into Harris. Harris has no real play here other than to work with Remo. He is completely fucked and they both know it. What does he have to lose?

"What do you want to do?" Harris asks.

"What do you mean?"

"About this. This situation."

"Oh." Remo thinks. He hadn't gotten that far. Squeezes his eyes tight, then says, "I can get Hollis, Lester and the other guy on board, but the other three might give me some static."

"We've got maybe a minute, two tops, before the entire world comes crashing down on us," Harris says. "This bridge looks more like Fallujah than New York state."

"If I can get the other three unarmed, down on the ground and hand them to you, can you guarantee me safe passage back to the city?"

"What?"

"I'll gift wrap you two goons who work for the Turkov brothers and some fat bastard who no doubt has ties to some large, big-ass criminal masterminds."

"Why, because he came in on a plane?"

Remo pauses. "Yes."

"And you want a ride to the city in exchange?"

"I want a car and for your trigger-happy assholes not to shoot me, Hollis, Lester or my other guy."

Now Harris stops to think. He turns back to the line of gun-wielding cops and vest boys behind him, then glances to Remo's side. Remo can see it in his eyes. He knows a cop's eyes better than anyone. It's as if Remo was reading a stop sign. Whatever is about to come out of Harris's mouth is a lie.

"Okay," Harris says. "You give me them with no blood loss and I'll get you into the city."

Remo's heart drops. He knows he's screwed in every direction, but at least he's got one side of this equation to stop shooting. Harris will at least not come charging in with guns blazing.

Maybe.

"But," Harris says, "you've got two minutes before I'm going have to take this bridge. I can't have this turn into a *Dog Day Afternoon* type deal all over the Internet. You got it?"

Remo's got it. He's got one hundred and twenty seconds before Harris comes charging in with guns blazing.

Remo nods.

Harris nods.

They both turn back to their sides.

17

Remo settles in behind the Camry with Lester, Hollis and his other bloodthirsty traveling companions.

His brain passed fried hours ago, headed toward full-on meltdown, and left Remo with a quivering mass of jelly between his ears. He looks to his watch. Seconds are ticking fast. There's none to waste.

"Well?" Three Bills asks with a bit of a tone.

Lester and Hollis look Remo over. They know something is up here, but not sure what. With Remo, anything is possible.

Oleg and Poe grunt, their eyes dancing between the other side of the bridge and Remo. Remo sucks in a deep breath, letting it creep out slowly. Remo has to let Hollis and Lester know what's up, but at the same time he needs to maintain full control of the Oleg, Poe and Three Bills situation. There's no time for a private conversation. No sidebar.

Remo closes his eyes, shutting them tight as he can.

"You gonna fucking speak?" Three Bills pushes.

The seconds tick.

"What's with this guy?"

Tick.

Lester puts a calming hand on Remo's shoulder.

Remo remembers his conversation with Hollis and Lester and something he learned from that chat.

Tick.

Bullshitting the people close to you is not always a great idea. Sometimes, if not always, the truth is the clearest, simplest path to getting what you want. Certainly the easiest thing to remember.

Tick.

Remo's eyes flip open. He readies his Glock, gives a quick side-eye to Hollis and Lester. So slight the other three don't even notice.

"We're going to take you down, hand you over to the other side without an ounce of shit from any of you."

Lester lands a fist to Poe's jaw then lunges for his throat knocking him back.

Hollis slams the butt of his AR into Oleg's nose. In a single motion, he rips Oleg's gun out from his hand, letting it skid down the bridge, then pins him to the side of the Camry by jamming his rifle sideways under his chin. Oleg's veins bulge out from under the rifle.

Remo jams his Glock between Three Bills's teeth, slipping the AR from his fumbling sausage fingers. Turning his head to Hollis and Lester, Remo finally feels some sense of control.

Tick.

"We also need to jump off the bridge and then steal a car," Remo says. "Like in less than thirty seconds."

Hollis and Lester both shrug. This sort of thing happens.

They quickly use the zip ties they had from the airport job to secure Oleg and Poe. Remo pulls a pair of zip ties from his pocket so he can do the same with Three Bills. The fat man calls Remo a cocksucker about fifteen times. It was hard to make out through the gun barrel in his mouth, but Remo was able to translate after a while. Remo allows himself to breathe easier. That went a helluva lot smoother than he thought.

Three Bills pulls back hard and Remo's gun slips out from his lips. He tries his best to slap the gun away from Remo. The gun goes off. Three Bills's head pops like a melon dropped from a ten-story building. What's left of him slumps, then falls off to the side. His thick neck pulses crimson, spraying out on the bridge like a deranged sprinkler. Remo's eyes bulge wide like plates.

Tick.

"Remo?" Harris says through the bullhorn across the bridge.

"We're cool," Remo yells back, standing up waving his arms as if landing a plane. "Nothing to worry about over here."

Harris scrunches his nose. "Clock's still running."

Remo gives two big thumbs-up then slumps back down behind the Camry.

"Don't we need that guy?" Hollis says.

"Hope not," Lester says, with eyes on Three Bills.

"No shit," Remo says.

"No." Hollis grabs Remo by the ears, turning his head behind them. "That guy."

J. Slim has escaped out from the back of the Yukon.

Tick.

18

"Shit," Remo yelps.

J. Slim stumble-runs, heading toward the 18-wheeler behind them. His legs are obviously not responding well after being knocked out and stuffed into the back of an SUV. Remo springs up to his feet, hauling ass toward J. Slim.

"Remo?" Harris calls out through the bullhorn.

Tick.

"Remo, goddammit!"

Remo ignores Harris's calls as his feet leave the bridge, lunging, landing NFL-style onto J. Slim's back. Piggyback-style, Remo twirls with arms wrapped around J. Slim's back, holding on for dear life. He's planted his face perfectly between the shoulder blades, like he was a human dart thrown by God. J. Slim twists then turns then spins around and round, eventually landing them both in a heap of flesh and bone onto the bridge's hard concrete floor.

J. Slim wiggles free, landing an elbow strike to Remo's face.

Remo's head jolts, whipping back then forward like his neck was a spring, only to be met by another strike to the face.

Remo throws a blind punch, reaching nothing but empty air.

He swings another. Nothing.

The third punch lands, tagging J. Slim square in the eye. Remo seizes the flash of a moment by contorting himself around, managing to get J. Slim in a headlock of sorts. It's not textbook, but it's working.

J. Slim stands, his strong legs lifting them both up with Remo still on his back, hanging on like a baby chimp. Slamming his back into the 18-wheeler, J. Slim is doing his damnedest to knock himself free from Remo's death grip. He slams again, again and again. Remo feels his back crack. The air leaving his lungs as his ribs crunch. Still he manages to hold on. But he knows it won't last. Through the haze of his failing fuzzy vision Remo can see what's unfolded up ahead near the Camry.

Poe is working hard to wrestle a gun away from Hollis, and Oleg has just kicked Lester in the skull, sending him falling backward. Oleg scramble-crawls toward an AR as fast as he can with his hands still zip tied.

Tick.

Another slam to Remo's back.

"Remo! We gotta wrap this up," Harris says through the bullhorn, pointing to the sky. "Hear that?"

Slam.

In the distance Remo can hear the helicopters. They're coming.

In this split second, Remo knows that Harris will never let this turn into a full-blown standoff video vomited all over social media for the masses to consume. He can't. It's going to be hard enough to explain why he was at the airport in the first place, let alone involved in this shit. It's going to be a massive challenge for Harris to talk his way around the eyewitnesses, but he can manage the message if he's smart. But if people—people meaning officials, FBI and the like—start digging too deep into this, it will all fall apart, and any value Harris would get for bagging Poe and Oleg will disappear fast. He doesn't even know that Three Bills is useless, on account of being deader than Dillinger.

"Shit," Remo says, defeated as hell.

Slam.

"Wait," Remo screams into J. Slim's ear. "Look. You see that shit?"

J. Slim stops. Up ahead he can see a line of cops and vest boys moving toward them. Guns raised and moving slowly but steadily toward them. They are using cars as cover, with the black sedans creeping ahead of them.

Hollis reaches Poe and punches the piss out of him. Poe has gotten hold of a gun, however.

Lester is now bashing Oleg's skull into the bridge. That won't last long.

J. Slim moves away from the 18-wheeler. As he does, he spins around, letting Remo flail while still holding on to his back. Behind them is another line of cops moving toward them from the other side.

J. Slim's face goes slack, resigning himself to the hopelessness of the situation he's woken up in. "Thoughts?" J. Slim asks, tilting his head back to Remo as he hangs there.

"I do." Remo resets. He knows he's got nothing, but he's got to keep working this thing as if he's got some cards left to play. "I know that cop, the one with the bullhorn. We can still be okay, but you have to tell me where that asshole has my ex and my son."

"Fuck you." J. Slim cracks a chuckle. "You really think I'm an idiot, don't you?"

"Fine. Take your chances. How do you think that cop over there knows my name? You think *Remo* was a lucky-ass guess?"

J. Slim's head is spinning and Remo can see it.

The lines of cops and vest boys are closing in from each side. Poe can now see them, and he raises his gun toward the cops. Bad idea. They carve him up with a stream of lead. Pops of gunfire rip him apart, starting at the head and moving down, leaving a meaty, bloody mess on the bridge.

Hollis spins away back behind the Camry for relative safety. He grabs Lester by the arm, dragging him away from what's left of Oleg. Remo locks eyes with Hollis and Lester.

Nothing said. Nothing to say.

Remo hopes silent mental communication is a thing.

"Gotta talk now or this goes horribly wrong for you, and I won't be able to help you," Remo says into J. Slim's ear. "What do you have to lose? This is just bad on top of bad." Remo slips from J. Slim's back, standing in front of him. Makes sure to hold eye contact. He doesn't have much time. There's a hint of fear in J. Slim's eyes. A crack in his armor. Remo presses on. "Anna and Sean have nothing to do with this. I'm the asshole. Me, only me, not them. Ray isn't going to gain anything by killing them." Remo waves his arms. "Look around. What the fuck am I going to do? How am I a threat anymore?"

J. Slim scans the bridge. They are completely boxed in. Nowhere to go, with an army of guns waiting to storm in. J. Slim begins to shake. This is the first time Remo has ever seen this man even vaguely concerned, let alone afraid.

J. Slim looks to Remo.

To the cops.

Back to Remo.

"You better not fuck me over," he says as he pulls a card from his back pocket. With a shaky hand, he hands it to Remo.

Remo snatches it and checks the back. There's an NYC address. He knows the neighborhood. It could easily match what Remo last saw on the iPad before it went black. He coughs, almost choking as he scans the address. He can't believe it worked. There's still a chance. He smiles huge.

"Thank you," Remo says, then nods to Hollis and Lester. "Now," Remo says to Hollis, then turns to J. Slim. "Go fuck yourself."

"What?" J. Slim stammers.

Hollis moves up quickly, jamming a Glock to the side of J. Slim's head. He pulls the trigger. Hollis and Remo both feel a sense of something undefined wash over them as J. Slim's brains blow out and his body slumps. Before his body even reaches the pavement, Remo, Lester and Hollis run hard toward the side of bridge.

"Remo!" Harris screams out.

The three remaining members of Mayhem Inc. jump off the bridge.

PART III

HOPE

19

When you hit the water from that height, shit happens.

Remo read once if you jump from the Golden Gate Bridge you'll more than likely die from blunt-force trauma. Death isn't a slam dunk, but if he remembers correctly something like ninety plus percent of people die. Now, he doesn't have the specs, but he's fairly certain this bridge is not an exact match to the fall from the Golden Gate, but this is the kind of shit that floats through your head as you're floating through the air after having just jumped from a bridge.

He's pretty sure his ribs will break, but he's also pretty sure they are already broken. He's also positive an organ or two will come unhooked or relocated inside of him, but there's not a whole hell of a lot he can do at the moment.

That ship has sailed, as they say.

In that moment before he hits the water, he remembers a little something from his childhood. He remembers breaking into a rich kids' country club and taking turns with his drunk, dumbass friends jumping off the ten-meter platform. It was the highest thing he'd ever seen. None of boys were expert divers, but one had done that jump before and did have a tip for Remo as the terrified teen stood at the end of the platform looking down at the cold water below.

"Jump and keep your damn body straight," he told Remo with beer-soaked breath, "with your shit pointed at the water at all times."

"My shit?" Remo asked, with his voice shaking.

"Your toes, boy, keep your damn toes pointed at the water. And when you hit the water, stretch your legs and arms out and arch your back."

Then that wise, learned asshole pushed Remo off the platform.

Remo hits the water hard with toes straight as can be. He knows it's so damn cold, but his body hasn't caught on yet. He managed to get his legs stretched and arms somewhat out, but definitely got his back arched. With no idea how far down he's sunk, he starts to feel the momentum of the fall slowing. He levels his body and swims with all he has toward what he's sure is land.

Reaching the surface, he lets his head come up just enough to grab some air and not give too much of a visual. As his ears get above water he can hear the sounds from the bridge. A quick blip of sirens and helicopters behind him. He goes back down and thrusts his arms forward, then back. While he was up he did steal a quick glimpse of land up ahead. At least he got pointed in the right direction.

Remo has no idea where Lester and Hollis are at the moment. He hopes they are right alongside him. He knows this is nothing to Hollis. The man has trained for every possible shitty situation there is, and jumping from a bridge is like playing jump rope to him. No need to rely on a buried teenage memory for survival, like Remo. He's more concerned that Lester even knows how to swim. No military in his background that Remo can remember. A pure badass on dry land, but in the water Remo doesn't know. He hopes for the best.

Now he feels it.

Oh yeah, it's really fucking cold.

Remo lands on the shore. He spits out what feels like gallon after gallon of dank river water. His lungs burn. His eyes at first provide him nothing but a view of a blurry world, but then his vision starts to work again.

Turning back, he takes a look at the bridge. From here it looks even worse than before. From this vantage point he can see the traffic is backed up on each side. Looks like it stretches for miles. Smoke twists upward, dissipating as it ascends up into the sky. He can hear the scream of squad cars cutting through the gridlock as they work to get closer and closer to the post-warzone bridge. Multiple helicopters are now hovering above and circling the bridge. A quick count gives him a tally of five crowding the blue sky. Three look to be media related, the others cops and feds. He can barely make out the cops and vest boys who are scurrying all over the bridge, looking much like upright ants racing around their hill that's been attacked. An image of Harris discovering that his prize criminal busts are dead on the bridge and that Remo, Hollis and Lester have slipped through his dirty fingers makes Remo smile.

He even giggles to himself a little. It's the small victories in life.

A thick hand grabs the back of Remo's Kevlar vest, pulling him all the way out of the water. It's Lester. They lie on the ground side by side. They both suck in huge gulps of air, trying to find some feeling of normal. Their eyes almost hang from their skulls. Remo is sure he is damaged in ways he can't even count, but, at the moment, he feels somewhat okay. Or at least what passes for okay these days. His mind slaps back on the here and now.

What's important. His eyes flare.

Got to get to Anna and Sean.

"We need a car. Now," Remo gets out between breaths. He looks around. "Where's Hollis?"

Lester shakes his head.

"What?" Remo asks. Fear spikes as he asks, "Is he dead?"

"No. Shit, no. He's cool. He took off."

Relief rockets through Remo. The idea that Hollis would die in all this would be too much. It's an idea Remo has had to wrestle with the last few days. The idea that a friend of his would be hurt, or worse, because of him is something Remo doesn't want to be a part of. After the relief subsides, Remo thinks. Then gets pissed off.

"What the hell do you mean, *he took off*?"

Lester's eyes slip over to the bridge. The sounds of the sirens are intensifying even from this distance. The choppers' whirling from above is getting louder and louder. They are starting to scan the water. Scanning for them. Lester gets Remo to his feet and motions for him to stay low. He moves them both into the woods. Out of sight from the watchers from above.

"Won't be long before they do a full-on search for us," Lester explains as they work their way through the thick brush.

"Where the hell is Hollis?" Remo asks as a branch thwacks him hard in the face.

"He's a smart man. They will be looking for three of us. Three of us together will be easier to find. He's been talking about finding his family anyway, so he took a stack or two out of the bags during all the chaos and decided it was time to go."

"Fucker didn't even say goodbye."

"Didn't want to make it a thing."

"Make it a *thing*?"

"He's not the sort."

"Unbelievable."

"There's more, Remo." Lester stops, then shows Remo several stacks of cash. "I took a little myself."

Remo's eyes meet Lester's. Remo knows where this is going before the man says another word to him.

"You're a smart man too, aren't ya, Lester my boy?"

Lester nods, then hands Remo a stack. "Take this and go get your son. Get your family."

"My son, yes, but not really my family. Anna hates every molecule of me, but I get what you're trying to say."

Lester, with the warmest of eyes, holds Remo's face in his hands. Hands that have killed more people than he'd care to count. Hands that cut off Dutch Mashburn's head and carried it around New York. Hands that have saved Remo's sorry ass and that have performed many a selfless act. Lester holds Remo's eyes with his for what seems like forever. Then he simply asks, "Did I save you, asshole?"

A part of Remo melts.

His stomach balls up inside. A lump rises up into his throat.

Lester's mission of mercy: *Kill multiple motherfuckers. Save one asshole.* A mantra Lester has held onto from the moment he left prison until now. A perfect little philosophy that Lester has used to guide him through the last few days, and for which Remo cannot begin to thank him.

Lester has saved his life on more than one occasion. Remo would have been dead a long time ago if not for this man. Probably gunned down by the Mashburns in New York, and definitely shot to hell in the Hamptons if it weren't for Lester. Remo knows that isn't the kind of saving Lester is talking about.

It's never been made clear if Lester fully intended for Remo to become a Sunday regular, sit in the first pew type of churchgoer, or study up and slide into being a man of the cloth. Remo hopes Lester will settle for Remo being a moderately better human being. If even only slightly. He's been in self-preservation mode recently so it's tough to separate the good from the bad given all the killing and such, but Remo feels like he has indeed changed. Hard to quantify or give a solid example, but incrementally, yeah maybe, Remo has become a better person. Certainly he's come to value others. Some more than others. Some more than himself. Remo can't begin to thank Lester for all he's done for him.

So, yes, in a larger sense, Lester has saved the asshole they call Remo Cobb.

Remo cracks a tiny grin and simply nods at his friend's question, unable to come up with the proper words.

"Good," Lester says as he releases his hands from Remo's face. He takes the Glock from Remo's waistband, checks the clip, puts one in the chamber and hands it back to him. He points straight ahead, showing Remo a new path. "Head that way. You'll hit a road. Get a car. Use cash or the gun, whatever works for you." Lester turns and walks to the right, away from the direction he pointed out to Remo. "Go do what you have to do to get to your son. Maybe Anna will come around ... now that you're saved."

Remo's face drops. This doesn't process.

He can't believe Lester, of all people, is leaving him. They've only been reacquainted for a short amount of time, but Remo has grown attached to the man. His right hand. His silent, wise man. His protector.

"Where are you going?"

"Not sure."

Lester is almost out of sight, slowly being swallowed whole by the trees.

"You can't leave me."

"I can."

"I need your help, man."

"You don't, but your boy needs yours," Lester says as he slips away.

Remo's heart pounds out of his chest. He's been alone for major chunks of his life. For the longest time, he thought alone was what he needed to be. That's all changed. Changed rapidly and recently. He sure as shit hasn't been alone since all this violence and insanity started. Not since he began down that unpleasant road. Not since he decided to grow a conscience and take on the criminal underworld.

Now Remo is more than a little pissed that Hollis and Lester have left him. Those fuckers should have let him die in the beginning. It would have been better for everyone concerned. Remo knows that's bullshit, but it's not complete bullshit. He's not sure that he remembers all the levels or circles or whatever of grief, but he's sure he's ripping through them, and he wishes they would just hurry the fuck up.

Remo stands in the woods, all alone.

Fights to not feel abandoned by his friends. He knows they are right, but hates them for it. He's better, not perfect. Cut a guy some slack.

The sounds of the helicopters and sirens offer a muted soundtrack in the background. Remo knows he has to move if he's going to have a single chance in hell. Alone or with an army, he has to put one foot in front of the other and go undo what he's done. What he's done to Anna and Sean.

Anna will be angry, and rightfully so.

Sean will be afraid, and rightfully so.

Remo hopes like hell they will both, at least, learn to forgive him.

20

R emo pulls himself through the wilds of the New York State jungle.

Each step hurts like hell. Every breath is a labor of love.

Self-love. Self-preservation.

He's running—well, to be honest, he's trotting—at an elevated speed though the uneven brush and dirt. The pain is real. His teeth grind. Eyes water. The desire to get to Anna and Sean drags him, pushes and pulls him, toward a road that lies only a few feet ahead. Could be a small highway. Hard to tell. Remo simply does not care.

He needs to get a car. Has to get a car. Must get to the city now.

Every moment is important. Every second he's not there is a waste of time.

Remo rushes out from the trees as if being birthed from the woods. He storms through a ditch that takes one of his shoes with it. As if a stray dog had snapped it off his foot. Remo slogs his way to the edge of the road.

He waits. Staring at an empty road like a zombie. He slaps himself to stay in tune with the world that is quickly fading into the background. The pain, the lack of sleep, the emotional beating he's taken is seconds away from turning his lights out.

He slaps himself again.

He hears something. Something coming his way.

There's a single car driving toward him. Like an angel from heaven, an Audi is barreling his way. Not too far away, but far enough for Remo to get his head together and ready his Glock. Perfect, Remo thinks. He can get out there, scare the shit out of this clown, take the car and get gone without a whole scene getting started. He stands out in the middle of the road and raises his gun, leveling it on the Audi.

The brakes lock up. The Audi skids to a stop a few feet from Remo's quivering knees. Remo races over to the driver's side window rapping the barrel of the gun hard against the glass.

"Get the fuck out of the car," Remo screams. "I'm not going to hurt you, but I need this Audi. Like fucking now, bro."

The thirtysomething man has no idea what to do. Frozen by the sight of Remo, he grips the wheel at ten and two and can only stare up at the crazy, wet man with a gun. Remo gets frustrated. He has no time for this guy's bullshit fear. Yes, Remo was afraid of guns a few short days ago. Yes, outside of a courtroom Remo had never been near guns prior to a few days ago. But shit has changed, and Remo needs Audi Boy to get up and get the fuck out of that car. Remo tries to open the door.

It's locked.

"Open the damn door, man."

Audi Boy panics and slams down the gas. Tires rip, scream as the Audio pulls away. Remo, simply on instinct, fires a single shot. The bullet blasts out the rear tire, shredding it all to hell. The Audi slows, twists and turns, dropping off into the ditch.

"Shit," Remo mutters.

He runs over best he can with his gun pointed at the driver's door. The door flies open. The thirtysomething Audi Boy comes out with his hands up. Remo lowers his gun. The car is stuck. The rear bumper and tires are an inch or two off the ground. Not going anywhere.

"What the hell, man?" Remo yells. "All you had to do was get out of the damn car."

"I got scared," Audi Boy says.

"I wasn't going to do shit to you. Just wanted your ride." Remo turns, looking all around the road. "Now what? Huh?"

"Don't shoot me." Audi Boy pulls out his wallet. "I've got cash."

"Fuck your cash," Remo says, then stops turning around.

Another car is coming.

An orange car. A taxi.

Remo's eyes go wide as plates, then he snatches the wallet away from Audi Boy. He points his gun at Audi Boy, waving him back into his car that's jammed into the ditch.

"What? You're robbing me now?"

"I am," Remo says. "Get your dumbass back in that German sleigh ride."

Audi Boy slumps, then slides back into his car behind the wheel with hands still up. The cab is almost there. Remo taps his gun on the window, motioning for him to roll it down.

"Toss me that phone of yours," Remo says.

"Oh come on."

Remo plants the gun on his forehead. Audi Boy hands him the phone with great haste. Remo pulls his arm back and tosses the phone into the woods with all he has. It flips and wobbles, bouncing off a tree before skidding through the leaves, landing God knows where.

"You can get it when I'm gone." Remo puts the gun back into his waistband and covers it with his shirt. "Now, get your ass down."

Audi Boy obeys, scrunching down into his seat, out of sight. Remo moves back out into the road, waving the wallet.

The cab stops.

"Here." Remo jumps into the back of the cab then hands the driver the card J. Slim gave him. It's soaking wet and barely holding together, but readable. The condition of the card, along with water dripping from it, plus the overall near-death look that Remo is sporting, earns a concerned stare from the driver.

"Go." Remo flashes some cash. "Go real fucking fast."

21

The cab ride started out by staying within the confines of the law.

Remo threw a few fresh dollars at the driver.

There was slightly more speed added, but the gusto Remo wanted was lacking.

Then he threw in a lot of dollars.

The driver is now cutting and weaving through the city like a man on a mission. A man driving beyond logic and reason. A man ripping through the city like he had a gun to his head. Oddly enough he doesn't, but Remo did consider it. The driver jams the gas. Lock-stomps the brakes. Whips the wheel back and forth, slamming and tossing Remo around in every direction in the back of the cab. Remo's faceprint can be seen on the Plexiglas that separates the two of them. Remo counts at least four times he's nailed the damn thing.

Remo has faded in and out during the drive. Allowing his body to be thrown around without much of a struggle, while trying to conserve his strength. Strength he knows he'll need. He's about to face the toughest test of his life, and any and all available strength would be appreciated.

Everything he's been through up until now was to prepare

himself for this. Remo knows it. He's not a deeply religious person, nor is he really spiritual in any way shape or form, but he does, from time to time at least, think things do happen for a reason. All of the violence, stress, bodily harm, wanton destruction—all of it—has brought him to here, and he'll need all of that to get through whatever is in store for him. There is a bad, bad man with his ex-wife and son. He has to remove this man without an ounce of harm coming to Anna and Sean.

He has no idea how to do this.

Who would?

Remo knows who.

He gets pissed at Hollis again for abandoning him. A little pissed at Lester too, but at least he did a little tearful goodbye thing. It was nice. But that son of bitch Hollis just bolted without a damn word. What a fucker. Remo could really use a friend like Hollis right now. His experience. His advice. Hell, him. Remo swallows hard as his head races through all the possible *what ifs* of this situation.

What if there's more than one bad, bad man?

What if there is only one, and Remo can't beat him?

And, the worst *what if* of all, what if that bad, bad man has seen the news and has already killed them both and decided to split before the shit comes down on him?

This is the one that has Remo frozen.

His eyes are in a deep stare, looking into the void. To a place only he can see. He fingers his Glock. Works the dryness in his mouth with his even drier tongue. His hands are trembling uncontrollably. He squeezes his eyes tight as the images of the last few days whip and blur, tearing his mind's eye to shreds. A flip-book of blood and chaos. Bodies rising and falling. Guns blasting. Anger. Danger. Hearts pounding to the point of near failure. All the mental games won and lost. The unmistakable truth that all of it was because of Remo.

All because Remo made a decision after watching a grainy security video.

All because Remo has a son.

Remo clucks his tongue, letting all that sink in. Letting that truth bury itself, finding a home deep inside his broken brain.

Fuck it, Remo thinks. *It was worth it.*

All of it.

Well, all of it *will* be worth it if a few things happen. All of it will be worth it if, and it's a big damn *if,* if Remo can take down this bad, bad man and get Anna and Sean safe again.

Remo's fear is unbearable. The worst idea yet is that all of this could end up being for nothing. The very thought that those previously mentioned *what ifs* could come to be true would make all of this a waste. Void any good created. Not much more defeating than a human being risking it all for a complete waste of time.

No.

Wait, there is something far greater. The lost lives. The dead and the living. There's been a river of blood and a pile of broken lives that can be pointed to through all of this little adventure. That's an idea that doesn't sit well with Remo. Not by a damn sight.

The cab stops in front of a busted-up apartment building. Graffiti-covered. Dumped-over trash cans. Homeless laid out at the doorsteps. Windows covered with plywood.

"This is it, man," the driver says, scrunching his nose while double-checking the address on the card Remo gave him.

Remo's eyes open. He checks his gun. Hands the driver some cash.

"Yes. Yes, it is."

22

T he building is the perfect place to house bad shit.

Remo's certain that more than a few people were killed, or at least maimed, here this morning alone. If Remo wanted to kidnap and hold some folks somewhere, this would be the place he'd choose, too. Nobody's going to ask questions here. Nobody is going to notice a scream in this neighborhood, or a gunshot or a stabbing. The cops sure as hell aren't coming into this building unless they absolutely have to.

Remo enters with great caution, stepping through a front door that's barely hanging on its hinges. There's a drunk beating his head against a wall in the lobby while arguing with someone who isn't there. A puddle of urine pooling around him. Down the hall are three teens who stop what they're doing long enough to take a good look at Remo. A good, hard look. Remo flashes his Glock, letting them get a good, hard look at that. They don't seem overly impressed, but decide it's not worth the effort to engage.

Remo takes to the stairs. The apartment number on the card J. Slim gave him reads three hundred and two. He takes a stab in the dark and decides the third floor is as good a starting place as any, but he takes each step as if he were navigating a minefield. As if death could pop up at any moment. His Glock is lowered by his side, but always at the ready. He's picked up some techniques by watching and listening to Hollis and Lester, but he's still far from Special Forces.

Reaching the third-floor landing, Remo can see a door marked by a three and a two, with an empty space between the numbers that looks like it held a zero at one time.

He takes in a deep breath.

Shakes his head hard side to side, trying to get his mind right. Once he feels like he's in a decent place, he releases the air from his lungs. His ribs ache off the simple act of breathing, but he doesn't give them much of a thought. Moving toward the door, quiet as a church mouse, he focuses on making as little movement as possible.

Nearing the door, he leans his back flat against a dirty wall directly to the right of the doorknob. He listens closely, hoping to get some kind of clue as to what's going on in there. He hears a TV. Children's show, best he can guess. There's high-pitched talking followed by rolling, exaggerated canned laughter. That's a good sign at least. Means there's a good chance there's a child in there, and that child is alive watching TV. Anything is possible, but Remo feels slightly better. He lets his fingers re-grip his Glock. He's been holding it so tightly that he lost feeling in parts of his hand.

He places his ear harder to the wall, trying to get a better listen inside. Muffled noises. A soup of sounds comprised of TV, air conditioning and pipes running. He does hear what could be footsteps, but still no voices speaking. His breathing quickens. Chest tightens. Time to do something.

He re-grips his Glock one last time.

Steps back. Remo has no great plan here. It's time to go in and he knows it. Time to take the last piece of advice Lester gave Remo.

Go do what you gotta do.

The *what ifs* are all done for now. Filed away.

Now it's all about the *what is,* and what is behind this damn door.

Remo raises his gun and kicks the door in with all he has.

The door explodes open, ripping apart the doorjamb and slamming the door back into the wall behind it. The knob punches a hole into the piece of shit wall. Remo charges inside hard with his Glock tracking the room. This is a level of focus he's never known before. Eyes scanning. Heart pounding. The place is small, but he doesn't see anyone in the area. He hears a TV playing in a bedroom to the side with the door closed. He can see light dancing under the door.

There's a flicker of something out the corner of his eye.

Remo whips himself around with his Glock leading the way.

The bad, bad, psycho man is facedown, motionless on the dirty carpet. At first glance, he seems to be resting peacefully, but there's something off about him. A major item of note. His head has been twisted around. Completely around. His chest is down on the floor with his mouth and bulging eyes wide open, staring blankly up at the ceiling.

Cloris sits at a card table in the corner of the room enjoying a sandwich.

She glances up at Remo, pauses, then gives him a casual, yet friendly wave.

23

"Where's Lester?" Cloris asks while choking down some ham.

Remo can't even begin to process what he's seeing in front of him. It shouldn't surprise him that Cloris was multiple steps ahead of him, but shock still rockets through every ounce of his being.

"Hello?" She waves again, annoyed by the lack of response she's receiving from Remo. She snaps her fingers. "Over here."

"He left." Remo finally gets some words out of his mouth. "We separated after the—after some things happened."

She shakes her head, taking another bite. "Well, shit." Cloris drops her sandwich, disgusted by what Remo just told her. She's clearly annoyed that she has wasted her time with all this here. She pushes herself away from the table with a hard shove. "Guess I'll go find his ass. Again."

She zips up a bag that's been sitting on the table. Remo caught a quick glance before she closed it up. It's stuffed with money and at least two guns. The bag she took off the Mashburn compound in New Mexico, no doubt. She moves toward the door, but not before thumping Remo in the balls.

Remo folds.

"Your ex and kid are fine. They're in the bedroom watching some dumb-as-shit TV program." She moves into the open doorway, but before she leaves: "You're welcome, fuckface."

Remo fights the flutter of nausea that Cloris's well-placed nut thump provided him. He sucks in a deep pull of air and stands up straight, then bends over again. He thinks of throwing up. Couldn't hurt at a time like this. Completely justified.

"Daddy?"

Remo spins around.

There he is. Remo can't believe it. His reason for all this is in the same room.

Remo can't fight it. The tears start slowly, then roll with reckless abandon. He shakes and falls to a knee, letting his gun fall to the floor. Sean runs to Remo, wrapping his arms tightly around his neck. Every inch of Remo screams in pain, but he doesn't care. He'll take that kind of hurt and more of the same to be right here, right now. This is the best moment of his life and Remo doesn't give a single damn about all the pain, mental and physical, he's endured to get here. He's getting a hug from his boy.

His first.

Ever.

Remo can't help it—the emotions roar out of him like a firehose. A surprising flood he didn't know existed inside of him, but he loves it. Letting go is freedom. He's a sobbing mess and he won't apologize to anyone for it. Sean still holds onto his dad's neck as he pulls back, getting a good look at the old man.

"You okay?" Sean asks, trying not to hurt his feelings, though Remo is clearly a disaster.

"No, but I'm getting better."

"Good." Sean smiles, then looks behind Remo at the twisted remains of the bad, bad man. "Aunt Cloris said he fell down."

The words *Aunt Cloris* have a nails-on-a-chalkboard kind of feel to them as they hit Remo's ears. He smiles, plays it off, tries to let go of the *Aunt Cloris* bit, then simply nods to his son's shining face. Remo has not a single clue how to address that or any of the shit Sean's seen or heard in the last few days. Can't even begin to explain what Remo's been through either. He knows one day he'll have to try, but for now? Remo only wants to soak up this moment as much as he can.

"Sean," Anna says from the doorway. Her face has escalated to a shade of Corvette red. She can barely contain the rage that is bubbling up within her body and soul. Remo freezes, as does Sean.

"Honey," she says to Sean through grinding teeth. "Honey, your father and I need to talk."

Sean looks to Remo.

Remo shakes his head *no*, hoping Sean will bail him out. Sean giggles.

No. No. No, Remo thinks. He'd rather fight all the Mashburns, Mr. Crow, Cormack, J. Slim, Godzilla and King Kong than have a *talk* with Anna right now.

24

To suggest the police, FBI and CIA were sympathetic to Remo's situation would be a gross exaggeration.

They listened to what Remo had to say.

They were helpful, to a certain extent.

They offered a solution.

Against his better judgement, Remo told them the truth. All of it. He told them about the Mashburns, Crow, Cormack, J. Slim, the Turkovs and all the finer points of disaster in between. The Cormack conversation was the one that captured their attention the most, just as Remo thought it would.

Apparently there had been whispers around the agency for a while about Cormack and his operations. Standard office gossip. Watercooler talk and the like, just like any other large organization. Only with the CIA, these types of things carry a little more weight. Require a little more concern and care. Cormack was a fast riser and had a reputation for getting shit done, which meant his superiors didn't question much as long as Cormack kept making them look good. He did just that, until he came across a man named Remo Cobb.

Many people have gone down in that deep ocean.

Remo also discussed Detective Harris's involvement, but he didn't want to. The man did help him to a certain degree on the bridge, but Harris was in way too deep and had way too much baggage. Remo framed it all the best he could, but he held no illusions that life was going to be pleasant for Detective Harris.

It was a tense room. The room in which Remo spilled his guts and gave it all up to the powers that be. It was a massive relief to Remo to let it all out. To unload, to unpack the last few days. The last few years, really. They put him up at a swank hotel with armed guards on the floor. He'd never slept so good. He ordered room service, three carts' worth, and took a shower that lasted at least an hour and a half. This rest and recovery time allowed Remo to find the proper mindset to sit in a chair and give it all up for the cops and feds.

After three solid days of his tell-all session, Remo finally struck a deal.

A deal that he never thought he'd make in a million and five years.

The CIA told him that there are still dozens of criminal organizations that want Remo dead. Ray is still out in the wild, and has people on the street hunting for him night and day. The CIA can't get a completely accurate measure as to the real numbers of questionable people who are searching for Remo, but it's high to be sure.

As they spoke in that room, Remo could see his life and career pass before his eyes. It's cliché as hell, but it's true. His formative years in Cut N' Shoot Texas. His dick of an old man. Law school. Moving up at the firm and all the cases that he won, and the handful he lost. Most notably the one case he threw that started a chain reaction, that landed him in the interrogation hot seat.

The Mashburn case was the one that started a raging bonfire that continues to burn.

The deal Remo struck will protect him, or at least try to. In exchange for the information Remo has given and will continue to give, Remo will go into the program. His continuing information is more or less an evergreen fountain of details via an off-the-record hard drive Remo produced from his old firm. The *in case of emergency* hard drive he went through a lot of trouble to get before his original meeting with Cormack. Somehow the drive survived all the shit from the last couple of days, and Remo couldn't be more thankful. This treasure trove of information will help supply law enforcement for years to come. None of it admissible in a court of law, of course, but it's great stuff to build off of, and will not be spoken of again by Remo or anyone else.

Remo's only condition before being placed in the program?

He wanted to make sure Anna and Sean were also taken care of. If Ray and the other members of the criminal element wanted Remo dead, then it's not a stretch to think they would go after the two of them just like Ray and J. Slim did.

The solution is not picture perfect, but it works in a strange way.

Remo doesn't know the stats on the success of divorced couples in WITSEC, but he feels like it's what's best for them. Anna, Sean and Remo have been set up in the same town, but not living together. Remo lives a few blocks over from Anna and Sean. Remo wanted to make sure, wherever they ended up, that the school district was good, the weather was decent at least, and they were in a location that most criminals couldn't find if you spotted them the state and the first letter of the town.

They now have different names.

Hair colors have changed.

And they're alive and together. Somewhat.

Remo managed to find a bag or two of cash stashed at the house in New Mexico where he, Lester, Hollis and Cloris stayed the night of the chicken pepperoni incident. Remo conveniently left that house out of all the info he gave the feds. It was tricky, but he managed to stop by there before he went into protection. That cash means that Remo can meet his healthy child support payment, and put Sean through college when the time comes.

Remo tends bar at a little beach place, and he loves it.

He sleeps with a gun under his pillow and an assault rifle in his closet. Anna and Sean's house is wired with more security equipment than Fort Knox.

Remo hopes Hollis found his family.

He hopes Lester finds whatever he's looking for.

He hopes Cloris never finds Lester.

He hopes Anna will forgive him and that Sean will adapt well to his new life.

For the first time in a long time, Remo has hope. Hope that the chaos is over. Hope for his family, as fragmented as it may be, and hope for the days to come.

Hope for better days, man.

That, folks, is all an asshole like Remo Cobb can want in this thing called life.

Mike McCrary's has been a screenwriter, a waiter, a securities trader, dishwasher, bartender, investment analyst and an unpaid Hollywood intern. He's quit corporate America, come back, been fired, been promoted, been fired again. Currently, he writes about questionable people who make questionable decisions.

Keep up with Mike at....

www.mikemccrary.com

mccrarynews@mikemccrary.com

GETTING UGLY - BONUS

BONUS PULP NOVELLA

PART I

FUCK YOU, GRANDE UGLY

1

L eon.

The man you'd rather be, or be with, depending on your preference. Twenty-five, whip-smart head, with a body crafted from Hanzo steel. Leon could very well be the spawn of an aggressive mud pit baby making session involving Han and Hope Solo. He's nothing like that pansy Skywalker. Leon used to like Luke. At one time wanted to be Luke. Hell, he *was* Luke one Halloween. Most days his features are just shy of perfection—even his minor imperfections are considered ruggedly handsome in most circles— but not today.

That was a long time ago, long before the events of today.

His time spent with the FBI has served him well. The hours working the Bureau's program have transformed him into a perfect physical machine. Not like the beefy boys of Venice Beach. No chest shaving or sweating through black and gold spandex so that he can look sweet in a pair of smiley face boxers. He looks nice in his boxers —boxer briefs actually—but that is not why he does it.

He's not out to impress, not trying to snatch up ladies. He has a wife he loves dearly, and that's more than enough for Leon. From the moment their eyes locked over a keg of Milwaukee's Beast at Dusty Ballard's house that summer, Leon knew she was the one. Still is. That was the summer before senior year. It's clichéd, he knows, but it's the truth: when you fall you fall, no matter when it is. What can you do? So, no, he's not killing himself at the gym, perfecting himself physically, to pull in some strange while out at Buffalo Wild Wings.

No, his body has been carefully honed for endurance and—if need be—fast, effective violence. The days and nights spent working through the different regimens, the grueling federally funded training is all for days like today.

Leon didn't use profanity for the majority of his life, considering it a simple language for simple, weak minds. But days like today have forced Leon rethink that philosophy.

Today Leon thinks, *Fuck Luke*.

Today those good looks hang from his bones like a shirt draped over a fat boy's treadmill. Today that cut from steel body resembles a turd that's been stepped in.

Haggard.

Beaten.

Of course, Leon never thought there would be days like this. No one does. Why would they?

He sports a bulging blood clot over one eye, a deep cut seeping above his brow. Crimson strands of saliva string from his bottom lip. Sleep's a distant memory, and Leon fights to stay focused, his mind drifting to thoughts of his wife—the way a child might cling to happy thoughts after waking from a nightmare. No lullaby here for Leon, only "Enter Sandman" as performed by Satan's garage band.

He stumbles through the dirt streets of Shit Town, Mexico. He's not sure of the town's actual name. His thoughts are starting to run together. Leon was given an assignment and began tracking this deranged man in LA. Then his quest took him to Chicago, and then to a tiny pothole in West Virginia. From there it was the Caymans (*That was nice.*), Warsaw (*Not so nice.*), Bangkok (*Just flat-out fucked up.*), and finally here, somewhere in the mountains outside of Mexico City.

But this man, Leon's target, is here.

He knows it.

Unmistakable signs are all around and cannot be ignored. Most notably, the swirling atmosphere of complete chaos. Behind Leon, a tiny town burns, small houses lit up like campfires. Dead bodies litter the dirt road, shell casings scattered amongst the pooling blood. An axe is planted in the chest of some poor soul. A goat runs like hell.

Leon's standard issue Glock 23 hangs in his chewed up excuse for a hand. A few locals from the town huddle behind him as if he's their only hope. Leon can't even begin to worry about them. Not because he's an unfeeling bastard—he wishes he could help—but because of the cold hard facts of the situation.

Leon can't do a damn thing for them.

He's tried before.

There was the guy at that Thai place in downtown Chicago who was kind enough to provide some useful information. Leon tried to help him.

Jesus, what was his name?

Leon struggles to remember. He does, however, remember that Thai Place Guy got up to go to the bathroom and was met by a dark stranger. Thai Place Guy received a lethal knife wound for his trouble, the blade starting at his navel and then ripping up to his sternum. Thai Place Guy's special reward for assisting the FBI? He got to watch his guts spill out over the urine-stained linoleum of a men's room. And Leon doesn't even want to think about what happened to that family in Poland who talked.

The FBI appreciates your sacrifice.

There are other helpful dead bodies scattered around the globe. The sum of those dead innocent people (well, some not so innocent) has caused Leon to think perhaps he shouldn't be so damn chatty with folks.

He pulls his cell while limping down the Mexican dirt road, his bloodied left leg dragging behind him. A torn Britney Spears t-shirt provides a makeshift tourniquet. Leon spins through his contacts and makes the call. After a one-ring pickup Leon spits out, "Cooper, I did it. Got a location on him."

Leon can't help but think back on the day he first sat down in Cooper's office.

That was two years, five months, eight days ago.

A lifetime ago.

2

L eon recalls the office being drab, sterile as hell, but with a magnificent view of the Los Angeles Westside.

Behind a cluttered oak desk sat a warhorse of a G-Man: LA Special Agent-in-Charge, A.L. Cooper, a living, breathing legend with thirty plus years on the books. The multitude of Cooper stories echo throughout the halls of the FBI. Cooper had worked offices across the U.S., as well as joint CIA gigs around the globe, and had his pick of offices years ago. After a fraction of thought, he selected swimming pools and movie stars. Of course he did. It's fucking seventy-two degrees and sunny three hundred and fifty days out of the year and, oh yeah, everybody's beautiful.

Even the homeless are fives and sixes.

Cooper needed to find a good man to track down a bad problem. He'd poured over the stack of potential candidates, and most of them didn't amount to a thimble full of warm cat piss.

One, however, caught his eye.

This kid, Leon, had only been on the bureau's roster for a couple of years, but it's been an impressive couple of years to say the least. The kid reminded Cooper of Cooper. They shared a similar blue-collar, lower-middle-class upbringing, Cooper born and bred in PA with Leon growing up in OH. Both played football. Cooper an All-District middle linebacker, Leon an All-District ball hawk of a safety with great run stuffing skills. Leon went from Quantico to a field office, then quickly made it onto an FBI SWAT team in Dallas. Currently, the kid was with the Tactical Section / Hostage Rescue Team (TS/HRT.) Just like Cooper's path years ago. In fact, Cooper was on the original TS/HRT team established in 1983 for the Los Angeles Olympics in response to that unfortunate shit that went on in Munich.

The major difference between Cooper and Leon?

Cooper had the benefit of a good, stable home. Leon, on the other hand, was raised in foster homes around Ohio. Cooper guesses Leon's parents bought it in a car crash, that's usually how they both die at the same time. He checks the file and sees they died in a company fire at the plant where they worked. Leon was six. The courts awarded some money, which his piece of shit aunt and uncle blew through most of it. The court-appointed trust did have some caveats baked in that stated how the money was to be used "for the benefit of the child," but Aunt Josie and Uncle John-John took that to mean buying them a new house, car and stocking their bar for the apocalypse. Fortunately, there was still enough for Leon to go to college and have a bit left over. By the look of that wife of Leon's, Cooper guesses most of what was left went to the rock on her finger and a down payment on a new house. And upon further review of Leon's bank records, yup, that's it.

All of this makes Cooper smile. Orphans with dependency issues and the need to excel make fantastic recruits.

Leon sits across Cooper's desk, a clean-cut, poster child of an FBI man, nervously twisting his wedding ring.

Newlyweds, Cooper thinks. *Adorable.*

Kid kinda reminds Cooper of Luke Skywalker.

Cooper likes the kid, make no mistake, but this is an interview for a very special project, so it's imperative to be a bit of an asshole and fuck with the young lamb Leon. Establish dominance; develop Cooper as a father figure and whatnot.

"Leon. Or is it Leo? Is Leo short for Leon?"

Leon wants this assignment as bad as anything he's ever wanted. Though he doesn't know what it is, he does know all about Cooper. Knows the war stories and the legends backward and forward. If even half of them are true, he wants to grow up to be Cooper, or at least his version of Cooper.

Leon fights back the nervous energy. It's okay to show respect but mustn't show any form of pussy tendencies. "Leo would only be losing an "n" so it's not really— Leon is fine, sir."

"Fuck it. Why the FBI?" Cooper fires back. What the kid says isn't nearly as important as how he responds. Does he freeze up? Shift in his seat? Or, Godforfuckingbid, start to sweat and stammer like a five-year-old ballerina.

Leon wants to impress. He thinks about how all great careers start with something like this, a defining moment. One of those points on the graph that signals an upward trend, heading for the stars, knocking a big assignment out of the park, blowing expectations out of the water. But, damn it all to hell, Leon does not know how to answer Cooper's question.

"Sir?"

"Why. Did. You. Join. The FBI?" Cooper presses. "You wanted to expand the cock n' balls via the Glock n' badge?"

Leon's response is nothing but free-flowing youthful sincerity. "I wanted to do something, you know, something good. Be proud of my job; be proud in general. I've got friends who jumped to Wall Street. Some became lawyers, chasing paychecks. Slaves to a salary…"

Cooper slices the air with his hand cutting him off. "Right. Right. Right. Enough, son. You already got the gig, stop the shit."

"No. No shit here, sir." Leon tries not to bounce up and down in his seat. *Did he say I got the gig?*

Cooper takes a moment to chew on the honest, wide-eyed little boy look plastered all over Leon. He remembers looking at the world through that lens. That was a long time ago, and Cooper knows that worldview simply does not exist—never has, never should. Cooper briefly entertains the idea of not allowing Leon to go through with this assignment. Save the kid from himself. Cooper allows a moment of silence to hang in the air while he lets his eyes tell him what he needs to know about Leon.

Is the boy completely full of crap?

No.

Will he survive?

Doubtful.

Do you have a choice?

Nope.

Cooper picks up Leon's file. "You come highly, highly recommended. Rising fast. Knocked the piss out of the test scores."

Cooper continues reviewing and discussing Leon's off the chart abilities: Leon rapid firing, speed loading, and ripping targets on the firing range to nothing before the instructors could begin to process his skill level; Leon tearing through the obstacle course like it wasn't even there. He was driven beyond reason, passing fellow cadets like they were disinterested sheep.

Leon's first day on the street?

He hunted down some stray dogs the FBI had eyes on, a beefy motorcycle gang that was selling meth to anything with a heartbeat. Leon ran up against two tatted-up Neanderthals who laid down some serious firepower with modified assault rifles—crazy, urban warfare shit. Very sophisticated for bike riding tweekers. Leon crept up behind the beasts, dove through the air, and tackled them both to the street like he was Riggs in *Lethal Weapon*. In a blink of an eye, Leon had disarmed them both and was on his feet, Glock leveled at their skulls.

"People still talk about it," Cooper wraps up with a swig of coffee.

"Thank you, sir."

Cooper glances at Leon as if trying to communicate with his mind. *Last chance to run, kid.* Leon doesn't receive Cooper's telepathy, only wants to devour whatever information Cooper has thrown his way.

Cooper shrugs. *Fuck it then.* He leans forward and gets to the meat of the conversation. "This is a manhunt. The man? Possibly the single most terrifying thing ever rendered by sperm and egg. Goddamn horror show who will kill and rob anything breathing. I need a young, aggressive agent with a healthy set of nuts. Most people are afraid to touch this shit show. You one of those homos?"

Young Leon wants to do well, excel, exceed. "Healthy nuts, yes. Homo, no."

Cooper hands Leon two, three-inch thick files. "Find this man. Bring him in to answer for the wicked he has done." Disturbing, grisly photos spill out from the files. The files have only two words on them: *BIG UGLY*

Leon lets a smile crack. He's heard stories about Big Ugly, the white whale, the Big Foot of the law enforcement community. Leon blurts, "Yes, sir." If he'd taken a moment from his race to impress Cooper to actually stop for a breath and look over the file, he wouldn't be smiling or thanking anybody for shit.

He'd bolt for the door and apply to the nearest grad school.

Cooper knows this, but he also knows where Leon's head is. He knows Leon's type: a young, strong kid who's blinded by a mix of ambition and cotton candy idealism, coupled with a not so great childhood. That cocktail has made and broken many a good man. Cooper feels some annoying need to offer a bit context. "Now, some consider this a fool's errand given who we're talking about. The levels of violence and so forth. It may take you some time. Might have to track this horrific cocksucker for months, maybe years. Can you do this for me, for the FBI?"

Leon doesn't even pretend to think about it. "Absolutely, sir." He smiles huge, completely forgetting about his wife, the one who will be left alone during Leon's crusade. Cooper cracks a half-smile. The death of idealism always hurts Cooper.

It'll pass.

~

THAT FATEFUL DAY in Cooper's office is now in Leon's rearview.

That was then.

This is now.

Leon's mind whips from that trip down memory lane to the present—his situation is problematic, at best. Today, Leon is beaten to hell, standing in the middle of a Mexican war zone.

He repeats firmly into his cell, "Cooper?"

Leon hears Cooper take a deep breath and then give an obligatory dramatic pause. He can almost see Cooper's shoulders shrug. The pause drags out for what seems like days.

Cooper finally says, "It's over. I'm being forced to end the hunt."

Disbelief rockets through Leon.

Cooper's words hit him like a spike puncturing his heart, draining his will. Hearing this news could only be matched by phrases like "inoperable tumor" or "no choice but to castrate." He feels his brain slosh inside his skull. "What? We got him. He's here. You hear me? He. Is. Here. Send in a team..."

Cooper's voice is clear and cold, as if reading ink from a page. "I want you to know, you've served the FBI admirably. Please understand, there was no other way."

"Oh bullshit...sir. I'm bringing him in."

Just before Cooper hangs up, he offers, "God be with you, son. I'm sorry."

"Agent Cooper? Cooper!"

Dead air.

3

Leon slumps, his back sliding down the wall of a shack that looks like it could crumble any second. He lets his cell drop to his side, his mind a swirling wad of confusion with no direction or place to go. Leon is a man without a country, his situation as bad as it gets. No backup, and the cavalry is not coming. His mentor, his hero, his surrogate father had abandoned him when he needed him the most. He has successfully tracked down the Devil, and in return Leon's been left to tangle with him alone.

Is this what the Thai Place Guy felt while watching his guts slip from his body?

The Mexican locals scatter as if it had started raining razor blades. Leon's confusion swells as he watches the people bolt in every direction, scrambling to avoid being anywhere near him, like rats that instinctively sense the ship is sinking. *What do they know?* His stomach twists with the fear that comes from being the last to know you're completely fucked.

A fist bursts through the thin wall behind Leon's head.

Thick, well-manicured fingers wrap around the back of his neck, like a mama cat snatching up her kitten. The unseen force yanks

Leon through the wall and into the dilapidated Third World home. In a single motion, Leon is thrown helicopter style, arms and legs spinning. He lands in a tumble-roll across the dirt floor.

Dust dances as Leon skids to a stop. He manages to squeeze off two blind shots. Prays he hit something, anything. Nicked a vital organ...please?

Nothing.

Silence.

Tiny dots of daylight shine through the bullet holes, with thin slivers of light creeping through where the walls don't completely meet up with the roof. A cockroach sprints across the dirt floor.

A John Lobb loafer steps on the roach with a moist squish, its high-dollar companion stomping Leon's gun hand with a twisting crunch of ligament and bone. The Glock slips out from his helpless fingers. Scrambling for the gun, Leon is met with a beatdown delivered by a master of ass kicking.

A blizzard of punches, kicks, chops, flips, elbows, palms of hands —all unpleasant shit. Leon fights back, giving him hell, but only lands every fourth or fifth fist or foot. It's not enough. Leon is fighting a beast way outside his class. Like the house of straw against the big, bad wolf, this piggy is in deep shit and sinking fast.

A Colt held by the figure shrouded in shadow jams into Leon's eye socket.

The dark figure speaks. "Hola."

Leon cannot, will not, give this man the satisfaction of knowing his fear. "Hi."

"Sucks when friends up and fuck you."

"That it does."

The dark figure readjusts his grip then continues. "What have I ever done to you? How long have you been on me?"

"Two years, five months, eight days."

"Seriously, when are you going to cease with the shit?"

"Maybe tomorrow."

"But not today?"

"Unlikely."

The dark figure playfully exaggerates a sigh then pulls back the hammer. "Buenos días, my little dead Fed."

Leon spits out a pulpy tooth. "Fuck you, Grande Ugly."

PART II

A FEW SHITTY YEARS LATER

4

It's a moist, sticky night inside a pay by the hour motel room.
Dirty, pink flowered paper clings to the walls. Even the room seems to sweat. An open window lets a breeze into this horrific excuse for living quarters. Graffiti marks the walls—something about big dicks and your mother—beer cans fill the bathtub, and what looks like old, dried-in blood stains on the carpet. A brown couch squeaks as if a jackrabbit were screwing an unwilling Tasmanian Devil.

A wiry twenty-something, Brobee is half-dressed in a *Wonder Pets!* T-Shirt, camo cargos down around his checkered Vans. Brobee huffs and puffs with a much, much older hooker riding him with the enthusiasm of a comatose cowgirl.

He's working way too hard.

She's bored-to-tears.

The hooker glances at her ancient Swatch, slightly bouncing up and down. "You've got five champ." Brobee goes faster, face beet red.

The door busts open, ripped out chain lock dangling impotently from the doorframe.

Three mean-spirited gents step in. Rasnick leads the charge, with two Eastern Bloc thugs named Vig and Oleg backing him up.

Brobee's eyes go wide but keeps at his squeaky sex. He's still on the clock, dammit.

Brobee knows Rasnick is a forty-four-year-old enforcer who's gone as high as he's going on the career ladder. It probably bothers him, sure, but what are you gonna do? He does his thing, makes a so-so living, dances when the boss says boogie and buys lottery tickets. Right now his boogie partner is Brobee.

Fucking Brobee.

Rasnick shields his eyes from the horrific intercourse as calmly he asks, "Brobee, where's the money?"

Brobee responds with hump-altered speech. "Look, Rasnick. Bro. Dude..." More squeaking. Oleg and Vig pull guns. The hooker gasps in between bounces. Rasnick's eyes never leave Brobee. "You lost twenty K on women's lacrosse."

Vig chimes in, "Who the fuck bets women's lacrosse?"

"What kind of shithead..." starts Oleg.

"That kind of shithead," Rasnick says. The room goes silent save the squeaking. Brobee is still at it. The kid's dedicated to getting his money's worth.

"Could you stop fucking her for five fucking seconds?" asks Rasnick. The squeaks stop. Bouncing hooker stops. Rasnick takes in a breath. "Tell me you have the money. Please tell me that I didn't make Oleg and Vig come down here for this sad-sack sex show."

Oleg and Vig could be twins—they're not, but they could be. Walls of former Soviet Union beef with tight crew cuts and Russian prison tats from neck to nuts. They'd joined up with Rasnick about a year ago, and things have gone well. Oleg and Vig are happy employees as long as they can drink the good stuff, get mouth-sex from time to time, and inflict pain on a daily basis.

Brobee looks over the situation and knows it's not favorable. His options are limited at best. Unfortunately, run like hell or certain death are the options Brobee usually faces. He thinks that a smart guy would find a better way to live. And he will, starting tomorrow. Tomorrow is personal inventory day for Brobee. Just gotta get *to* tomorrow, and right now that's a problem.

He tosses the naked hooker towards them with a yelp.

Rasnick and company are knocked off balance as they open fire. Their blasts crater the walls, taking out fistfuls of drywall. Brobee does a two hop, penguin walk with his cargos around his ankles. The pounding bullets barely miss as he takes a bare ass dive out the window.

Brobee hits the trash cans ass first, his tailbone screaming as his lower back locks up. He spins from the cans as Vig and Oleg hang out the window looking for a shot. Brobee manages to pull his pants up and gain speed as they open up on him. He runs like he's never run before, bare feet slapping hard on the pavement. Brobee remembers hearing something about how running barefoot is better for you, had read the first paragraph of an article about that somewhere. Thinks, *This is the start, the start of a new Brobee.*

He'll almost definitely take up barefoot running, eating right—well, better at least—and he will, without question, poke fewer hookers.

5

A cab pulls into LAX.

Brobee tosses a few bills to the cabbie. It's not enough. The cabbie screams as Brobee storms into the airport.

Always keeping his head on a swivel while he waits in line at the American Airlines ticket counter. He takes an opportunity to cut in line as the family in front of him wrestles with a stroller and three kids. At the counter a chipper ticket agent asks, "Where will you be traveling this evening?"

"Next flight the fuck outta here. Doesn't matter where," Brobee fires back as he slams down an AmEx he stole from a Persian guy he knows who churns out credit cards using stolen identities.

On the plane, Brobee starts seat dancing with headphones planted on his head, his cocktail sloshing all over his hand. He flips off the window in rhythm with Katy Perry. Other passengers pretend not to notice.

Hours later he lands at some bumfuck airport just north of nowhere. Brobee didn't even bother really checking where he was going, and he didn't recognize the name of the place on the ticket— someplace that starts with a B or an M, maybe in Montana...perhaps

Idaho. He'd had to change planes three times, and he's hammered out of his skull from the Jack and Cokes.

Brobee walks through the parking lot, looking over the available vehicles as if he was shopping for a new ride. The booze is starting to fade and he lost his ticket at some point. He still has no idea where he is. Could be Oregon. Could be Canada. Could be Sweden. There are woods in the distance, with mountains. Brobee selects a slick, old school Cadillac and smashes a brick through the passenger window.

The freshly stolen Caddie weaves and winds down a serpentine, country road that's completely surrounded by thick walls of trees. The headlights cut through the dark, foggy night. Inside the Caddie, Brobee has the 10-speaker, 2 subwoofer, 200 watt sound system booming classic rock. He's enjoying Golden Earring so much he doesn't notice the red blinking fuel light.

Brobee's new ride slows down to a crawl, then rolls to a stop as "Radar Love" shuts off.

"Fuck."

Brobee exits, nothing for miles but trees, crickets and moonlight. He fumbles around the glove box and finds a flashlight. He hears a muffled noise coming from the trees far away. Distant, but it almost sounds like someone is there.

"Hello?" Brobee asks the dark.

The sound comes from deep within the woods. Brobee hates this: still half-buzzed, alone in the wild, no gas, had to bail the motel without his cell, and his only food is that extra bag of nuts he swiped from the plane. He moves into the heavy woods with the flashlight in hand.

After what seems like hours of pushing through this dark maze of bark and vegetation, Brobee's out of breath. He's been at this awhile, and hasn't begun his exercise program yet. That's tomorrow, he reminds himself as he leans on a tree.

The sound has stopped. Brobee asks, "Hello?" Nothing. Complete silence greets him from the darkness in every direction.

Dense.

Claustrophobic.

This sucks and I'm not happy.

Then the sound is back. This time it's much louder and sounds like it's just up ahead; sounds a lot like singing.

What the fuck?

Brobee pushes through the seemingly endless forest until he finally reaches a clearing.

"Thank Christ," Brobee exhales. He's saved. He's so excited and happy he starts to bounce a bit. The singing continues, belting an almost operatic version of AC/DC.

Brobee strains to get a good look at something out into the distance. Something located in a large clearing has grabbed his attention by the throat. He freezes, not believing what his eyes are reporting back to his brain. He mutters to himself, "Is that? No. No fuckin' way."

Confusion fills his feeble mind as recognition shakes his flimsy body. Pure fear mixed with terror, topped off with an asshole clenching panic. Lips tremble. Eyes twitch. Flashlight drops.

He hears the sound of water trickling. Looking down, he sees piss rolling down his leg splashing all over the flashlight—so terrified he didn't even notice he was pissing himself. A new low, even for Brobee. All of this, the twitching, trembling, pissing...all of it because of what is up ahead in the clearing.

Brobee unleashes the scream of thousand girly men as he hauls ass back into the woods, running for his life. With no regard for his body, he bounces off trees, falls, skids, slides, and claws his way through the darkness, maintaining his feminine wail throughout his frantic journey to safety. Bat outta hell style, Brobee flies from the woods and lands sprawled in the road. A truck skids to a stop inches from plastering him. A portly driver steps out, but the nice guy doesn't even get the chance ask *"Are you okay?"* before Brobee jumps him. He puts a foot to the driver's balls and a knee to his chin, then steals his truck.

Brobee lets the tires peel as he continues his screaming, tears streaming and fists beating the dashboard. At the airport parking lot he brings the stolen truck to a skidding stop, leaving the engine running as he bolts for the terminal with arms flailing.

After the plane takes off, Brobee gulps down two Jack Daniel's mini bottles, skips the Coke. He sniffle-cries between breaths like a two-year-old. Far from okay, but at least he's not screaming or pissing himself. Calming down he tries to think. The wheels in his head turn as he takes a moment to piece together what he saw.

Correction.

Who he saw.

6

B robee flies through the doors of the dark, nasty bar with purpose, ignoring everything in his path. It's a hardcore drinker's bar, where people throw a few back while minding their own business... until there's an opportunity to kill or fuck someone. A dirty mirror clings to the wall behind the bar with tattered bras hung with care like a rainbow. A burly, aging bartender wipes down glasses with a rag that looks like used Charmin. He pulls down the tail of his flannel shirt to cover the .38 tucked in his waistband.

The bartender tries to stop Brobee. "Hey, asshole!" But nothing can stop him as he burns a trail to a back room, throwing open the reinforced steel door.

He enters a room that serves both as an office and criminal playpen and finds Rasnick, Oleg and Vig playing pool. Nothing shocks these guys, but even they are a bit taken aback at seeing Brobee here.

Brobee runs toward them, forgetting these guys tried to kill him not long ago. Rasnick's punch to the face reminds him quickly. Brobee stumbles back, then tries to soothe the mood of the room. "Let me talk..." Rasnick slams a pool stick to Brobee's gut, followed by a fist to the jaw. Brobee drops to a knee and screams, "Wait!" Before

Brobee has a chance to utter another word, two 9mms are jammed into his skull.

"Please listen, motherfuckers," yelps Brobee.

"Really, guy?" Rasnick slaps him.

Hammers pull back.

"I got something, fuckheads."

Earns another slap.

Oleg and Vig tighten their trigger fingers.

"I found Big Ugly!"

The room goes quiet. Oleg and Vig look to each other. They know the name, and that name scares the shit out of even them. Rasnick lowers himself to eye level with Brobee. "You mind repeating that?"

"Big Ugly," Brobee pants. "I know where he is."

"Bullshit," barks Oleg.

"He knows shit," agrees Vig.

Rasnick looks into Brobee's eyes trying to get a read. "How do I know, huh? How do I know?"

"Oh, fuck you. When have I ever lied to you..."

Rasnick slaps him again.

"Fine, fine. Okay, I've lied. But I'm telling you the truth." Brobee gets to his feet. Oleg and Vig keep their guns on his head. While adjusting his shirt, Brobee, unfortunately, feels the need to say, "Now, if you cocksucking faggots aren't interested in finding the biggest prize on the planet, then maybe you could go fuck yourselves."

Not well received.

An avalanche of fists and feet rain down on Brobee. He's beaten to the floor, curling into a ball covering his face with his arms. This is a defensive stance that Brobee has perfected over the years. Rasnick, Oleg, and Vig take turns kicking the various parts of Brobee still available.

"Stop," barks a commanding voice from a dark corner of the room.

Rasnick, Oleg, and Vig follow the order, immediately pulling back as if scalded. Out of the dark wheels a man in a chair. Face covered with burns and scars, the man looks as if he was pulled from an industrial accident seconds before death. He wears a suit and tie, partly to keep a certain level of respect, but mainly to cover up his disfigured body. His legs are useless, but he opted for multiple surgeries to avoid amputation. This is a fifty-year-old crime lord, Doren.

Doren eyes Brobee carefully, trying to assess if he can believe this man. "Tell me everything."

Brobee swallows big at the sight of Doren. He knows not many people get to speak to this man... or at least not many live long after speaking to this man. He nods and begins to explain. "Big Ugly. I swear to whateverthefuck you worship, Doren, I can give you Big Ugly—spin the wheel, let's make a deal."

Doren's hard stare burns through Brobee. Bubbling rage spikes through him as Doren's memory flips through a ton of pain and unpleasantness. Big Ugly left Doren scarred from head to toe, but it's the unseen scars that truly eat away at Doren. His eyes stop just short of popping as he commands, "Call a meeting."

7

D oren, a king on wheels, rolls across the floor of a gorgeous penthouse hotel suite, Rasnick pushing the chair with Vig and Oleg close behind. It's a room tailored for the illusion of royalty: crystal, glass, brass, oak, fresh flowers. All at the price tag of ten grand a day.

Doren is focused, mind churning behind cold eyes that burn with a hate that few will ever know. They glide past the floor to ceiling windows overlooking the LA skyline. A family of fifteen could live here, quite comfortably. You could feed a small country for the price of the art hanging on the walls. Rasnick eyes a painting closely—he's pretty sure he can lift it out of here without a problem.

They stop as they reach a dining room that holds massive, circular granite table. Seated at the table are the other three crime bosses of Los Angeles. Knights in the round. Nothing happens in this town without these guys and Doren earning a piece of it. Outside of a random domestic violence case here and there, there isn't a drop of blood spilled in LA without these guys knowing about it. These are the lords of the city.

Cherrito: middle-aged Latino hood, but worth multi-millions.

Bosko: fifty-something, full-fledged Irish mob.

Waingrow: late sixties, but tough as nails with style and class—his blue hearing aid even matches his tie.

Doren is wheeled to the front of the table, as he should be. Doren has the respect of the room, and he has earned it, the hard way. Rasnick, Oleg, and Vig take their places against the wall. Dorn addresses the room. "Thank you for your timely response. I called you here to discuss an urgent matter that concerns all of us. Today, right now, someone can lead us to Big Ugly."

The mood at the table turns electric, tension gravy-thick. It's as if Doren just announced that Lucifer is alive and well. Waingrow rubs his ear, adjusting his hearing aid to get it just right—wants to make sure that the guys outside got all that.

Parked outside the hotel is a standard, non-descript, trying-hard-not-to-be-noticed van. Inside the metal cube of a workspace is wall-to-wall surveillance equipment. Stacks and stacks of Federal tax dollar funded audio and video equipment. The van's interior is dark save for the bouncing red and green levels, B&W images light up the screens.

Two G-Men watch, soaking it all in. Cooper stands behind a tech, paying close attention to everything the young lad does. Shitty coffee in hand, they listen in on the crime lords' penthouse suite conversation.

Cooper's blood pressure flares at the words Big Ugly.

Over his headphones he strains to listen, wanting each and every word. He presses the headphones tight to his ears with his fingertips as Bosko says, "Big Ugly. That's a name I'd love to fuckin' forget."

The tech, too young to know what's what asks, "Who? Big what?"

Cooper doesn't bother explaining. "Grab me a cup of coffee, would ya?"

"Cooper, you've got a full..."

"How about you get the fuck outta here."

The tech understands that. He gets up immediately, thinks of asking how Cooper wants his coffee but thinks better of it and exits. Cooper takes a seat, and with laser focus pushes the headphones even tighter. If he could shove them into his brain, he would. He picks up a small mic that gives him a direct line into Waingrow's hearing aid; a nice link to Waingrow's head whenever he wants it.

Cooper listens in as Doren explains. "A degenerate named Brobee stumbled across Big Ugly. Simply blind luck and, after some negotiations, he has agreed to lead us to him."

Cooper speaks low into the handset. "Clear your throat if you hear me, butt fucker."

Waingrow grinds his teeth. He thinks about how long he's been at this game and never got picked up on anything. Nothing. Not one damn thing. Then, at his age no less, he gets tagged on some bullshit gambling bit. Just because some bitch got nervous and blabbed. He broke one of his steadfast rules: always pay for pussy. Paid pussy keeps quiet. But Waingrow got soft; he liked that waitress with the green eyes and big knockers. And what does he have to show for it? He's sitting here with these good people, people he's known forever, and he has to fuck them.

He's forced to snap out of his pity party as he hears Cooper in his ear again. "Hello, butt fucker? Clear your throat if you hear me. Butt-fucker?" Waingrow clears his throat, clears his head, then says, "Think we all can agree our lives would be better if we never met Big Ugly." He hates himself, but the table bought it.

Bosko sounds off, anger-fueled tears about to flow. "Soulless, shady, fucking..."

Cherrito interrupts. "Motherfuckin' misery master is what he is. There's no God while Big Ugly roams the earth."

Bosko raises his right hand; he's missing three fingers. "Monster took my digits."

Doren regains control of the table. "True. We've all lost something to Big Ugly." Nobody there has to dig too deep to recall a *favorite* Big Ugly memory.

There was that sunny SoCal afternoon in a Ralphs parking lot when some heavy-hitting, gun-toting bad boys took down an armored car in broad daylight. Guards were on the ground hog-tied, bags of money being thrown into a getaway van. It was an easy peasy job for Bosko's people. Until a wall of bullets carved them all to hell.

Bosko's men dropped. No last words. No death rattle. Just a pile of dead bad boys. All the carnage was done by a lone, at the time anonymous, "Dark Figure" who scooped up the money bags and took off without a trace. A mysterious thief of thieves.

Then there was that time at Cherrito's little grow house outside of Manhattan Beach. He had a team of topless immigrants working day and night, surgical masks over their faces, gloves over their hands, nothing over their chests. Mixing. Bagging. Processing. A goon with a sawed-off manning the door, an accountant with an industrial money-counting machine to keep track of the stacks upon stacks of dead presidents.

Then, without warning, a knife slammed down through the top of the goon's skull, blood spurting out like Old Faithful. The accountant took a few pops to the face from a Colt. That same Dark Figure grabbed the bloodstained money, but before leaving wiped the crimson hundreds across the surgical mask and bare breasts of one of the trembling immigrants. He wanted someone to tell the tale that time. He whispered in her ear simply, "Big Ugly was here."

Waingrow tells the story of how his brother was in the comfort of his bedroom, banging a very attractive girl who he paid good money for, when the Dark Figure showed up, stopping his brother mid doggy-style. Didn't even let the man finish. The Dark Figure handed the girl a stack of cash and escorted her to the door. Waingrow's bro tried to go at him, but he got bitch slapped back onto the bed, where he could only look on terrified, frozen by the sight of the Dark Figure holding an ignited blowtorch. He held the torch in one hand, a thick, blood-caked chain in the other. Brother Waingrow's screams echoed, his fingers gripping the mattress, chest split open and toes charred from the torch. He told Big Ugly everything he wanted, and more. Gave up safe houses, drop spots, jobs, account numbers, phone numbers, addresses... you name it. He gave up enough info for Big Ugly to sink his teeth in and really go to work. Big Ugly thanked him and set the bed on fire.

When this conversation about Big Ugly's deeds started, the stories were deliberately spoken, clearly told. Now, they start to turn into lightning fast blips of description as floods of memories burst out—memories they've all pushed far back in their heads to just get through life. CliffsNotes versions of Big Ugly doing dirty deeds are spit out left and right, everyone talking over the top of one another, one sentence overlapping the next.

The time two of Bosko's best earners got cut to chunks by a samurai sword in Santa Monica.

Waingrow's Irish Bar downtown blown to shit by the rhythmic pumping of a 12-gauge in the hands of a skilled killing machine. The bartender was tagged point-blank, the top half of his body found across the bar from his legs.

The chainsaw story on La Brea.

An axe was used here.

A baseball bat used there.

Hemo-soaked money shoved into bags.

Suitcases.

Trash bags.

Guns loaded then unload.

Doren slams his palm hard to the table commanding everyone's attention. The table falls silent, all eyes on Doren as he points a finger to the burns and scars that litter his face, neck, and hands. He doesn't bother pointing out the wheelchair. "No one has lost more than me." His stare is cold. Dead. Black. The table gives a silent nod out of respect. Doren continues, "This man. This thing..." He trails off, unable to finish his thought.

Cherrito jumps in. "The last time we heard from Big Ugly, he went rip-shit fucking riot. He killed a hundred and four of our people in less than twenty-four hours. Emptied our pockets..."

"Then disappeared," says Bosko. "Went ghost. Nothing. Not one fucking blip for fucking years." He turns to Doren. "What do you propose?" Doren takes a moment, wrapped up in his thoughts. He rubs his disfigured hands across the smooth table. He can't feel it, hasn't felt anything in his hands for years but imagines the cool feeling of fine craftsmanship along with the granite. He gets lost thinking of all the things he will never feel again, all of the things that were taken from him.

Taken by that man.

That monster.

That disease.

"Doren, what do you propose?"

Doren looks up and, as calm as he can says, "Assemble a crew and execute Big Ugly."

Looks fire around the table, eyes dancing at the very thought of it. Bosko asks the question on the tip of everyone's tongue. "Kill Big Ugly? One might consider that a futile enterprise."

Cherrito adds, "Dangerous man. Not one to fuck around with. Go at him, go strong. Swing and miss...God help us all."

"Big Ugly can lay down a ton of unpleasant," agrees Bosko.

Waingrow thinks, *amen to that shit.*

Doren attempts to calm the room by breaking it down the way only a true leader can. "Vengeance is a great motivator, but should never be the only motivation. We are men of business. He took lives, but also he took assets, our liquidity. According to my accounting, he got away with just over one hundred and sixty million of our hard earned dollars. Any of you recovered from that economic setback?" Stares burn around the table.

That would be a no.

"He has to have kept that money close. We have ties to every Swiss bank, every bank in Belize, Mexico. That's too much money to not draw attention. My proposal? We each nominate some of our own to man this crew so that we are all fairly represented. Choose your best. They will go kill this man and find what's left of our money."

The table chews on that for a second. Bosko is the first to speak. "Requires a special breed."

"Requires serious loco fuckers," mumbles Cherrito.

"For incentive," Doren adds, "We give this crew twenty cents for every dollar returned to us."

From his spot against the wall, Rasnick zeros in. Something big going on behind those eyes of his, something that Doren said has set his brain ablaze.

Waingrow does the simple math. "Two hundred K per million? That'll motivate a motherfucker or two."

"With a kicker," adds Doren. "The one who puts Big Ugly's head on this table, I'll give one million personally." They allow this to make a lap around their heads. Doren goes on. "We have to move. We have hours, not days. To put it mildly, Big Ugly is a flight risk. My representatives are ready." He motions and Rasnick, Vig and Oleg step up, looking like they could chew raw meat off the bone. Doren gives the table his final words. "I know we've had our differences, but it brings a smile to my face knowing that we can meet as men and form a plan to destroy this disease. This will work. It will work, and heal a lot of pain from our pasts. Friends, I ask you with an open heart and mind... in or out?"

Cooper cracks an ever so slight smile as he listens in on Doren's proposal. Ideas are taking hold in Cooper's big brain. A giddy feeling tingles in his stomach.

In the suite Bosko, Cheritto and Waingrow share a look.

Bosko gives his answer. "In."

Then Cherrito. "Fuckin' A Wally World, all in."

Everyone looks to the member who hasn't chimed in yet. Waingrow. He picks at his hearing aid, uncomfortable, fidgeting like a child that needs to pee.

"Jesus," Cooper says as he fumbles with the handset that provides the link to Waingrow's ear. He grips the mic and speaks as clearly as possible, explaining to the crime lord as he would an infant. "You're in. You are so fucking in. And guess what, sport, I got a representative you *will* nominate."

Waingrow shifts in his chair, hating this. Cooper doesn't care what Waingrow likes or hates. "Asshole, speak up or die in prison."

Waingrow gives up. "Yes. Of course, I am in."

Doren rubs a burn on his wrist with a satisfied grin. He was pretty sure that everyone would come to their senses, but you never really knew with this group. "I have a Gulfstream fueled and ready to go where the degenerate leads. Have your people ready in two hours."

In the van, Cooper tosses the handset, runs his fingers through his hair. His mind zooming from zero to a hundred.

Rasnick leans against the wall next to Oleg and Vig, catching his smile before it spreads too far across his face. The men in this room don't appreciate smiles from their hired muscle; they question smiles, wonder what the hell is so damn funny. Rasnick keeps his thoughts to himself, but there is some serious planning going on in his head.

8

A rundown, shitbox apartment building in the dead of night. The SWAT team—tactical gear, laser sights, alpha dog attitudes— glides stealth-like from car to car, getting closer and closer to the apartment. A beefy team member applies a ram to the front door, which explodes into splinters. The team storms in, and muffled yells come from inside: *Motherfucker!* This and *Don't fucking move!* that. All punctuated by controlled machine gun bursts. A spray of blood splats against a window before the glass blows out, then dead silence. It's over before it started.

The SWAT team comes out spreading around high fives, yuk-yuks, and fist bumps. From behind a van steps Rasnick, Oleg, and Vig nowhere to be seen. Rasnick leans in and whisper-yells to two of the SWAT guys. "Buster! Talley!"

Buster and Talley, who happen to be brothers, break from the rest of the team. Talley's a 6'5" brick shithouse of a man, while Buster is a five-foot-nothing spark plug, but surprisingly strong. His lack of height, coupled with older brother Talley's defensive end body, has Buster in a classic Napoleonic twist.

Talley squints at Rasnick, then smiles with recognition. "Your case over?"

"Mom know?" Buster asks.

"No, I'm still on the job," says Rasnick.

Talley winces. "You should call Mom, man."

"Shit bro, you can't be around here," says Buster. "You get made hanging with your cop family? Not good."

Rasnick puts a hand up to stop the verbal barrage from his brothers. "Got something huge and no time." His brothers are all ears.

In a small house, their mother's house, Buster, Talley, and Rasnick sit around a kitchen table, its beaten up wooden showing the signs of raising three boys. Chunks are missing, with words carved by butter knives on the top. Things like, *Buster sux, Talley sux dicks* and *Go Lakers*. Currently, the table is home to guns, a box of Ritz crackers, a twelve of High Life, and a heaping pile of coke. Talley snorts a line, passing a pink pig shaped cutting board to Buster.

After a hard sniff, Buster grunts, "How much you thinking?"

Rasnick does the math in his head. "Even if he blew half of it, there's got to be eighty plus million. Maybe fifty on the low side."

"Fuuuuuck." from Buster.

"That's what I'm saying. I go in first with this crew. I'm so up their ass, they have no idea I'm a badge. You two show up, we dead the lot of them, grab the cash, and be done with all this low tax bracket, law enforcement shit."

Talley likes the idea but has concerns. "That's lotto dollars, no doubt, but you're not talking about just matching six numbers man. This lotto ticket carries a gun."

Rasnick sits back, taking a swig of High Life. "Granddad, Pops, our uncles...all cops. We're stuck in a damn cycle, an endless loop. No way for this family to get above it. This how you want to spend the next twenty years?"

"Not me, dog," says Buster.

Talley gets it, but he's always been the most sensible of the three. "I hear ya, man. But this Big Ugly thing? You don't even know where you're going. So how do we get to you?"

"Not sure yet. That paranoid shit stain, Brobee, he's going to search us all before we leave. No cells."

Talley thinks, then pulls a 9mm Beretta and slides it to Rasnick. "New thing. Has a GPS in the grip in case we lose it, get kidnapped or some shit." Talley's way of letting his brother know he's on board.

Buster's eyes glow like wildfire. "Fuck yes. We'll track you, roll in like cowboys from hell, and put some fire on those motherfuckers."

Talley rolls his coked-up, pie-eyes to his younger brother. "Why don't you shut the fuck up? *We're gonna roll in like cowboys from hell.*"

"Fuck you, prick."

Talley loves pushing buttons, keeps it going. "Maybe we can hold our TECs and Gats sideways. Rat-a-tat-tat. Bust some caps in a nigga's ass while pumping NWA, idiot."

Buster is beginning to get offended. "Why do you have to talk to me like this?"

"You keep yapping retarded banter."

"Your attitude is horrible," Buster fires back.

Rasnick breaks it up. "Please stop," takes a big coke snort, "We do this together, like family, and we can do anything we want for the rest of our days."

Talley lets the Buster bashing go, for the moment. He thinks, adding it all up. "Doren, those guys...they're going to know something's up when you don't come back."

Rasnick pats his gun with a grin. "I gotta plan for that too."

Buster gets it, loves it. "Fuck yeah. Boom!" Snorts a line as his exclamation point. Talley rolls his eyes again, fighting the urge to lay into his brother. Calmly he says, "This crew you're going in with, what's the roster?"

"Doren has me with two standard, off the boat Eastern Bloc boys, Oleg and Vig." Rasnick goes on to describe the rogues' gallery that will make up the crew, telling the story about when Vig and Oleg unleashed on a BMW at a red light at the corner of Melrose and Fairfax one Saturday morning. They left the poor souls in the BMW bloody, mangled, twitching and flopping. Rasnick calls them the vodka and AK crowd. "They're good boys."

"Then there's the pair Bosko is bringing in," says Rasnick. "Good God." He recounts the day Bosko sat behind a desk across from Pike and Patience, both of the twenty-somethings pulsing with an unnerving, psycho-fueled energy. Still, a cute young couple, though. Patience twirled a gun with her right hand while jerking Pike's junk under the table with her left. If Sid and Nancy and Bonnie and Clyde had a foursome, these two nut jobs would be the product. Their claim to fame was this job they did where they had the tellers and customers face down on the floor next to the dead security guards, while in the back room Pike and Patience had sex on top of a massive pile of cash —actually bumping uglies on the money were stealing. They sat the scared shitless manager against the wall, apple on his head, and forced him to watch. Pike blasted the apple off of the man's head, all while never breaking is love stroke. Patience loved it. Weird sex, killing and money... that's what Pike and Patience are about. No particular order.

"Next is Cherrito's man, Chats. From what I hear Chats is, well... Chats is everything that's wrong in the world." Rasnick takes a hard swig and fills his brothers in.

Chats sat cross-legged next to a rusted bathtub in a busted up motel bathroom—a single bulb hanging from the ceiling, a new level of filthy kind of place. A scar runs down one side of Chat's face, his left eye dead and glossy. Another scar runs along his neck. His chilling, rock-hard stare focuses somewhere out in the void as he tears at a grilled cheese sandwich.

There's a dead body face down in the toilet. A large burlap sack shoots up from the tub, muffled screams seep out as the sack shifts wildly. Chats doesn't blink, doesn't even bother setting down his sandwich. He whips out a tactical knife and rips a single slice, cutting through the sack and the throat of the poor bastard inside with razor precision. The sack drops back down into the tub with a thump, crimson pouring down the drain. Chats calmly nibbled his grilled cheese.

Rasnick takes a big snort, taking down the last line of coke with authority. "The last asshole? Waingrow? No idea what the hell he's sending out."

9

A lump of a security guard sits at a desk across the sprawling marble lobby of a nondescript office building. His post, his place in life as it were, rests among this vast tomb of a space. It's the kind of building you'd hate to work in, but have to.

The burned-out shell of a man nurses a cup of the building's complementary, horrible, coffee. Starbucks? Coffee Bean? Those are a fantasy on his salary. Hell, it's not even fucking Folgers.

He wears a fading gold name tag which reads LEON.

It sags crooked on his semi-pressed uniform. No gun, but he does have a belt with a walkie and a stick. Leon figures if something should actually happen he could use the stick to tap S.O.S into the walkie as he waits to bleed out from the bullet wounds. All this *gear* is designed to give the illusion of safety, the appearance of actual police; it's not fooling anyone.

Dressed in his gray, unflattering guard garb, Leon stares out into the empty office floor. He's barely hanging onto the handsome he once had, his once Greek God body now a shadow of its former glory. He can still gut through a mile run, maybe, but he's not going to pass any tests at Quantico. Leon has seen some tough days since Mexico.

He spins his wedding ring on the desk, eyes drifting back and forth from the hypnotic spinning ring to a slow-as-hell clock on the wall.

When is this shit over?

A janitor buffs the floor, adding a layer of white noise to the deafening silence. He glances over to Leon, feels for the man. Leon sits there night after night sucking down bad coffee, never saying more than four or five words. The janitor forces eye contact with an exaggerated wave. "Later, Leon. You be well."

Leon slaps his hand down, stopping the spinning wedding ring cold. "Yeah."

At the employee lockers just off the lower level parking garage, Leon changes from his guard duds into street wear. These clothes aren't much better: tube socks, bad jeans, bad flannel...bad look overall.

He grabs his thermos.

Takes a squirt.

Clocks out.

As part of his nightly routine, he hits a bar on Wilshire not far from the building. At least it's his routine when he works. On his nights off he rarely gets out of bed. Leon sits alone at the bar, whiskey shots five deep with a Bud chaser close behind. LA's elite passes around him as if he was a pothole. The cocaine and boob job crowd have better things to do than pay attention to a guy they write off as some homeless dude at the bar.

Leon drains his shots one by one. It's an assembly line process that he's worked out—the assembly line of a fully functional alcoholic. He makes a face, upset that his head is still racing. The booze is supposed to at least slow that down. It doesn't, and that pisses Leon off. The booze actually cranks up his thoughts, hands them a microphone, and shoves them into the spotlight. That myth he heard about drinking to forget? Utter shit.

Leon remembers everything. He can even recall a time in his life when he didn't drink at all. Wasn't so long ago. He used to have a nice home with a great Labrador, surrounded by nice crap from Pottery Barn. He used to have a kind, beautiful wife. There were friends and cookouts and football parties and talked about having children. His head keeps spinning back to the kind, beautiful wife back to his is time with her. Remembers the laughter and smiles, the time when he didn't hate everyone and everything.

Not like now.

Now? Life consists of work, drinking, *Seinfeld* and *Family Guy* reruns, then some quick masturbation to free porn clips online before passing out. He doesn't speak to anyone he doesn't have to. Even prefers the drive-thru to communicating face-to-face at a counter. Orders things online when he can. Leon's built a life that is contained, controlled and void of an emotional interaction of any kind. It's how he wants it.

He wanted that other life gone. Eased. Stuffed in a furnace and set ablaze. Wanted that house, the Lab and the wife to go away. And fuck you, Pottery Barn. He pushed it all away after Mexico, after Big Ugly took him captive.

Those days, weeks and months with that man have all bled together in Leon's head. Time meant nothing after awhile. Leon doesn't remember everything, which is probably best. He remembers flashes of dark places, moments of terror, sudden violence then days of nothing but breathing.

Oh yeah, there was the humiliation too.

Then, completely out of nowhere, there would be a random day where a steak dinner would appear, served by a gorgeous blonde offering body massages and sex. Leon took the steak, but thanked the blonde for the offer and declined the sex. Sometimes Big Ugly would read Leon poetry. Or children's books, Or pull Leon's eyelids open forcing him to watch *The Sound of Music* spliced together with German snuff films.

On the last day, Big Ugly announced he was bored with Leon.

He calmly stated they were going to fight to the death. Leon's mind was gone by then, but somehow he understood. He even thanked Big Ugly for the opportunity. Leon was brought to a room, a very nice room that had crystal chandeliers... and a cage filled with medieval weapons. It was a real gladiator style affair, complete with an audience of half-naked women and men in suits. After what Leon had been through, none of this seemed strange at all. Almost expected.

It took a few minutes for Leon's eyes to adjust after being in the dark during all the days prior. It's mostly a blur, but Leon does clearly recall Big Ugly coming at him with an axe to start. There were punches thrown, along with near misses from weapon strikes. It was a brutal struggle that seemed to last for hours.

Then there was a moment that changed everything.

A tiny sliver of time where luck and skill came together. Leon landed a punch that caught Big Ugly completely off guard. It was nothing special, not some special martial arts kick or a devastating combination drawn from Krav Maga. Just a wildly thrown haymaker that happened to catch Big Ugly just right; a fist that crash-landed to the temple and knocked Big Ugly out cold.

The audience went silent when Big Ugly dropped like a sack of meat. They all stopped breathing. Their master was down for the count.

That didn't happen. Big Ugly didn't lose.

Leon gathered himself and dragged his battered remains to the door of the cage. A group of the suits quickly beat him unconscious, of course, but later Leon woke up on a beach in Santa Monica. He couldn't believe it.

He was free, sort of.

Leon returned to the FBI and his wife. He tried to get back to his old life, tried hard to fall back into routines, but it wasn't easy. He was a P.O.W returning home, and everyone knew it was going to take time. There were medical and physiological evaluations and lots of counseling. But life was slowly beginning to take shape again until that video went viral.

Big Ugly released highlights of Leon's captivity. Moments that Leon didn't even remember, locked away out of self-defense. Now they were posted online and subsequently emailed to the FBI, Leon's family, friends, and a special private message sent to his wife. What was on that video could not be unseen that could never be forgotten?

No one ever talked directly to Leon about what was on the video, and Leon decided never to watch it. The expressions on their faces and the tone of their voices told Leon all he wanted to know. He heard the snickers in the hallways, the hushed tones that would go silent just as he entered a room. Ultimately it was the look in his wife's eyes. She tried to hide it, but it was there.

He started to resent others for not living through what he had, began to hate them for not being him.

He hated himself.

Everyone told Leon it was okay, but he knew it wasn't. He retreated deep inside himself, put himself into his own private exile. He pushed everything and everyone away. Knowing that his time with Big Ugly changed him forever and there was no going back, Leon left the FBI, his wife, and his life. Hopefully, his wife would find someone else who loved her, someone who wasn't broken and could never be put back together again. Someone who'd love her enough to let her go if that's what it took... like Leon did.

All of this passes through Leon's mind each night as he relentlessly pounds booze, and every night it doesn't get any easier.

He takes another shot, chases it, then slams another even faster. Leon's machine is working overtime, but his little pity party routine is stopped dead in its tracks by a voice behind him.

"Leon?"

10

A mushroom cloud blooms behind Leon's eyes as Cooper takes a seat next to him, motioning to the bartender for another round. He looks to Leon with great sympathy. "Sorry doesn't seem to quite cut it..."

Smash.

Leon shatters his bottle of Bud on Cooper's head, exploding from the bar stool and ramming Cooper into the wall. "What the fuck man?" yells the bartender. Cooper pulls his badge and calls out so everyone can hear him clearly. "FBI. Please give us the room." No one moves.

"Now!"

The bartender and the few remaining tipsy stragglers stumble to the exit. Leon is on fire. His eyes bulge. He can taste strangling the life from of this man and decides to give it a shot. "You left me to die in Mexico."

Cooper fights for air. "I'm here to make it right."

"Make it right? Look at me. I'm leftover scraps, a fraction of a fraction. Make it fucking right?" Leon lets him go and takes a seat—goes back to his booze. "What do you want, Cooper?"

Cooper puts pressure on his bleeding head. "I have an offer."

Leon throws back a final drink then heads for the door. "I'll counter with fuck your mother."

"There's been a Big Ugly sighting."

Cooper's words stop Leon dead in his tracks. He can't help but think of the implications of Cooper's statement. Cooper knows he has his full attention as he continues. "Doren and the other heads of state are putting together some fellowship of psychos to go after him. I can get you in."

"To do what?" asks Leon.

"Kill Big Ugly."

Leon turns to face Cooper.

"I'm offering you a chance for the big payback. A chance to silence all that shit rattling around your head," says Cooper. He shifts his tone, uncomfortable to even talk about it. "I know what he did you to."

Leon explodes, "You know shit!"

"I know you escaped within an inch of your life. I know you got laughed out of the FBI. I know you swept your wife from your life. And I know Big Ugly's been a big fuckin' pain in your ass." Cooper sucks in through his teeth. "Sorry, wrong thing to say."

Leon fires *eat shit* eyes at Cooper—that last statement was unnecessary, a cheap shot. He resets, explains as if to a child. "I escaped, and there's a lot I don't remember."

Cooper lets it go. "Look, I can give him to you. I can serve him up real special, but there's something you need to do for me."

"Takes some serious balls to show up looking for a favor. I lost everything. I got within a foot of that monster, and you served *me* up real special to *him*."

"Everybody was ordered off of him, even though we had an ocean of evidence. They destroyed his files, closed all open cases and investigations against him. They wiped him off the books, off the grid...off the earth."

"Why?" Leon asks.

"Big Ugly took out a den of high-end call girls before he disappeared. Killed the madam, shot the girls, then tore the place apart.

Back at the Bureau there's a belief, one I happen to share, that Big Ugly found something, dirt on people who don't like to be dirty. Senators, Supreme Court justices. Don't know what he's got for sure. Could be video, audio, accounting records. Nobody's talking, but whatever it is, it's made Big Ugly untouchable. That's why you were left twisting in Mexico."

Leon slides back onto his stool, reaches across and pulls a Wild Turkey bottle from the other side of the bar. Taking it up a notch.

Cooper knows he has to get to the point, fast. "I can't send anybody else. Any involvement by me or the Bureau and word will spread. You're not FBI, you're not on anybody's radar. There are no eyes on you. Technically, this conversation isn't happening. But I'll set you up right; I got a big fucking bag of guns out in the car."

Leon takes a pull straight from the bottle. Cooper drags up a stool next to him. "I can't do a thing about the wife, but I can get your pension back. Get ya back your badge, maybe some of your pride and a bit of your soul. But that's if, and only if, you can get whatever Big Ugly has. We can put away some serious assholes and do some real good, Leon." Cooper is getting to him. Leon takes another gulp. "You used to care about that kinda shit, Leon."

A slow burn snakes up Leon's spine.

He lowers the Wild Turkey from his lips.

"You had me at kill Big Ugly."

11

———

Brobee, Rasnick, Oleg and Vig stand waiting next to a small hanger which houses a Gulfstream G280. Brobee is not happy. "The fuck is everybody?"

Rasnick, annoyed beyond reason, is forced to suffer this fool. "They'll be here."

Brobee bites a nail. "Fuckin' hungry."

"Stop talking," Rasnick snaps.

"A bit parched too..."

Brobee's bitching is stopped short as he's distracted by the sight of Pike and Patience strutting in. Pike is shirtless, a black blazer barely covering his two shoulder holsters. Patience's sundress clings to her sultry body. She loosely holds a Beretta in hand, a submachine gun slung over a shoulder. A Rambo-worthy strap of clips parts her breasts. A little extra accessory, just to make sure you notice them.

Brobee notices. He stares, bug-eyed. "I just might love her."

Pike and Patience take positions in front of the group. They speak over each other, completing the sentence started by the other. Not in a rude way, or that *I know this person so well, married 20 years* kind of way. Their speech reflects the deep bond between them. It's a reckless, bottomless well that borders on—well, not borders...it is—violent obsession.

Pike announces, "Pike and Patience, ready to..."

"Make a buck and..." Patience continues.

"Kill a fuck," Pike finishes.

Rasnick's eyes roll. *Are you kidding me?*

Pike and Patience lock into a deep, tongue-wrapped kiss. It's nice for them but dammed uncomfortable for everybody else. Brobee stutters, "Ahhh, I gotta frisk ya." He moves toward Patience, trying to figure out how to touch her in a way that won't repulse her, too much, and still work in his needs. Pike slaps him with a firm, open hand. At least he spared Brobee the embarrassment.

Next to join the party is Chats. It's as if ice could walk. Everybody immediately tightens up, not even really knowing why. They are all armed and have been in some pretty ugly spots, but when this guys walks in—*shit.* Chats walks past them without even a hint of eye contact and boards the plane without ceremony.

Pike looks to Brobee. "Gonna frisk him, ya fuckin' freak?"

"I'll...maybe later." Brobee motions to Pike. "Come on, tough guy. Open the jacket. Arms up." Pike humors the little guy and allows Brobee to pat him down.

Leon hovers outside the hangar watching it all. He can't believe he's here. *What the hell am I doing?* He pulls a flask and fires down a swig. He lets the whiskey burn down his chest, knowing he has to do this, has to go in there and do this thing. This is a once in a lifetime opportunity, the kind of second chance most people will never get. It's what people fantasize about after someone does something shitty to them. *If I'd only done X or said Y to that asshole.* Most fantasy do-over's don't contain the levels of violence and human suffering as Leon's case, but it's all relative. Leon takes another swig, swishes it around his mouth and makes his move inside.

Everyone gives Leon a look as he walks in. The group of killers lay hard eyes on him with blank expressions, giving Leon nothing in the way of greeting. None of them recognize him. Leon takes in their stares. *Nothing new,* he thinks. *Just tough guys being tough.*

Patience looks him up and down, perhaps a bit too long for Pike's taste. Brobee pats down Pike finds a cell. Drops it in a bag and says, "Nobody's calling anybody, nobody's tracking us anywhere."

"Why's that, Sports Fan?" Pike asks.

"You motherfuckers are on a need-to-fucking-know basis, and you don't need to fucking know where the fuck we're going. I know how this movie ends—I tell you how to get to Big Ugly, you don't need Brobee anymore, you shoot Brobee. Not today, bitches."

Rasnick tries not to smirk.

Brobee tries not to drool over Patience. "You're next, beautiful." Patience is all too aware of her gifts and their ability to crush the superficial male. Her words glide from her tongue. "Be gentle." She lets her guns and ammo drop...then her sundress.

Patience is a jaw-dropping display of a woman. A Victoria's Secret model, criminally insane edition. Brobee doesn't know what to do.

She locks eyes on Leon. "See anything?"

Pike can't take it. He slaps Patience with a hard backhand. Everybody goes silent. Patience touches her lip with hurt in her eyes, but she's no garden-variety abused spouse. She puts a foot to Pike's balls, releases a war cry and pounces with reckless abandon. The lovers punch, spit and claw at each other. Rasnick motions to Vig and Oleg to break it up. They pull the two off each other, Patience's feet still flying as she's dragged away from Pike.

Patience and Pike catch their breath, then shove Vig and Oleg aside. They rush to each other, colliding in an anger-soaked kiss. Hands are groping. Moans are vibrating. Bloody lips pressed hard together. The others share a look between them.

That's fucked up.

THE RAGTAG CREW cruises through the clouds toward their mission of murder, surrounded by the Gulfstream's plush leather and luxury.

Leon keeps an eye on everything and everyone, sizing them up one by one. Breaking up his analysis is a constant, dull, thumping coming from the bathroom. Pike and Patience are joining the mile high club. Muffled, awkward grunts and moans seep out from the lavatory, along with bits of dirty talk.

"Spit in my mouth," barks Pike.

Leon shifts uncomfortably in his seat. Rasnick looks at the ceiling. Vig and Oleg share a vodka bottle. Chats locks an icy stare out into nothing while he cleans his teeth with a tactical knife.

Brobee eyes Leon. "I know you." Leon turns to find Brobee about two inches from his face.

"No, you don't."

"Yeah, yeah I do. Where do I fucking know you?" Brobee asks.

The pleasure moans and thumps from the bathroom get louder, now sounding like rabid monkeys trapped in a box.

Brobee doesn't let it go with Leon. "You been on TV?"

"No."

"Prison?"

"No."

"Punch my nipple," orders Patience.

Vig leans over, offering Leon a hit from his bottle. Leon declines. Vig insists. "Drink."

Leon tries being polite. "I'm good."

Rasnick joins the conversation. "You should take that drink."

"You my sponsor?" asks Leon.

"You a gay?" asks Oleg.

Vig pushes the bottle at him again. "Drink it."

Leon works to remain cool. "I'd rather keep a clear head before this...exercise."

Rasnick says, "Sauce helps Vig and Oleg. Frees the mind."

"The soul," add Vig and Oleg in harmony.

"And the soul," grins Rasnick.

Leon flashes a blank stare. "Congratulations." A knife flies, sticking with a thunk about an inch from Leon's face. He whips around to see Chats staring. "What the fuck, man?"

Rasnick puts a hand on Leon. "Chats doesn't talk. That's his way of asking, 'What's your fucking problem, fucko?' His words, not mine."

"Ever consider sign language?" Leon asks. Chats shakes his head. *Nope.*

A Comanche war-cry booms from the bathroom as Pike's climax rattles the cabin. A moment of silence, then Pike exits. "Now I can get my murder on." Patience slips out adjusting her dress, flicks something from her finger. She notices the eyes on Leon, the tension in the cabin. She lets the words slip out like releasing a pressure valve. "What's up boys?"

Rasnick turns back to Leon. "Who are you, dude?"

Pike joins in. "Yeah, chief. I know these other bitches from around the way. Work acquaintances and so on..." Pike's words are cut short by Patience sliding in with sleepy, bedroom eyes on Leon. She wipes the corner of her mouth with the back of her hand then addresses Leon. "Who the hell are you?"

Tension picks up a notch.

People start fingering weapons.

Brobee addresses the cabin. "Easy, you animals. I've seen this guy somewhere, just can't place him."

Leon takes a breath. He thought this wouldn't come up, but realizes now there is no way to ignore the situation. He clears his throat. "Waingrow asked me to come as a favor to him. I know Big Ugly. Been tracking him for years. Came close in Mexico, but he got the jump on me."

"But you're alive," states Rasnick, a note of disbelief in his voice.

"Yeah, this motherfucker, this Big Ugly?" Pike says. "From what I hear, live and let live ain't his way."

Leon tries to deflect the subject. "It's not important. What is important is we need to..."

"Fairly important, I think," says Pateince.

Pike wraps an arm around her waist. "Yup."

"I agree," Rasnick adds. "I mean, we need to know everything about our team and our target, right?" Chats flips his knife with a nod. Leon takes a beat trying to sort through his words. "He wanted to make an example of me, send a message. So he set me free."

Brobee heads snaps up. A light bulb goes off, then shatters. He can barely contain himself, fumbling to get the words out as fast as he can. "Holy fucking shit! I remember. Ah man, it's you! I'm fucking sorry, man. Oh my God."

"What?" asks Rasnick.

"Nothing. He's got the wrong guy," says Leon.

"No, no I do not," Brobee continues. "Big Ugly and this poor bastard...there was a video online."

Eyes around the cabin go wide, even Chats. Leon's lip trembles ever so slightly as he speaks. "I escaped, and that's it."

Brobee keeps riding his train of thought. "Fucking awful, horrific. Bad, bad, bad."

Pike just wants to know. "What happened?" Brobee leans in and whispers into Pike's ear. Pike makes a face like he swallowed a bug wrapped in dog shit. Can't even look at Leon, all he can do is glance to his shoes.

Leon spits out, "Nothing happened. I busted out and escaped. Nothing happened."

Patience is almost bouncing out of her seat wanting to know. Pike whispers in her ear and her gorgeous features melt into a response similar to Pike's. She looks to Brobee in disbelief.

Brobee says, "It was all over the web. There was this comment forum; it was big deal."

Leon's anger ripples just below his skin. "I said nothing happened." He stops as he watches the whisper-wave spreads the story through the cabin and the remaining members of the crew.

Brobee asks, "Somebody got a laptop? I'll pull it up."

Leon loses it. Cover be damned. "Nothing fucking happened, you fucking half-wit cocksuckers! Now shut the fuck up before I execute every fucking last one of you."

The cabin goes silent.

Really, what do you say?

Leon takes a shaky breath, pulling it together best he can. "Do you people have any idea who we are going after? This guy will burn down your dreams and eat your soul. If he likes you, he'll *just* kill you." Silence as the crew shares looks. "He is absent conscience, heart, or any form of reason. Living, breathing evil with 2400 SAT score. Do not, please, do not take him lightly or we will all die, badly."

The crew takes a moment to soak in Leon's words, his sincerity. It's all over him; he has seen things that no man should see.

Slowly the cabin begins to swell with laughter. The crew can't contain themselves. Patience is close to rolling in the isle. Chat snorts.

Pike busts out, "It was on the web?"

"Oh yeah, man, it was epic," wails Brobee.

A good time, all at Leon's expense.

12

In the hall in front of the penthouse suite, the same penthouse where the crime lords met, two armed goons guard the door, another at the elevator. The elevator doors open, and as the goon on elevator duty turns he catches a silenced 9mm to the head.

Goon one down.

Buster and Talley spring from the elevator wearing ski masks, black painter coveralls zipped to the neck, shoes covered. Buster blasts out the camera overhead while Talley takes out the two remaining goons at the door with head shots. The whole thing takes four seconds, maybe. Impressive, to say the least.

Inside the penthouse stand more goons, shoulder holsters heavy with guns at the ready. Cherrito and Waingrow are watching a Lakers game. Bosko sits in a chair reading *People*. Doren is resting comfortably in another room.

The room's door lock clicks, the light going green. The door flies open as the masked Buster and Talley storm in. Their movement is constant, efficient, with not a single motion or bullet wasted. Controlled three round bursts. These are not meth-zombies shooting up a trailer park in search of a hundred bucks and a roll of quarters. These are highly trained individuals who do this kind of thing for a paycheck, pension, and dental. The goons are dead before they can even draw their weapons, let alone fire a shot.

Cherrito and Waingrow are next.

They are unceremoniously removed from this Earth with a shots between the eyes. Bosko barely looks from his magazine, a crime lord thinking he's untouchable, that nobody would have the sack to even think about doing what they are doing. Bosko mutters, "Cocksucking..." before being silenced by Buster's bullet between the eyes. A plum of blood pops as Bosko's body is blown back over his chair.

Buster and Talley scan the room for Doren. The cowboys from hell slip into a side bedroom, where they find Doren sitting up in bed, enjoying soup. Doren looks them over, acknowledges his fate. He knew this day would come. Rarely do people like Doren die naturally. He says, "Just do it."

Done.

Buster and Talley remove their masks, quickly moving back to the living room. They tear away their coveralls, revealing blazers and slacks that look a lot like private security garb. Much like the uniforms the dead goons in the hallway were wearing. They exit into the hallway, where they stand on either side of the penthouse doors with 9mms drawn as if they are about to go into the room for the first time. They wait. Buster rolls his eyes, impatient as hell. Talley knows his brother and instructs him, "Wait for it." Buster's eyes dance, his impulsive streak running wild as he spits out, "Fucking useless security shit stains."

"Shut. The. Fuck. Up."

"You shut up."

Elevator dings.

Buster and Talley get into character, snapping on the looks of panicked, dumbfounded, dipshit security guards. They start with the heavy breathing and plant looks of fear and concern on their faces. A team of security guards pours out of the elevator with guns drawn. Everything about them is identical to Buster and Talley. The lead guard slips up next to them, looks them over. He doesn't recognize them, but they are wearing the correct uniform, and a good supervisor tries to avoid looking like an idiot at all costs. "What happened?"

The two brothers give the performance of a lifetime. Talley pants like a mutt, fakes terror and stutters while saying, "I think...I think... they're still in there, sir." Buster squeaks out, "They're armed, sir." The lead guard puts a calming hand on Buster's shoulder. Buster looks into his eyes and nods. *I'll be strong for you sir.* The lead guard motions for the rest of the team to move in around the door. As they do, Buster and Talley slip back toward the elevator. The lead guard address whoever he thinks is in the room in his best movie badass voice. "Okay, let's not get anybody hurt."

The elevator door closes.

Buster and Talley are gone baby gone. In the elevator, Buster giggles. *That was enjoyable.* Talley pulls out the GPS monitor that's tracking their brother, Rasnick.

"Where the fuck are they?" asks Buster.

Talley scrunches his nose. "They keep going in circles. It's like they're..."

13

"Lost?"

Rasnick stares out in the wilderness. "Fucking lost? You have no clue where we are?"

The bus of an SUV cruises down a one-lane road that snakes through a seemingly endless patch of dense woods. The crew fills the three rows of Chevy seating, Patience nestled in Pike's lap. A lot of pissed off looks fire in Brobee's direction, and he tries to hide the truth as he rides shotgun, Rasnick at the wheel.

"I'm not lost."

"Really? Fantastic. Where are we?" snaps Rasnick.

"We're close."

"Bullshit," snorts Vig. On cue Oleg chimes in, "Fucking bullshit, man."

Brobee can't believe this; he knows what he saw dammit. "It was dark as shit that night. Take it easy, you animals, I'll find it."

Pike fidgets, annoyed. This makes Patience annoyed. She barks, "This is a joke, right?" Leon keeps to himself, but his face says it all. *Fuck me.* His mind even drifts to a place that thinks his office building security gig maybe wasn't all that bad.

Brobee is completely flustered. "Look, goddammit, I am trying here. I'm trying, damn, ok?"

Chats jams a knife into the headrest next to his ear. Leon looks to Chats then taps Brobee. "Think he's saying trying is for pussies." Leon leans into Chats. "Close?" Chats nods.

Brobee's eyes lock.

Just over the hill.

In the distance, shining like a diamond in a goat's ass.

Brobee yelps, "There!" His stolen Caddie sits on the side of the road like a hooker's corpse, right where he left it. "Stop!"

The Suburban's brakes lock.

THE CREW MOVES through the same woods Brobee braved less than 48 hours ago. A heavily armed band of the most ill-tempered, badass Cub Scouts ever known, Brobee leads the way, still not completely confident where he's going. They've been trudging through these woods for a while, and the natives are getting restless, again.

Pike looks up, down, all around the suffocating woods. "He build a nest or some shit?", "You'll see, fuck face," spits Brobee.

"Been staring at trees for two hours now," says Patience.

"We're good. Trust. Please?" begs Brobee.

Rasnick and Leon are bringing up the rear, staying a few steps behind the rest of the pack. Rasnick turns to Leon. "You said you tracked Big Ugly for a time, right?" Leon nods, not sure where this is going. "Who is he?" Rasnick asks. Leon fights off a grin. "Nobody knows for sure. Some think he was a Marine once, maybe CIA. Maybe trained in Asia. Contract killer for a time. Some even believe he was a cop for awhile."

"About to be a broke, dead bitch," interrupts Pike.

"Absolutely," purrs Patience.

Leon hopes they're right.

Pike keeps spewing testosterone. "Don't know everything, but I know my skills, and they are sharp, tight and ready to light some fire on his ass." Patience throws an arm around him, and Pike spanks her backside. Leon thinks about using a nail and hammer to keep his eyes from rolling. Instead, he says, "Confidence is cute, but a healthy dose of fear might keep you alive."

Patience stops cold, stares at Leon as if he slapped her Mama. "Fear? You be afraid, pillow-bitter." That earns a laugh from the rest of the crew.

Leon looks to Rasnick. *Be afraid.*

Rasnick gets it.

The crew stops under a massive tree, its roots spiraling out of the ground and back in like a ride at a water park. They've reached a bullet-riddled body slumped against the tree's trunk. Brobee recognizes the face. "Ahhh, man."

"You knew him?" asks Rasnick.

"I—yeah, I stole his truck when I left. Feel bad, a little responsible."

Leon looks on. *A little? These people are unbelievable.*

Rasnick motions for them to keep moving and they continue their march through the thick woods. Something bothers Leon, a question he needs answered. "Hey, Brobee."

"Yo."

"Did he see you?"

"Who?"

"Santa. Who do you think? Big Ugly, asshole."

"No, no way."

Leon's face tightens. "You sure about that?"

Rasnick joins in. "If we're walking into a goddamn slaughter, so fucking help me." Brobee attempts to reassure them. "I'm damn positive, man. C'mon." Everybody stops. All eyes bore through Brobee. He can't believe the lack of trust from his brothers and sisters in arms. "He did not fucking see me."

He's sure.

Damn sure.

So sure.

Kinda sure.

PART III

SOME KINDA WILLY WONKA PRICK COCKSUCKER

14

L *ess than 48 hours ago...*

BROBEE STOOD at the edge of the clearing, mouth, and eyes agape.

Up ahead was the object of his horror.

Up ahead...

Big Ugly.

Forty-something, dressed in a slick, tailored Fioravanti suit and, oddly enough, not ugly at all. Better looking than probably 99% of men walking the earth. Cigar in his mouth, scotch in hand, and his baby blues locked on Brobee from across the yard. Big Ugly flashed a chilling smile, took a beat, then gave a tiny finger wave to Brobee.

Piss flowed.

Brobee bolted.

Big Ugly stood in front of a 28,000 square foot sprawling mega mansion. *His* mansion. Aside from the open land that immediately encircles the home, the area is completely surrounded, protected by the dense trees and wilderness. This place won't show up on any map. A stable of cows sits to the side of the jaw-dropping home. There is no visible road that leads in or out of Big Ugly's land.

This is a lap of luxury that does not want to be found.

Big Ugly's right-hand man, Bobby, runs from the house. Big Ugly's gaze is still fixed out into the distance as Bobby races up to him. He's knee-deep in a thinking man's trance. Bobby controls his breath. "Big Ugly, I saw something breached the red line." Big Ugly doesn't bother with eye contact as he cuts Bobby off. "Somebody. Somebody breached, Bobby.

"I'll get the dogs." Bobby pulls an old school Uzi while springing into Code Blue mode.

"No, Bobby. Not this time."

Bobby stops. "Did they see you?"

Big Ugly cracks a grin. "Oh, yes. Saw me... knows me."

"Interpol? CIA?"

"No."

"How did he find you?"

Big Ugly puffs his cigar. "Luck. Fate. Doesn't matter."

"I need to get you out of here. They'll send people."

Big Ugly finally turns to Bobby. "Oh, people will come, Bobby. Nasty, filthy, scary people. People with bad childhoods and questionable morals will descend on me with guns, bloodlust, and visions of murderous mayhem dancing in their heads. But Bobby, make no mistake..." Big Ugly puts the cigar out in his palm with a sizzle. "I'm not fuckin' going anywhere."

Inside the mega mansion, Big Ugly glides through a foyer that rivals the lobby of Caesars Palace. Bobby stays close, trying to reason with the unreasonable. "I know you haven't been yourself recently." Big Ugly appreciates the concern—not really. Bobby continues, "Depression is a natural response..."

Big Ugly spins, jamming his Smith & Wesson down Bobby's throat. "Depression is for cock deprived housewives. Do you find me cock deprived?"

Bobby gurgles a "No."

"I've walked on water, turned water into scotch. I've cleaned out the Gods—stuffed their balls in my pocket and then simply walked away. You know the win/loss record for people who nail the big score and then retire to the sweet life?" Bobby shakes his head. Big Ugly completes his sermon. "There's one winner and two million, six hundred and fifty-eight thousand limp-dick losers. And Bobby-Boy, I'm the one."

Big Ugly slips his gun from Bobby's lips. "Warriors are born to war, not to hide. Sure, I've done the cocaine and orgy thing for good while..."

Bobby wants to appear agreeable. "And done it well."

Big Ugly chews on that a bit. "I have, haven't I? I need to...need something. Killing the occasional hiker ain't cutting it anymore. Oh yeah, there's a guy out on the road who just lost his truck. Would you kill him and leave him in the woods for me?"

Bobby doesn't bother answering. He knows it's neither needed or appreciated. Big Ugly pauses, wants to frame this the proper way. "I'm bored, man."

Bobby looks into his master's crestfallen eyes. Bobby even feels sorry for him. "I understand, but are you sure?"

"I fucked a goat yesterday, Bobby. A goat."

Bobby can only stare back. Really, there's not much to say to that.

Big Ugly spins a finger in the air, a signal for Bobby to round up the staff.

～

BIG UGLY and Bobby enter an oversize formal dining room. This is where royalty grazes. Standing in a long line at full attention are maids, butlers, kitchen help and a scholarly-looking man. He wears a lab coat and a stethoscope. Not because he has to, but because Big Ugly has him on staff to be a doctor and, by God, in Big Ugly's mind he should look like a doctor.

Big Ugly walks down the line, Bobby next to him carrying a basket filled with stacks of rubber band bound cash. As Big Ugly

shakes the hand of each staff member, he hands him or her a severance stack.

Big Ugly reaches an attractive maid and gives her a nipple twist.
She smiles. She gets an extra stack. He reaches the doctor.

"I'm not leaving you here," announces the doctor.

Big Ugly nods.

"You need help. Treatments need to..."

Blam!

Big Ugly drops him with a bullet to the brain. The staff barely
flinches; this happens somewhat frequently around here. Bobby
motions to an open door leading to an adjacent room. The nondescript room contains a lone bed, a sandbox, and walls padded with
blue foam egg crates.

Brobee asks, "And them?"

Looking toward the room, Big Ugly eyes a row of five semi-nude
hookers. "Get rid of them." Bobby moves towards them, not
completely sure if he's supposed to kill them or just set them free. Big
Ugly places a hand on Bobby. "On second thought, leave two."

The remaining staff and hookers exit with Bobby, who is carrying
the dead doctor. They all pile into waiting Escalades. Bobby stuffs the
doctor's body into the back of one Escalade and turns to his master
with watery eyes. *Goodbyes are hard.*

Big Ugly shows a flicker of humanity. "Bobby, words do not do
justice." Bobby extends a hand. "It's been an honor and a privilege."
Big Ugly hands him four stacks, pauses, then takes back one.

Bobby gets in, and the Escalades drive off into the woods. Big
Ugly watches them leave. He'll miss them, some of them.

Not really.

He snaps his fingers.

The Escalades explode, bursting into multiple fireballs.

～

INSIDE HIS HOME, Big Ugly stands in front of a sound system that
reaches from floor to ceiling. A hand carefully loads a CD. Yes, he still

uses CDs. Can't very well have an iTunes account when you're trying to be a ghost, can you? The windows shake, and the walls rattle as the rock anthem *For Those About to Rock (We Salute You)* booms. Big Ugly moves through the mansion with the music following him.

It's time to prepare for his guests.

Instruments of murder are laid out on an Olympic-size table, a white linen cloth underneath. Glocks, Colts, submachine guns, a sawed-off pistol-grip 12 gauge, an axe, a samurai sword, tactical knives, a whip, bullets, and shells piled high. Weapons served up buffet style.

Big Ugly practices knife play in a mirror.

He tries out a different gun at the in-house range, fine tuning his game.

Cleans each of his guns with the greatest of care, carefully inspecting every detail and then going over them again. He polishes a handcrafted samurai sword with a fine shammy.

Big Ugly sits naked in the middle of an indoor basketball court.

Old bullet wounds, knife scars, teeth marks decorate his chiseled body like medals of honor. With legs crossed, he lets his mind cleanse itself. Letting himself go, he releases his soul into deep mediation. The battle is won before it's fought. Big Ugly visualizes his war without knowing whom he will be fighting. It doesn't matter. They will die and die badly. Big Ugly will be entertained. His mind weaves in and out of reality, and the false reality he's created over the years.

The lies, the covers, the truth... none of it is clear anymore. The stories he's used over the years range from him being an orphan to the son of a dentist, from an only child to the third child in a family of ten. He's been straight, homosexual, bi-sexual—there was also that thing with the goat, whatever that was. He's been married, divorced, murdered wives strangled gay lovers and was the live-in penis for two bi Israel chicks for a bit.

He's deep down in his head now.

The one thing, the only thing he wanted to hold onto, was his memory mother's face. No matter what happened, no matter how many false versions of him there were, he wanted to remember the face of his mother. The details of her life and the life Big Ugly had with her were not important—he sure as hell can't keep all that straight anymore—but if he could just hold onto Mom's beautiful face he could hang onto something that was still his own.

His mind fumbles through images of women he's known, fucked, killed, and seen on TV, but none of them are Mom. *Where is she? She's here somewhere, right?* He squeezes his eyes tight. Sweat trickles down his forehead as the faces spin faster and faster in his mind. *She's not there.* His brain is out of control, flipping through an endless loop, unable to find her.

Big Ugly pops his eyes open.

Snaps his fingers.

Fuck Mama.

Big Ugly surveys the impressive wardrobe in his gigantic walk-in closet. Silk button-downs, polished shoes, pristine suits hand-tailored by the finest craftsmen around the globe. He slips on a black Brioni suit that carries the price tag of a BMW. He tightens a blood red tie. He chooses socks with care. Shines a loafer.

All of this as if he was a knight selecting armor, suiting up in proper battle attire. Choosing the clothes he'd like to die in perhaps.

The room Big Ugly selected for his office is the size of the average tech start-up's entire building. It's filled with the best of everything, and when that best is outdated, he gets the new best of everything.

Big Ugly takes a seat in front of a wall of monitors sporting a look that would make most GQ cover boys run away shrieking like frightened, homely bitches. He waits. His eyes bounce off each screen, one after the other. He syncs a handheld, wireless LG video surveillance tablet. The touch screen now buzzes through the same views as the wall of monitors, missing nothing.

A touch of the screen... a bird flies.

Touch... Brobee's Cadi on the road, the crew's empty Suburban parked next to it.

Touch...a squirrel scampers.

Touch... big smile from Big Ugly. "Hola."

15

Out from the woods steps the crew, armed with enough firepower to invade a small country.

Brobee points to the mega mansion with great vindication and whisper-yells, "There. There, ya dicks. Everybody happy?"

Everyone soaks in the scope of the place.

Pike utters, "Ya fuckin' kidding me?"

"I pray the bastard did not spend all our money," says Vig.

"Pray the bastard is home," says Oleg.

Leon's focus is razor sharp as he takes note of everything. He feels it—something is off. "He knows we're here."

Rasnick studies Leon. "How do you know?"

In the distance, there is the low hum of something coming their way. They turn to the hum, two four-wheel ATVs motoring toward them. One ATV rides behind the other in a very careful, precise straight line. Manning the ATVs are two naked hookers, one blonde, one brunet. The male crewmembers' heads follow the dancing double Ds rolling their way. The off-road tires of the ATVs leave ruts in their wake.

Patience notices Pike taking in every not so subtle boob bounce and presses a .45 to Pike's head. Pike coughs, then recovers by quickly looking at his shoes. Chats scratches his nuts with a knife.

The ATVs come to a stop in front of the crew. The blonde hooker, the dumber of the two—cheerfully dumb, but dumb none-theless—calls out like a medieval messenger. "I bring word from Big Ugly." She pauses to read her hand. "If you want blood, you got it."

Leon can't help but stare at the small black heart tattoo nestled just above her right breast.

The hookers blow the crew a kiss and ride off.

The crew looks to Brobee. He shrugs. "Perhaps he did see me." Brobee pulls a Glock while backing up toward the woods. "Well, kids, I'm outta here."

"No really, can't you stay?" Leon asks with fake sincerity.

Brobee keeps drifting backward, making his getaway. "Cute. My role in this circle-jerk is done. Soooo, good luck with that Big Ugly thing. Looks hard..." A sudden crack from a high-powered rifle sounds, a bullet ripping Brobee's head off, ending his exit strategy. A heartbeat later his body flops to the grass.

The crew hits the dirt. Pike begins to shake, showing signs of his false bravado crumbling. He mutters, "Holy fuck—shit." Oleg jumps up, pulls his AK, and sprints toward the house.

Leon doesn't like the feel of this either. It's too...something. He calls out to Oleg, "Wait!" Oleg makes it maybe three steps before...

Boom!

A landmine sends Oleg's body flying. Earth scatters. Oleg's charred remains thump to the ground in three clumps of human-like pieces. A new level of fear has reached the crew.

Vig freezes at the sight his dead buddy.

Chats fires up a cigar.

Pike continues his shaking. Patience looks to her man, or what she thought was her man—this one has turned into a complete pansy.

Rasnick turns to the one person in the crew who seems to have a clue, Leon. "The fuck do we do now?" Leon has no real answer other than, "Try to stay alive." Patience is losing hers. "I'm gonna gut this piece of shit," she says to Pike. "Right, baby?"

Pike is jello.

Leon looks around, searching for inspiration. He spots the ruts left by the hookers' ATVs. He calls out the remaining members of the once proud crew. "There. Follow the tracks to the house."

Pike offers a counter strategy. "We could go back in the woods, regroup a bit?"

"Like Brobee?" asks Rasnick.

Leon keeps looking over the land, the situation, trusts his gut—he gets it now. He knows Big Ugly. As if thinking out loud he says, "He wants us to come inside."

Rasnick asks, "For what?"

Leon looks to the house. *Not sure yet.* He is sure that he has to either lead this pack of whackos into the house or sit there and die. Leon gets up, swallows hard, and starts walking along the tire ruts.

The rest of the crew shares a look. *Is he nuts?* Chats rises, then follows Leon. Rasnick is next. Patience motions for Pike to go. The man is a puddle. Patience punches him in the jaw with a crunch. Pike shakes his head. Patience jabs at him again, this time to the nose. Nothing. Patience stands up and attempts to stomps his balls. Pike finally snaps out of it, grabbing her foot and spinning her to the ground. He jams a Glock under Patience's chin. His breathing is hard, his eyes wild like a frightened animal. Patience smiles, getting to her feet. "There's my baby, come on now." She holds out a hand. Pike pulls it together, takes her hand, and the two follow Leon's lead.

The crew moves along the ruts with Vig bringing up the rear. He looks back to his fallen comrade Oleg and the hate swells. Vig racks his AK. The crew is halfway between the woods and the Big Ugly's mansion. All is quiet for now, but their thoughts bounce, roll and catch fire knowing that anything could happen at any moment. Their breathing is accelerated, hearts racing, but down deep inside, each of them love this.

The crack of whip snaps in the distance. A voice booms with a cowboy yell. "Yeee-haaa!" The crew stops.

What.

The.

Hell?

A low rumble slowly rolls, quickly growing into rapid thumping. The ground shakes and trembles. Leon realizes what it is. *Shit!*

It's the heart-stopping sound of a stampede coming their way.

The herd of cattle runs riot from the stables in the distance, moving at amazing speed and kicking up the earth in their path, storming headlong at Leon and company. This something not even Leon anticipated. Guns? *Sure.* Blood? *You bet.* Pain and anguish? *Without question.* But rumbling cattle driving at them with reckless abandon? No, that did not enter their minds.

Boom!

A cow goes flying as it hits a landmine. Beef sent flying end over end. Across the flood of livestock, a cow shoots up in the air every couple of seconds, with the shock and awe of the landmines causing the herd to stampede even harder towards the crew.

The crew is frozen by the remarkable sight. They can only look on. *Dear God!*

"Run!" screams Leon.

They sprint hard, legs pumping and knees riding high, all while trying to remain in the tire tracks. The rampaging cattle bear down on them like a bovine tsunami.

Boom!

Another cow is hurled airborne, flopping down within inches of Leon. He hurdles the meaty mess, landing in a pile at a side door to the mansion. He throws open the door and is immediately met by a shotgun blast. He manages to flip the door shut just in time. The door takes the shot, blasting it back open.

Leon tumbles back planting himself spread eagle against the wall, taking safety in the inches available to him as the stampede is almost there.

The remaining crew does the same, lining up as close to the wall as they can on the other side of the door. Everyone is as tight against the wall as humanly possible, all except for Vig.

Vig's grief-fueled rage gets the better of him when he sees Big Ugly through the blown-out door. His veins pop. His mind unsnaps. Vig runs full tilt, crashing through what's left of the door while unloading his AK into the mansion. His wild bullets miss Big Ugly who, bored with this, calmly fires his sawed-off shotgun.

The scatter blast hits Vig, sending him flying backward just as the rambling stampede blows by, ripping Vig along with them. His body bounces along limply, contorting like a rag doll atop the raging grain-fed mass.

Along the wall the crew braces themselves as the rush of cattle rips past, trying to make themselves one with the bricks and mortar behind them. The cattle roar by, heading off into the woods. The crew gathers themselves. Leon moves closer to his side of the door as Rasnick does the same on the other side. They share a look.

A shotgun pump echoes from inside the house.

Leon pulls a tactical smoke grenade. Rasnick nods, turning to Pike, Patience and Chats huddled behind him. *Ready?* Leon tosses the grenade into the doorway. Smoke quickly spreads, overtaking the room and seeping back outside.

They hear a cough.

The crew all looks to Leon.

He gives the signal.

The crew unleashes a hellfire maelstrom of relentless fire, unloading buckets of bullets into the smoke. Leon empties his Glock, slam loads, and waits. The others keep pounding away. Leon yells out, "Stop!" They don't. The bullets continue to run ripshit. Leon screams out again, nearly tearing a vocal cord. "Stop, dammit!" The rest of the crew finally ceases fire. They hold smoking guns at the ready.

The smoke starts to thin out.

All's quiet.

Leon slips inside the house, swinging his tricked out assault rifle from left to right. Checks the corners first, sweeping, clearing like a good boy should. Rasnick follows suit, sweeping the room like a pro, just like Leon. Leon takes note of Rasnick's technique.

The once Caesars Palace-like room is now a war-torn shit pile. Bullet holes decorate the walls, marble and granite gouged in chunks. Not a hint of Big Ugly. Pike, Patience and Chats file in with guns drawn.

Leon speaks low to Rasnick. "He's somewhere in the house."

"How do you know he didn't slip out the back?" asks Rasnick. "Maybe hauled ass to Switzerland or some shit?"

"Does it look like he's running scared?" asks Leon.

Chats pumps his shotgun, moseying up the spiral marble stairs toward a massive set of double doors. "Where are you going?" asks Leon. Nothing from Chats as he checks the knives that decorate his chest, then the 9mm at his side, before slipping through the doors. Patience agrees. "He's right. Divide and conquer." Pike finds his nuts again. "Hell yeah, baby doll." They start moving toward another set of doors on the right.

Leon grabs Pike's shoulder. "Let him go."

Pike whips his arm free. "He's gonna take all the money."

"Think. We're on his home field. This guy will chew us up one by one if we separate." Leon stops just short of adding *you fucking idiot* to the end of that sentence.

Pike fails to see the logic. "Fuck that. We split up and..."

"Dead this fool," Patience finishes.

Leon hates these people, he really does, but he realizes he needs them to survive this thing. He moves in front of Pike and Patience, working to maintain eye contact. Not unlike training animals, he realizes he needs to speak on their terms while maintaining some form of dominance. Leon says, "Our strength, our only strength, is we are four hard-hitting, ball-busting, badass fuckers here with some death to deal, and get paid to do it. Right?" It's a lot of work and hurts his head to talk this way, but Leon sees he's winning Pike and Patience over by spewing their special brand of bullshit. Leon now has their complete attention and keeps at it. "I need to know something. You got the heart for this?"

Rasnick watches, trying not to smirk. He does enjoy the show Leon is putting on.

"Let me think about it. How 'bout fuck you?" says Pike.

Patience nods, eating it all up with a spoon.

Leon smiles. "Good. Because you need to ask yourselves a serious question—are you here to cut the Devil's nuts off, or piss your panties?" Pike and Patience are all ears. Leon is feeling it now. He jerks his thumb. "Behind those doors is a nightmare greased for war." He turns an eye to Pike. "You go pussy on me, I'll fucking leave you dead on the floor."

Now all eyes are now on Pike.

He shrinks, knowing he can't hide the way he reacted moments ago in the front yard. "I lost it a bit, okay? I'm better now." Leon raises an eyebrow. Patience knows Leon's concern is warranted—hell, she's concerned too—but Pike is her man, dammit. She blurts out, "He's fucking good, ok?"

Rasnick shifts, eyes the 9mm Berretta with the GPS grip that Talley gave him. He glances to the door, knowing his SWAT brothers are coming in at some point. Wishes they'd hurry the hell up.

Leon turns his attention to Rasnick. "And you?" Rasnick knows he needs to squash any doubters right here and now. He responds, "Don't waste my time. You? Questioning me? You fucking..."

"Then let's go," Leon says.

16

The Gentlemen's room.

This room is a finely woven mix of a high-end strip joint and a Best Buy. Deep leather couches, plush chairs, massive screens everywhere showing various ESPN channels, along with three stripper stages complete with polished brass poles. Colored lights twirl above the stages, with the rest of the room dimly lit. Along the far wall is a fully stocked bar that stretches up to a skylight in the ceiling. Rain starts to spatter on the windows, giving a new eerie feel to an already odd place. Nothing like walking through a madman's home equipped with in-house version of Scores.

Leon, Rasnick, Patience and Pike push through the doors, entering with caution. Rasnick and Leon sweep with trained efficiency, again checking corners and clearing the area.

Rasnick's method is perfect, and this isn't lost on Leon. "You ever in the military?"

Rasnick gives a defensive snarl. "Fuck no. Why?"

Patience jumps up on the center stage and begins working a stripper pole. Pike loves it. Leon doesn't hate it but feels the need to put this fire out before it gets out of control. "Not the time." Patience fires off a sexual blast with a simple flicker of her eyes, a curl of her lip and an ever so slight hip roll. She works the pole like a pro, driving Pike crazy. He folds a dollar bill and bites down on it. Rasnick doesn't like them getting careless either. He ratchets up a harsh tone. "He's right, we need to move."

Patience slithers and slides, sexy pumping full stream. She crawls over to Pike, taking the dollar from his mouth with her teeth. They hold their stare. Leon thinks, *Don't do it on the stage, don't do it on the stage...*

A stream of gunfire cuts up the hardwood stage.

Pike rips Patience away. He comes up with a hand cannon in each fist, screaming and firing blindly at anything and everything. Patience follows suit laying down M4 submachine gun bursts. They fire in no particular direction, bullets searing air, rounds popping spastic. The bar shatters. Bottles pop. Booze rains. Sixty-inch screens get cut up to shit. Leon pushes over a table, taking cover with his tricked out AR-15 ready. Rasnick dives next to him. They scan the area.

There's nobody else in the room.

No Big Ugly.

"Stop!" yells Leon. Pike and Patience continue screaming and unloading bullets at nothing in particular. Leon gets to his feet. "Stop fucking shooting. Please!" Gunfire stops. *What the fuck?* Glances all around. They all turn to Leon looking for something in the way of wisdom.

"He's not here. He's just fucking with us."

"How do you know?" asks Rasnick.

"Because we're all alive." Leon turns to Patience and Pike. "You wanna dance a little more, or can we get the fuck on with this?"

LEON LEADS WITH HIS AR, the rest following behind him with weapons tracking. They've entered a long corridor of a room that contains two-foot thick glass walls on either side. It's a room-sized fish tank holding thousands of gallons of water and various aquatic life forms. What little light there is gives off a soft bluish glow to the room. Fish streak by the glass. Hundreds of them cut through the water surrounding the crew. It's as if SeaWorld had a Gun-Toting Wild Bunch Day. Pike taps the glass, pissing off the fish. Patience joins him. They stare childlike at the marine life, like two kids who've only seen fish on TV.

A large chunk of raw meat floats in the water. Leon takes note of a skeleton, stares hard. "Is that...a cow?"

Pike presses his nose to the glass.

A shark rips through the water inches from the Pike's face, jaws snapping taking the chunk of meat down whole. Pike almost shits himself. Pulls his guns, ready to blast away. Leon stops him. "Easy, Tex." Patience plays with Pike's hair, trying to sooth her boyfriend.

After Pike's blood pressure comes down to a manageable level he says, "This guy's some kinda Willy Wonka prick cocksucker."

17

C hats enters the Great Room, a room mammoth in scale with twenty-foot high ceilings. The crystal chandeliers seem to float in the air. Chats charges through; he couldn't care less about the décor or the fine craftsmanship or the time and effort required to put together a room like this. He moves with purpose, void of any skill or concern, without regard for clearing the room first for safety.

That shit's for Johnny Law.

Chats plows along like Michael Myers stalking a teenager, the big difference being that Chats doesn't give two shits about his prey's sex life and does not bother with a mask. He's extremely confident he'll kill whatever comes his way. He tries a set of doors. Locked. Pumps a round, blasts it open.

A sharp noise sounds from a stairway to the right.

Chats marches down a hallway to the set of stairs. Enters with sawed-off first. There's a heart-freezing stillness to the open space, only the rain from outside patters against the windows. This is the point when a weaker mind, a sane mind, would start to rethink strategy. Perhaps think of doing something other than driving into the heart of a certified killer's home. Others might even take this moment to analyze where they are in life, think about maybe making some changes. Chats does not take such a moment. Chats presses on with his hunt.

A platinum hatchet cuts through the air.

Chats pivots right, the hatchet thudding deep in the wall about a half-inch from his skull. All Chats sees is Big Ugly's shoe slipping through an exit. Chats unleashes a 12-guage fury while rushing the doorway. The door blows open, torn off its hinges from the pulverizing shotgun force.

~

BACK IN THE AQUARIUM HALL, Leon, Rasnick, Pike, and Patience jump at the sound of the shotgun blasts. They rush to the doors.

~

CHATS PUSHES THROUGH THE DOORWAY. No Big Ugly to be found. He's reached a locker room type shower area. Gold fixtures. Etched glass. Flat screens show a sharply edited montage of porn with fast cuts of gruesome Japanese horror movie death.

Something else catches Chats's attention. Up ahead, at the far end of the lockers stands Big Ugly.

Five Big Uglys, actually.

Multiple mirrors are angled perfectly to give five full-length reflections of Big Ugly in his exquisite suit... and the steel axe strapped to his back. Big Ugly gives him the finger—five fingers, actually.

Chats pumps and unloads, shattering the mirrors as if twenty disco balls exploded into a confetti shower. Chats shoves in fresh shells as the gentle tinkle of mirror bits fall.

A flat-hand chops Chats in the throat as Big Ugly twists the shotgun loose from his grip, throwing it against the shower wall. Chats recovers with hard foot to Big Ugly's knee, putting him on the tile. Chats dives, wrapping his hands tight around Big Ugly's throat.

Big Ugly counters by unsheathing the axe from his back, whipping it around like a windshield wiper.

Chats falls back, but not before the axe snips the tip of his nose. Blood spreads down his mouth and chin. Chats spits red, pulling his 9mm from his belt. Big Ugly springs like a cat from a bathtub, spinning, pivoting, and slipping away from the gun blasts into the next room, leaving Chats with nothing but the sound of empty shells bouncing off the tile. Chats can only grin as blood drips from his snipped nose.

LEON and the remaining crew rush down the hallway into the locker room.

～

CHATS FOLLOWS BIG UGLY, entering mid-court onto a full-size basketball court marked with NBA specs, complete with a big-ass Jumbotron. On the other side of the court stands Big Ugly, who slips his axe behind his back and pulls his favorite Colt. Chats keeps his 9mm on Big Ugly, and the two hold guns on each other, taking a moment to size up their competition. Big Ugly takes a second to glance at the surveillance monitor app on his tablet, where he sees Leon, Rasnick, Pike and Patience entering the shower room. With a flick of his thumb, the Jumbotron lights up with a full image of Chats and Big Ugly on the court. He flicks his thumb again.

As Leon and company enter the shower room, a side door to another room swings open by itself. They glance at each other. *The fuck?* With guns raised they creep through the door, slipping into a room filled with rows of theater seating ten rows deep. But not your average bleacher seating. These are plush leather captain chairs with the initials BU embroidered on the backs.

The door slams behind them with a metal thunk.

The wall in front of them rolls down revealing a glassed-in view of the basketball court. Pike tries a door leading to the court. "Locked."

Rasnick pulls at the door they came through, and it opens a bit. He keeps that info to himself. "Yeah, we're locked in."

Leon checks the glass. It's thick as hell, surely bulletproof.

All they can do is watch the two gladiators on the court. Sound is piped in through Bose speakers. On the basketball court is the show. The war. Guns on guns, psycho on psycho, Chats on Big Ugly.

Chats and Big Ugly lock eyes, grins spreading across their faces. Two warriors who know what is happening here—only one gets out alive. *It's cool.* They nod respectfully.

They go at each other in an all-out sprint. Both blasting, each weaving just enough for the bullets to whizz by. Chats dodges left, then right. Big Ugly spins and rolls, comes back up firing. The hardwood court is chewed up and spit out. They steamroll, bulls raging toward one another, getting closer and closer to impact.

They collide at center court. Chats jams his 9mm to Big Ugly's temple, who swats it away as a bullet plows into center court. The battle, in all its glory, is mirrored up on the Jumbotron.

Big Ugly shoves his Colt into Chats heart. Chats grabs Big Ugly's wrist, twisting it away with a crack of ligaments. The Colt slides across the court, a stray bullet firing toward the glass viewing wall.

The bullet digs into the glass wall directly in front of Leon's face. He doesn't even blink as he watches on.

Chats and Big Ugly twist, tug, and pull as Big Ugly holds on to Chats's gun hand. Chats throws a head-butt into Big Ugly's face, which Big Ugly returns with an even harder forehead slam to what's left of Chats's nose. Chats stumbles back and Big Ugly rips the axe free, cutting off Chats's right hand in a single, clean swipe. The severed hand bounces to the hardwood, still gripping the 9mm.

Chats's body trembles. His eyes bulge, water, swell red. Still not a single sound from the man as blood spits from his wrist stump. Big Ugly leaps, plunging his axe downward for the mother of all death chops. Chats rolls and the axe slams full force into the foul line, completely stuck in the wood.

Chats pulls a tactical knife from his ankle with his remaining hand. He flips the knife into an overhand grip. He swings and rips at Big Ugly with lightning fast, wind-cutting swipes, pushing Big Ugly away from the axe planted in the court. Big Ugly throws a quick jab, then lands a roundhouse. Chats takes the hits but keeps coming.

From the bleacher room, the remaining crew watches on like they were at a UFC brawl. The hell-bent warriors on the court are getting closer and closer to the glass. Chats has his back to them. Big Ugly goes for a knockout uppercut. Chats pivots and comes up slicing Big Ugly's cheek.

Big Ugly takes a step back. Like Bruce Lee in *Enter the Dragon*, he touches his finger to his bleeding cheek, tastes it. Then, as if a switch was flipped, as if Big Ugly suddenly decided enough is enough, he grabs Chats's arm with amazing speed and force. The arm cracks, knife popping up, airborne. Big Ugly grabs another tactical knife from Chats's belt, then snatches the first blade in midair.

The crew is stone cold silent. Leon closes his eyes; he knows how this is going to end.

Holding the Ginsu-sharp tactical knives in each hand with an overhand grip, Big Ugly slices both hands in a scissor-whip across Chats's throat.

Chats's head slowly slides from his neck, landing with a single bounce. Blood pumps from the carotid arteries in the open neck. Big Ugly looks into the bleacher room at his captive audience. His stare is blank, calm, and chilling. He drops the knives, picks up his Colt, grabs Chats's head and calmly walks away, leaving a chill in the air and an O negative spitting neck-fountain on the court. All televised on the Jumbotron above.

The crew is shell-shocked, disbelief so thick you could bite it.

All except Leon. He looks around. Sees Pike. Sees Patience.

"Where's Rasnick?"

18

R asnick moves with life-threatening urgency through the house, knowing that he has to find that money and quick. In a perfect world, he would find the stash before his brothers got there and be ready to load up and slip out when they arrive, while Leon and company distract that maniac who owns this manor.

He tracks his weapon over the sprawling area he's entered, a space dedicated to Big Ugly's surprising dedication to art and culture. The room is peppered with marvelous ancient stone sculptures of Greek Gods in exile, along with a rich collection of Buddhist artifacts from Indonesia. Rare, eclectic collections of paintings are hung up and down the walls: Botticelli, Vermeer, Whistler, Munch, Dali, Warhol... and a photo of Jenna Jameson autographed in lipstick.

Rasnick tosses a Warhol Big Electric Chair, checking the wall behind it. He pushes at the wall seeking out a secret door. *There's got to be something.* He finds nothing. *Where's the fucking money?*

Rasnick tries another wall.

Flicks the balls of a Hermes statue.

He utters an adrenaline-fueled whisper to himself. "Come on. Come on..." Stepping back, he bumps into Chats's head. It has been mounted on the wall—right next to a Pollock that looks like a yak vomited up a bag of Skittles—like a hunting prize in Big Ugly's collection.

Rasnick leaps from his skin. His face drains pale, just shy of translucent. There's a row of ten other heads displayed just like Chats's.

"Fuck!" Rasnick fights to pull it together.

He works to control his breathing as he looks into Chats's dead eyes, thinks about the kind of man Chats was. He was a cold-blooded killer, a crazed fighter. He was a bad motherfucker. If Big Ugly took him down, what the hell is he going to do to Rasnick? He knows he can't afford to think this way. He's here on a mission of commerce and must stay focused. This is about dollars, not dick size.

Rasnick swallows his fear. *You're a bad man. Anybody can be gotten to. Big Ugly just got the jump on Chats, that's all. You got to move on.*

He squeezes his GPS Beretta. "Where the hell are they?

19

T he sun slips down for the day, framing the mega mansion in a warm, purple glow. The rain has slowed to a peaceful rate, falling gently on the woods. The soft pat, pat of drops landing on leaves gives the lull of a sleepy hideaway.

A vulture yanks and gnaws at the insides of a dead cow.

Zwips whisper-blast the feathered fucker.

Out from the woods step Buster and Talley, officially joining the party. They're dressed head to toe in black SWAT tactical gear: urban assault body armor, laser-sighted modified assault rifles, Glocks, riot helmets with steel grid face shields and cervical neck protectors. The light rain picks up, pissing down on them.

They survey the mess, the carnage-laden wasteland that is Big Ugly's front yard. Soil cut up by landmines, smoldering cow remains, what's left of Oleg and Vig. It's a form of repulsive yard art, cold, hard indicators of what has happened

"Holy hell!" blurts Talley.

Buster snickers, "Fuckin' dope, man."

Talley looks at his brother with disgust.

Buster doesn't get his moods. "What, bro?"

"Do you remember the day you became a fucking idiot?"

"Dude, easy..."

"Was it cold that day? Sunny?"

"Asking you, go easy. Please."

"No really? When was it?"

Buster's eyes well. "Begging you..."

"Is it something I did?" asks Talley.

Angry tears form from Buster. "Now I'm warning you."

Talley keeps at it. "If I did, I want to apologize. I'm sorry for assisting you in your quest to become a complete fucking idiot."

"Goddammit, Talley! Lay off me. I'm a person. If you can't accept who I am then...then... I don't fucking know what, but will you please stop judging and accept me like a brother, you complete fucking asshole?"

Talley starts to retort but stops himself when he sees his brother's hurt expression. Buster wipes away the tears. They stand silent, observing a moment of brotherly reflection.

"Done?" Talley asks.

Buster snorts. "Yes."

Talley nods.

They trudge toward the mega mansion without making eye contact.

20

L eon, Pike, and Patience check each door that spread out along a long hallway carpeted in thick red shag.

Leon half expects to see twin girls and something about *Red Rum*. They push on, guns at the ready as they perform a room-to-room sweep. Leon flings open the first door. They find what can only be described as an artillery room, packed wall-to-wall with weapons, ammo, and explosives. Leon thinks he sees a trident in the corner; maybe it's a pitchfork. He motions to the others that it's clear.

Something bothers Pike. "That prick Rasnick went after the money on his own, didn't he?"

Patience seethes.

Leon knows he's right, but they have to stay on task. "Greed's a bitch. Keep your damn voice down." He throws open another door, finding an empty spa-like bathroom. Scans the area. Clear.

Patience looks to Leon. "That your big plan? Dash with cash?"

Leon doesn't answer, thinking, *It's not the worst idea.*

Pike chimes in. "It's always about the money, my man."

"I have other goals, my man," says Leon.

Patience's voice goes soft. "Do tell. What's this all about to you?"

Leon readies himself at the next door. "Not important."

Pike senses his woman's interest in Leon. "If the man don't wanna talk, he don't wanna talk."

Patience zeroes in on Leon, trying to strip away at his defenses with her ample sexuality. It's an effective strategy that's served her well. "Come on Leon, give it up," she purrs.

Leon looks at her. For a second she seems like a human being, an actual real, caring female. Her green eyes glow. "C'mon. Please?" Leon is a strong, disciplined man, but he *is* a still a man, and men can be weaker than shit. It's nature. The basic heterosexual need for female attention fueled by the primitive need to procreate. Not to mention, it's been awhile since a woman gave Leon the time of day, let alone acted like she wanted to hump him.

Leon gets lost her gaze as he explains, "It's about taking back what was taken from me. Finding something positive in all this bad. I lost everything to that man, a life and a woman I loved more than anything. I can never get it all back; I've been reduced to next to nothing. So now, I guess, it's all about just getting back to good."

Pike and Patience look moved by his honesty.

Patience takes Leon's face in her hands. "That's the best reason I've heard yet. I'm sorry you've been hurt, you gorgeous man." She gently caresses his cheek with the tips of her fingers then whispers, "But you're a complete pussy."

Pike and Patience roll with laughter.

Leon moves on.

Why do I bother?

21

R asnick moves through an area of the house that looks like a luxury hotel lobby was picked up and dropped directly into the mansion. Brass fixtures, wall-to-wall hardwood floors, and antique furniture placed around the room with perfect symmetry.

Rasnick scans the open space for signs of where the money could be hidden, as well as signs of a crazy fucker trying to kill him. There's an elevator at the far end of the room, with an open stairway next to it. Various doors lead everywhere as if the room is the connector to the various arteries of the house.

BACK IN THE red shag hallway, Pike and Patience are still giggling. Leon is pissed but hides it fairly well. "Can we?" He gestures down the hallway.

Leon throws open the next door, which leads into a swinger's style love shack equipped with mirrored walls and ceiling. An Olympic-size bed takes up half the room. A sex swing hangs in the center of the room. Leather hoods, whips... you name it line the far wall. It's as if Hustler threw up in here.

Pike and Patience step in. One would think this would be Toys"R"Us to these two. She pushes the sex swing. "Gross." Pike nods in complete agreement. The two of look around, disgusted by what they see. Patience looks at her man and asks, "Since when is that making love?" Leon can only stare in utter disbelief.

The lights go out.

Complete darkness.

Pike barks out, "Cocksucker."

"Take it easy." Urges Leon.

RASNICK IS ALSO NOW in complete darkness. Can't see a damn thing save for the few shards of streaking lightning firing off outside, flickering, flashing, and bouncing light off the polished floor. Rasnick clicks on his tactical flashlight, illuminating the wood paneling that lines the walls of the room.

Just off his left shoulder, he hears the sound of a door opening.

Rasnick fumbles, quickly shutting off the flashlight plunging the lobby into darkness again. A lightning strike cuts the blackness just for a moment, followed by the roll of rumbling thunder. Rasnick presses himself against the wall trying to become invisible.

A shadowy figure slips through the darkness.

Big Ugly.

Rasnick watches, holding his breath, gulping to keep his pounding heart out of his throat. Every part of his being is taut, trying to hide as pure evil walks past. Rasnick pushes harder against the wall. The wall gives a click.

Rasnick's cells freeze.

Big Ugly stops in front of the elevator doors, scans the darkness.

Flipping on the laser sight on his Colt, Big Ugly looks around the room. The red beam carves through the darkness. The wall behind Rasnick has opened up revealing a secret door. Rasnick slides through as quickly and quietly as possible, closing the door just a fraction of a second before Big Ugly's laser sight scans over the wall.

In the secret room is nothing but black in every direction. He can't make out where he is.

Rasnick listens closely outside, praying to a merciful God that Big Ugly does not find him.

Big Ugly sweeps his laser sight around the room again. Pauses. Listens closely. Once satisfied there's nothing there, he moves on.

Rasnick listens. *Sounds like he's gone.* He allows himself to breathe again. Hopes he didn't piss himself. He clicks his flashlight on, revealing a steep concrete stairway leading down to a steel door at the bottom. He moves down the stairs toward to the door. Readies his weapon, takes a deep breath, yanks the door open.

Pitch black.

Rasnick sweeps the room with his flashlight, stopping as the light illuminates something. He can't make out what it is, but it's something displayed on a small pedestal. A display case of some kind. It's damn peculiar.

Rasnick's jaw goes slack as the contents of the case finally register. "What the fuck?"

PART IV

PATIENCE, WAIT!

22

L eon, Pike, and Patience are still in darkness. Patience breaks the silence. "Not loving this shit."

Leon keeps his voice calm and flat. "Hold it together. I got a flashlight here, somewhere…"

There's a thick slap of flesh, a crack of bone followed by a muffled yell trailing off into the darkness. Then nothing. Not a sound. Only a bone-chilling silence.

"What the hell happened?" Patience frantically asks.

"I don't know," says Leon.

Thunder crackles.

Fear splits Patience in two. "Babydoll?"

Nothing.

Patience's voice shakes. "Baby?"

"Pike?" calls Leon.

The lights kick back on.

Patience and Leon are all alone among the perverse tools and sexual aids. No Pike. A rippling wave of panic pours over Patience. "Where is he? Where the fuck is he?"

Leon spins, checking all the angles of the room. "I don't know."

Patience spits out the only question that matters. "What did that fucker do to him?"

"We'll find him."

"If he even thinks about hurting him, I'll kill him. I will fuck-ing..." She suddenly stops raging as a cold shard fires up her spine. Her eyes have found a trickle of blood leading out the door. Leon sees it. *Shit.* He tires to put a soothing hand on her, but she throws it aside.

"Patience, I know what you're thinking, but we have to be careful here. He wants us to get pissed, get emotional, and make a mistake. This is what he does. Please hear what I'm saying," Leon pleads.

Patience lights caution on fire, pisses on its ashes. She throws open the door. In the hallway, the blood trail snakes down the thick red shag carpet to a door at the far end. The blood is just enough of a shade off the carpet's red to be easily seen. Patience races at full speed, Leon chasing behind her trying to keep up. With guns drawn she flings the door open and rushes through, Leon trailing.

They find themselves in the elevator lobby, now fully lit. The blood trail runs across the hardwood floor, ending in front of the elevator doors.

Leon and Patience aren't allowed time to process information, not given the luxury of time to think. Not even a single second for Leon to try and talk Patience off the ledge.

The elevator dings.

It's coming down.

Patience's breathing becomes low and controlled, her delicate balance of love and hate pulsing. Her emotional levels are spiking beyond normal comprehension.

She commands Leon, "Be. Fucking. Ready."

Leon looks on. *Yes, ma'am.* He tightens his grip on the AR-15, taking aim on the elevator doors. Patience has her M4 ready to rock, rage rippling under her skin. It's hard to contain, but she keeps a steady hand, aim dialed in.

Ding.

It's as if the air is sucked out of the room. Nerves are pulled taut.

Waiting. The seconds tick away, seeming to last forever. Finally, the elevator doors spread open.

Blood pours out from the elevator like a wild river spreading across the marble floor, covering it. It's as if gallons of dark red paint had been dumped out.

Patience and Leon double-blink, jumping back to avoid the crimson wave. Leon fears the worst. Patience is already there. Her body tremors with anger as if volts of electricity were coursing through her.

Pike's body slips out of the elevator, sliding out on a wave of his own blood. He has been cut open from neck to nuts.

Patience goes apeshit. It's a Titanic-size crush of psychosis that most chemically balanced people will never know, and never should.

From the elevator steps Big Ugly. Leon's pupils flare with hate.

Big Ugly blows Patience a kiss.

All.

Hell.

Breaks.

Loose.

Leon opens up, spewing bursts of AR fire at the elevator. Obliterating pillars. Sending fistfuls of marble flying. Big Ugly returns fire with thumping blasts from his Colt.

Bullets? Not personal enough for Patience. She needs to, has to, must kill Big Ugly with her bare hands. She runs screaming with the finesse of a rabid boar toward Big Ugly, bare feet sloshing through the blood-drenched floor. Big Ugly keeps laying down firepower to keep Leon at bay. He turns his Colt to Patience at the last second, but not before she lunges at him. She wraps her hands around his throat with the force of a sledgehammer shot from a cannon, the collision sending them both hurtling backward into the elevator.

Leon yells, "Patience, wait!"

The doors shut. Elevator dings. Leon is left in the lobby alone with the pools of blood and Pike's corpse. He races to the stairway next to the elevator.

In the elevator rages an all-out war.

Combat in a tight, confined space.

If you took two orangutans, fed them cocaine, then dumped them in an elevator with weapons, this would be the result. Unseemly violence. No style points awarded here. Patience alternates lightning fast jabs to every part of Big Ugly she can hit, unleashing an avalanche of hurt.

Big Ugly gets a good grip on her and tosses her against the opposite wall. He pulls his Colt. Patience springs up with mouth wide, biting down hard on his hand. Blood drips from her lips. Big Ugly pulls back, but her jaw is locked. His Colt drops.

At the stairway, Leon takes the stairs on two, three at a time racing to meet the elevator.

Big Ugly tears Patience's jaws from his hand, but not before she takes some skin and meat with her. Blood smears across her pretty face.

Ding.

The door opens. Patience grabs the Colt. Big Ugly's eyes go wide, and he blurs out the door as Patience fires with reckless abandon.

Big Ugly spins out into the hall, only to be met by multiple shots snaking up the carpet toward him from Leon's AR. Big Ugly flips a tactical blade at Leon, planting it in his leg. A high-velocity splash of blood flies as Leon drops to a knee with a yelp.

Big Ugly makes a jolting leap back into the elevator, ducking Patience's wild, emotional gun blasts.

Leon wails as he pulls the knife from his thigh, the blade taking a piece of him with it.

The sounds of muted, ultra-violent insanity echo from inside the closed elevator.

Ding.

Doors open.

Out comes Big Ugly with Patience attached to him. She faces him, legs wrapped tight around his waist. She has one of her thumbs dug into his eye socket as she fights to angle the Colt with her free hand. She can't get a good shot, but that doesn't stop her. A blast fires off harmlessly, missing Big Ugly's face completely.

Big Ugly wobble-walks through the lobby while fighting and pulling her hands away the best he can. They make their way to the mansion's kitchen, a magnificent room built for gourmets to lust over. Over an island hangs a rack of pots and pans above a butcher's block of ceramic knives.

Outside the door are the sounds of the storm, along with a pack of dogs going berserk. They bark and howl, paws clawing at the door.

Big Ugly can't get Patience off of him. She wails and swipes her long black nails at his face, head, and neck with a terrifying level of persistence. She jams the Colt to the top of his head, but he swats it away. The stray bullet blows out the sink, water spraying into the air. Big Ugly's hands grab, reaching for anything he can find. His fingers fumble, finding the handle to a hanging pot. He whips it around.

A dull fwap of Calphalon slaps Patience's face, sending her skidding across the tile. Big Ugly yanks a massive ceramic knife from the island. He turns, only to be met by a double blast from his own Colt courtesy of Patience, who is laid out flat on her back. Both shots pound his chest, the brutal force sending him over the kitchen island.

Dogs still bark their balls off from outside.

Lightning fires off.

Patience gets to her feet; she knows damn well he has on a vest. She steps around the island, her back to an open steel door that leads to a huge Sub-Zero walk-in freezer.

Thunk.

The handle of the ceramic knife bobs from her chest.

A gift courtesy of Big Ugly. Most MLB catchers couldn't make that throw from their knees. Patience's expression drifts to a remote place in the universe, a place far from this kitchen. Her hand releases the Colt, letting it bounce to the tile.

Big Ugly gets to his feet, his ballistic vest now visible through the bullet holes in his exquisite silk shirt. Patience shakes. She summons her remaining shreds of rage as she stumbles toward Big Ugly. Big Ugly pulls another knife from the block, plunging the blade in her stomach with another expert-level throw. He takes a moment to acknowledge how good he is.

The dogs outside continue barking through a storm that is gaining strength.

Patience makes a bounce backward toward the walk-in freezer but does not go down. Will not go down. She pulls a hidden .38 from under her dress, firing as she lets loose her last death yell.

Big Ugly ducks, spinning toward the back door. He throws the door open to a mad rush of rabid Rottweilers and Dobermans. They leap on Patience with jaws spread wide, the pile of dogs and crazy woman falling back into the walk-in freezer. Big Ugly slams the freezer door shut.

Chewing.

Gnawing.

Tearing.

A few gun shots.

Extremely unpleasant sounds echo and bump from inside the freezer. Big Ugly fixes his hair and adjusts his tie, vanity still on the job.

"Uppity bitch," grunts Big Ugly. He picks up his Colt. Peels a banana on his way out the back door.

The storm rages on.

23

B uster and Talley clear a six-lane bowling alley with their SWAT proficiency, pausing at the rumbling sound of distant barking.

"Dogs?" Talley asks.

Buster stands still, staring mesmerized by the porn blazing on the hanging HD screens. Wrinkles his nose. "Dude, I have this one."

"Move," says Talley.

"You think those girls are like, ya know, down–to–earth and shit? Can they talk about things, ya know? Life or whateverthefuck. Anything other than penetration and semen?"

Talley can't look at him.

"What? Seriously. If we're gonna have this kinda jingle in our pockets, we're gonna attract these type of ladies so. Therefore, I need to know these type of ladies, right?"

Talley puts up a finger for silence. *For the love of sweet Christ, silence.*

Buster pulls back, hurt. "Rude, dog. You're improving your delivery, slightly, but still flat-out fucking rude."

They reach a door and move into the elevator lobby. Talley and

Buster sweep the room, stopping at the river of Pike's blood that's spread across the floor.

"Jesus," Buster says.

A muffled yell.

Buster and Talley spin around, fingers on triggers. It sounds like a voice is coming from inside the wall. Stranger still, it sounded like their brother. Buster and Talley look to each other. *No way.*

The secret doorway cracks open just a bit. Buster and Talley ready their guns. Their brother peaks his head out.

"About motherfuckin' time," Rasnick whisper-yells.

"What the hell is going on here?" asks Talley.

"Don't ask. We need to get gone. C'mon. I've got two bags loaded, but there's a shitload of cash, and you won't believe..."

"Hello." Leon limps down the stairs, favoring his leg with the gash. He keeps his AR alternating between the three brothers.

Buster and Talley whip guns around on Leon.

"Who are you?" asks Leon.

"Cleaning ladies," snorts Buster.

"You're cops," says Leon. He looks at Rasnick. "Criminals don't sweep rooms like you."

"Watch a lot of TV," offers Rasnick.

"Who is this clown?" asks Talley.

"I'm former FBI."

Buster rubs the trigger. "He's a lyin' little bitch."

"You think I'm lying, Rasnick?" asks Leon.

Rasnick isn't sure. Eyes lock all around.

"You guys can have the money. I could give a shit less. I'm here to kill Big Ugly and find something for somebody."

Rasnick motions to the open secret door. "Think I found the *something*, but if the *somebody* is the FBI? We've got issues."

"It's got nothing to do with you, man," says Leon.

"The fuck it doesn't," barks Talley.

"You think we can take the money and let you roll up to the F-B-fucking-I?" asks Buster.

"I won't tell a soul."

"Fucking well right you won't," cracks Buster.

Tension high. Three guns on Leon against his one. Fingers itch on triggers. Then...

A goat walks across the floor.

Big silence.

A strange pause in this Mexican standoff as Big Ugly's "friend" trots across the bloody floor. The goat clears the room, on its way to the kitchen. Eyes bounce among the four men. Talley looks to Rasnick. "Call it, man."

Leon knows the answer before it's said.

"Kill him," says Rasnick.

A wave of bullets plow toward Leon. He returns fire with his AR, pumping rapid bursts, but the firepower coming from the other side is a monster. Talley sidesteps while firing, getting a new angle. His foot slips on the slick blood that coats the hardwood, causing his legs to fly out from under him. His finger involuntarily squeezes the trigger as his legs fold. As he lands, the stray bullet-spray carves up his neck and face, the barrel landing on his temple for the final kill shot.

Talley's body flops to the floor.

Rasnick hasn't noticed and keeps up the pounding fire on Leon, pushing Leon out of the room. Buster's brain circuits crossfire with overloading emotions, his head a synaptic car fire.

Leon skids into a room filled with a jaw-dropping display of flowers and plants, birds flying above a sanctuary that is complete with a retractable glass roof that is currently closed. The rain pours down through the moonlight, providing a drum solo rhythm on the glass. Leon reloads, limping his way through the massive, Garden of Eden area.

In the elevator lobby, Rasnick lumbers catatonic over to Buster, who stands over their dead brother neither of them knows exactly what happened. Buster is a frantic, mumbling mess. "Fucking shit."

"You killed Talley?" asks Rasnick.

"What?"

"You were his primary backup, and you failed him."

Buster's mind scrambles, no idea how to respond to his brother's analysis of the situation. "I didn't mean to, dog. He was repositioning and I...I...I..."

"You may as well have shot our brother."

Buster swallows hard. "Oh come on, man..."

"You always hated him."

"Not true. Take that shit back. Unfucking true..."

"Bullshit! From day one, you never liked him."

"We had differences for sure, but not like this."

"The Green Machine incident of 1985?"

Buster's eyes moisten. "You gonna throw that in my face? Now, asshole, at a time like this?"

A whistle sounds out from across the room. Buster and Rasnick swivel. Rasnick squints at a man cloaked in shadow.

Buster asks, "Who the fuck are you?"

Rasnick knows. He raises his weapon in an attempt to take down the devil.

A second splits in two.

Buster and Rasnick are each met by a single bullet to the brain. They flop in a heap next to their brother.

24

L eon scramble-limps though the doors of an indoor water haven that destroys even the best Cancun party pools. That kick-ass cement pond you saw on Cribs a few years ago? Bullshit compared to this. BIG UGLY is etched in gold, centered perfectly under the rippling water of the gargantuan pool. A raging waterfall lies at the far end, with rock cliffs designed for diving. The retractable glass roof that began in the garden room stretches into this room.

Leon holds his seeping knife wound. The blood doesn't show too badly through his black REI cargos, just looks like he's pissed himself —perhaps the only time in his life that Leon wishes that was the case.

He looks up.

The glass roof has begun to retract, opening up and allowing the rain to dump down. The driving rain pounds Leon. The thunder and lightning dance in the moonlight, providing the mood for his perfect little reunion with...

Big Ugly.

In steps the world's leading producer of misery, the master of disaster.

He stands on the cliff just behind the waterfall, taking a stance like the God of War—at least in his mind. Slightly battered from his battles with his various guests, but he knows he's still the goods. The waterfall parts like curtains for him as he steps forward. A samurai sword is sheathed behind his back, a Colt tucked into his lizard skin belt.

Leon's face goes slack. The object of his personal demise stands a mere pool length away. The man who ruined his existence on this planet, who killed his dreams and pissed on his soul. Leon's very DNA burns. His face darkens, hate pushing the needle to the point of mental implosion.

Big Ugly grins wide. "Leon."

"Big Ugly."

"Been awhile."

"Too long."

Big Ugly cocks his head birdlike. "You look like shit, buddy." Leon flashes a fake smile. Big Ugly keeps pushing buttons. "How's your ass? Heard you needed stitches. Were there stitches?"

Leon drops the smile.

"I get it confused. If you're sodomized by a guy wearing a strap-on, does that make you gay? Or is the guy wearing the strap-on gay? I don't feel gay. Do you feel gay, Leon?"

Leon grips his AR.

Big Ugly cracks his knuckles. *Showtime.*

Leon can't hold back any longer. He unleashes years worth of hostility, unloading hyper-burst of relentless lead. With Olympic precision, Big Ugly dives into the pool with very little splash. He cuts underwater like a jet-propelled merman.

Leon continues firing round after round into the pool. He pulls back seeing no sign of Big Ugly. He holds his fire, conserving his ammo. The ripples in the water fade. Only the plops of heavy rain churn the pool as the storm continues to pour down from the dark skies above.

Lightning flashes.

Thunder cracks.

From the dark water springs Big Ugly, swiping his sword at Leon's legs. Leon hops, the blade barely missing as he fights to take aim on Big Ugly. Before he can get a shot off, Big Ugly whips the sword around cutting the AR in half. Leon drops what's left of weapon to the tile. Big Ugly leaps from the pool, sword poised for mutilation. Leon tosses a deck chair with everything he has, slipping and sliding trying to make his way to an exit.

Big Ugly dodges the chair with minimal effort. Leon grabs another chair, letting it fly. Big Ugly cuts it into a non-threat. Leon trips over a fallen table. Big Ugly's sword comes slicing down. Leon rolls, the blade sparking off the tile. Leon lands a foot to Big Ugly's face, giving him enough of an opening to bolt to for the door.

Leon stumbles through, landing outside the house. Squinting through the driving rain, he realizes he's entered an MLB level batting cage. He gets to his feet and backs away from the door, waiting, anticipating, Big Ugly's arrival.

Fwoomp.

A baseball tags him square in the ribs. Leon feels an internal crunch of bone which robs the air from his lungs.

Fwoomp.

Another ball nails his thigh, taking his leg out from under him. Big Ugly charges through the door like an insane Apache, plunging the sword at Leon's face. He dodges hard left; the blade misses his ear by an inch. Leon falls back, his fingers finding a Louisville Slugger. He slams it into Big Ugly's nuts.

Gut.

Face.

Big Ugly stumbles from side to side, swallowing back the snot and blood. He fights to clear his vision while tremors rocket from his groin to his feet. He staggers toward a cage door that leads back into the house. Fastballs whizz around them. Some miss. Some don't. Big Ugly swings his sword with one hand, trying to hold back the blood pouring from his nose with his free hand. He cuts a ball in half.

Leon swings his bat. Big Ugly dodges, returning with a quick jab to Leon's eye. Leon whips his bat around. Big Ugly can't get a full swipe but gets in position enough to block the blow with his blade. The sword and bat lock together, the sword stuck deep into the wood. They tug and pull, tumbling back through the door into elevator lobby. They've entered the now familiar room from the opposite side.

War rages.

Punches rock.

They are engaged in full-on brutality as they fight to free the sword from the bat. Behind their struggle, the heavy coating of blood spreads across the slick floor glistening in the moonlight. The secret door Rasnick found is wide open.

Leon spots the door just over Big Ugly's shoulder, catching a glimpse of the stairs leading down. He glances down to the Colt still in Big Ugly's belt. Leon pumps the sword/bat combo hard into Big Ugly's face.

Once.

Twice.

Three times.

Big Ugly's face busts to shit. His eyes glaze over, his equilibrium thrown off. The sword/bat hits the floor. Leon rears back then bull-rushes, ramming a shoulder hard into Big Ugly like a runaway train striking a tackling dummy. The tangled pair hit the blood-soaked marble at ramming speed, gliding along the blood while tracking a straight line directly toward the secret doorway.

They rip through the door and down the stairs like riding a horrific Slip 'N Slide.

PART V

CHESTER

25

An angry tumbleweed of humanity screams down the stairs. A shard of light from the open door cuts through the dark, perfectly framing the pile of Big Ugly and Leon. A mutated mess of arms, legs, and hate barrels through, skidding to a stop leaving them in an inert lump on the cold floor.

Leon peels off, wobbling to find his balance. "Do not fucking move." Leon has managed to get his hands on the Colt during the tumble. He holds it dead on Big Ugly.

Big Ugly is laid out on the floor in a somewhat broken, blood-soaked pile. It's been a damn rough day. Leon wipes the blood from his face and feels around for a way to get the lights on.

Leon's eyes pop. "Son of a bitch."

As the room lights up, he realizes he's in a room full of money. A vault made for kings. Leon can't help but think of when Bugs and Daffy found the genie's treasure. Stacks of hundreds reach for the ceiling. All the money Big Ugly has taken over the years. The sum of all his labor, his big score. Leon takes a moment to drink it all in. On the floor are two cash-stuffed Nike bags—the ones Rasnick never got a chance to come back to. Big Ugly regards the bags. "Movies make people stupid. Million dollars weighs about twenty pounds. You can't carry two thousand pounds in two fucking bags."

"Where is it?" Leon asks.

Big Ugly spits out a tooth. "Where's what, love?"

Leon spins around looking. "Where's the video, the records, the files. Whatever you have that is keeping you safe?"

"Oh. You mean, Chester."

Leon looks to him. *Chester?*

Big Ugly motions behind him. Just over his right shoulder is a small platform lit with a warm glow. This is what Rasnick saw.

Leon is dumbstruck. "You've got to be kidding me."

Displayed like the Mona Lisa in a sealed glass case, lit by a beam overhead, is a gargantuan dildo. Big Ugly grins ear-to-ear. "Had some people put the display together. Vacuum sealed to lock in dead hooker DNA and keep fingerprints crystal clear and incriminating as shit, the way God intended them to be."

Leon's mind spins trying to piece together what this could possibly mean. His thoughts come together, only to explode into insane theories. He attempts to work this mental Silly Putty into some form logic. "Senators and Supreme Court judges were mixed up with call girls, and you had this? That thing?"

"Who?" asks Big Ugly.

Leon starts over. "Senators. Judges. They don't want you to give that over to the authorities."

"What the fuck are you talking about, Nature Boy?"

A gun clicks.

A familiar voice speaks.

"Love to have that dildo, son."

26

Leon spins around to find Cooper holding a 9mm in each hand, the right one for Leon, the left for Big Ugly.

Leon, mouth agape, struggles to find the best word. "Fucker."

"All the guns and goodies I gave you were bugged with tracking devices," says Cooper.

Leon levels a death stare that sears through his onetime hero slash father figure. His current hate object.

"Sorry, kid. I am a lifer, dedicated to God, country and all that. Believe me, I had every intention of bringing that son of a bitch to justice when I recruited you. Truly did. But I've got weaknesses, like everybody else. I like the hookers."

"Who doesn't?" adds Big Ugly. Cooper plants a shoe to his gut and Big Ugly coughs up some blood with a giggle.

Cooper explains, "This prick got to me while you were in Mexico." Cooper leans down to Big Ugly. "You really didn't have to kill all the girls."

"Yeah, kinda did. See, that's what makes Chester so sweet, like pumpkin pie. He gives the impression you killed the skanks. Get it?"

Cooper kicks him again. Harder.

"You understand," coughs Big Ugly.

Leon's mind churns. "You were the lead on his case. You asked me to go after him, and then when he got dirt on you--you sold me out, made all the charges, all intelligence just simply go away?"

"Yes, yes I did."

Leon explodes, "You fucking piece of shit!"

"Be that as it may."

"You two need a moment?" asks Big Ugly.

"Shut that goddam mouth," barks Cooper.

Leon's guts twist like bread ties. An all too familiar feeling to Leon, that same old feeling that can only come from the being the last to know you've been completely fucked over. "I wanted to be a good agent—get it right, live a life to be proud of." Leon's eyes glaze over. "You people, you fucking people used me up and shit on what was left."

"Yeah, kid. I'm gonna need that dildo," says Cooper dismissively.

Big Ugly slow rolls into laughter. Cooper joins the joke with a snicker. He knows it's not funny, but there's something about joining in on a joke that's irresistible, a *thank God I'm not that guy* sort of thing.

Leon is not remotely amused.

Vibrates with anger.

Blam!

Leon fires a single bullet between Cooper's eyes. A jet of red pulp shoots across the Nike bags as his body drops. Even Big Ugly is surprised. Leon turns the Colt on him.

Big Ugly springs.

Blam!

Leon's stray shot misses Big Ugly but shatters the glass case. Chester wiggles free and flops to the concrete.

Big Ugly's head fires up like a piston, pulverizing Leon's chin from below. The Colt skips across the floor, and Leon falls as Big Ugly bolts for a back door. Big Ugly hauls ass, retreating beyond the stacks of cash.

Leon's fingers scramble and claw for something, anything. He finds Chester. He hums it with everything he has. Chester catches Big Ugly on the ankle, just enough to trip him up. Big Ugly hits the floor, skidding into the library.

Leon launches into the air, landing on top of Big Ugly. Big Ugly flips around, throwing Leon, who sails over a leather couch. He comes up grabbing for a lamp, which he smashes on Big Ugly's head. Leon grabs a book from a towering bookcase and slams the spine into Big Ugly's face. Big Ugly counters by flipping a coffee table up and jamming the edge into Leon's throat.

Punches land with a constant smack of flesh. Kicks miss, then hit. Bones crunch. Ligaments tear as limbs twist. Blood spits and spills on the fine Persian rugs. It's a brawl of biblical proportions.

The thing that separates them, gives Leon the edge, is that Leon fucking hates Big Ugly, while Big Ugly just wants to fight. Leon is driven beyond reason. His blood burns hot, the needle passed rage a long time ago. Leon pushes himself to another level of violence, a new emotion that is yet to be defined.

He beats Big Ugly with a left, then a right. Throws a hammer kick sending Big Ugly hard against a far wall covered with large velvet curtains. Something behind the curtains gives an odd crunch; there's glass behind it. Could be windows, not sure.

Leon comes at him, a man possessed, kicks and punches thrown with every ounce of his being. Big Ugly can barely defend himself from the blitz of hand-to-hand hell. With every blow, the glass behind Big Ugly crunches a little more. Leon grabs Big Ugly's neck, spit flying from his lips as he slams Big Ugly's head repeatedly against the glass until...

Crash.

They tumble through the shattered glass, hurtling and smashing into a new room as the busted glass showers the floor. They land in a pile, bouncing on the white tile with Leon on top riding Big Ugly to a jolting stop.

Leon finds his feet. Big Ugly leans forward, resting on his elbows. He's bloodied, his face a mess, but still manages a smile. Leon pulls the Colt, poking Big Ugly in the eye with the barrel. It's similar to the scene in Mexico when Big Ugly had the jump on Leon, but things have changed.

"Hola, my little Fed friend," says Big Ugly.

"Hi," says Leon, seething. He fights to control his breathing and pounding heart.

"Seriously, when are you going cease with the shit?"

Leon pulls back the hammer. "Thinking today's the day." Leon stops, thrown by Big Ugly's expression—he almost appears happy. *Wants to be shot?*

Big Ugly says, "I wanted it to be you, but you had to earn it. Couldn't just give it to you."

Leon scans the area. They've landed in a room that looks like a high-end hospital room via W Hotel. There's a king-size adjustable bed, glass cases lined with prescription bottles, syringes, blood tests... way too much medical equipment for the average human being.

Leon gets it. "You're sick."

"Understatement of the year."

"What's with the private hospital?"

"My body's a temple."

Leon inspects some of the drug bottles. "These aren't TUMS. This is serious medication. What do you have? Cancer? What?"

"Oh, it's some nasty, nasty shit," sneers Big Ugly.

Leon spots the handheld surveillance monitor that Big Ugly has been carrying around. It peeks from his suit jacket, strapped to Big Ugly by a shoulder strap. Leon rips it away. He touches the screen, flipping through the different views. On the monitor, he sees Chats's headless body on the basketball court. Swipe. The carnage of Pike at the elevators. Then the kitchen, the brothers, the vault with dead Agent Cooper and, finally, the crew's Chevy Suburban and Brobee's Caddie parked on the road outside the woods.

A light bulb goes off for Leon, then explodes. "Nobody gets near here without you knowing about it." Leon mind plays through events, stringing together his thoughts, the stories he's heard, the things he knows. Rearranges them in some form of order in an attempt to apply logic where it has no business being used. In his mind's eye, it starts to play out clear as day.

The country road. Brobee's stolen Caddie running out of gas, sputtering to a stop near the woods. Leon connects the dots. Brobee stumbled onto Big Ugly by accident, but he could've gone in any direction, up or down the road, even stayed at the car.

The Office. Big Ugly sitting in his designer suit in front of his sea of security monitors. He spotted the Caddie, saw Brobee get out of the car. Big Ugly's eyes slammed into focus, recognizing. Big Ugly raced down the hall passing his staff and hookers, cigar and scotch still in hand.

Big Ugly storming out the door into the night air, checking his handheld surveillance monitor looking at Brobee. He starts to sing at the top of his lungs, wanting to make sure Brobee comes his way. Brobee walks into the woods. Big smile from Big Ugly.

Back into the mansion, Big Ugly glides through the foyer talking with Bobby. "I know you haven't been yourself," says Bobby. "Depression is a natural response."

"Appreciate your concern," replies Big Ugly.

Big Ugly moves down the line in the formal dining room handing out stacks of money to his staff. He reaches the Doctor. "I'm not leaving here. You need help."

Big Ugly nods.

Leon eyes flare. "You wanted us to come here." He stands over Big Ugly, holding the Colt at his side. Big Ugly's smile still shines through the blood.

"You wanted one last battle."

"Warriors were made to war, not die in bed."

"You wanted us to kill you, go down in flames."

"C'mon, Leon. Don't pussy out now." Big Ugly grabs Leon's gun hand, directing the Colt at his own face. "You've dreamed of killing me. Pull that trigger. This is it. Do it. Take it. Get some release, man. Nobody's been able to take me out. You can be the one. Conquering FBI hero who got his man."

Big Ugly licks the gun barrel.

Leon is wrapped in complete disbelief. Big Ugly recites an earlier line he used with Bobby. "You know the win/loss record for people who make the big score and retire to the sweet life? One winner and a fucking piss-load of losers. I'm the one."

"No, you're not," says Leon with glazed eyes.

"Pardon?"

Leon rips the Colt away from Big Ugly's puzzled face. Safely lowers the hammer. Shoves his hate down with a better idea. "You don't get to win. You don't get to die like a gladiator. No blaze of glory." Big Ugly works another angle, other buttons to push. "Think, boy. Cooper destroyed my records. Feds got nothing on me."

"I know."

"Whatever the fuck Cooper promised you, it died with him."

"You're under arrest."

"You think you can just walk back into your old life? Get fucking real."

He's getting to Leon.

"Maybe not," admits Leon.

"Maybe? Seriously? You're nothing. You're a cum stain on a tranny's skirt."

Leon starts to raise the gun, so Big Ugly pours it on. "I'll be out of lockup before I finish my McMuffin, and once I'm out, I'm going to run a killing spree that'll make cancer look like a fun way to check out. I'm a bad man. Baddest motherfucker in the history of bad motherfuckers." Leon whips the butt of the Colt across Big Ugly's jaw, putting him on the floor. Ending Big Ugly's sermon.

Leon leans in close, wants to make sure Big Ugly gets this. "They are going to find you in a house littered with bodies. In particular, three dead cops and an FBI agent. And, oh yeah, millions of unaccounted for dollars that I'll bet my balls isn't on your last tax return. Yeah, I'm pretty sure that'll fuckin' stick, Billy Badass."

Big Ugly's stomach drops farther and farther with every word.

"You get to die in a cage you pathetic, silly cunt." This is the first time Big Ugly's ever had a sliver of fear in his life. Leon is enjoying this moment, the moment he's earned. "First day, they'll probably kick your teeth out, so your mouth gives that smooth vagina-like feel."

Big Ugly panics.

A new side to the scariest man alive.

He jumps at Leon. Twisting the Colt away, he jams it under his own chin attempting to shoot himself. Leon pounces on his back, pushing the gun away at the last second. The shot rings out harmlessly as they struggle for control of the gun.

Fighting against Leon's grip, Big Ugly uses every fiber of his being trying to stick the gun in his own mouth, fighting to pull the trigger. Dying to kill himself.

Both their faces burn red. Veins pop. Spit flies. Fingers fumble around the trigger.

An Odd change in circumstances, one Leon never could have imagined—him trying to save Big Ugly's life, Big Ugly trying to end it.

Grunts.

Punches.

Profanity.

A gunshot rings out.

Silence... then a crack of thunder.

"Fuck you, Grande Ugly."

27

T he clang of steel sliding shut rattles behind Big Ugly as he walks though the maximum security facility. Draped in an orange jumpsuit, his new identity is stenciled neatly above his breast pocket—he's just a number now. His hard gaze burns as the bars slam with that unmistakable sound. No longer the untouchable master of darkness in a ten grand suit, today he's just another guest of the U.S. Correctional System.

In the yard, Big Ugly keeps to himself. Even here he's confident he has no equal and would rather not mix with the local yokels. From behind Big Ugly, a mix of tattoo-skinned, shaved-head felons move toward him, a gleam twinkles in their eyes.

The smallest one is six four, two sixty, and they are not fans seeking an autograph. Big Ugly has only been here a few days, and so far he's already killed an inmate, paralyzed two, and sent three guards home for some much needed time for healing and reflection. Some of the prison officials unofficially decided that Big Ugly needed "socialization" with other inmates in order to facilitate a smoother transition. They even went as far as to allow this very group of shaved-head felons some extra shop time to create something special for the task.

They huddle in, surrounding Big Ugly.

The Guards look the other way.

Big Ugly turns, facing the pack of hostile inmates he finds a defiant grin. He still holds onto his edge, still able to find just the right thing to say to people.

"Who's fucking first?"

The crazed felons attack.

Big Ugly thinks of Leon.

Leon would enjoy this.

~

THE BLUEST of water kisses the white sand, sun beaming through the slight, whispering breeze. A gorgeous bikini-clad waitress snakes down the beach of the remote island paradise, delivering a cocktail.

She reaches Leon, who's sprawled out in a chair like a lazy feline. Healing cuts and scars pepper his face and tanning body. His leg is still strapped in a brace, and his arm hangs in a sling from a gunshot wound.

The waitress hands him a towering Bloody Mary with a sexy smile. Leon digs into the tattered Nike bag that rests in the sand next to his chair, pulling a hundred from under the beach towel on top. The waitress takes the bill, pausing as she notices the dried bloodstains.

"Sorry," says Leon as he fumbles around, finding her a clean, fresh hundred. He sips the cocktail as he lies back, waving off the change. The waitress thanks him with a smile, her blonde hair rippling in the ocean breeze.

Leon returns the smile then asks, "You know the win/loss record for people who make the big score and retire to the sweet life? One winner and many, many losers."

She smiles through her confusion. "Que?"

Leon offers a big smile. "I'm the one."

Leon coughs hard.

Wheezes.

Gasps.

His lungs struggle to find a breath through his closing throat.

The waitress giggles and leans down to Leon's ear, speaking perfect English. "Sorry, sweetheart." Leon's eyes bulge as he grabs his throat, panic spiking as his brain starts to process the very real possibility of dropping dead from lack of oxygen.

The waitress kisses his forehead. Leon notices the small black heart tattoo above her right breast. His mind splits in two.

She's the blonde ATV driving hooker!

The last thing Leon sees is the blonde pouring the drink into the sand before picking up his Nike bag. She checks the contents, finding his room key along with various papers and a keychain. She proudly walks down the beach, raising the bag above her head as if showing off a trophy or championship belt for all to see.

Just on the horizon, near the water, the other girl, the brunet ATV hooker, stands with her double Ds muted under a tasteful dress. She waits for her girl with a warm smile. She thinks of the time spent in captivity with Big Ugly. It was a rough time, but today she and her girl get what they've earned. All that weird shit with that monster of a man took its toll, and most of the girls at the mansion relied heavily on the drugs and booze to get them through the endless days and nights with Big Ugly.

Not the brunet and the blonde.

They paid attention.

To everything.

They took note of the details, of the devil performing those details. They watched Big Ugly, how he got information, how he processed that info, how he did his business. It's easy to dismiss two hookers with fake double Ds who spread the dumb girl act on thick as molasses while being used so casually for sex.

Now? Today? It's a much different time.

Their time.

They didn't leave the woods that day. No, after they gave Big Ugly's message to Leon and the crew they hung around. They laid low and paid close attention. They watched Leon kill Cooper and take Big Ugly kicking and screaming to the proper law enforcement authorities. They studied Leon's patterns, tracked the man, picked up the trail that led them here to this perfect little island paradise.

The blonde reaches her love, Nike bag in hand. She wraps her arm around the brunet's waist. "I've got the key to his room."

"The storage shed?"

"Yup." The blonde dangles the keychain. "Gotta be where he keeps the rest of it."

They get lost in one another's eyes. So much shared between them, so much endured. No words are needed. The blonde and brunet lock their finger together, holding hands as they walk along the sand watching the waves roll in.

Two winners in a world of so many losers.

THE END

Made in the USA
Monee, IL
24 June 2022

98574709R00402